Steve Harrison's Casebook

Robert E. Howard

Introduction by Don Herron
Edited by Rob Roehm

THE
Robert E. Howard
FOUNDATION PRESS

Special thanks to Glenn Lord for supplying the vast majority of original Robert E. Howard typescripts, manuscripts, and transcripts thereof.

Edition 2.0

Published by The Robert E, Howard Foundation Press by arrangement with Robert E. Howard Properties, Inc.

http://www.rehfoundation.org

Cover art by Mark Wheatley.

Contents

Acknowledgements

The first Steve Harrison yarn I ever read was "The House of Suspicion," first published in *The Second Book of Robert E. Howard* in 1976. At the time, it was just another good story in a great collection. I remember being intrigued by Howard's private eye, but no other Harrison yarns were available, as far as I knew. Years later, after the Howard bug had bitten me, I wished I had paid a little more attention to the fan press of the day. It turned out there were a few more stories featuring Howard's hard-boiled hero, but I didn't discover that until I started collecting his works in earnest around 1999.

To obtain all of Harrison's adventures took some work. Besides the above-mentioned paperback, I had to hunt down and acquire several other volumes—often for only one or two Harrison yarns—including a couple of chapbooks produced by Cryptic Publications: *Bran Mak Morn: A Play and Others*, and *Two-Fisted Detective*. Each of those slender booklets cost me more individually than the volume now in your hands. Remembering the trouble I went through to acquire the complete Harrison collection, I was happy to finally move forward with the present volume.

The typescripts for these stories are spread around a bit. Glenn Lord provided copies of most, some of which came to me via Patrice Louinet, and the Cross Plains Public Library has the rest. Paul Herman, John Bullard, and Rusty Burke provided the initial e-text as well as information about story titles and copies of pulp magazine appearances. Once the text was prepared, Barbara Barrett provided an additional set of eyes to catch some of my mistakes, as well as invaluable moral support.

When it came time for the book's introduction, I immediately thought of my 2007 traveling companion, Don Herron. Besides accompanying me to Cross Plains for Howard Days that year, Don is the author of what I consider the finest essay on Howard's works, "Hard-Boiled Heroic Fantasist," as well as many others.

Without the support and assistance of those mentioned above this volume would still be a half-finished project buried in the stacks. My thanks to all.

All of the items in *Steve Harrison's Casebook* were taken from copies of Robert E. Howard's original typescripts and carbons, which were provided by Glenn Lord and the Cross Plains Public Library.

Note: The February 1934 issue of *Strange Detective Stories* carried two tales by Robert E. Howard: "The Tomb's Secret" and "Fangs of Gold." At some point during production, it appears that the titles were inadvertently switched, as there are no "fangs of gold" or anything similar in "Fangs of Gold" as published; however, the other story, credited in that magazine to Howard's pseudonym Patrick Ervin, works quite well with that title. To further complicate matters, Howard's agent, Otis Adelbert Kline, kept a list of titles and the magazines that purchased them. Above "The Teeth of Doom" on Kline's list, someone has added "The Tomb's Secret"; above "The People of the Serpent," someone has added "Fangs of Gold." The original titles work well for the stories in question and are probably the titles that Howard himself used when they were submitted. For the current publication, we have corrected the errors that appeared when the stories were first published. "The Tomb's Secret" appears as "The Teeth of Doom"; "Fangs of Gold" appears as "The People of the Serpent."

Hard-Boiled in Texas
by Don Herron

"I find it more and more difficult to write anything but western yarns," Robert E. Howard told H. P. Lovecraft toward the end of a long letter dated May 13, 1936. "I have definitely abandoned the detective field, where I never had any success anyway, and which represents a type of story I actively detest. I can scarcely endure to read one, much less write one."

Yet write detective stories he did—at the same time he leaned fast-fingered over his Underwood and knocked out the last tales of Conan of Cimmeria he would finish, returned to new adventures of one of his earliest creations in the figure of El Borak, spun out more series of humorous westerns as well as standalone serious oaters, plus the usual boxing fiction, horror stories. . . . Howard's assault on the pulp jungle was nothing less than volcanic, stories and poems erupting non-stop from his small room in a house in Cross Plains, Texas—the scattered detritus of false starts and fragments alone enough to fill several volumes. For someone who detested detective fiction, the Texan nonetheless proved he could shove a gat in the mitt of a gumshoe and set the sleuthing game afoot.

Less than a month after he made those comments in the letter to Lovecraft, on June 11, the prolific young writer committed suicide at the age of only thirty, throwing into sudden sharp relief each remark dropped into the surviving correspondence. If he had not fired the fatal bullet, would Howard in fact have devoted his creative energies strictly to western stories? The commercial forces of the marketplace soon might have commanded a return to crime fiction—where his natural penchant for headlong action and sudden violence could well have made the creator of Conan a major tough guy writer during the paperback explosion of the 1950s, someone who effortlessly could have out-Spillaned a Mickey Spillane.

Intriguingly, as the last year of his life dawned, it looked as if Howard not only had called quits on his tentative fling with crime fiction, but that his spectacular marathon run as the originator of fantastic tales of Sword-and-Sorcery finally had ended, as well. In an earlier letter to Lovecraft, dated February 11, 1936, he informed his fellow *Weird Tales* contributor: "As for my own fantastic writing, whether or not I do any future work in that field depends a good deal on the editors themselves. I would hate to abandon weird writing entirely, but my financial needs are urgent, immediate and imperious. Slowness of payment in the fantastic field forces me into other lines against my will."

Howard's first professional story saw print in *Weird Tales* in 1925, and by 1932 he had created an enduring icon of popular culture in Conan—thief, pirate, king, assassin, even a bit of a detective if that's what the fictioneer wanted as he sat at the typewriter keys, dreaming scarlet dreams, carving out a career at a penny-a-word. Today "Rogues in the House" remains as ruthlessly hard-boiled a read as any of the stories Dashiell Hammett, Raymond Chandler and company sold to *Black Mask*, the flagship magazine of the tough guy detective school of crime writing. The memorable scenes of Shevatas the thief in "Black Colossus" or the youthful Cimmerian as a wall-scaling burglar in "The Tower of the Elephant" also toy with the themes of pulp crime fiction.

The Conan series stands as Howard's defining work in part because he created a concept into which he could merge all his interests, including touches of the humor fully showcased in his boxing and tall tale western yarns—or a dash of science fiction, a full-scale desert adventure. "The God in the Bowl" even tosses a little murder mystery into the Hyborian Age setting. Genre-bending in the frontline trenches of genre-bending—writers and game-creators at work today follow in the footsteps of one of the first modern masters.

That postwar era in which Howard lived was no doubt crucial to his success—the period when literature jumped full force into works meant for the modern sensibility, shaking off Victorian dust and giving readers who had lived through the First World War something fresh, tough-minded, realistic—in the parlance of the day, hard-boiled.

In San Francisco in 1922 and 1923 an ex-Pinkerton's detective named Dashiell Hammett began writing crime fiction for the pulp *Black Mask*, soon centered on the casework of a short fat nameless operative for the Continental Detective Agency. By 1924 average enough outings featuring the Continental Op such as "One Hour" published in the April 1924 issue of the *Mask* were followed by a full-fledged masterpiece titled "The Girl with the Silver Eyes" in June. In 1925 Hammett's talent reached white-heat as he saw into print "The Whosis Kid," "The Scorched Face," "Corkscrew," "Dead Yellow Women," and "The Gutting of Couffignal" one after the other, a series run that would be hard to equal in the history of pulp fiction—to get close, you would have to cherry-pick five of the best Conan stories and pretend they appeared back-to-back, say, "The Tower of the Elephant," "Queen of the Black Coast," "Rogues in the House," "Beyond the Black River," and "Red Nails." In that year Hammett raced ahead of his fellow contributors to *Black Mask* and became the modern master of the detective story, with his Continental Op series the Gold Standard of pulp sleuthing action.

In the exact period when Hammett hard-boiled the detective story Ernest Hemingway lived in Paris and wrote his early short stories under the influence of Gertrude Stein and other modernists, finishing his first novel *The Sun Also Rises* in 1924—its book publication in 1926 revolutionized fiction in general. And in 1926 a new editor, Captain Joseph T. Shaw, took the reins of *Black Mask* and decided if you wanted to write for him, then you'd better do your damndest to write like Hammett, and even more importantly he encouraged the ex-detective to top himself with novels such as *The Big Knockover*, *Red Harvest* and an instant classic in 1930 entitled *The Maltese Falcon*.

Coming into that heady era, Howard also had the talent to change the face of fiction, carving out his own niche in the modern pantheon as, single-handed, he brought the fantastic tale from its roots in saga and legend up to date, imbuing his stories with the tough realism of the day. From his fledgling sales he worked his magic with each new adventure of the wandering Puritan Solomon Kane, Bran Mak Morn of the Caledonian Picts, King Kull of Atlantis, the outlawed Black Turlogh O'Brien. By 1932 it was a hardened professional writer who launched Conan on his way. Possibly the most significant quote underlining this point appears in a 1935 letter from the Texan to Clark Ashton Smith, another of his peers in the pages of *Weird Tales*, concerning the creation of Conan: "It may sound fantastic to link the term 'realism' with Conan; but as a matter of fact—his supernatural adventures aside—he is the most realistic character I ever evolved. He is simply a combination of a number of men I have known. . . . Some mechanism in my sub-consciousness took the dominant characteristics of various prize-fighters, gunmen, bootleggers, oil field bullies, gamblers, and honest workmen I had come in contact with, and combining them all, produced the amalgamation I call Conan the Cimmerian."

Talent, timing—and a third factor you cannot underestimate when assessing the lasting prominence of at least Howard and Hammett: They made their reps in the ever changing and uncertain world of the wood pulp fiction magazines.

"Spear and Fang," the first story sold by the young writer from Cross Plains, saw print in *Weird Tales* for July 1925—as he told Lovecraft during their intense correspondence: "I was eighteen when I wrote 'Spear and Fang,' 'The Lost Race,' 'The Hyena'; nineteen when I wrote 'In the Forest of Villefère' and 'Wolfshead.' And after that it was two solid years before I sold another line of fiction. I don't like to think about those two years." The leading Howard scholar Glenn Lord once noted, "despite extensive efforts, *Weird Tales* remained Howard's sole market prior to 1929." An October 1928 letter Howard sent to his friend Tevis Clyde Smith detailed the stirring saga of the mere eight stories and seven poems placed by that point with *Weird Tales*: "Here I am, slugging away at a cheap, little known magazine which may already be bankrupt, weaving fanciful and impossible tales and absolutely unknown outside that magazine's limited clientele."

Soon Howard began to land stories in other markets and in other genres—boxing tales, historical fiction, adventure, westerns—and by 1933 he was able to hire Otis Adelbert Kline as his agent. By 1936 Howard was a regular byline in not only *Weird Tales* but also *Fight Stories* and *Action Stories*—even as the Kline agency splashed the exploits of the desert daredevil El Borak across the pages of the December 1934, June 1935, and July 1935 issues of *Top-Notch*—then *Complete Stories* for August 1936 and finally *Thrilling Adventures* for December 1936.

In that May 13, 1936 letter to Lovecraft, Howard also mentioned, "The new editor of *Argosy* has asked me to create a new western character on the order of Breckinridge Elkins, and I've made one in the person of Pike Bearfield of Wolf Mountain. I don't know how he'll turn out. If I can get a series running in *Argosy*, keep the Breck Elkins series running in *Action Stories*, now a monthly, and the Buckner J. Grimes yarns in *Cowboy Stories*, I'll feel justified in devoting practically all my time to the writing of western stories." But for his suicide, who can doubt that Jack Byrne, that new editor of *Argosy*, then hitting the newsstands with an issue each and every week, could have done for Howard what Cap Shaw did for Hammett at *Black Mask*, fully uncorking the volcano. In his previous post as editor of *Fight Stories* and *Action Stories*, Byrne had welcomed Howard as a regular contributor, and provided a source of income as other pulp markets dried up.

Even though the popularity of the Conan series is said to have carried *Weird Tales* through the worst years of the Great Depression, the editor who had discovered Howard—the erratically capricious Farnsworth Wright—seemed unable or unwilling to pay his star writer in a timely fashion. In a letter to Wright dated May 6, 1935, Howard made his case bluntly: "*Weird Tales* owes me over eight hundred dollars for stories already published and supposed to be paid for on publication—enough to pay all my debts and get back on my feet again if I could receive it all at once. Perhaps this is impossible. I have no wish to be unreasonable; I know times are hard for everybody. But I don't believe that I am being unreasonable in asking you to pay a check each month until the accounts are squared. Honestly, at the rate we're going now, I'll be an old man before I get paid up! And my need for money now is urgent. . . . I may not—may never be a great writer, but no writer ever worked with more earnest sincerity than I have worked on the tales that have appeared in *Weird Tales*. . . . Of late when I write of Conan's adventures I have to struggle against the disheartening reflection that if the story is accepted, it may be years before I get paid for it."

By the time of his death on June 11, 1936, Wright would owe Howard over a thousand dollars. Reading the writing on that wall, Howard had stopped submitting to his first market after sending in what would be the last adventure of Conan, "Red Nails," a full-tilt drum-symphony of claustrophobic violence, the definitive Howardian action tale, which began serialization in the July 1936 issue of *Weird Tales*—providing an epic Viking funeral, incantations in prose-poetry blazing across the wood pulp pages to transport the fallen author to literary Valhalla, a testament to the Texan's tremendous talent that very few other writers have ever equaled in farewell to a character, a mood, a genre—or a life. . . .

The typescript of "Red Nails" had arrived in the offices of *Weird Tales* in July 1935, a full year before, while previous inventory remained unpaid, and the professional pulp writer sought other sources of income—including a barrage of new fiction aimed at the detective field.

"Lately I've been trying to write detective yarns, something entirely new for me," Howard reported in a letter to Lovecraft circa September or October 1933, "and haven't had much success— in fact none, so far, except for a short yarn, 'Talons in the Dark,' written in San Antonio last spring, and which Kline, as my agent, sold to a magazine called *Strange Detective Stories*. Kline has been a big help in teaching me the technique of detective story writing; whether I am able to profit by his teaching remains to be seen."

Then Howard added a parenthetical note: "(Kline marketed another yarn for me since I wrote the above.)" That unnamed yarn is thought to be the manuscript "The Teeth of Doom," which would see print under the title "The Tomb's Secret"—and while "Talons in the Dark" was a stab at a standalone crime story, "The Tomb's Secret" marked the Texan turning to one of the things he did again and again: creating yet another new series in explosive sessions on the typewriter.

The casework of private eye Steve Harrison does not match the exploits of Conan for either number written or actual stories sold in Howard's lifetime—nor the Sailor Steve Costigan boxing tales or the humorous westerns featuring Breck Elkins. But look at the nine tales gathered here, plus the extras, that smoldering residue of fragments and miscellaneous drafts Howard left behind for every concept. "Fangs of Gold" and "The Tomb's Secret" both appeared in *Strange Detective Stories* for February 1934—the latter under Howard's occasional penname "Patrick Ervin." Two stories in one issue! "Names in the Black Book" saw print in *Super-Detective Stories* for May 1934 and "Graveyard Rats" in *Thrilling Mystery* for February 1936.

Four out of nine sold. Not as impressive as Howard's set of six stories featuring Bran Mak Morn, where four appeared in *Weird Tales*, but consider the no less than fourteen stories and fragments about King Kull, where only three saw contemporary publication—and among those was "Kings of the Night," also one of the four Mak Morn tales sold! Against Kull, the new detective series does not sound like such an abject commercial failure.

The worst thing you can say about the Steve Harrison stories is that the Texan never equaled his finest moments—no "Beyond the Black River," no "Red Nails." Yet you can see his talent kicking into gear, and realize that if he had kept at it, at some point the Howard we read and read again would have surged onto the page. A touch of that definitive Howard—evoking the time-lost mysterious past—appears in "Names in the Black Book" in the lines "'Allah shield us against Shaitan the Damned!' ejaculated Khoda Khan, making a sign with his fingers that antedated Islam by some thousands of years." When modern religions were young, the world was an ancient and unknowable place.

I would not hint that Howard's private eye series is equal to Hammett's Continental Op—the Conan series is equal to the Op. But against typical hard-boiled crime fiction of the period the writer from Cross Plains holds up pretty well indeed, as witnessed in the 1993 anthology *Tough Guys and Dangerous Dames* edited by Robert E. Weinberg, Stefan Dziemianowicz and Martin H. Greenberg, a thick compilation from a variety of detective pulps. They close out the volume with "Names in the Black Book," and Howard's ghost has no need for embarrassment, even included alongside mainstay authors from *Black Mask*, *Dime Detective* and other magazines—pulps to which Howard could have contributed more crime fiction of his own, hotter and more violent crime fiction, if he had lived.

The last yarn in the Steve Harrison run, "Graveyard Rats," shows off the solid professional fictioneer really starting to punch it, conjuring up a fever pitch of fear, while keeping the hard-boiled detective action on the straight and narrow. And finally, anyone who wants to read Robert E. Howard's only private eye series has it all under one set of boards. What the hell—from a writer with *no interest* in detective stories, *enough tough guy sleuthing to fill an entire book.* This book!

Steve Harrison's
Casebook

Lord of the Dead

The onslaught was as unexpected as the stroke of an unseen cobra. One second Steve Harrison was plodding profanely but prosaically through the darkness of the alley—the next, he was fighting for his life with the snarling, mouthing fury that had fallen on him, talon and tooth. The thing was obviously a man, though in the first few dazed seconds Harrison doubted even this fact. The attacker's style of fighting was appallingly vicious and beast-like, even to Harrison who was accustomed to the foul battling of the underworld.

The detective felt the other's teeth in his flesh, and yelped profanely. But there was a knife, too; it ribboned his coat and shirt, and drew blood, and only blind chance that locked his fingers about a sinewy wrist, kept the point from his vitals. It was dark as the backdoor of Erebus. Harrison saw his assailant only as a slightly darker chunk in the blackness. The muscles under his grasping fingers were taut and steely as piano wire, and there was a terrifying suppleness about the frame writhing against his which filled Harrison with panic.

The big detective had seldom met a man his equal in strength; this denizen of the dark not only was as strong as he, but was lither and quicker and tougher than a civilized man ought to be.

They rolled over into the mud of the alley, biting, kicking and slugging, and though the unseen enemy grunted each time one of Harrison's maul-like fists thudded against him, he showed no signs of weakening. His wrist was like a woven mass of steel wires, threatening momentarily to writhe out of Harrison's clutch. His flesh crawling with fear of the cold steel, the detective grasped that wrist with both his own hands, and tried to break it. A blood-thirsty howl acknowledged this futile attempt, and a voice, which had been mouthing in an unknown tongue, hissed in Harrison's ear: "Dog! You shall die in the mud, as I died in the sand! You gave my body to the vultures! I give yours to the rats of the alley! *Wellah!*"

3

A grimy thumb was feeling for Harrison's eye, and fired to desperation, the detective heaved his body backward, bringing up his knee with bone-crushing force. The unknown gasped and rolled clear, squalling like a cat. Harrison staggered up, lost his balance, caromed against a wall. With a scream and a rush, the other was up and at him. Harrison heard the knife whistle and chunk into the wall beside him, and he lashed out blindly with all the power of his massive shoulders. He landed solidly, felt his victim shoot off his feet backward, and heard him crash headlong into the mud. Then Steve Harrison, for the first time in his life, turned his back on a single foe and ran lumberingly but swiftly up the alley.

His breath came pantingly; his feet splashed through refuse and clanged over rusty cans. Momentarily he expected a knife in his back. "Hogan!" he bawled desperately. Behind him sounded the quick lethal patter of flying feet.

He catapulted out of the black alley mouth head on into Patrolman Hogan who had heard his urgent bellow and was coming on the run. The breath went out of the patrolman in an agonized gasp, and the two hit the sidewalk together.

Harrison did not take time to rise. Ripping the Colt .38 Special from Hogan's holster, he blazed away at a shadow that hovered for an instant in the black mouth of the alley.

Rising, he approached the dark entrance, the smoking gun in his hand. No sound came from the Stygian gloom.

"Give me your flashlight," he requested, and Hogan rose, one hand on his capacious belly, and proffered the article. The white beam showed no corpse stretched in the alley mud.

"Got away," muttered Harrison.

"Who?" demanded Hogan with some spleen. "What is this, anyway? I hear you bellowin' 'Hogan!' like the devil had you by the seat of the britches, and the next thing you ram me like a chargin' bull. What—"

"Shut up, and let's explore this alley," snapped Harrison. "I didn't mean to run into you. Something jumped me—"

"I'll say somethin' did." The patrolman surveyed his companion in the uncertain light of the distant corner lamp. Harrison's coat hung in ribbons; his shirt was slashed to pieces, revealing his broad hairy chest which heaved from his exertions. Sweat ran down his corded neck, mingling with blood from gashes on arms, shoulders and breast muscles. His hair was clotted with mud, his clothes smeared with it.

"Must have been a whole gang," decided Hogan.

"It was one man," said Harrison; "one man or one gorilla; but it talked. Are you coming?"

"I am not. Whatever it was, it'll be gone now. Shine that light up the alley. See? Nothin' in sight. It wouldn't be waitin' around for us to grab it by the tail. You better get them cuts dressed. I've warned you against short cuts through dark alleys. Plenty men have grudges against you."

"I'll go to Richard Brent's place," said Harrison. "He'll fix me up. Go along with me, will you?"

"Sure, but you better let me—"

"What ever it is, no!" growled Harrison, smarting from cuts and wounded vanity. "And listen, Hogan—don't mention this, see? I want to work it out for myself. This is no ordinary affair."

"It must not be—when *one* critter licks the tar out of Iron Man Harrison," was Hogan's biting comment; whereupon Harrison cursed under his breath.

Richard Brent's house stood just off Hogan's beat—one lone bulwark of respectability in the gradually rising tide of deterioration which was engulfing the neighborhood, but of which Brent, absorbed in his studies, was scarcely aware.

Brent was in his relic-littered study, delving into the obscure volumes which were at once his vocation and his passion. Distinctly the scholar in appearance, he contrasted strongly with his visitors. But he took charge without undue perturbation, summoning to his aid a half course of medical studies.

Hogan, having ascertained that Harrison's wounds were little more than scratches, took his departure, and presently the big detective sat opposite his host, a long whiskey glass in his massive hand.

Steve Harrison's height was above medium, but it seemed dwarfed by the breadth of his shoulders and the depth of his chest. His heavy arms hung low, and his head jutted aggressively forward.

His low, broad brow, crowned with heavy black hair, suggested the man of action rather than the thinker, but his cold blue eyes reflected unexpected depths of mentality.

"'—As I died in the sand,'" he was saying. "That's what he yammered. Was he just a plain nut—or what the hell?"

Brent shook his head, absently scanning the walls, as if seeking inspiration in the weapons, antique and modern, which adorned it.

"You could not understand the language in which he spoke before?"

"Not a word. All I know is, it wasn't English and it wasn't Chinese. I do know the fellow was all steel springs and whale bone. It was like fighting a basketfull of wild cats. From now on I pack a gun regular. I haven't toted one recently, things have been so quiet. Always figured I was a match for several ordinary humans with my fists, anyway. But this devil wasn't an ordinary human; more like a wild animal."

He gulped his whiskey loudly, wiped his mouth with the back of his hand, and leaned toward Brent with a curious glint in his cold eyes.

"I wouldn't be saying this to anybody but you," he said with a strange hesitancy. "And maybe you'll think I'm crazy—but—well, I've bumped off several men in my life. Do you suppose— well, the Chinese believe in vampires and ghouls and walking dead men— and with all this talk about being dead, and me killing him—do you suppose—"

"Nonsense!" exclaimed Brent with an incredulous laugh. "When a man's dead, he's dead. He can't come back."

"That's what I've always thought," muttered Harrison. "But what the devil *did* he mean about me feeding him to the vultures?"

"I will tell you!" A voice hard and merciless as a knife edge cut their conversation.

Harrison and Brent wheeled, the former starting out of his chair. At the other end of the room one of the tall shuttered windows stood open for the sake of the coolness. Before this now stood a tall rangy man whose ill-fitting garments could not conceal the dangerous suppleness of his limbs, nor the breadth of his hard shoulders. Those cheap garments, muddy and blood-stained, seemed incongruous with the fierce dark hawk-like face, the flame of the dark eyes. Harrison grunted explosively, meeting the concentrated ferocity of that glare.

"You escaped me in the darkness," muttered the stranger, rocking slightly on the balls of his feet as he crouched, catlike, a wicked curved dagger gleaming in his hand. "Fool! Did you dream I would not follow you? Here is light; you shall not escape again!"

"Who the devil are you?" demanded Harrison, standing in an unconscious attitude of defense, legs braced, fists poised.

"Poor of wit and scant of memory!" sneered the other. "You do not remember Amir Amin Izzedin, whom you slew in the Valley of the Vultures, thirty years ago! But I remember! From my cradle I remember. Before I could speak or walk, I knew that I was Amir Amin, and I remembered the Valley of Vultures. But only after deep shame and long wandering was full knowledge revealed to me. In the smoke of Shaitan I saw it! You have changed your garments of flesh, Ahmed Pasha, you Bedouin dog, but you can not escape me. By the Golden Calf!"

With a feline shriek he ran forward, dagger on high. Harrison sprang aside, surprisingly quick for a man of his bulk, and ripped an archaic spear from the wall. With a wordless yell like a warcry, he rushed, gripping it with both hands like a bayonet. Amir Amin wheeled toward him lithely, swaying his pantherish body to avoid the onrushing point. Too late Harrison realized his mistake—knew he would be spitted on the long knife as he plunged past the elusive Oriental. But he could not check his headlong impetus. And then Amir Amin's foot slipped on a sliding rug. The spear head ripped through his muddy coat, ploughed along his ribs, bringing a spurting stream of blood. Knocked off balance, he slashed wildly, and then Harrison's bull-like shoulder smashed into him, carrying them both to the floor.

Amir Amin was up first, minus his knife. As he glared wildly about for it, Brent, temporarily stunned by the unaccustomed violence, went into action. From the racks on the wall the scholar had taken a shotgun, and he wore a look of grim determination. As he lifted it, Amir Amin yelped and plunged recklessly through the nearest window. The crash of splintering glass mingled with the thunderous roar of the shotgun. Brent, rushing to the window, blinking in the powder fumes, saw a shadowy form dart across the shadowy lawn, under the trees, and vanish. He turned back into the room, where Harrison was rising, swearing luridly.

"Twice in a night is too danged much! Who is this nut, anyway? I never saw him before!"

"A Druse!" stuttered Brent. "His accent—his mention of the golden calf—his hawk-like appearance—I am sure he is a Druse."

"What the hell is a Druse?" bellowed Harrison, in a spasm of irritation. His bandages had been torn and his cuts were bleeding again.

"They live in a mountain district in Syria," answered Brent; "a tribe of fierce fighters—"

"I can tell that," snarled Harrison. "I never expected to meet anybody that could lick me in a stand-up fight, but this devil's got me buffaloed. Anyway, it's a relief to know he's a living human being. But if I don't watch my step, I won't be. I'm staying here tonight, if you've got a room where I can lock all the doors and windows. Tomorrow I'm going to see Woon Sun."

2

Few men ever traversed the modest curio shop that opened on dingy River Street and passed through the cryptic curtain-hung door at the rear of that shop, to be amazed at what lay beyond: luxury in the shape of gilt-worked velvet hangings, silken cushioned divans, tea-cups of tinted porcelain on toy-like tables of lacquered ebony, over all which was shed a soft colored glow from electric bulbs concealed in gilded lanterns.

Steve Harrison's massive shoulders were as incongruous among those exotic surroundings as Woon Sun, short, sleek, clad in close-fitting black silk, was adapted to them.

The Chinaman smiled, but there was iron behind his suave mask.

"And so—" he suggested politely.

"And so I want your help," said Harrison abruptly. His nature was not that of a rapier, fencing for an opening, but a hammer smashing directly at its objective.

"I know that you know every Oriental in the city. I've described this bird to you. Brent says he's a Druse. You couldn't be ignorant of him. He'd stand out in any crowd. He doesn't belong with the general run of River Street gutter rats. He's a wolf."

"Indeed he is," murmured Woon Sun. "It would be useless to try to conceal from you the fact that I know this young barbarian. His name is Ali ibn Suleyman."

"He called himself something else," scowled Harrison.

"Perhaps. But he is Ali ibn Suleyman to his friends. He is, as your friend said, a Druse. His tribe live in stone cities in the Syrian mountains—particularly about the mountain called the Djebel Druse."

"Muhammadans, eh?" rumbled Harrison. "Arabs?"

"No; they are, as it were, a race apart. They worship a calf cast of gold, believe in reincarnation, and practice heathen rituals abhorred by the Moslems. First the Turks and now the French have tried to govern them, but they have never really been conquered."

"I can believe it, alright," muttered Harrison. "But why did he call me 'Ahmed Pasha'? What's he got it in for *me* for?"

Woon Sun spread his hands helplessly.

"Well, anyway," growled Harrison, "I don't want to keep on dodging knives in back alleys. I want you to fix it so I can get the drop on him. Maybe he'll talk sense, if I can get the cuffs on him. Maybe I can argue him out of this idea of killing me, whatever it is. He looks more like a fanatic than a criminal. Anyway, I want to find out just what it's all about."

"What could I do?" murmured Woon Sun, folding his hands on his round belly, malice gleaming from under his drooping lids. "I might go further and ask, *why* should I do anything for you?"

"You've stayed inside the law since coming here," said Harrison. "I know that curio shop is just a blind; you're not making any fortune out of it. But I know, too, that you're not mixed up with anything crooked. You had your dough when you came here—plenty of it—and how you got it is no concern of mine.

"But, Woon Sun," Harrison leaned forward and lowered his voice, "do you remember that young Eurasian Josef La Tour? I was the first man to reach his body, the night he was killed in Osman

Pasha's gambling den. I found a note book on him, and I kept it. Woon Sun, your name was in that book!"

An electric silence impregnated the atmosphere. Woon Sun's smooth yellow features were immobile, but red points glimmered in the shoe-button blackness of his eyes.

"La Tour must have been intending to blackmail you," said Harrison. "He'd worked up a lot of interesting data. Reading that note book, I found that your name wasn't always Woon Sun; found out where you got your money, too."

The red points had faded in Woon Sun's eyes; those eyes seemed glazed; a greenish pallor overspread the yellow face.

"You've hidden yourself well, Woon Sun," muttered the detective. "But double-crossing your society and skipping with all their money was a dirty trick. If they ever find you, they'll feed you to the rats. I don't know but what it's my duty to write a letter to a mandarin in Canton, named—"

"Stop!" The Chinaman's voice was unrecognizable. "Say no more, for the love of Buddha! I will do as you ask. I have this Druse's confidence, and can arrange it easily. It is now scarcely dark. At midnight be in the alley known to the Chinese of River Street as the Alley of Silence. You know the one I mean? Good. Wait in the nook made by the angle of the walls, near the end of the alley, and soon Ali ibn Suleyman will walk past it, ignorant of your presence. Then if you dare, you can arrest him."

"I've got a gun this time," grunted Harrison. "Do this for me, and we'll forget about La Tour's note book. But no double-crossing, or—"

"You hold my life in your fingers," answered Woon Sun. "How can I double-cross you?"

Harrison grunted skeptically, but rose without further words, strode through the curtained door and through the shop, and let himself into the street. Woon Sun watched inscrutably the broad shoulders swinging aggressively through the swarms of stooped, hurrying Orientals, men and women, who thronged River Street at that hour; then he locked the shop door and hurried back through the curtained entrance into the ornate chamber behind. And there he halted, staring.

Smoke curled up in a blue spiral from a satin divan, and on that divan lounged a young woman—a slim, dark supple creature, whose night-black hair, full red lips and scintillant eyes hinted at blood more exotic than her costly garments suggested. Those red lips curled in malicious mockery, but the glitter of her dark eyes belied any suggestion of humor, however satirical, just as their vitality belied the languor expressed in the listlessly drooping hand that held the cigarette.

"Joan!" The Chinaman's eyes narrowed to slits of suspicion. "How did you get in here?"

"Through that door over there, which opens on a passage which in turn opens on the alley that runs behind this building. Both doors were locked—but long ago I learned how to pick locks."

"But why—?"

"I saw the brave detective come here. I have been watching him for some time now—though he does not know it." The girl's vital eyes smoldered yet more deeply for an instant.

"Have you been listening outside the door?" demanded Woon Sun, turning grey.

"I am no eavesdropper. I did not have to listen. I can guess why he came. And you promised to help him?"

"I don't know what you are talking about," answered Woon Sun, with a secret sigh of relief.

"You lie!" The girl came tensely upright on the divan, her convulsive fingers crushing her cigarette, her beautiful face momentarily contorted. Then she regained control of herself, in a cold resolution more dangerous than spitting fury. "Woon Sun," she said calmly, drawing a stubby black automatic from her mantle, "how easily, and with what good will could I kill you where you stand. But I do not wish to. We shall remain friends. See, I replace the gun. But do not tempt me, my friend. Do not try to eject me, or to use violence with me. Here, sit down and take a cigarette. We will talk this over calmly."

"I do not know what you wish to talk over," said Woon Sun, sinking down on a divan and mechanically taking the cigarette she offered, as if hypnotized by the glitter of her magnetic black eyes—and the knowledge of the hidden pistol. All his Oriental immobility could not conceal the fact that he feared this young pantheress—more than he feared Harrison. "The detective came here merely on a friendly call," he said. "I have many friends among the police. If I were found murdered they would go to much trouble to find and hang the guilty person."

"Who spoke of killing?" protested Joan, snapping a match on a pointed, henna-tinted nail, and holding the tiny flame to Woon Sun's cigarette. At the instant of contact their faces were close together, and the Chinaman drew back from the strange intensity that burned in her dark eyes. Nervously he drew on the cigarette, inhaling deeply.

"I have been your friend," he said. "You should not come here threatening me with a pistol. I am a man of no small importance on River Street. You, perhaps, are not as secure as you suppose. The time may come when you will need a friend like me—"

He was suddenly aware that the girl was not answering him, or even heeding his words. Her own cigarette smoldered unheeded in her fingers, and through the clouds of smoke her eyes burned at him with the terrible eagerness of a beast of prey. With a gasp he jerked the cigarette from his lips and held it to his nostrils.

"She-devil!" It was a shriek of pure terror. Hurling the smoking stub from him, he lurched to his feet where he swayed dizzily on legs suddenly grown numb and dead. His fingers groped toward the girl with strangling motions. "Poison—dope—the black lotus—"

She rose, thrust an open hand against the flowered breast of his silk jacket and shoved him back down on the divan. He fell sprawling and lay in a limp attitude, his eyes open, but glazed and vacant. She bent over him, tense and shuddering with the intensity of her purpose.

"You are my slave," she hissed, as a hypnotizer impels his suggestions upon his subject. "You have no will but my will. Your conscious brain is asleep, but your tongue is free to tell the truth. Only the truth remains in your drugged brain. Why did the detective Harrison come here?"

"To learn of Ali ibn Suleyman, the Druse," muttered Woon Sun in his own tongue, and in a curious lifeless sing-song.

"You promised to betray the Druse to him?"

"I promised but I lied," the monotonous voice continued. "The detective goes at midnight to the Alley of Silence, which is the Gateway to the Master. Many bodies have gone feet-first through that gateway. It is the best place to dispose of his corpse. I will tell the Master he came to spy upon him, and thus gain honor for myself, as well as ridding myself of an enemy. The white barbarian will stand in the nook between the walls, awaiting the Druse as I bade him. He does not know that a trap can be opened in the angle of the walls behind him and a hand strike with a hatchet. My secret will die with him."

Apparently Joan was indifferent as to what the secret might be, since she questioned the drugged man no further. But the expression on her beautiful face was not pleasant.

"No, my yellow friend," she murmured. "Let the white barbarian go to the Alley of Silence—aye, but it is not a yellow-belly who will come to him in the darkness. He shall have his desire. He shall meet Ali ibn Suleyman; and after him, the worms that writhe in darkness!"

Taking a tiny jade vial from her bosom, she poured wine from a porcelain jug into an amber goblet, and shook into the liquor the contents of the vial. Then she put the goblet into Woon Sun's limp fingers and sharply ordered him to drink, guiding the beaker to his lips. He gulped the wine mechanically, and immediately slumped sidewise on the divan and lay still.

"You will wield no hatchet this night," she muttered. "When you awaken many hours from now, my desire will have been accomplished—and you will need fear Harrison no longer, either—whatever may be his hold upon you."

She seemed struck by a sudden thought and halted as she was turning toward the door that opened on the corridor.

"'Not as secure as I suppose'—" she muttered, half aloud. "What could he have meant by that?" A shadow, almost of apprehension, crossed her face. Then she shrugged her shoulders. "Too late to make him tell me now. No matter. The Master does not suspect—and what if he did? He's no Master of mine. I waste too much time—"

She stepped into the corridor, closing the door behind her. Then when she turned, she stopped short. Before her stood three grim figures, tall, gaunt, black-robed, their shaven vulture-like heads nodding in the dim light of the corridor.

In that instant, frozen with awful certainty, she forgot the gun in her bosom. Her mouth opened for a scream, which died in a gurgle as a bony hand was clapped over her lips.

3

The alley, nameless to white men, but known to the teeming swarms of River Street as the Alley of Silence, was as devious and cryptic as the characteristics of the race which frequented it. It did not run straight, but, slanting unobtrusively off River Street, wound through a maze of tall, gloomy structures, which, to outward seeming at least, were tenements and warehouses, and crumbling forgotten buildings apparently occupied only by rats, where boarded-up windows stared blankly.

As River Street was the heart of the Oriental quarter, so the Alley of Silence was the heart of River Street, though apparently empty and deserted. At least that was Steve Harrison's idea, though he could give no definite reason why he ascribed so much importance to a dark, dirty, crooked alley that seemed to go nowhere. The men at headquarters twitted him, telling him that he had worked so much down in the twisty mazes of rat-haunted River Street that he was getting a Chinese twist in his mind.

He thought of this, as he crouched impatiently in the angle formed by the last crook of that unsavory alley. That it was past midnight he knew from a stealthy glance at the luminous figures on his watch. Only the scurrying of rats broke the silence. He was well hidden in a cleft formed by two jutting walls, whose slanting planes came together to form a triangle opening on the alley. Alley architecture was as crazy as some of the tales which crept forth from its dank blackness. A few paces further on the Alley ended abruptly at the cliff-like blankness of a wall, in which showed no windows and only a boarded-up door.

This Harrison knew only by a vague luminance which filtered greyly into the alley from above. Shadows lurked along the angles darker than the Stygian pits, and the boarded-up door was only a vague splotch in the sheer of the wall. An empty warehouse, Harrison supposed, abandoned and rotting through the years. Probably it fronted on the bank of the river, ledged by crumbling wharfs, forgotten and unused in the years since the river trade and activity had shifted into a newer part of the city.

He wondered if he had been seen ducking into the alley. He had not turned directly off River Street, with its slinking furtive shapes that drifted silently past all night long. He had come in from a wandering side street, working his way between leaning walls and jutting corners until he came out into the dark winding alley. He had not worked the Oriental quarter for so long, not to have absorbed some of the stealth and wariness of its inhabitants.

But midnight was past, and no sign of the man he hunted. Then he stiffened. Some one was coming up the alley. But the gait was a shuffling step; not the sort he would have connected with a man like Ali ibn Suleyman. A tall stooped figure loomed vaguely in the gloom and shuffled on past the detective's covert. His trained eye, even in the dimness, told Harrison that the man was not the one he sought.

The unknown went straight to the blank door and knocked three times with a long interval between the raps. Abruptly a red disk glowed in the door. Words were hissed in Chinese. The man on the outside replied in the same tongue, and his words came clearly to the tensed detective: *"Erlik Khan!"* Then the door unexpectedly opened inward, and he passed through, illumined briefly in the reddish light which streamed through the opening. Then darkness followed the closing of the door, and silence reigned again in the alley of its name.

But crouching in the shadowed angle, Harrison felt his heart pound against his ribs. He had recognized the fellow who passed through the door as a Chinese killer with a price on his head; but it was not that recognition which sent the detective's blood pumping through his veins. It was the pass-word muttered by the evil-visaged visitant: "Erlik Khan!" It was like the materialization of a dim nightmare dream; like the confirmation of an evil legend.

For more than a year rumors had crept snakily out of the black alleys and crumbling doorways behind which the mysterious yellow people moved phantom-like and inscrutable. Scarcely rumors, either; that was a term too concrete and definite to be applied to the maunderings of dope-fiends, the ravings of madmen, the whimpers of dying men—disconnected whispers that died on the midnight wind. Yet through these disjointed mutterings had wound a dread name, fearsomely repeated, in shuddering whispers: *"Erlik Khan!"*

It was a phrase always coupled with dark deeds; it was like a black wind moaning through midnight trees; a hint, a breath, a myth, that no man could deny or affirm. None knew if it were the name of a man, a cult, a course of action, a curse, or a dream. Through its associations it became a slogan of dread: a whisper of black water lapping at rotten piles; of blood dripping on slimy stones; of death whimpers in dark corners; of stealthy feet shuffling through the haunted midnight to unknown dooms.

The men at headquarters had laughed at Harrison when he swore that he sensed a connection between various scattered crimes. They had told him, as usual, that he had worked too long among the labyrinths of the Oriental district. But that very fact made him more sensitive to furtive and subtle impressions than were his mates. And at times he had seemed almost to sense a vague and monstrous Shape that moved behind a web of illusion.

And now, like the hiss of an unseen serpent in the dark, had come to him at least as much concrete assurance as was contained in the whispered words: *"Erlik Khan!"*

Harrison stepped from his nook and went swiftly toward the boarded door. His feud with Ali ibn Suleyman was pushed into the background. The big dick was an opportunist; when chance presented itself, he seized it first and made plans later. And his instinct told him that he was on the threshold of something big.

A slow, almost imperceptible drizzle had begun. Overhead, between the towering black walls, he got a glimpse of thick grey clouds, hanging so low they seemed to merge with the lofty roofs, dully reflecting the glow of the city's myriad lights. The rumble of distant traffic came to his ears faintly and faraway. His environs seemed curiously strange, alien and aloof. He might have been stealing through the gloom of Canton, or forbidden Peking—or of Babylon, or Egyptian Memphis.

Halting before the door, he ran his hands lightly over it, and over the boards which apparently sealed it. And he discovered that some of the bolt-heads were false. It was an ingenious trick to make the door appear inaccessible to the casual glance.

Setting his teeth, with a feeling as of taking a blind plunge in the dark, Harrison rapped three times as he had heard the killer, Fang Yim, rap. Almost instantly a round hole opened in the door, level with his face, and framed dimly in a red glow he glimpsed a yellow Mongoloid visage. Sibilant Chinese hissed at him.

Harrison's hat was pulled low over his eyes, and his coat collar, turned up against the drizzle, concealed the lower part of his features. But the disguise was not needed. The man inside the door was no one Harrison had ever seen.

"Erlik Khan!" muttered the detective. No suspicion shadowed the slant eyes. Evidently white men had passed through that door before. It swung inward, and Harrison slouched through, shoulders hunched, hands thrust deep in his coat pockets, the very picture of a waterfront hoodlum. He heard the door closed behind him, and found himself in a small square chamber at the end of a narrow corridor. He noted that the door was furnished with a great steel bar, which the Chinaman was now lowering into place in the heavy iron sockets set on each side of the portal, and the hole in the center was covered by a steel disk, working on a hinge. Outside of a squatting-cushion beside the door for the doorman, the chamber was without furnishings.

All this Harrison's trained eye took in at a glance, as he slouched across the chamber. He felt that he would not be expected, as a denizen of whatever resort the place proved to be, to remain long in the room. A small red lantern, swinging from the ceiling, lighted the chamber, but the corridor seemed to be without lumination, save such as was furnished by the aforesaid lantern.

Harrison slouched on down the shadowy corridor, giving no evidence of the tensity of his nerves. He noted, with sidelong glances, the firmness and newness of the walls. Obviously a great deal of work had recently been done on the interior of this supposedly deserted building.

Like the alley outside, the corridor did not run straight. Ahead of him it bent at an angle, around which shown a mellow stream of light, and beyond this bend Harrison heard a light padding step approaching. He grabbed at the nearest door, which opened silently under his hand, and closed as silently behind him. In pitch darkness he stumbled over steps, nearly falling, catching at the wall, and cursing the noise he made. He heard the padding step halt outside the door; then a hand pushed against it. But Harrison had his forearm and elbow braced against the panel. His groping fingers found a bolt and he slid it home, wincing at the faint scraping it made. A voice hissed something in Chinese, but Harrison made no answer. Turning, he groped his way hurriedly down the stairs.

Presently his feet struck a level floor, and in another instant he bumped into a door. He had a flashlight in his pocket, but he dared not use it. He fumbled at the door and found it unlocked. The edges, sill and jambs seemed to be padded. The walls, too, seemed to be specially treated, beneath his sensitive fingers. He wondered with a shiver what cries and noises those walls and padded doors were devised to drown.

Shoving open the door, he blinked in a flood of soft reddish light, and drew his gun in a panic. But no shouts or shots greeted him, and as his eyes became accustomed to the light, he saw that he was looking into a great basement-like room, empty except for three huge packing cases. There were doors at either end of the room, and along the sides, but they were all closed. Evidently he was some distance under the ground.

He approached the packing cases, which had apparently but recently been opened, their contents not yet removed. The boards of the lids lay on the floor beside them, with wads of excelsior and tow packing.

"Booze?" he muttered to himself. "Dope? Smugglers?"

He scowled down into the nearest case. A single layer of tow sacking covered the contents, and he frowned in puzzlement at the outlines under that sacking. Then suddenly, with his skin crawling, he snatched at the sacking and pulled it away—and recoiled, choking in horror. Three yellow faces, frozen and immobile, stared sightlessly up at the swinging lamp. There seemed to be another layer underneath—

Gagging and sweating, Harrison went about his grisly task of verifying what he could scarcely believe. And then he mopped away the beads of perspiration.

"Three packing cases full of dead Chinamen!" he whispered shakily. "Eighteen yellow stiffs! Great cats! Talk about wholesale murder! I thought I'd bumped into so many hellish sights that nothing could upset me. But this is piling it on *too* thick!"

It was the stealthy opening of a door which roused him from his morbid meditations. He wheeled, galvanized. Before him crouched a monstrous and brutish shape, like a creature out of a nightmare. The detective had a glimpse of a massive, half-naked torso, a bullet-like shaven head split by a toothy and slavering grin—then the brute was upon him.

Harrison was no gunman; all his instincts were of the strong-arm variety. Instead of drawing his gun, he dashed his right mauler into that toothy grin, and was rewarded by a jet of blood. The creature's head snapped back at an agonized angle, but his bony fingers had locked on the detective's lapels. Harrison drove his left wrist-deep into his assailant's midriff, causing a green tint to overspread the coppery face, but the fellow hung on, and with a wrench, pulled Harrison's coat down over his shoulders. Recognizing a trick meant to imprison his arms, Harrison did not resist the movement, but rather aided it, with a headlong heave of his powerful body that drove his lowered head hard against the yellow man's breastbone, and tore his own arms free of the clinging sleeves.

The giant staggered backward, gasping for breath, holding the futile garment like a shield before him, and Harrison, inexorable in his attack, swept him back against the wall by the sheer force of his rush, and smashed a bone-crushing left and right to his jaw. The yellow giant pitched backward, his eyes already glazed; his head struck the wall, fetching blood in streams, and he toppled face-first to the floor where he lay twitching, his shaven head in a spreading pool of blood.

"A Mongol strangler!" panted Harrison, glaring down at him. "What kind of a nightmare is this, anyway?"

It was just at that instant that a blackjack, wielded from behind, smashed down on his head; the lights went out.

4

Some misplaced connection with his present condition caused Steve Harrison to dream fitfully of the Spanish Inquisition just before he regained consciousness. Possibly it was the clank of steel chains. Drifting back from a land of enforced dreams, his first sensation was that of an aching head, and he touched it tenderly and swore bitterly.

He was lying on a concrete floor. A steel band girdled his waist, hinged behind, and fastened before with a heavy steel lock. To that band was riveted a chain, the other end of which was made fast to a ring in the wall. A dim lantern suspended from the ceiling lighted the room, which seemed to have but one door and no window. The door was closed.

Harrison noted other objects in the room, and as he blinked and they took definite shape, he was aware of an icy premonition, too fantastic and monstrous for credit. Yet the objects at which he was staring were incredible, too.

There was an affair with levers and windlasses and chains. There was a chain suspended from the ceiling, and some objects that looked like iron fire tongs. And in one corner there was a massive, grooved block, and beside it leaned a heavy broad-edged axe. The detective shuddered in spite of himself, wondering if he were in the grip of some damnable medieval dream. He could not doubt the significance of those objects. He had seen their duplicates in museums—

Aware that the door had opened, he twisted about and glared at the figure dimly framed there—a tall, shadowy form, clad in night-black robes. This figure moved like a shadow of Doom into the chamber, and closed the door. From the shadow of a hood, two icy eyes glittered eerily, framed in a dim yellow oval of a face.

For an instant the silence held, broken suddenly by the detective's irate bellow.

"What the hell is this? Who are you? Get this chain off me!"

A scornful silence was the only answer, and under the unwinking scrutiny of those ghostly eyes, Harrison felt cold perspiration gather on his forehead and among the hairs on the backs of his hands.

"You fool!" At the peculiar hollow quality of the voice, Harrison started nervously. "You have found your doom!"

"Who are you?" demanded the detective.

"Men call me Erlik Khan, which signifies Lord of the Dead," answered the other. A trickle of ice meandered down Harrison's spine, not so much from fear, but because of the grisly thrill in the realization that at last he was face to face with the materialization of his suspicions.

"So Erlik Khan is a man, after all," grunted the detective. "I'd begun to believe that it was the name of a Chinese society."

"I am no Chinese," returned Erlik Khan. "I am a Mongol—direct descendant of Genghis Khan, the great conqueror, before whom all Asia bowed."

"Why tell me this?" growled Harrison, concealing his eagerness to hear more.

"Because you are soon to die," was the tranquil reply, "and I would have you realize that it is into the hands of no common gangster scum you have blundered.

"I was head of a lamasery in the mountains of Inner Mongolia, and, had I been able to attain my ambitions, would have rebuilt a lost empire—aye, the old empire of Genghis Khan. But I was opposed by various fools, and barely escaped with my life.

"I came to America, and here a new purpose was born in me: that of forging all secret Oriental societies into one mighty organization to do my bidding and reach unseen tentacles across the seas into hidden lands. Here, unsuspected by such blundering fools as you, have I built my castle. Already I have accomplished much. Those who oppose me die suddenly, or—you saw those fools in the packing cases in the cellar. They are members of the Yat Soy, who thought to defy me."

"Judas!" muttered Harrison. "A whole tong scuppered!"

"Not dead," corrected Erlik Khan. "Merely in a cataleptic state, induced by certain drugs introduced into their liquor by trusted servants. They were brought here in order that I might convince them of their folly in opposing me. I have a number of underground crypts like this one, wherein are implements and machines calculated to change the mind of the most stubborn."

"Torture chambers under River Street!" muttered the detective. "Damned if this isn't a nightmare!"

"You, who have puzzled so long amidst the mazes of River Street, are you surprized at the mysteries within its mysteries?" murmured Erlik Khan. "Truly, you have but touched the fringes of its secrets. Many men do my bidding—Chinese, Syrians, Mongols, Hindus, Arabs, Turks, Egyptians."

"Why?" demanded Harrison. "Why should so many men of such different and hostile religions serve you—"

"Behind all differences of religion and belief," said Erlik Khan, "lies the eternal *Oneness* that is the essence and root-stem of the East. Before Muhammad was, or Confucius, or Gautama, there were signs and symbols, ancient beyond belief, but common to all sons of the Orient. There are cults stronger and older than Islam or Buddhism—cults whose roots are lost in the blackness of the dawn ages, before Babylon was, or Atlantis sank.

"To an adept, these young religions and beliefs are but new cloaks, masking the reality beneath. Even to a dead man I can say no more. Suffice to know that I, whom men call Erlik Khan, have power above and behind the powers of Islam or of Buddha."

Harrison lay silent, meditating over the Mongol's words, and presently the latter resumed: "You have but yourself to blame for your plight. I am convinced that you did not come here tonight to spy upon me—poor, blundering, barbarian fool, who did not even guess my existence. I have learned that you came in your crude way, expecting to trap a servant of mine, the Druse Ali ibn Suleyman."

"You sent him to kill me," growled Harrison.

A scornful laugh put his teeth on edge.

"Do you fancy yourself so important? I would not turn aside to crush a blind worm. Another put the Druse on your trail—a deluded person, a miserable, egoistic fool, who even now is paying the price of folly.

"Ali ibn Suleyman is, like many of my henchmen, an outcast from his people, his life forfeit.

"Of all virtues, the Druses most greatly esteem the elementary one of physical courage. When a Druse shows cowardice, none taunts him, but when the warriors gather to drink coffee, some one spills a cup on his *abba*. That is his death-sentence. At the first opportunity, he is obliged to go forth and die as heroically as possible.

"Ali ibn Suleyman failed on a mission where success was impossible. Being young, he did not realize that his fanatical tribe would brand him as a coward because, in failing, he had not got himself killed. But the cup of shame was spilled on his robe. Ali was young; he did not wish to die. He broke a custom of a thousand years; he fled the Djebel Druse and became a wanderer over the earth.

"Within the past year he joined my followers, and I welcomed his desperate courage and terrible fighting ability. But recently the foolish person I mentioned decided to use him to further a private feud, in no way connected with my affairs. That was unwise. My followers live but to serve me, whether they realize it or not.

"Ali goes often to a certain house to smoke opium, and this person caused him to be drugged with the dust of the black lotus, which produces a hypnotic condition, during which the subject is amenable to suggestions, which, if continually repeated, carry over into the victim's waking hours.

"The Druses believe that when a Druse dies, his soul is instantly reincarnated in a Druse baby. The great Druse hero, Amir Amin Izzedin, was killed by the Arab shaykh Ahmed Pasha, the night Ali ibn Suleyman was born. Ali has always believed himself to be the reincarnated soul of Amir Amin, and mourned because he could not revenge his former self on Ahmed Pasha, who was killed a few days after he slew the Druse chief.

"All this the *person* ascertained, and by means of the black lotus, known as the Smoke of Shaitan, convinced the Druse that you, detective Harrison, were the reincarnation of his old enemy Shaykh Ahmed Pasha. It took time and cunning to convince him, even in his drugged condition, that an Arab shaykh could be reincarnated in an American detective, but the *person* was very clever, and so at last Ali was convinced, and disobeyed my orders—which were never to molest the police, unless they got in my way, and then only according to my directions. For I do not woo publicity. He must be taught a lesson.

"Now I must go. I have spent too much time with you already. Soon one will come who will lighten you of your earthly burdens. Be consoled by the realization that the foolish person who brought you to this pass is expiating her crime likewise. In fact, separated from you but by that padded partition. Listen!"

From somewhere near rose a feminine voice, incoherent but urgent.

"The foolish one realizes her mistake," smiled Erlik Khan benevolently. "Even through these walls pierce her lamentations. Well, she is not the first to regret foolish actions in these crypts. And now I must begone. Those foolish Yat Soys will soon begin to awaken."

"Wait, you devil!" roared Harrison, struggling up against his chain. "What—"

"Enough, enough!" There was a touch of impatience in the Mongol's tone. "You weary me. Get you to your meditations, for your time is short. Farewell, Mr. Harrison—*not* au revoir."

The door closed silently, and the detective was left alone with his thoughts which were far from pleasant. He cursed himself for falling into that trap; cursed his peculiar obsession for always working alone. None knew of the tryst he had tried to keep; he had divulged his plans to no one.

Beyond the partition the muffled sobs continued. Sweat began to bead Harrison's brow. His nerves, untouched by his own plight, began to throb in sympathy with that terrified voice.

Then the door opened again, and Harrison, twisting about, knew with numbing finality that he looked on his executioner. It was a tall, gaunt Mongol, clad only in sandals and a trunk-like garment of yellow silk, from the girdle of which depended a bunch of keys. He carried a great bronze bowl and some objects that looked like joss sticks. These he placed on the floor near Harrison, and squatting just out of the captive's reach, began to arrange the evil-smelling sticks in a sort of pyramidal shape in the bowl. And Harrison, glaring, remembered a half-forgotten horror among the myriad dim horrors of River Street: a corpse he had found in a sealed room where acrid fumes still hovered over a charred bronze bowl—the corpse of a Hindu, shriveled and crinkled like old leather—mummified by a lethal smoke that killed and shrunk the victim like a poisoned rat.

From the other cell came a shriek so sharp and poignant that Harrison jumped and cursed. The Mongol halted in his task, a match in his hand. His parchment-like visage split in a leer of appreciation, disclosing the withered stump of a tongue; the man was a mute.

The cries increased in intensity, seemingly more in fright than in pain, yet an element of pain was evident. The mute, rapt in his evil glee, rose and leaned nearer the wall, cocking his ear as if unwilling to miss any whimper of agony from that torture cell. Slaver dribbled from the corner of his loose mouth; he sucked his breath in eagerly, unconsciously edging nearer the wall—Harrison's foot shot out, hooked suddenly and fiercely about the lean ankle. The Mongol threw wild arms aloft, and toppled into the detective's waiting arms.

It was with no scientific wrestling hold that Harrison broke the executioner's neck. His pent-up fury had swept away everything but a berserk madness to grip and rend and tear in primitive passion. Like a grizzly he grappled and twisted, and felt the vertebrae give way like rotten twigs.

Dizzy with glutted fury he struggled up, still gripping the limp shape, gasping incoherent blasphemy. His fingers closed on the keys dangling at the dead man's belt, and ripping them free, he hurled the corpse savagely to the floor in a paroxysm of excess ferocity. The thing struck loosely and lay without twitching, the sightless face grinning hideously back over the yellow shoulder.

Harrison mechanically tried the keys in the lock at his waist. An instant later, freed of his shackles, he staggered in the middle of the cell, almost overcome by the wild rush of emotion—hope, exultation, and the realization of freedom. He snatched up the grim axe that leaned against the darkly stained block, and could have yelled with bloodthirsty joy as he felt the perfect balance of the weighty weapon, and saw the dim light gleaming on its flaring razor-edge.

An instant's fumbling with the keys at the lock, and the door opened. He looked out into a narrow corridor, dimly lighted, lined with closed doors. From one next to his, the distressing cries were coming, muffled by the padded door and the specially treated walls.

In his berserk wrath he wasted no time in trying his keys on that door. Heaving up the sturdy axe with both hands, he swung it crashing against the panels, heedless of the noise, mindful only of his frenzied urge to violent action. Under his flailing strokes the door burst inward and through its splintered ruins he lunged, eyes glaring, lips asnarl.

He had come into a cell much like the one he had just quitted. There was a rack—a veritable medieval devil-machine—and in its cruel grip writhed a pitiful white figure—a girl, clad only in a scanty chemise. A gaunt Mongol bent over the handles, turning them slowly. Another was engaged in heating a pointed iron over a small brazier.

This he saw at a glance, as the girl rolled her head toward him and cried out in agony. Then the Mongol with the iron ran at him silently, the glowing, white-hot steel thrust forward like a spear. In the grip of red fury though he was, Harrison did not lose his head. A wolfish grin twisting his thin lips, he side stepped, and split the torturer's head as a melon is split. Then as the corpse tumbled down, spilling blood and brains, he wheeled catlike to meet the onslaught of the other.

The attack of this one was silent as that of the other. They too were mutes. He did not lunge in so recklessly as his mate, but his caution availed him little as Harrison swung his dripping axe. The Mongol threw up his left arm, and the curved edge sheared through muscle and bone, leaving the limb hanging by a shred of flesh. Like a dying panther the torturer sprang in turn, driving in his knife with the fury of desperation. At the same instant the bloody axe flailed down. The thrusting knife point tore through Harrison's shirt, ploughed through the flesh over his breastbone, and as he flinched involuntarily, the axe turned in his hand and struck flat, crushing the Mongol's skull like an egg shell.

Swearing like a pirate, the detective wheeled this way and that, glaring for new foes. Then he remembered the girl on the rack.

And then he recognized her at last. "Joan La Tour! What in the name—"

"Let me go!" she wailed. "Oh, for God's sake, let me go!"

The mechanism of the devilish machine balked him. But he saw that she was tied by heavy cords on wrists and ankles, and cutting them, he lifted her free. He set his teeth at the thought of the ruptures, dislocated joints and torn sinews that she might have suffered, but evidently the torture had not progressed far enough for permanent injury. Joan seemed none the worse, physically, for her experience, but she was almost hysterical. As he looked at the cowering, sobbing figure, shivering in her scanty garment, and remembered the perfectly poised, sophisticated, and self-sufficient beauty as he had known her, he shook his head in amazement. Certainly Erlik Khan knew how to bend his victims to his despotic will.

"Let us go," she pleaded between sobs. "They'll be back—they will have heard the noise—"

"Alright," he grunted; "but where the devil are we?"

"I don't know," she whimpered. "Somewhere in the house of Erlik Khan. His Mongol mutes brought me here earlier tonight, through passages and tunnels connecting various parts of the city with this place."

"Well, come on," said he. "We might as well go somewhere."

Taking her hand he led her out into the corridor, and glaring about uncertainly, he spied a narrow stair winding upward. Up this they went, to be halted soon by a padded door, which was not locked. This he closed behind him, and tried to lock, but without success. None of his keys would fit the lock.

"I don't know whether our racket was heard or not," he grunted, "unless somebody was nearby. This building is fixed to drown noise. We're in some part of the basement, I reckon."

"We'll never get out alive," whimpered the girl. "You're wounded—I saw blood on your shirt—"

"Nothing but a scratch," grunted the big detective, stealthily investigating with his fingers the ugly ragged gash that was soaking his torn shirt and waist-band with steadily seeping blood. Now that his fury was beginning to cool, he felt the pain of it.

Abandoning the door, he groped upward in thick darkness, guiding the girl of whose presence he was aware only by the contact of a soft little hand trembling in his. Then he heard her sobbing convulsively.

"This is all my fault! I got you into this! The Druse, Ali ibn Suleyman—"

"I know," he grunted; "Erlik Khan told me. But I never suspected that you were the one who put this crazy heathen up to knifing me. Was Erlik Khan lying?"

"No," she whimpered. "My brother—Josef. Until tonight I thought you killed him."

He started convulsively.

"*Me?* I didn't do it! I don't know who did. Somebody shot him over my shoulder—aiming at me, I reckon, during that raid on Osman Pasha's joint."

"I know, now," she muttered. "But I'd always believed you lied about it. I thought you killed him, yourself. Lots of people think that, you know. I wanted revenge. I hit on what looked like a sure scheme. The Druse doesn't know me. He's never seen me, awake. I bribed the owner of the opium-joint that Ali ibn Suleyman frequents, to drug him with the black lotus. Then I would do my work on him. It's much like hypnotism.

"The owner of the joint must have talked. Anyway, Erlik Khan learned how I'd been using Ali ibn Suleyman, and he decided to punish me. Maybe he was afraid the Druse talked too much while he was drugged.

"I know too much, too, for one not sworn to obey Erlik Khan. I'm part Oriental and I've played in the fringe of River Street affairs until I've got myself tangled up in them. Josef played with fire, too, just as I've been doing, and it cost him his life. Erlik Khan told me tonight who the real murderer was. It was Osman Pasha. He wasn't aiming at you. He intended to kill Josef.

"I've been a fool, and now my life is forfeit. Erlik Khan is the king of River Street."

"He won't be long," growled the detective. "We're going to get out of here some how, and then I'm coming back with a squad and clean out this damned rat hole. I'll show Erlik Khan that this is America, not Mongolia. When I get through with him—"

He broke off short as Joan's fingers closed on his convulsively. From somewhere below them sounded a confused muttering. What lay above, he had no idea, but his skin crawled at the thought of being trapped on that dark twisting stair. He hurried, almost dragging the girl, and presently encountered a door that did not seem to be locked.

Even as he did so, a light flared below, and a shrill yelp galvanized him. Far below he saw a cluster of dim shapes in a red glow of a torch or lantern. Rolling eyeballs flashed whitely, steel glimmered.

Darting through the door and slamming it behind them, he sought for a frenzied instant for a key that would fit the lock and not finding it, seized Joan's wrist and ran down the corridor that wound among black velvet hangings. Where it led he did not know. He had lost all sense of direction. But he did know that death grim and relentless was on their heels.

Looking back, he saw a hideous crew swarm up into the corridor: yellow men in silk jackets and baggy trousers, grasping knives. Ahead of him loomed a curtain-hung door. Tearing aside the heavy satin hangings, he hurled the door open and leaped through, drawing Joan after him, slamming the door behind them. And stopped dead, an icy despair gripping at his heart.

5

They had come into a vast hall-like chamber, such as he had never dreamed existed under the prosaic roofs of any Western city.

Gilded lanterns, on which writhed fantastic carven dragons, hung from the fretted ceiling, shedding a golden lustre over velvet hangings that hid the walls. Across these black expanses other dragons twisted, worked in silver, gold and scarlet. In an alcove near the door reared a squat idol, bulky, taller than a man, half hidden by a heavy lacquer screen, an obscene, brutish travesty of nature, that only a Mongolian brain could conceive. Before it stood a low altar, whence curled up a spiral of incense smoke.

But Harrison at the moment gave little heed to the idol. His attention was riveted on the robed and hooded form which sat cross-legged on a velvet divan at the other end of the hall—they had blundered full into the web of the spider. About Erlik Khan, in subordinate attitudes sat a group of Orientals, Chinese, Syrians and Turks.

The paralysis of surprise that held both groups was broken by a peculiarly menacing cry from Erlik Khan, who reared erect, his hand flying to his girdle. The others sprang up, yelling and fumbling for weapons. Behind him, Harrison heard the clamor of their pursuers just beyond the door. And in that instant he recognized and accepted the one desperate alternative to instant capture. He sprang for the idol, thrust Joan into the alcove behind it, and squeezed after her. Then he turned at bay. It was the last stand—trail's end. He did not hope to escape; his motive was merely that of a wounded wolf which drags itself into a corner where its killers must come at it from in front.

The green stone bulk of the idol blocked the entrance of the alcove save for one side, where there was a narrow space between its misshapen hip and shoulder, and the corner of the wall. The space on the other side was too narrow for a cat to have squeezed through, and the lacquer screen stood before it. Looking through the interstices of this screen, Harrison could see the whole room, into which the pursuers were now storming. The detective recognized their leader as Fang Yim, the hatchet-man.

A furious babble rose, dominated by Erlik Khan's voice, speaking English, the one common language of those mixed breeds.

"They hide behind the god; drag them forth."

"Let us rather fire a volley," protested a dark-skinned powerfully built man whom Harrison recognized—Ak Bogha, a Turk, his fez contrasting with his full dress suit. "We risk our lives, standing here in full view; he can shoot through that screen."

"Fool!" The Mongol's voice rasped with anger. "He would have fired already if he had a gun. Let no man pull a trigger. They can crouch behind the idol, and it would take many shots to smoke them out. We are not now in the Crypts of Silence. A volley would make too much noise; one shot might not be heard in the streets. But one shot will not suffice. He has but an axe; rush in and cut him down!"

Without hesitation Ak Bogha ran forward, followed by the others. Harrison shifted his grip on his axe haft. Only one man could come at him at a time—

Ak Bogha was in the narrow strait between idol and wall before Harrison moved from behind the great green bulk. The Turk yelped in fierce triumph and lunged, lifting his knife. He blocked the entrance; the men crowding behind him had only a glimpse, over his straining shoulder, of Harrison's grim face and blazing eyes.

Full into Ak Bogha's face Harrison thrust the axe head, smashing nose, lips and teeth. The Turk reeled, gasping and choking with blood, and half blinded, but struck again, like the slash of a dying panther. The keen edge sliced Harrison's face from temple to jaw, and then the flailing axe crushed in Ak Bogha's breastbone and sent him reeling backward, to fall dying.

The men behind him gave back suddenly. Harrison, bleeding like a stuck hog, again drew back behind the idol. They could not see the white giant who lurked at bay in the shadow of the god, but they saw Ak Bogha gasping his life out on the bloody floor before the idol, like a gory sacrifice, and the sight shook the nerve of the fiercest.

And now, as matters hovered at a deadlock, and the Lord of the Dead seemed himself uncertain, a new factor introduced itself into the tense drama. A door opened and a fantastic figure swaggered through. Behind him Harrison heard Joan gasp incredulously.

It was Ali ibn Suleyman who strode down the hall as if he trod his own castle in the mysterious Djebel Druse. No longer the garments of western civilization clothed him. On his head he wore a silken *kafiyeh* bound about the temples with a broad gilded band. Beneath his voluminous, girdled *abba* showed silver-heeled boots, ornately stitched. His eye-lids were painted with *kohl*, causing his eyes to glitter even more lethally than ordinarily. In his hand was a long curved scimitar.

Harrison mopped the blood from his face and shrugged his shoulders. Nothing in the house of Erlik Khan could surprize him any more, not even this picturesque shape which might have just swaggered out of an opium dream of the East.

The attention of all was centered on the Druse as he strode down the hall, looking even bigger and more formidable in his native costume than he had in western garments. He showed no more awe of the Lord of the Dead than he showed of Harrison. He halted directly in front of Erlik Khan, and spoke without meekness.

"Why was it not told me that mine enemy was a prisoner in the house?" he demanded in English, evidently the one language he knew in common with the Mongol.

"You were not here," Erlik Khan answered brusquely, evidently liking little the Druse's manner.

"Nay, I but recently returned, and learned that the dog who was once Ahmed Pasha stood at bay in this chamber. I have donned my proper garb for this occasion." Turning his back full on the Lord of the Dead, Ali ibn Suleyman strode before the idol.

"Oh, infidel!" he called, "come forth and meet my steel! Instead of the dog's death which is your due, I offer you honorable battle—your axe against my sword. Come forth, ere I hale you thence by your beard!"

"I haven't any beard," grunted the detective. "Come in and get me!"

"Nay," scowled Ali ibn Suleyman; "when you were Ahmed Pasha, you were a man. Come forth, where we can have room to wield our weapons. If you slay me, you shall go free. I swear by the Golden Calf!"

"Could I dare trust him?" muttered Harrison.

"A Druse keeps his word," whispered Joan. "But there is Erlik Khan—"

"Who are you to make promises?" called Harrison. "Erlik Khan is master here."

"Not in the matter of my private feud!" was the arrogant

reply. "I swear by my honor that no hand but mine shall be lifted against you, and that if you slay me, you shall go free. Is it not so, Erlik Khan?"

"Let it be as you wish," answered the Mongol, spreading his hands in a gesture of resignation.

Joan grasped Harrison's arm convulsively, whispering urgently: "Don't trust him! He won't keep his word! He'll betray you and Ali both! He's never intended that the Druse should kill you—it's his way of punishing Ali, by having some one else kill you! Don't—don't—"

"We're finished anyway," muttered Harrison, shaking the sweat and blood out of his eyes. "I might as well take the chance. If I don't they'll rush us again, and I'm bleeding so that I'll soon be too weak to fight. Watch your chance, girl, and try to get away while everybody's watching Ali and me." Aloud he called: "I have a woman here, Ali. Let her go before we start fighting."

"To summon the police to your rescue?" demanded Ali. "No! She stands or falls with you. Will you come forth?"

"I'm coming," gritted Harrison. Grasping his axe, he moved out of the alcove, a grim and ghastly figure, blood masking his face and soaking his torn garments. He saw Ali ibn Suleyman gliding toward him, half crouching, the scimitar in his hand a broad curved glimmer of blue light. He lifted his axe, fighting down a sudden wave of weakness—there came a muffled dull report, and at the same instant he felt a paralyzing impact against his head. He was not aware of falling, but realized that he was lying on the floor, conscious but unable to speak or move.

A wild cry rang in his dulled ears and Joan La Tour, a flying white figure, threw herself down beside him, her fingers frantically fluttering over him.

"Oh, you dogs, dogs!" she was sobbing. "You've killed him!" She lifted her head to scream: "Where is your honor now, Ali ibn Suleyman?"

From where he lay Harrison could see Ali standing over him, scimitar still poised, eyes flaring, mouth gaping, an image of horror and surprize. And beyond the Druse the detective saw the silent group clustered about Erlik Khan; and Fang Yim was holding an automatic with a strangely misshapen barrel—a Maxim silencer. One muffled shot would not be noticed from the street.

A fierce and frantic cry burst from Ali ibn Suleyman.

"Aie, my honor! My pledged word! My oath on the Golden Calf! You have broken it! You have shamed me to an infidel! You robbed me both of vengeance and honor! Am I a dog, to be dealt with thus! *Ya Maruf!*"

His voice soared to a feline screech, and wheeling, he moved like a blinding blur of light. Fang Yim's scream was cut short horribly in a ghastly gurgle, as the scimitar cut the air in a blue flame. The Chinaman's head shot from his shoulders on a jetting fountain of blood and thudded on the floor, grinning awfully in the golden light. With a yell of terrible exultation, Ali ibn Suleyman leapt straight toward the hooded shape on the divan. Fezzed and turbaned figures ran in between. Steel flashed, showering sparks, blood spurted, and men screamed. Harrison saw the Druse scimitar flame bluely through the lamplight full on Erlik Khan's coifed head. The hood fell in halves, and the Lord of the Dead rolled to the floor, his fingers convulsively clenching and unclenching.

The others swarmed about the maddened Druse, hacking and stabbing. The figure in the wide-sleeved *abba* was the center of a score of licking blades, of a gasping, blaspheming, clutching knot of straining bodies. And still the dripping scimitar flashed and flamed, shearing through flesh, sinew and bone, while under the stamping feet of the living rolled mutilated corpses. Under the impact of struggling bodies, the altar was overthrown, the smoldering incense scattered over the rugs. The next instant flame was licking at the hangings. With a rising roar and a rush the fire enveloped one whole side of the room, but the battlers heeded it not.

Harrison was aware that someone was pulling and tugging at him, someone who sobbed and gasped, but did not slacken their effort. A pair of slender hands were locked in his tattered shirt, and he was being dragged bodily through billowing smoke that blinded and half strangled him. The tugging hands grew weaker, but did not release their hold, as their owner fought on in a heart-breaking struggle. Then suddenly the detective felt a rush of clean wind, and was aware of concrete instead of carpeted wood under his shoulders.

He was lying in a slow drizzle on a sidewalk, while above him towered a wall reddened in a mounting glare. On the other side loomed broken docks, and beyond them the lurid glow was reflected on water. He heard the screams of fire sirens, and felt the gathering of a chattering, shouting crowd about him.

Life and movement slowly seeping back into his numbed veins, he lifted his head feebly, and saw Joan La Tour crouched beside him, oblivious to the rain as to her scanty attire. Tears were streaming down her face, and she cried out as she saw him move: "Oh, you're not dead—I thought I felt life in you, but I dared not let *them* know—"

"Just creased my scalp," he mumbled thickly. "Knocked me out for a few minutes—seen it happen that way before—you dragged me out—"

"While they were fighting. I thought I'd never find an outer door—here come the firemen at last!"

"The Yat Soys!" he gasped, trying to rise. "Eighteen Chinamen in that basement—my God, they'll be roasted!"

"We can't help it!" panted Joan La Tour. "We were fortunate to save ourselves. Oh!"

The crowd surged back, yelling, as the roof began to cave in, showering sparks. And through the crumpling walls, by some miracle, reeled an awful figure—Ali ibn Suleyman. His clothing hung in smoldering, bloody ribbons, revealing the ghastly wounds beneath. He had been slashed almost to pieces. His head-cloth was gone, his hair crisped, his skin singed and blackened where it was not blood-smeared. His scimitar was gone, and blood streamed down his arm over the fingers that gripped a dripping dagger.

"Aie!" he cried in a ghastly croak. "I see you, Ahmed Pasha, through the fire and mist! You live, in spite of Mongol treachery! That is well! Only by the hand of Ali ibn Suleyman, who was Amir Amin Izzedin, shall you die! I have washed my honor in blood, and it is spotless!

> *" 'I am a son of Maruf,*
> *Of the mountain of sanctuary;*
> *When my sword is rusty*
> *I make it bright*
> *With the blood of my enemies!'"*

Reeling, he pitched face first, stabbing at Harrison's feet as he fell; then rolling on his back he lay motionless, staring sightlessly up at the flame-lurid skies.

The People of the Serpent

"This is the only trail into the swamp, mister." Steve Harrison's guide pointed a long finger down the narrow path which wound in and out among the live-oaks and cypresses. Harrison shrugged his massive shoulders. The surroundings were not inviting, with the long shadows of the late afternoon sun reaching dusky fingers into the dim recesses among the moss-hung trees.

"You ought to wait till mornin'," opined the guide, a tall lanky man in cowhide boots and sagging overalls. "It's gittin' late, and we don't want to git catched in the swamp after night."

"I can't wait, Rogers," answered the detective. "The man I'm after might get clean away by morning."

"He'll have to come out by this path," answered Rogers as they swung along. "Ain't no other way in or out. If he tries to push through to high ground on the other side, he'll shore fall into a bottomless bog, or git et by a 'gator. There's lots of them. I reckon he ain't much used to swamps?"

"I don't suppose he ever saw one before. He's city-bred."

"Then he won't dast leave the beaten path," confidently predicted Rogers.

"On the other hand, he might, not realizing the danger," grunted Harrison.

"What'd you say he done?" pursued Rogers, directing a jet of tobacco juice at a beetle crawling through the dark loam.

"Knocked an old Chinaman in the head with a meat-cleaver and stole his life-time savings—ten thousand dollars, in bills of a thousand each. The old man left a little granddaughter who'll be penniless if this money isn't recovered. That's one reason I want to get this rat before he loses himself in a bog. I want to recover that money, for the kid."

"And you figure the Chinaman seen goin' down this path a few days ago was him?"

"Couldn't be anybody else," snapped Harrison. "We've hounded him half way across the continent, cut him off from the borders and the ports. We were closing in on him when he slipped through, somehow. This was about the only place left for him to hide. I've chased him too far to delay now. If he drowns in the swamp, we'll probably never find him, and the money will be lost, too. The man he murdered was a fine, honest old Chinaman. This fellow, Woon Shang, is bad all the way through."

"He'll run into some bad folks down here," ruminated Rogers. "Nothin' but niggers live in these swamplands. They ain't regular darkies like them that live outside. These came here fifty or sixty years back—refugees from Haiti, or somewhere. You know we ain't far from the coast. They're yaller-skinned, and don't hardly ever come out of the swamp. They keep to theirselves, and they don't like strangers. *What's that?*"

They were just rounding a bend in the path, and something lay on the ground ahead of them—something black, and dabbled with red, that groaned and moved feebly.

"It's a nigger!" exclaimed Rogers. "He's been knifed."

It took no expert to deduce that. They bent over him and Rogers voiced profane recognition. "Why, I know this feller! He ain't no swamp rat. He's Joe Corley, that razored up another nigger at a dance last month and lit out. Bet he's been hidin' in the swamp ever since. Joe! Joe Corley!"

The wounded man groaned and rolled up his glassy eyes; his skin was ashy with the nearness of approaching death.

"Who stabbed you, Joe?" demanded Rogers.

"De Swamp Cat!" The gasp was scarcely audible. Rogers swore and looked fearfully about him, as if expecting something to spring on them from the trees.

"I wuz tryin' to git outside," muttered the negro.

"What for?" demanded Rogers. "Didn't you know you'd git jailed if they catched you?"

"Ruther go to de jail-house dan git mixed up—in de devilment—dey's cookin' up—in de swamp." The voice sank lower as speech grew more difficult.

"What you mean, Joe?" uneasily demanded Rogers.

"Voodoo niggers," muttered Corley disjointedly. "Took dat Chinaman 'stead uh me—didn't want me to git away, though—then John Bartholomew—uuuugh!"

A trickle of blood started from the corner of his thick lips, he stiffened in brief convulsion and then lay still.

"He's dead!" whispered Rogers, staring down the swamp path with dilated eyes.

"He spoke of a Chinaman," said Harrison. "That clinches it that we're on the right trail. Have to leave him here for the time being. Nothing we can do for him now. Let's get going."

"You aim to go on, after this?" exclaimed Rogers.

"Why not?"

"Mr. Harrison," said Rogers solemnly, "you offered me a good wage to guide you into this here swamp. But I'm tellin' you fair there ain't enough money to make me go in there now, with night comin' on."

"But why?" protested Harrison. "Just because this man got into a fight with one of his own kind—"

"It's more 'n just that," declared Rogers decisively. "This nigger was tryin' to git out of the swamp when they got him. He knowed he'd git jailed on the outside, but he was goin' anyway; that means somethin' had scared the livin' daylights out of him. You heard him say it was the Swamp Cat that got him?"

"Well?"

"Well, the Swamp Cat is a crazy nigger that lives in the swamp. It's been so long since any white folks claimed they seen him, I'd begun to believe he was just a myth the 'outside' niggers told to scare people away from the swamp. But this shows he ain't. He killed Joe Corley. He'll kill us if he catches us in the dark. Why, by golly, he may be watchin' us right now!" This thought so disturbed Rogers that he drew a big six-shooter with an enormous length of barrel, and peered about, masticating his quid with a rapidity that showed his mental perturbation.

"Who's the other follow he named, John Bartholomew?" inquired Harrison.

"Don't know. Never heard of him. Come on, let's shove out of here. We'll git some boys and come back after Joe's body."

"I'm going on," growled Harrison, rising and dusting his hands. Rogers stared. "Man, you're plumb crazy! You'll git lost—"

"Not if I keep to the path."

"Well, then the Swamp Cat'll git you, or them 'gators will—"

"I'll take my chance," answered Harrison brusquely. "Woon Shang's somewhere in this swamp. If he manages to get out before I get my hands on him, he may get clean away. I'm going after him."

"But if you'll wait we'll raise a posse and go after him first thing in the mornin'," urged Rogers.

Harrison did not attempt to explain to the man his almost obsessional preference for working alone. With no further comment he turned and strode off down the narrow path. Rogers yelled after him: "You're crazy as hell! If you git as far as Celia Pompoloi's hut, you better stay there tonight! She's the big boss of them niggers. It's the first cabin you come to. I'm goin' back to town and git a posse, and tomorrow mornin' we'll—" The words became unintelligible among the dense growth as Harrison rounded a turn that shut off the sight of the other man.

As the detective strode along he saw that blood was smeared on the rotting leaves, and there were marks as if something heavy had been dragged over the trail. Joe Corley had obviously crawled for some distance after being attacked. Harrison visualized him dragging himself along on his belly like a crippled snake. The man must have had intense vitality to have gotten so far with a mortal wound in his back. And his fear must have been desperate to so drive him.

Harrison could no longer see the sun, but he knew it was hanging low. The shadows were gathering, and he was plunging deeper and deeper into the swamp. He began to glimpse patches of scummy ooze among the trees, and the path grew more tortuous as it wound to avoid these slimy puddles. Harrison plunged on without pausing. The dense growth might lend concealment to a desperate fugitive, but it was not in the woods, but among the scattered cabins of the swamp dwellers that he expected to find the man he hunted. The city-bred Chinaman, fearful of solitude and unable to fend for himself, would seek the company of men, even of black men.

The detective wheeled suddenly. About him, in the dusk, the swamp was waking. Insects lifted strident voices, wings of bats or owls beat the air, and bullfrogs boomed from the lily pads. But he had heard a sound that was not of these things. It was a stealthy movement among the trees that marched in solid ranks beside the trail. Harrison drew his .45 and waited. Nothing happened. But in primitive solitudes a man's instincts are whetted. The detective felt that he was being watched by unseen eyes; he could almost sense the intensity of their glare. Was it the Chinaman, after all?

A bush beside the trail moved, without a wind to stir it. Harrison sprang through the curtain of creeper-hung cypresses, gun ready, snarling a command. His feet sank in slimy ooze, he stumbled in rotting vegetation and felt the dangling strands of moss slap against his face. There was nothing behind the bush, but he could have sworn that he saw a shadowy form move and vanish among the trees a short distance away. As he hesitated, he glanced down and saw a distinct mark in the loam. He bent closer; it was the print of a great, bare, splay foot. Moisture was oozing into the depression. A man *had* been standing behind that bush.

With a shrug Harrison stepped back into the trail. That was not the footprint of Woon Shang, and the detective was not looking for anybody else. It was natural that one of the swamp dwellers would spy on a stranger. The detective sent a hail into the gathering darkness, to assure the unseen watcher of his friendly intentions. There was no reply. Harrison turned and strode on down the trail, not feeling entirely at ease, as he heard, from time to time, a faint snapping of twigs and other sounds that seemed to indicate someone moving along a course paralleling the path. It was not soothing to know that he was being followed by some unseen and possibly hostile being. His thoughts kept reverting to that grisly wound in the dead Joe Corley's back.

It was so dark now that he kept the path more by feel than by sight. About him sounded weird cries of strange birds or animals, and from time to time a deep grunting reverberation that puzzled him until he recognized it as the bellow of a bull alligator. He wondered if the scaly brutes ever crawled up on the trail, and how the fellow that was shadowing him out there in the darkness managed to avoid them. With the thought another twig snapped, much closer to the trail than before. Harrison swore softly, trying to peer into the Stygian gloom under the moss-festooned branches. The fellow was closing in on him with the growing darkness.

There was a sinister implication about the thing that made Harrison's flesh creep a bit. This reptile-haunted swamp-trail was no place for a fight with an insane negro—for it seemed probable that the unknown stalker was the killer of Joe Corley. Harrison was meditating on the matter when a light glimmered through the trees ahead of him. Quickening his steps he came abruptly out of the darkness into a grey twilight.

He had reached an expanse of solid ground, where the thinning trees let in the last grey light of the outer dusk. They made a black wall with waving fringes all about a small clearing, and through their boles, on one side, Harrison caught a glimmer of inky water. In the clearing stood a cabin of rough-hewn logs, and through a tiny window shone the light of an oil lamp.

As Harrison emerged from among the growth he glanced back, but saw no movement among the ferns, heard no sound of pursuit. The path, dimly marked on the higher ground, ran past the cabin and vanished in the further gloom. This cabin must be the abode of that Celia Pompoloi Rogers had mentioned. Harrison strode to the sagging stoop and rapped on the hand-made door.

Inside there was movement, and the door swung open. Harrison was not prepared for the figure that confronted him. He had expected to see a bare-footed slattern; instead he saw a tall, rangily powerful man, neatly dressed, whose regular features and light skin portrayed his mixed blood.

"Good evening, sir." The accent hinted of education above the average.

"Name's Harrison," said the detective abruptly, displaying his badge. "I'm after a crook that ran in here—a Chinese murderer, named Woon Shang. Know anything about him?"

"Yes, sir," the man replied promptly. "That man went past my cabin three days ago."

"Where is he now?" demanded Harrison.

The other spread his hands in a curiously Latin gesture.

"I can not say. I have little intercourse with the other people who live in the swamp, but it is my belief that he is hiding among them somewhere. I have not seen him pass my cabin going back up the path."

"Can you guide me to these other cabins?"

"Gladly, sir; by daylight."

"I'd like to go tonight," growled Harrison.

"That's impossible, sir," the other protested. "It would be most dangerous. You ran a great risk in coming this far alone. The other cabins are further back in the swamp. We do not leave our huts at night; there are many things in the swamp which are dangerous to human beings."

"The Swamp Cat, for instance?" grunted Harrison.

The man cast him a quick glance of interrogation.

"He killed a colored man named Joe Corley a few hours ago," said the detective. "I found Corley on the trail. And if I'm not mistaken, that same lunatic has been following me for the past half hour."

The mulatto evinced considerable perturbation and glanced across the clearing into the shadows.

"Come in," he urged. "If the Swamp Cat is prowling tonight, no man is safe out of doors. Come in and spend the night with me, and at dawn I will guide you to all the cabins in the swamp."

Harrison saw no better plan. After all, it was absurd to go blundering about in the night, in an unknown marsh. He realized that he had made a mistake in coming in by himself, in the dusk; but working alone had become a habit with him, and he was tinged with a strong leaven of recklessness. Following a tip he had arrived at the little town on the edge of the swamplands in the mid-afternoon, and plunged on into the woods without hesitation. Now he doubted the wisdom of the move.

"Is this Celia Pompoloi's cabin?" he asked.

"It was," the mulatto replied. "She has been dead for three weeks. I live here alone. My name is John Bartholomew."

Harrison's head snapped up and he eyed the other with new interest. John Bartholomew; Joe Corley had muttered that name just before he died.

"Did you know Joe Corley?" he demanded.

"Slightly; he came into the swamp to hide from the law. He was a rather low grade sort of human, though naturally I am sorry to hear of his death."

"What's a man of your intelligence and education doing in this jungle?" the detective asked bluntly.

Bartholomew smiled rather wryly. "We can not always choose our environments, Mr. Harrison. The waste places of the world provide retreat for others than criminals. Some come to the swamps like your Chinaman, fleeing from the law. Others come to forget bitter disappointments forced upon them by circumstances."

Harrison glanced about the cabin while Bartholomew was putting a stout bar in place across the door. It had but two rooms, one behind the other, connected by a strongly built door. The slab floor was clean, the room scantily furnished; a table, benches, a bunk built against the wall, all hand-made. There was a fireplace, over which hung primitive cooking utensils, and a cloth covered cupboard.

"Would you like some fried bacon and corn pone?" asked Bartholomew. "Or perhaps a cup of coffee? I do not have much to offer you, but—"

"No, thanks; I ate a big meal just before I started into the swamp. Just tell me something about these people."

"As I said, I have little intercourse with them," answered Bartholomew. "They are clannish and suspicious, and keep much to themselves. They are not like other colored people. Their fathers came here from Haiti, following one of the bloody revolutions which have cursed that unfortunate island in the past. They have curious customs. Have you heard of the worship of Voodoo?"

Harrison nodded.

"These people are Voodooists. I know that they have mysterious conclaves back in the swamps. I have heard drums booming in the night, and seen the glow of fires through the trees. I have sometimes felt a little uneasy for my safety at such times. Such people are capable of bloody extremes, when their primitive natures are maddened by the bestial rites of the Voodoo."

"Why don't the whites come in here and stop it?" demanded Harrison.

"They know nothing about it. No one ever comes here unless he is a fugitive from the law. The swamp people carry on their worship without interference.

"Celia Pompoloi, who once occupied this very hut, was a woman of considerable intelligence and some education; she was the one swamp dweller who ever went 'outside,' as they call the outer world, and attended school. Yet, to my actual knowledge, she was the priestess of the cult and presided over their rituals. It is my belief that she met her fate at last during one of those saturnalias. Her body was found in the marshes, so badly mangled by the alligators that it was recognizable only by her garments."

"What about the Swamp Cat?" asked Harrison.

"A maniac, living like a wild beast in the marshes, only sporadically violent; but at those times a thing of horror."

"Would he kill the Chinaman if he had a chance?"

"He would kill anyone when his fit is on him. You said the Chinaman was a murderer?"

"Murderer and thief," grunted Harrison. "Stole ten grand from the man he killed."

Bartholomew looked up as with renewed interest, started to speak, then evidently changed his mind.

Harrison rose, yawning. "Think I'll hit the hay," he announced. "I'm tired, and I want to be up by daylight in the morning."

Bartholomew took up the lamp and led his guest into the back room, which was of the same size as the other, but whose furnishings consisted only of a bunk and a bench.

"I have but the one lamp, sir," said Bartholomew. "I shall leave it with you."

"Don't bother," grunted Harrison, having a secret distrust of oil lamps, resultant from experiencing an explosion of one in his boyhood. "I'm like a cat in the dark. I don't need it."

With many apologies for the rough accommodations and wishes for a good night's sleep, Bartholomew bowed himself out, and the door closed. Harrison, through force of habit, studied the room. A little starlight came in through the one small window, which he noticed was furnished with heavy wooden bars. There was no door other than the one by which he had entered. He lay down on the bunk fully dressed, without even removing his shoes, and pondered rather glumly. He was beset by fears that Woon Shang might escape him, after all. Suppose the Chinaman slipped out by the way he had come in? True, local officers were watching at the edge of the swampland, but Woon Shang might avoid them in the night. And what if there *was* another way out, known only to the swamp people? And if Bartholomew was as little acquainted with his neighbors as he said, what assurance was there that the mulatto would be able to guide him to the Chinaman's hiding place? These and other doubts assailed him while he lay and listened to the soft sounds of his host's retiring, and saw the thin line of light under the door vanish as the lamp was blown out. At last Harrison consigned his doubts to the devil, and fell asleep.

.2.

It was a noise at the windows, a stealthy twisting and wrenching at the bars, that awakened him. He woke quickly, with all his facilities alert, as was his habit. Something bulked in the window, something dark and round, with gleaming spots in it. He realized with a start that it was a human head he saw, with the faint starlight shining on rolling eyes and bared teeth. Without shifting his body, the detective stealthily reached for his gun; lying as he was in the darkness of the bunk, the man watching him could scarcely have seen the movement. But the head vanished, as if warned by some instinct.

Harrison sat up on his bunk, scowling, resisting the natural impulse to rush to the window and look out. That might be exactly what the man outside was wanting. There was something deadly about this business; the fellow had evidently been trying to get in. Was it the same creature that had followed him through the swamp? A sudden thought struck him. What was more likely than that the Chinaman had set a man to watch for a possible pursuer? Harrison cursed himself for not having thought of it before.

He struck a match, cupped it in his hand, and looked at his watch. It was scarcely ten o'clock. The night was still young. He scowled abstractedly at the rough wall behind the bunk, minutely illuminated in the flare of the match, and suddenly his breath hissed between his teeth. The match burned down to his fingers and went out. He struck another and leaned to the wall. Thrust in a chink between the logs was a knife, and its wicked curved blade was grimly smeared and clotted. The implication sent a shiver down Harrison's spine. The blood might be that of an animal—but who would butcher a calf or a hog in that room? Why had not the blade been cleansed? It was as if it had been hastily concealed, after striking a murderous blow.

He took it down and looked at it closely. The blood was dried and blackened as if at least many hours had elapsed since it had been let. The weapon was no ordinary butcher knife—Harrison stiffened. *It was a Chinese dagger.* The match went out and Harrison did what the average man would have done. He leaned over the edge of the bunk, the only thing in the room that would conceal an object of any size, and lifted the cloth that hung to the floor. He did not actually expect to find the corpse of Woon Shang beneath it. He merely acted through instinct. Nor did he find a corpse. His hand, groping in the dark, encountered only the uneven floor and rough logs; then his fingers felt something else—something at once compact and yielding, wedged between the logs as the knife had been.

He drew it forth; it felt like a flat package of crisp paper, bound with oiled silk. Cupping a match in his hand, he tore it open. Ten worn bills met his gaze; on each bill was the numeral $1,000. He crushed the match out and sat in the dark, mental pictures tumbling rapidly across his consciousness.

So John Bartholomew had lied. Doubtless he had taken in the Chinaman as he had taken in Harrison. The detective visualized a dim form bending in the darkness above a sleeping figure in that same bunk—a murderous stroke with the victim's own knife.

He growled inarticulately, with the chagrin of the cheated man-hunter, certain that Woon Shang's body was rotting in some slimy marsh. At least he had the money. Careless of Bartholomew to hide it there. But was it? It was only by an accidental chain of circumstances that he had found it—

He stiffened again. Under the door he saw a thin pencil of light. Had Bartholomew not yet gone to bed? But he remembered the blowing out of the lamp. Harrison rose and glided noiselessly to the thick door. When he reached it he heard a low mumble of voices in the outer room. The speakers moved nearer, stood directly before the door. He strained his ears and recognized the crisp accents of John Bartholomew. "Don't bungle the job," the mulatto was muttering. "Get him before he has a chance to use his gun. He doesn't suspect anything. I just remember that I left the Chinaman's knife in a chink over the bunk. But the detective will never see it, in the dark. He had to come butting in here, this particular night. We can't let him see what he'd see if he lived through this night."

"We do de job quick and clean, mastah," murmured another voice, with a guttural accent different from any Harrison had ever heard, and impossible to reproduce.

"Alright; we haven't anything to fear from Joe Corley. The Swamp Cat carried out my instructions."

"Dat Swamp Cat prowlin' 'round outside right now," muttered another man. "Ah don't like him. Why can't he do dis job?"

"He obeys my orders; but he can't be trusted too far. But we can't stand here talking like this. The detective will wake up and get suspicious. Throw open that door and rush him. Knife him in his bunk—"

Harrison always believed that the best defense was a strong offensive. There was but one way out of this jam. He took it without hesitation. He hurled a massive shoulder against the door, knocking it open, and sprang into the outer room, gun leveled, and barked: "Hands up, damn you!"

There were five men in that room; Bartholomew, holding the lamp and shading it with his left hand, and four others, four lean, rangy giants in nondescript garments, with yellow, sinister features. Each man of the four had a knife in his hand.

They recoiled with yells of dismay as Harrison crashed upon them. Automatically their hands went up and their knives clattered on the floor. For an instant the white man was complete master of the situation, Bartholomew turning ashy as he stared, the lamp shaking in his hands.

"Back against that wall!" snapped Harrison.

They obeyed dumbly, rendered incapable of action by the shock of surprize. Harrison knew that it was John Bartholomew, more than these hulking butchers, that he had to fear.

"Set that lamp on the table," he snapped. "Line up there with them—*ha!*"

Bartholomew had stooped to lower the lamp to the table— then quick as a cat he threw it crashing to the floor, ducking behind the table with the same motion. Harrison's gun crashed almost simultaneously, but even in the bedlam of darkness that followed, the detective knew he had missed. Whirling, he leaped through the outer door. Inside the dark cabin he would have no chance against the knives for which the negroes were already groping on the floor, mouthing like rabid dogs.

As Harrison raced across the clearing he heard Bartholomew's furious voice yelling commands. The white man did not take the obvious route, the beaten trail. He rounded the cabin and darted toward the trees on the other side. He had no intention of fleeing until he was run down from behind. He was seeking a place where he could turn at bay and shoot it out with a little advantage on his side. The moon was just coming up above the trees, emphasizing, rather than illuming the shadows.

He heard the negroes clamoring out of the cabin and casting about, momentarily at a loss. He reached the shadows before they rounded the hut, and glancing back through the bushes, saw them running about the clearing like hunting dogs seek a spoor, howling in primitive blood-lust and disappointment. The growing moonlight glittered on the long knives in their hands.

He drew back further among the trees, finding the ground more solid underfoot than he had expected. Then he came suddenly upon the marshy edge of a stretch of black water. Something grunted and thrashed amidst it, and two green lamps burned suddenly like jewels on the inky water. He recoiled, well knowing what those twin lights were. And as he did so, he bumped full into something that locked fierce arms like an ape about him, hissing inarticulate menace in his ear.

Harrison ducked and heaved, bowing his powerful back like a great cat, and his assailant tumbled over his head and thumped on the ground, still clutching the detective's coat with the grip of a vise. Harrison lunged backward, ripping the garment down the back, wrenching his arms from the sleeves, in his frenzy to free himself.

The man leaped to his feet on the edge of the pool, snarling like a wild beast. Harrison saw a gaunt half naked black man with wild strands of hair caked with mud hanging over a contorted mask of a face, the thick loose lips drooling foam. This indeed, he knew, was the dread Swamp Cat.

Still grasping Harrison's torn coat brainlessly in his left hand, his right swept up with a sheen of sharp steel, and even as he sensed the madman's intention, the detective ducked and fired from the hip. The thrown knife hummed by his ear, and with the crash of the shot the Swamp Cat swayed and pitched backward into the black pool. There was a threshing rush, the waters stormed foamily, there was a glimpse of a blunted, reptilian snout, and the trailing body vanished with it.

Harrison stepped back, sickened, and heard behind him the shouting progress of men through the bushes. His hunters had heard the shot. He drew back into the shadows among a cluster of gum trees, and waited, gun in hand. An instant later they rushed out upon the bank of the pool, John Bartholomew and his dusky knife-fighters.

They ranged the bank, gaping, and then Bartholomew laughed and pointed to a blood-stained piece of cloth that floated soggily on the foam-flecked waters.

"The fool's coat! He must have run right into the pool, and the 'gator's got him! I can see them tearing at something, over there among the reeds. Hear those bones crack?" Bartholomew's laugh was fiendish to hear.

"Well," said the mulatto, "we don't have to worry about him. If they send anybody in after him, we'll just tell them the truth: that he fell into the water and got grabbed by the 'gators, just like Celia Pompoloi."

"She wuz a awful sight when us foun' huh body," muttered one of the swamp negroes.

"We'll never find that much of him," prophesied Bartholomew.

"Did he say what de Chinaman done?" asked another of the men.

"Just what the Chinaman said; that he'd murdered a man."

"Wish he'd uh robbed uh bank," murmured the swamp dweller plaintively. "Wish he'd uh brung uh lot uh money in wid him."

"Well, he didn't," snapped Bartholomew. "You saw me search him. Now get back to the others and help them watch him. These Chinese are slippery customers, and we can't take any chances with him. More white men may come looking for him tomorrow, but if they do, they're welcome to all of him they can find!" He laughed with sinister meaning, and then added abruptly: "Hurry and get out of here. I want to be alone. There are spirits to be communed with before the hour arrives, and dread rites that I must perform alone. Go!"

The others bent their heads in a curious gesture of subservience, and trooped away, in the direction of the clearing. He followed leisurely.

Harrison glared after them, turning what he had heard over in his mind. Some of it was gibberish, but certain things were clear. For one thing, the Chinaman was obviously alive, and imprisoned somewhere. Bartholomew had lied about his own relations with the swamp people; one of them he certainly was not; but he was just as certainly a leader among them. Yet he had lied to them about the Chinaman's money. Harrison remembered the mulatto's expression when he had mentioned it to him. The detective believed that Bartholomew had never seen the money; that Woon Shang, suspicious, had hidden it himself before he was attacked.

Harrison rose and stole after the retreating negroes. As long as they believed him dead, he could conduct his investigations without being harried by pursuit. His shirt was of dark material and did not show in the darkness, and the big detective was trained in stealth by adventures in the haunted dives of Oriental quarters where unseen eyes always watched and ears were forever alert.

When he came to the edge of the trees, he saw the four giants trooping down the trail that led deeper into the swamp. They walked in single file, their heads bent forward, stooping from the waist like apes. Bartholomew was just going into the cabin. Harrison started to follow the disappearing forms, then hesitated. Bartholomew was in his power. He could steal up on the cabin, throw his gun on the mulatto and make him tell where Woon Shang was imprisoned—maybe. Harrison knew the invincible stubbornness of the breed. Even as he ruminated, Bartholomew came out of the cabin and stood peering about with a strange furtiveness. He held a heavy whip in his hand. Presently he glided across the clearing toward the quarter where the detective crouched. He passed within a few yards of Harrison's covert, and the moonlight illumined his features. Harrison was astounded at the change in his face, at the sinister vitality and evil strength reflected there.

Harrison altered his plans and stole after him, wishing to know on what errand the man went with such secrecy. It was not difficult. Bartholomew looked neither back nor sidewise, but wound a tortuous way among inky pools and clusters of rotting vegetation that looked poisonous, even in the moonlight. Presently the detective crouched low; ahead of the mulatto there was a tiny hut, almost hidden among the trees which trailed Spanish moss over it like a grey veil. Bartholomew looked carefully about him, then drew forth a key and manipulated a large padlock on the door. Harrison was convinced that he had been led to the prison of Woon Shang.

Bartholomew disappeared inside, closing the door. A light gleamed through the chinks of the logs. Then came a mumble of voices, too indistinct for Harrison to tell anything about them; that was followed by the sharp, unmistakable crack of a whip on bare flesh, and a shrill cry of pain. Enlightenment came to Harrison. Bartholomew had come secretly to his prisoner, to torture the Chinaman—and for what reason but to make him divulge the hiding place of the money, of which Harrison had spoken? Obviously Bartholomew had no intentions of sharing that money with his mates.

Harrison began to work his way stealthily toward the cabin, fully intending to burst in and put a stop to that lashing. He would cheerfully have shot down Woon Shang himself, had the occasion arisen, but he had a white man's abhorrence of torture. But before he reached the hut, the sounds ceased, the light went out and Bartholomew emerged, wiping the perspiration of exertion from his brow. He locked the door, thrust the key in his pocket, and turned away through the trees, trailing his whip in his hand. Harrison, crouching in the shadows, let him go. It was Woon Shang he was after. Bartholomew could be dealt with later.

When the mulatto had disappeared, Harrison rose and strode to the door of the hut. The absence of guards was rather puzzling, after the conversation he had overheard, but he wasted no time on conjecture. The door was secured by a chain made fast to a big hasp driven deep into a log. He thrust his gun barrel through this hasp, and using it as a lever, pried out the hasp with no great difficulty, though it was a feat calling for considerable strength.

Pulling open the door he peered in; it was too dark to see, but be heard somebody's breath coming in jerky hysterical sobs. He struck a match, looked—then glared. The prisoner was there, crouching on the dirt floor. But it was not Woon Shang. It was a woman.

She was a mulatto, young, and handsome in her way. She was clad only in a ragged and scanty chemise, and her hands were bound behind her. From her wrists a long strand of rawhide ran to a heavy staple in the wall. She stared wildly at Harrison, her dark eyes reflecting both hope and terror. There were tear-stains on her checks.

"Who the devil are you?" demanded the detective.

"Celia Pompoloi!" Her voice was rich and musical despite its hysteria. "Oh, white man, for God's sake let me go! I can't stand it any more. I'll die; I know I will!"

"I thought you *were* dead," he grunted.

"John Bartholomew did it!" she exclaimed. "He persuaded a yellow girl from 'outside' into the swamp, and then he killed her and dressed her in my clothes, and threw her into the marsh where the alligators would chew the body till nobody could tell it wasn't me. The people found it and thought it was Celia Pompoloi. He's kept me here for three weeks and tortured me every night."

"Why?" Harrison found and lighted a candle stump stuck on the wall. Then he stooped and cut the rawhide thongs that bound her hands. She climbed to her feet, chafing her bruised and swollen wrists. In her scanty garb the brutality of the floggings she had received was quite apparent.

"He's a devil!" Her dark eyes flashed murderously; whatever her wrongs, she obviously was no meek sufferer. "He came here posing as a priest of the Great Serpent. He said he was from Haiti, the lying dog. He's from Santo Domingo, and no more priest than you are. *I* am the proper priestess of the Serpent, and the people obeyed me. That's why he put me out of the way. I'll kill him!"

"But why did he lick you?" asked Harrison.

"Because I wouldn't tell him what be wanted to know," she muttered sullenly, bending her head and twisting one bare foot behind the other ankle, school-girl fashion. She did not seem to think of refusing to answer his questions. His white skin put him beyond and outside swamp-land politics.

"He came here to steal the jewel, the heart of the Great Serpent, which we brought with us from Haiti, long ago. He is no priest. He is an impostor. He proposed that I give the Heart to him and run away from my people with him. When I refused, he tied me in this old hut where none can hear my screams; the swamp people shun it, thinking it's haunted. He said he'd keep beating me until I told him where the Heart was hidden. But I wouldn't tell him—not though he stripped all the flesh from my bones. I alone know that secret, because I am a priestess of the Serpent, and the guardian of its heart."

This was Voodoo stuff with a vengeance; her matter-of-fact manner evinced an unshaken belief in her weird cult.

"Do you know anything about the Chinaman, Woon Shang?" he demanded.

"John Bartholomew told me of him in his boastings. He came running from the law and Bartholomew promised to hide him. Then he summoned the swamp men, and they seized the

Chinaman, though he wounded one of them badly with his knife. They made a prisoner of him—"

"Why?"

Celia was in that vengeful mood in which a woman recklessly tells everything, and repeats things she would not otherwise mention.

"Bartholomew came saying he was a priest of old time. That's how he caught the fancy of the people. He promised them an *old* sacrifice, of which there has not been one for thirty years. We have offered the white cock and the red cock to the Great Serpent. But Bartholomew promised them the *goat-without-horns*. He did that to get the Heart into his hands, for only then is it taken from its secret hiding place. He thought to get it into his hands and run away before the sacrifice was made. But when I refused to aid him, it upset his plans. Now he can not get the Heart, but he must go through with the sacrifice anyway. The people are becoming impatient. If he fails them, they will kill him.

"He first chose the 'outside' black man, Joe Corley, who was hiding in the swamp, for the sacrifice; but when the Chinaman came, Bartholomew decided he would make a better offering. Bartholomew told me tonight that the Chinaman had money, and he was going to make him tell where he hid it, so he would have the money, and the Heart, too, when I finally gave in and told him—"

"Wait a minute," interposed Harrison. "Let me get this straight. What is it that Bartholomew intends doing with Woon Shang?"

"He will offer him up to the Great Serpent," she answered, making a conventional gesture of conciliation and adoration as she spoke the dread name.

"A *human* sacrifice?"

"Yes."

"Well, I'll be damned!" he muttered. "If I hadn't been raised in the South myself, I'd never believe it. When is this sacrifice to take place?"

"Tonight!"

"Eh, what's that?" He remembered Bartholomew's cryptic instructions to his henchmen. "The devil! Where does it happen, and what time?"

"Just before dawn; far back in the swamp."

"I've got to find Woon Shang and stop it!" he exclaimed. "Where is he imprisoned?"

"At the place of the sacrifice; many men guard him. You'd never find your way there. You'd drown and get eaten by the 'gators. Besides, if you did get there, the people would tear you to pieces."

"You lead me there and I'll take care of the people," he snarled. "You want revenge on Bartholomew. All right; guide me there and I'll see that you get plenty. I've always worked alone," he ruminated angrily, "but the swamp country isn't River Street."

"I'll do it!" Her eyes blazed and her white teeth gleamed in a mask of passion. "I'll guide you to the 'Place of the Altar.' We'll kill him, the yellow Dominican dog!"

"How long will it take us to get there?"

"I could go there in an hour, alone. Guiding you, it will take longer. Much longer, the way we must go. You can't travel the road I would take, alone."

"I can follow you anywhere you walk," he grunted, slightly nettled. He glanced at his watch, then extinguished the candle. "Let's get going. Take the shortest route and don't worry about me. I'll keep up."

She caught his wrist in a fierce grasp and almost jerked him out of the door, quivering with the eagerness of a hunting hound.

"Wait a minute!" A thought struck him. "If I go back to the cabin and capture Bartholomew—"

"He will not be there; he is well on his way to the Place of the Altar; better that we beat him there."

.3.

As long as he lived Harrison remembered that race through the swamp, as he followed Celia Pompoloi along pathless ways that seemed impossible. Mire caught at his feet, and sometimes black scummy water lapped about his ankles, but Celia's swift sure feet always found solid ground where none seemed possible, or guided him over bogs that quaked menacingly beneath their weight.

She sprang lightly from hummock to hummock, or slid between turgid pools of black slime where unseen monsters grunted and wallowed. Harrison floundered after her, sweating, half nauseated with the miasmic reek of the oozy slime that plastered him; but all the bulldog was roused in him, and he was ready to wade through swamps for a week if the man he hunted were at the other end of the loathsome journey. Dank misty clouds had veiled the sky, through which the moon shone fitfully, and Harrison stumbled like a blind man, depending entirely on his guide, whose dusky, half-naked body was all but invisible to him at times in the darkness.

Ahead of them he began to hear a rhythmic throbbing, a barbaric pulsing that grew as they advanced. A red glow flickered through the black trees.

"The flames of the sacrifice!" gasped Celia, quickening her pace. "Hasten!"

Somewhere in his big, weary body Harrison found enough reserve energy to keep up with her. She seemed to run lightly over bogs that engulfed him to the knees. She possessed the swamp dweller's instinct for safe footing. Ahead of them Harrison saw the shine of something that was not mud, and Celia halted at the verge of a stretch of noisome water.

"The Place of the Altar is surrounded by water on all sides but one," she hissed. "We are in the very heart of the swamp, deeper than anyone ever goes except on such occasions as these. There are no cabins near. Follow me! I have a bridge none knows of except myself."

At a point where the turgid stream narrowed to some fifty feet, a fallen tree spanned it. Celia ran out upon it, balancing herself upright. She swayed across, a slim ghostly figure in the cloudy light. Harrison straddled the log and hitched himself ignominiously along. He was too weary to trust *his* equilibrium. His feet dangled a foot or so above the black surface, and Celia, waiting impatiently on the further bank as she peered anxiously at the distant glow, cast him a look over her shoulder and cried a sudden urgent warning.

Harrison jerked up his legs just as something bulky and grisly heaved up out of the water with a great splash and an appalling clash of mighty fangs. Harrison fairly flung himself over the last few feet and landed on the further bank in a more demoralized condition than he would have admitted. A criminal in a dark room with a knife was less nerve-shaking than these ghoulish slayers of the dark waters.

The ground was firmer; they were, as Celia said, on a sort of island in the heart of the marshes. The girl threaded her way supply among the cypresses, panting with the intensity of her emotions. Perspiration soaked her; the hand that held Harrison's wrist was wet and slippery.

A few minutes later, when the glow in the trees had grown to an illuminating glare, she halted and slipped to the damp mold, drawing her companion with her. They looked out upon a scene incredible in its primitive nakedness.

There was a clearing, free of underbrush, circled by a black wall of cypress. From its outer edge a sort of natural causeway wandered away into the gloom, and over that low ridge ran a trail, beaten by many feet. The trail ended in the clearing, the ultimate end of the path that Harrison had followed into the swamp. On the other side of the clearing there was a glimpse of dusky water, reflecting the firelight.

In a wide horseshoe formation, their backs to the causeway, sat some fifty men, women and children, resembling Celia Pompoloi in complexion. Harrison had not supposed that so many people inhabited the swamp. Their gaze was fixed on an object in the center of the opening of the human horseshoe. This was a great block of dark wood that had an unfamiliar appearance, as of an altar, brought from afar. There was an intolerable suggestion about that block, and the misshapen, leering figure that rose behind it—a fantastically carven idol, to whose bestial features the flickering firelight lent life and mobility. Harrison intuitively knew that this monstrosity was never carved in America. The yellow people had brought it with them from Haiti, and surely their black ancestors had brought it originally from Africa. There was an aura of the Congo about it, the reek of black squalling jungles, and squirming faceless shapes of a night more primeval than this. Harrison was not superstitious, but he felt gooseflesh rise on his limbs. At the back of his consciousness, dim racial memories stirred, conjuring up unstable and monstrous images from the dim mists of the primitive, when men worshipped such gods as these.

Before the idol, near the block, sat an old crone, striking a bowl tom-tom with quick staccato strokes of her open hands; it growled and rumbled and muttered, and the squatting negroes swayed and chanted softly in unison. Their voices were low, but they hummed with a note of hysteria. The firelight struck gleams from their rolling eyeballs and shining teeth.

Harrison looked in vain for John Bartholomew and Woon Shang. He reached out a hand to get his companion's attention. She did not heed him. Her supple figure was tense and quivering as a taut wire under his hand. A sudden change in the chanting, a wild wolfish baying, brought him about again.

Out of the shadows of the trees behind the idol strode John Bartholomew. He was clad only in a loin cloth, and it was as if he had doffed his civilized culture with his clothing. His facial expression, his whole bearing, were changed; he was like an image of barbarism incarnate. Harrison stared at the knotted biceps, the ridged body muscles which the firelight displayed. But something else gripped his whole attention. With John Bartholomew came another, unwillingly, at the sight of whom the crowd gave tongue to another bestial yell.

About Bartholomew's mighty left hand was twisted the pigtail of Woon Shang, whom he dragged after him like a fowl to the chopping block. The Chinaman was stark naked, his yellow body gleaming like old ivory in the fire. His hands were bound behind his back, and he was like a child in the grasp of his executioner. Woon Shang was not a large man; beside the great mulatto he seemed slimmer than ever. His hysterical panting came plainly to Harrison in the silence that fell tensely as the shouting ceased and the negroes watched with eyes that gleamed redly. His straining feet tore at the sod as he struggled against the inexorable advance of his captor. In Bartholomew's right hand shone a great razor-edged crescent of steel. The watchers sucked in their breath loudly; in a single stride they had returned to the jungle whence they had crawled; they were mad for the bloody saturnalia their ancestors had known.

In Bartholomew's face Harrison read stark horror and mad determination. He sensed that the mulatto was not enjoying this ghastly primordial drama into which he had been trapped. He also realized that the man must go through with it, and that he would go through with it. It was more than the jewel-heart of the serpent-god for which Bartholomew strove now; it was the continued dominance of these wolfish devil-worshippers on which his life depended.

Harrison rose to one knee, drew and cocked his revolver and sighted along the blue barrel. The distance was not great, but the light was illusive. But he felt he must trust to the chance of sending a slug crashing through John Bartholomew's broad breast. If he stepped out into the open and tried to arrest the man, the negroes, in their present fanatical frenzy, would tear him to pieces. If their priest was shot down, panic might seize them. His finger was crooking about the trigger when something was thrown into the fire. Abruptly the flames died down, throwing everything into deep shadow. As suddenly they flared up again, burning with a weird green radiance. The dusky faces looked like those of drowned corpses in the glow.

In the moment of darkness Bartholomew had reached the block. His victim's head was thrust down upon it, and the mulatto stood like a bronze image, his muscular right arm lifted, poising above his head the broad steel crescent. And then, before could strike the blow that would send Woon Shang's head rolling to the misshapen feet of the grinning idol, before Harrison could jerk the trigger, something froze them all in their places.

Into the weird glow moved a figure, so lithely that it seemed to float in the uncertain light rather than move on earthly feet. A groan burst from the negroes and they came to their feet like automatons. In the green glow that lent her features the aspect of death, with perspiration dripping from her draggled garment, Celia Pompoloi looked hideously like the corpse of a drowned woman newly risen from a watery grave.

"Celia!"

It was a scream from a score of gaping months. Bedlam followed.

"Celia Pompoloi!" "Oh, Gawd, she done come back from de watah!" "Done come back from hell!" "Go back whah you belong, Celia, don' ha'nt us!" "Oh Gawd, it's huh for sho'!"

"Yes, you dogs!" It was a most unghostly scream from Celia. "It's Celia Pompoloi, come back from hell to send John Bartholomew there!"

And like a fury she rushed across the green-lit space, a knife she had found somewhere glittering in her hand. Bartholomew, momentarily paralyzed by the appearance of his prisoner, came to life. Releasing Woon Shang he stepped aside and swung the heavy beheading knife with all his power. Harrison saw the great muscles leap up under his glossy skin as he struck. But Celia's spring was that of a swamp panther. It carried her inside the circular sweep of the weighted blade, and her knife flashed as it sank to the hilt under John Bartholomew's heart. With a strangled cry he reeled and fell, dragging her down with him as she strove to wrench her blade free.

Abandoning it she rose, panting, her hair standing on end, her eyes starting from her head, her red lips writhing back in a curl of devilish rage. The people shrieked and gave back from her, still evidently in the grip of the delusion that they looked on one risen from the dead.

"Dogs!" she screamed, an incarnation of fury. "Fools! Swine! Have you lost your reason, to forget all my teachings, and let this dead dog make of you the beasts your fathers were? Oh—!" Glaring about for a weapon she caught up a blazing fire-brand and rushed at them, striking furiously. Men yelped as the flames bit them, and the sparks showered. Howling, cursing, and screaming they broke and fled, a frenzied mob, streaming out across the causeway, with their maddened priestess at their heels, screaming maledictions and smiting with the splintered fagot. They vanished in the darkness and their clamor came back faintly.

Harrison rose, shaking his head in wonder, and went stiffly up to the dying fire. Bartholomew was dead, staring glassily up at the moon which was breaking through the scattering clouds. Woon Shang crouched babbling incoherent Chinese as Harrison hauled him to his feet.

"Woon Shang," said the detective wearily, "I arrest you for the murder of Li-keh-tsung, and I warn you that anything you say will be used against you."

That familiar formula seemed to invest the episode with some sanity, in contrast to the fantastic horror of the recent events. The Chinaman made no struggle. He seemed dazed, muttering: "This will break the heart of my honorable father; he had rather see me dead than dishonored."

"You ought to have thought of that before," said Harrison heavily. Through force of habit he cut Woon Shang's cords and reached for his handcuffs before he realized that they had been lost with his coat.

"Oh, well," he sighed. "I don't reckon you'll need them. Let's get going."

Laying a heavy hand on his captive's naked shoulder, Harrison half guided, half pushed him toward the causeway. The detective was dizzy with fatigue, but combined with it was a muddled determination to get his prisoner out of the swamp and into a jail before he stopped. He felt he had no more to fear from the swamp people, but he wanted to get out of that atmosphere of decay and slime in which he seemed to have been wandering for ages. Woon Shang took note of his condition with furtive side-long glances, as the stark fear died out of the Chinaman's beady black eyes to be replaced by one of craft.

"I have ten thousand dollars," he began babbling. "I hid it before the negroes made me prisoner. I will give you all of it if you will let me go—"

"Oh, shut up!" groaned Harrison wearily, giving him an exasperated shove. Woon Shang stumbled and went to his knees, his bare shoulder slipping from Harrison's grasp. The detective was stooping, fumbling for him when the Chinaman rose with a chunk of wood in his hand, and smote him savagely on the head. Harrison staggered back, almost falling, and Woon Shang, in a last desperate bid for freedom, dashed, not for the neck of land between himself and which Harrison stood, but straight toward the black water that glimmered beyond the fringe of cypresses. Harrison fired mechanically and without aim, but the fugitive kept straight on and hit the dusky water with a long dive. Harrison, following, lifted his gun and tried to sight at the swimmer's head; his hammer snapped on a faulty cartridge. Woon Shang's bobbing head was scarcely visible in the shadows of the overhanging ferns. Then a wild shriek cut the night; the water threshed and foamed, there was the glimpse of a writhing, horribly contorted yellow body and of a longer, darker shape, and then the blood-streaked waters closed over Woon Shang forever.

Harrison exhaled gustily and sank down on a rotting log.

"Well," he said wearily, aloud, "that winds *that* up. It's better this way. Woon's family had rather he died this way than in the chair, and they're decent folks, in spite of him. If this business had come to trial, I'd have had to tell about Celia shoving a knife into that devil Bartholomew, and I'd hate to see her on trial for killing that rat. This way it can be smoothed over. He had it coming to him. And I've got the money that's coming to old Li-keh-tsung's granddaughter. And it's me for the feather beds and fried steaks of civilization."

The Teeth of Doom

When James Willoughby, millionaire philanthropist, realized that the dark, lightless car was deliberately crowding him into the curb, he acted with desperate decision. Snapping off his own lights, he threw open the door on the opposite side from the onrushing stranger, and leaped out, without stopping his own car. He landed sprawling on all fours, shredding the knees of his trousers and tearing the skin on his hands. An instant later his auto crashed cataclysmically into the curb, and the crunch of crumpled fenders and the tinkle of breaking glass mingled with the deafening reverberation of a sawed-off shotgun as the occupants of the mysterious car, not yet realizing that their intended victim had deserted his automobile, blasted the machine he had just left.

Before the echoes died away, Willoughby was up and running through the darkness with an energy remarkable for his years. He knew that his ruse was already discovered, but it takes longer to swing a big car around than for a desperately frightened man to burst through a hedge, and a flitting figure in the darkness is a poor target. So James Willoughby lived where others had died, and presently came on foot and in disheveled condition to his home, which adjoined the park beside which the murderous attempt had been made. The police, hastening to his call, found him in a condition of mingled fear and bewilderment. He had seen none of his attackers; he could give no reason for the attack. All that he seemed to know was that death had struck at him from the dark, suddenly, terribly and mysteriously.

It was only reasonable to suppose that death would strike again at its chosen victim, and that was why Steve Harrison, detective, kept a rendezvous the next evening with one Joey Glick, a nondescript character of the underworld who served his purpose in the tangled scheme of things.

Harrison bulked big in the dingy backroom appointed for the meeting. His massive shoulders and thick body dwarfed his height. His cold blue eyes contrasted with the thick black hair that crowned his low broad forehead, and his civilized garments could not conceal the almost savage muscularity of his hard frame.

Opposite him Joey Glick, never an impressive figure, looked even more insignificant than usual. And Joey's skin was a pasty grey, and Joey's fingers shook as he fumbled with a bit of paper on which was drawn a peculiar design.

"Somebody planted it on me," he chattered. "Right after I phoned you. In the jam on the uptown train. Me, Joey Glick! They plant it on me and I don't even know it. Only one man in this burg handles dips that slick—even if I didn't know already.

"Look! It's the death-blossom! The symbol of the Sons of Erlik! They're after me! They've been shadowing me—tapping wires—they know I know too much—"

"Come to the point, will you?" grunted Harrison. "You said you had a tip about the gorillas who tried to put the finger on Jim Willoughby. Quit shaking and spill it. And tell me, cold turkey—who was it?"

"The man behind it is Yarghouz Barolass."

Harrison grunted in some surprise.

"I didn't know murder was his racket."

"Wait!" Joey babbled, so scared he was scarcely coherent. His brain was addled, his speech disjointed. "He's head of the American branch of the Sons of Erlik—I know he is—"

"Chinese?"

"No—Mongol. He's a Mongol. His racket is blackmailing nutty old dames who fall for his black magic. You know that. But this is bigger. Listen, you know about Richard Lynch?"

"Sure; got smashed up in an auto wreck by a hit-and-run speed maniac a week ago. Lay unidentified in a morgue all night before they discovered who he was. Some crazy loon—or body-snatcher—tried to steal the corpse off the slab. What's that got to do with Willoughby?"

"It wasn't an accident." Joey was fumbling for a cigarette.

"They meant to get him—Yarghouz's mob. It was them after the body that night—"

"Have you been hitting the pipe?" demanded Harrison harshly.

"No, damn it!" shrilled Joey. "I tell you, Yarghouz was after Richard Lynch's corpse, just like he's sending his mob after Job Hopkins' body tomorrow night—"

"*What?*" Harrison came erect, glaring incredulously.

"Don't rush me," begged Joey, striking a match. "Gimme time. That death-blossom has got me jumping sideways. I'm jittery—"

"I'll say you are," grunted Harrison. "You've been babbling a lot of stuff that don't mean anything, except that it's Yarghouz Barolass who had Lynch bumped off, and now is after Willoughby. Why? That's what I want to know. Straighten it out and give me the low-down."

"Alright," promised Joey, sucking avidly at his cigarette. "Lemme have a drag—I been so upset I haven't even smoked since I reached into my pocket for a fag and found that damned death-flower. This is straight goods. I know why they want the bodies of Richard Lynch, Job Hopkins and James Willoughby—"

With appalling suddenness his hands shot to his throat, crushing the smoldering cigarette in his fingers. His eyes distended, his face purpled. Without a word he swayed upright, reeled and crashed to the floor. With a curse Harrison sprang up, bent over him, ran skilled hands over his body.

"Dead as Judas Iscariot," swore the detective. "What an infernal break! I knew his heart would get him some day, if he kept hitting the pipe—"

He halted suddenly. On the floor where it had fallen beside the dead man lay the bit of ornamented paper Joey had called the blossom of death, and beside it lay a crumpled package of cigarettes.

"When did he change his brand?" muttered Harrison. "He never smoked any kind but a special Egyptian make before; never saw him use this brand." He lifted the package, drew out a cigarette and broke it into his hand, smelling the contents gingerly. There was a faint but definite odor which was not part of the smell of the cheap tobacco.

"The fellow who slipped that death-blossom into his pocket could have shifted fags on him just as easy," muttered the detective. "They must have known he was coming here to talk to me. But the question is, how much do they know now? They can't know how much or how little he told me. They evidently didn't figure on him reaching me at all—thought he'd take a draw before he got here. Ordinarily he would have; but this time he was too scared even to remember to smoke. He needed dope, not tobacco, to steady his nerves."

Going to the door, he called softly. A stocky bald-headed man answered his call, wiping his hands on a dirty apron. At the sight of the crumpled body he recoiled, paling.

"Heart attack, Spike," grunted Harrison. "See that he gets what's needed." And the big dick thrust a handful of crumpled bills into Spike's fingers as he strode forth. A hard man, Harrison, but one mindful of his debts to the dead as well as the living.

A few minutes later be was crouched over a telephone.

"This you, Hoolihan?"

A voice booming back over the wires assured him that the chief of police was indeed at the other end.

"What killed Job Hopkins?" he asked abruptly.

"Why, heart attack, I understand." There was some surprise in the chief's voice. "Passed out suddenly, day before yesterday, while smoking his after-dinner cigar, according to the papers. Why?"

"Who's guarding Willoughby?" demanded Harrison without answering.

"Laveaux, Hanson, McFarlane and Harper. But I don't see—"

"Not enough," snapped Harrison. "Beat it over there yourself with three or four more men."

"Say, listen here, Harrison!" came back the irate bellow. "Are you telling *me* how to run my business?"

"Right now I am." Harrison's cold hard grin was almost tangible in his voice. "This happens to be in my particular domain. We're not fighting white men; it's a gang of River Street yellow-bellies who've put Willoughby on the spot. I won't say any more right now. There's been too damned much wire-tapping in this burg. But you beat it over to Willoughby's as fast as you can get there. Don't let him out of your sight. Don't let him smoke, eat or drink anything till I get there. I'll be right on over."

"Okay," came the answer over the wires. "You've been working the River Street quarter long enough to know what you're doing. When it comes to yellow-bellies, I'm following your lead."

Harrison snapped the receiver back on its hook and strode out into the misty dimness of River Street, with its furtive hurrying forms—stooped alien figures which would have fitted less incongruously into the scheme of Canton, Bombay or Stamboul.

The big dick walked with a stride even springier than usual, a more aggressive lurch of his massive shoulders. That betokened unusual wariness, a tension of nerves. He knew that he was a marked man, since his talk with Joey Glick. He did not try to fool himself; it was certain that the spies of the man he was fighting knew that Joey had reached him before he died. The fact that they could not know just how much the fellow had told before he died, would make them all the more dangerous. He did not underestimate his own position. He knew that if there was one man in the city capable of dealing with Yarghouz Barolass, it was himself, with his experience gained from years of puzzling through the devious and often grisly mysteries of River Street, with its swarms of brown and yellow inhabitants.

"Taxi?" A cab drew purring up beside the curb, anticipating his summoning gesture. The driver did not lean out into the light of the street. His cap seemed to be drawn low, not unnaturally so, but, standing on the sidewalk, it was impossible for the detective to tell whether or not he was a white man.

"Sure," grunted Harrison, swinging open the door and climbing in. "540 Park Place—and step on it."

The taxi roared through the crawling traffic, down shadowy River Street, wheeled off onto 35th Avenue, crossed over, and sped down a narrow side street.

"Taking a short cut?" asked the detective.

"Yes, sir." The driver did not look back. His voice ended in a sudden hissing intake of breath. There was no partition between the front and back seats. Harrison was leaning forward, his gun jammed between the shoulders of the driver.

"Take the next right-hand turn and drive to the address I gave you," he said softly. "Think I can't tell the back of a yellow neck by the street lamps? You drive, but you drive careful. If you try to wreck us, I'll fill you full of lead before you can twist that wheel. No monkey business now; you wouldn't be the first man I've plugged in the course of duty."

The driver twisted his head about to stare briefly into the grim face of his captor; his wide thin mouth gaped, his coppery features were ashy. Not for nothing had Harrison established his reputation as a man-hunter among the sinister denizens of the Oriental quarter.

"Joey was right," muttered Harrison between his teeth. "I don't know your name, but I've seen you hanging around Yarghouz Barolass's joint when he had it over on Levant Street. You won't take me for a ride, not tonight. I know that trick, old copper-face. You'd have a flat, or run out of gas at some convenient spot. Any excuse for you to get out of the car and out of range while a hatchet-man hidden somewhere mows me down with a sawed-off. You better hope none of your friends see us and try anything, because this gat has a hair-trigger, and it's cocked. I couldn't die quick enough not to pull the trigger."

The rest of that grim ride was made in silence, until the reaches of South Park rose to view--darkened, except for a fringe of lights around the boundaries, because of municipal economy which sought to reduce the light bill.

"Swing into the park," ordered Harrison, as they drove along the street which passed the park, and, further on, James Willoughby's house. "Cut off your lights, and drive as I tell you. You can feel your way between the trees."

The darkened car glided into a dense grove and came to a halt. Harrison fumbled in his pockets with his left hand and drew out a small flashlight, and a pair of handcuffs. In climbing out, he was forced to remove his muzzle from close contact with his prisoner's back, but the gun menaced the Mongol in the small ring of light emanating from the flash.

"Climb out," ordered the detective. "That's right--slow and easy. You're going to have to stay here awhile. I didn't want to take you to the station right now, for several reasons. One of them is

I didn't want your pals to know I turned the tables on you. I'm hoping they'll still be patiently waiting for you to bring me into range of their sawed-offs--ha, would you?"

The Mongol, with a desperate wrench, struck the flashlight from the detective's hand, plunging them into darkness.

Harrison' clutching fingers locked like a vise on his adversary's coat sleeve, and at the same instant he instinctively threw out his .45 before his belly, to parry the stroke he knew would instantly come. A knife clashed venomously against the blue steel cylinder, and Harrison hooked his foot about an ankle and jerked powerfully. The fighters went down together, and the knife sliced the detective's coat as they fell. Then his blindly driven gun barrel crunched glancingly against a shaven skull, and the straining form went limp.

Panting and swearing beneath his breath, Harrison retrieved the flashlight and cuffs, and set to work securing his prisoner. The Mongol was completely out; it was no light matter to stop a full-arm swing from Steve Harrison. Had the blow landed solidly it would have caved in the skull like an eggshell.

Handcuffed, gagged with strips torn from his coat, and his feet bound with the same material, the Mongol was placed in the car, and Harrison turned and strode through the shadows of the park, toward the eastern hedge beyond which lay James Willoughby's estate. He hoped that this affair would give him some slight advantage in this blind battle. While the Mongols waited for him to ride into the trap they had undoubtedly laid for him somewhere in the city, perhaps he could do a little scouting unmolested.

.2.

James Willoughby's estate adjoined South Park on the east. Only a high hedge separated the park from his grounds. The big three-storied house—disproportionately huge for a bachelor—towered among carefully trimmed trees and shrubbery, amidst a level, shaven lawn. There were lights in the two lower floors, none in the third. Harrison knew that Willoughby's study was a big room on the second floor, on the west side of the house. From that room no light issued between the heavy shutters. Evidently curtains and shades were drawn inside. The big dick grunted in approval as he stood looking through the hedge.

He knew that a plainclothes man was watching the house from each side, and he marked the bunch of shrubbery amidst which would be crouching the man detailed to guard the west side. Craning his neck, he saw a car in front of the house, which faced south, and he knew it to be that of Chief Hoolihan.

With the intention of taking a short cut across the lawn, he wormed through the hedge, and, not wishing to be shot by mistake, he called softly: "Hey, Harper!"

There was no answer. Harrison strode toward the shrubbery.

"Asleep at the post?" he muttered angrily. "Eh, what's this?"

He had stumbled over something in the shadows of the shrubs. His hurriedly directed beam shone on the white, upturned face of a man. Blood dabbled the features, and a crumpled hat lay nearby, an unfired pistol near the limp hand.

"Knocked stiff from behind!" muttered Harrison. "What—"

Parting the shrub he gazed toward the house. On that side an ornamental chimney rose tier by tier, until it towered above the roof. And his eyes became slits as they centered on a window on the third floor within easy reach of that chimney. On all other windows the shutters were closed, but these stood open.

With frantic haste he tore through the shrubbery and ran across the lawn, stooping like a bulky bear, amazingly fleet for one of his weight. As he rounded the corner of the house and rushed toward the steps, a man rose swiftly from among the hedges lining the walk, and covered him, only to lower his gun with an exclamation of recognition.

"Where's Hoolihan?" snapped the detective.

"Upstairs with old man Willoughby. What's up?"

"Harper's been slugged," snarled Harrison. "Beat it out there; you know where he was posted. Wait there until I call you. If you see anything you don't recognize trying to leave the house, plug it! I'll send out a man to take your place here."

He entered the front door and saw four men in plain clothes lounging about in the main hall.

"Jackson," he snapped, "take Hanson's place out in front. I sent him around to the west side. The rest of you stand by for anything."

Mounting the stair in haste, he entered the study on the second floor, breathing a sigh of relief as he found the occupants apparently undisturbed.

The curtains were closely drawn over the windows, and only the door letting into the hall was open. Willoughby was there, a tall, spare man, with a scimitar sweep of nose and a bony aggressive chin. Chief Hoolihan, big, bear-like, rubicund, boomed a greeting.

"All your men downstairs?" asked Harrison.

"Sure; nothin' can get past 'em, and I'm stayin' here with Mr. Willoughby—"

"And in a few minutes more you'd both have been scratching gravel in hell," snapped Harrison. "Didn't I tell you we were dealing with Orientals? You concentrated all your force below, never thinking that death might slip in on you from above—but I haven't time to talk. Turn out that light. Mr. Willoughby, get over there in that alcove. Chief, stand in front of him, and watch that door that leads into the hall. I'm going to leave it open. Locking it would be useless, against what we're fighting. If anything you don't recognize comes through it, shoot to kill."

"What the devil are you driving at, Harrison?" demanded Hoolihan.

"I mean one of Yarghouz Barolass's killers is in this house!" snapped Harrison. "There may be more than one; anyway, he's somewhere upstairs. Is this the only stair, Mr. Willoughby? No back stair?"

"This is the only one in the house," answered the millionaire. "There are only bedrooms on the third floor."

"Where's the light button for the hall on that floor?"

"At the head of the stairs, on the left; but you aren't—"

"Take your places and do as I say," grunted Harrison, gliding out into the hallway.

He stood glaring at the stair which wound up above him, its upper part masked in shadow. Somewhere up there lurked a soulless slayer—a Mongol killer, trained in the art of murder, who lived only to perform his master's will. Harrison started to call the men below, then changed his mind. To raise his voice would be to warn the lurking murderer above. Setting his teeth, he glided up the stair. Aware that he was limned in the light below, he realized the desperate recklessness of his action; but he had long ago learned that he could not match subtlety against the Orient. Direct action, however desperate, was always his best bet. He did not fear a bullet as he charged up; the Mongols preferred to slay in silence; but a thrown knife could kill as promptly as tearing lead. His one chance lay in the winding of the stair.

He took the last steps with a thundering rush, not daring to use his flash, plunged into the gloom of the upper hallway, frantically sweeping the wall for the light button. Even as he felt life and movement in the darkness beside him, his groping fingers found it. The scrape of a foot on the floor beside him galvanized him, and as he instinctively flinched back, something whined past his breast and thudded deep into the wall. Then under his frenzied fingers, light flooded the hall.

Almost touching him, half crouching, a copper-skinned giant with a shaven head wrenched at a curved knife which was sunk deep in the woodwork. He threw up his head, dazzled by the light, baring yellow fangs in a bestial snarl.

Harrison had just left a lighted area. His eyes accustomed themselves more swiftly to the sudden radiance. He threw his left like a hammer at the Mongol's jaw. The killer swayed and fell, out cold.

Hoolihan was bellowing from below.

"Hold everything," answered Harrison. "Send one of the boys up here with the cuffs. I'm going through these bedrooms."

Which he did, switching on the lights, gun ready, but finding no other lurking slayer. Evidently Yarghouz Barolass considered one would be enough. And so it might have been, but for the big detective.

Having latched all the shutters and fastened the windows securely, he returned to the study, whither the prisoner had been taken. The man had recovered his senses and sat, handcuffed, on a divan. Only the eyes, black and snaky, seemed alive in the copperish face.

"Mongol alright," muttered Harrison. "No Chinaman."

"What is all this?" complained Hoolihan, still upset by the realization that an invader had slipped through his cordon.

"Easy enough. This fellow sneaked up on Harper and laid him cold. Some of these fellows could steal the teeth right out of your mouth. With all those shrubs and trees it was a cinch. Say, send out a couple of the boys to bring in Harper, will you? Then he climbed that fancy chimney. That was a cinch, too. I could do it myself. Nobody had thought to fasten the shutters on that floor, because nobody expected an attack from that direction.

"Mr. Willoughby, do you know anything about Yarghouz Barolass?"

"I never heard of him," declared the philanthropist, and though Harrison scanned him narrowly, he was impressed by the ring of sincerity in Willoughby's voice.

"Well, he's a mystic fakir," said Harrison. "Hangs around Levant Street and preys on old ladies with more money than sense—faddists. Gets them interested in Taoism and Lamaism and then plays on their superstitions and blackmails them. I know his racket, but I've never been able to put the finger on him, because his victims won't squeal. But he's behind these attacks on you."

"Then why don't we go grab him?" demanded Hoolihan.

"Because we don't know where he is. He knows that I know he's mixed up in this. Joey Glick spilled it to me, just before he croaked—. Yes, Joey's dead—poison; more of Yarghouz's work. By this time Yarghouz will have deserted his usual hangouts, and be hiding somewhere—probably in some secret underground dive that we couldn't find in a hundred years, now that Joey is dead."

"Let's sweat it out of this yellow-belly," suggested Hoolihan.

Harrison grinned coldly. "You'd sweat to death yourself before he'd talk. There's another tied up in a car out in the park. Send a couple of boys after him, and you can try your hand on both of them. But you'll get damned little out of them. Come here, Hoolihan."

Drawing him aside, he said: "I'm sure that Job Hopkins was poisoned in the same manner they got Joey Glick. Do you remember anything unusual about the death of Richard Lynch?"

"Well, not about his death, but that night somebody apparently tried to steal and mutilate his corpse—"

"What do you mean, mutilate?" demanded Harrison.

"Well, a watchman heard a noise and went into the room and found Lynch's body on the floor, as if somebody had tried to carry it off, and then maybe got scared off. And a lot of the *teeth* had been pulled or knocked out!"

"Well, I can't explain the teeth," grunted Harrison. "Maybe they were knocked out in the wreck that killed Lynch. But this is my hunch: Yarghouz Barolass is stealing the bodies of wealthy men, figuring on screwing a big price out of their families. When they don't die naturally or quick enough, he bumps them off."

Hoolihan cursed in shocked horror.

"But Willoughby hasn't any family."

"Well, I reckon they figure the executors of his estate will kick in. Now listen: I'm borrowing your car for a visit to Job Hopkins' vault. I got a tip that they're going to lift his corpse tomorrow night. I believe they'll spring it tonight, on the chance that I might have gotten the tip. I believe they'll try to get ahead of me. They may have already, what with all this delay. I figured on being out there long before now.

"No, I don't want any help. Your flat-feet are more of a hindrance than a help in a job like this. You stay here with Willoughby. Keep men upstairs as well as down. Don't let Willoughby open any packages that might come, don't even let him answer a phone call. I'm going to Hopkins' vault, and I don't know when I'll be back; may roost out there all night. It just depends on when—or if— they come for the corpse."

A few minutes later he was speeding down the road on his grim errand. The graveyard which contained the tomb of Job Hopkins was small, exclusive, where only the bones of rich men were laid to rest. The wind moaned through the cypress trees which bent shadow-arms above the gleaming marble.

Harrison approached from the back side, up a narrow, tree-lined side street. He left the car, climbed the wall, and stole through the gloom, beneath the pallid shafts, under the cypress shadows. Ahead of him Job Hopkins' tomb glimmered whitely, and he stopped short, crouching low in the shadows. He saw a glow—a spark of light—it was extinguished, and through the open door of the tomb trooped half a dozen shadowy forms. His hunch had been right, but they had gotten there ahead of him. Fierce anger sweeping him at the ghoulish crime, he leaped forward, shouting a savage command.

They scattered like rats, and his crashing volley re-echoed futilely among the sepulchers. Rushing forward recklessly, swearing savagely, he came into the tomb, and turning his light into the interior, winced at what he saw. The coffin had been burst open, but the tomb itself was not empty. In a careless heap on the floor lay the embalmed corpse of Job Hopkins—*and the lower jawbone had been sawed away.*

"What the hell!" Harrison stopped short, bewildered at the sudden disruption of his theory. "They didn't want the body—what did they want? His *teeth?* And they got Richard Lynch's teeth—"

Lifting the body back into its resting place, he hurried forth, shutting the door of the tomb behind him. The wind whined through the cypress, and mingled with it was a low moaning sound. Thinking that one of his shots had gone home, after all, he followed the noise, warily, pistol and flash ready.

The sound seemed to emanate from a bunch of low cedars near the wall, and among them he found a man lying. His beam revealed the stocky figure, the square, now convulsed face of a Mongol. The slant eyes were glazed, the back of the coat soaked with blood. The man was gasping his last, but Harrison found no trace of a bullet wound on him. In his back, between his shoulders, stood up the hilt of a curious skewer-like knife. The fingers of his right hand had been horribly gashed, as if he had sought to retain his grasp on something which his slayers desired.

"Running from me he bumped into somebody hiding among these cedars," muttered Harrison. "But who? And why? By God, Willoughby hasn't told me everything."

He stared uneasily at the crowding shadows. No stealthy shuffling footfall disturbed the sepulchral quiet. Only the wind whimpered through the cypress and the cedars. The detective was alone with the dead—with the corpses of rich men in their ornate tombs, and with the staring yellow man whose flesh was not yet rigid.

.3.

"You're back in a hurry," said Hoolihan, as Harrison entered the Willoughby study. "Do any good?"

"Did the yellow boys talk?" countered Harrison.

"They did not," growled the chief. "They sat like pot-bellied idols. I sent 'em to the station, along with Harper. He was still in a daze."

"Mr. Willoughby," Harrison sank down rather wearily into an arm-chair and fixed his cold gaze on the philanthropist, "am I right in believing that you and Richard Lynch and Job Hopkins were at one time connected with each other in some way?"

"Why do you ask?" parried Willoughby.

"Because somehow the three of you are connected in this matter. Lynch's death was not accidental, and I'm pretty sure that Job Hopkins was poisoned. Now the same gang is after you. I thought it was a body-snatching racket, but an apparent attempt to steal Richard Lynch's corpse out of the morgue, now seems to resolve itself into what was in reality a successful attempt to get his *teeth*. Tonight a gang of Mongols entered the tomb of Job Hopkins, obviously for the same purpose—"

A choking cry interrupted him. Willoughby sank back, his face livid.

"My God, after all these years!"

Harrison stiffened.

"Then you do know Yarghouz Barolass? You know why he's after you?"

Willoughby shook his head. "I never heard of Yarghouz Barolass before. But I know why they killed Lynch and Hopkins."

"Then you'd better spill the works," advised Harrison. "We're working in the dark as it is."

"I will!" The philanthropist was visibly shaken. He mopped his brow with a shaking hand, and reposed himself with an effort.

"Twenty years ago," he said, "Lynch, Hopkins and myself, young men just out of college, were in China, in the employ of the warlord Yuen Chin. We were chemical engineers. Yuen Chin was a far-sighted man—ahead of his time, scientifically speaking.

He visioned the day when men would war with gasses and deadly chemicals. He supplied us with a splendid laboratory, in which to discover or invent some such element of destruction for his use.

"He paid us well; the foundations of each of our fortunes were laid there. We were young, poor, unscrupulous.

"More by chance than skill we stumbled onto a deadly secret—the formula for a poisonous gas, a thousand times more deadly than anything yet dreamed of. That was what he was paying us to invent or discover for him, but the discovery sobered us. We realized that the man who possessed the secret of that gas, could easily conquer the world. We were willing to aid Yuen Chin against his Mongolian enemies; we were not willing to elevate a yellow mandarin to world empire, to see our hellish discovery directed against the lives of our own people.

"Yet we were not willing to destroy the formula, because we foresaw a time when America, with her back to the wall, might have a desperate need for such a weapon. So we wrote out the formula in code, but left out three symbols, without any of which the formula is meaningless and undecipherable. Each of us then had a lower jaw tooth pulled out, and on the gold tooth put in its place was carved one of the three symbols. Thus we took precautions against our own greed, as well as against the avarice of outsiders. One of us might conceivably fall so low as to sell the secret, but it would be useless without the other two symbols.

"Yuen Chin fell and was beheaded on the great execution ground at Peking. We escaped, Lynch, Hopkins and I, not only with our lives, but with most of the money which had been paid us. But the formula, scrawled on parchment, we were obliged to leave, secreted among musty archives in an ancient temple.

"Only one man knew our secret: an old Chinese tooth-puller, who aided us in the matter of the teeth. He owed his life to Richard Lynch, and when he swore the oath of eternal silence, we knew we could trust him."

"Yet you think somebody is after the secret symbols?"

"What else could it be? I can understand it. The old tooth-puller must have died long ago. Who could have learned of it? Torture would not have dragged the secret from him. Yet it can be for no other reason that this fellow you call Yarghouz Barolass murdered and mutilated the bodies of my former companions, and now is after me.

"Why, I love life as well as any man, but my own peril shrinks into insignificance compared to the world-wide menace contained in those little carven symbols—two of which are now, according to what you say, in the hands of some ruthless foe of the western world.

"Somebody has found the formula we left hidden in the temple, and has learned somehow of its secret. Anything can come out of China. Just now the bandit warlord Yah Lai is threatening to overthrow the National government—who knows what devilish concoction that Chinese caldron is brewing?

"The thought of the secret of that gas in the hands of some Oriental conqueror is appalling. My God, gentlemen, I fear you do not realize the full significance of the matter!"

"I've got a faint idea," grunted Harrison. "Ever see a dagger like this?" He presented the weapon that had killed the Mongol.

"Many of them, in China," answered Willoughby promptly.

"Then it isn't a Mongol weapon?"

"No, it's distinctly Chinese; there is a conventional Manchu inscription on the hilt."

"Ummmmmm!" Harrison sat scowling, chin on fist, idly tapping the blade against his shoe, lost in meditation. Admittedly, he was all at sea, lost in a bewildering tangle. To his companions he looked like a grim figure of retribution, brooding over the fate of the wicked. In reality he was cursing his luck.

"What are you going to do now?" demanded Hoolihan.

"Only one thing to do," responded Harrison. "I'm going to try to run down Yarghouz Barolass. I'm going to start with River Street—God knows, it'll be like looking for a rat in a swamp. I want you to contrive to let one of those Mongols escape, Hoolihan. I'll try to trail him back to Yarghouz's hangout—"

The phone tingled loudly.

Harrison reached it with a long stride.

"Who speaks, please?" Over the wire came a voice with a subtle but definite accent.

"Steve Harrison," grunted the big dick.

"A friend speaks, detective," came the bland voice. "Before we progress further, let me warn you that it will be impossible to trace this call, and would do you no good to do so."

"Well?" Harrison was bristling like a big truculent dog.

"Mr. Willoughby," the suave voice continued, "is a doomed man. He is as good as dead already. Guards and guns will not save him, when the Sons of Erlik are ready to strike. But *you* can save him, without firing a shot?"

"Yeah?" It was a scarcely articulate snarl humming bloodthirstily from Harrison's bull-throat.

"If you were to come alone to the House of Dreams on Levant Street, Yarghouz Barolass would speak to you, and a compromise might be arranged whereby Mr. Willoughby's life would be spared."

"Compromise, hell!" roared the big dick, the skin over his knuckles showing white. "Who do you think you're talking to? Think I'd fall into a trap like that?"

"You have a hostage," came back the voice. "One of the men you hold is Yarghouz Barolass's brother. Let him suffer if there is treachery. I swear by the bones of my ancestors, no harm shall come to you!"

The voice ceased with a click at the other end of the wire.

Harrison wheeled.

"Yarghouz Barolass must be getting desperate to try such a child's trick as that!" he swore. Then he considered, and muttered, half to himself: "By the bones of his ancestors! Never heard of a Mongolian breaking *that* oath. All that stuff about Yarghouz's brother may be the bunk. Yet—well, maybe he's trying to outsmart me—draw me away from Willoughby—on the other hand, maybe he thinks that I'd never fall for a trick like that—aw, to hell with thinking! I'm going to start acting!"

"What do you mean?" demanded Hoolihan.

"I mean I'm going to the House of Dreams, alone. I've got an idea that taking this meeting is the very last thing Yarghouz will be expecting me *to* do. Maybe I'll get under his guard that way, somehow."

"You're crazy!" exclaimed Hoolihan. "Take a squad, surround the house, and raid it!"

"And find an empty rat-den," grunted Harrison, his peculiar obsession for working alone again asserting itself. "You're needed here, with all the men you can have. If it's a trap—well, I've slugged my way in and out of plenty of traps in my time."

"If you wasn't the fightin'est fool in the world you'd been dead and forgotten long ago," said Hoolihan, half in admiration, half in irritation. "You big, dumb, reckless bull-ape!"

.4.

Dawn was not far away when Harrison entered the smoky den near the waterfront which was known to the Chinese as the House of Dreams, and whose dingy exterior masked a subterranean opium joint. Only a pudgy Chinaboy nodded behind the counter; he looked up with no apparent surprise. Without a word he led Harrison to a curtain in the back of the shop, pulled it aside, and revealed a door. The detective gripped his gun under his coat, nerves taut with excitement that must come to any man who has deliberately walked into what might prove to be a death-trap. The boy knocked, lifting a sing-song monotone, and a voice answered from within. Harrison started. He recognized that voice. The boy opened the door, bobbed his head and was gone. Harrison entered, pulling the door to behind him.

He was in a room heaped and strewn with divans and silk cushions. If there were other doors, they were masked by the black velvet hangings, which, worked with gilt dragons, covered the walls. On a divan near the further wall squatted a stocky, pot-bellied shape, in black silk, a close-fitting velvet cap on his shaven head.

"So you came, after all!" breathed the detective. "Don't move, Yarghouz Barolass. I've got you covered through my coat. Your gang can't get me quick enough to keep me from getting you first."

"Why do you threaten me, detective?" Yarghouz Barolass's face was expressionless, the square, parchment-skinned face of a Mongol from the Gobi, with wide thin lips and glittering black eyes. His English was perfect.

"See, I trust you. I am here, alone. The boy who let you in said that you are alone. Good. You kept your word, I keep my promise. For the time there is truce between us, and I am ready to bargain, as you suggested."

"As *I* suggested?" demanded Harrison.

"I have no desire to harm Mr. Willoughby, any more than I wished to harm either of the other gentlemen," said Yarghouz Barolass. "But knowing them all as I did—from report and discreet observation—it never occurred to me that I could obtain what I wished while they lived. So I did not enter into negotiations with them."

"So you want Willoughby's tooth, too?"

"Not I," disclaimed Yarghouz Barolass. "It is an honorable person in China, the grandson of an old man who babbled in his dotage, as old men often do, drooling secrets torture could not have wrung from him in his soundness of mind. The grandson, Yah Lai, has risen from a mean position to that of warlord. He listened to the maunderings of his grandfather, a tooth-puller. He found a formula, written in code, and learned of symbols on the teeth of old men. He sent a request to me, with promise of much reward. I have one tooth, procured from the unfortunate person, Richard Lynch. Now if you will hand over the other—that of Job Hopkins—as you promised, perhaps we may reach a compromise by which Mr. Willoughby will be allowed to keep his life, in return for a tooth, as you hinted."

"As *I* hinted?" exclaimed Harrison. "What are you driving at? I made no promises; and I certainly haven't Job Hopkins' tooth. You've got it, yourself."

"All this is unnecessary," objected Yarghouz, an edge to his tone. "You have a reputation for veracity, in spite of your violent nature. I was relying upon your reputation for honesty when I accepted this appointment. Of course, I already knew that you had Hopkins' tooth. When my blundering servants, having been frightened by you as they left the vaults, gathered at the appointed rendezvous, they discovered that he to whom was entrusted the jaw-bone containing the precious tooth, was not among them. They returned to the graveyard and found his body, but not the tooth. It was obvious that you had killed him and taken it from him."

Harrison was so thunderstruck by this new twist, that he remained speechless, his mind a tangled whirl of bewilderment.

Yarghouz Barolass continued tranquilly: "I was about to send my servants out in another attempt to secure you, when your agent phoned me—though how he located me on the telephone is still a mystery into which I must inquire—and announced that you were ready to meet me at the House of Dreams, and give me Job Hopkins' tooth, in return for an opportunity to bargain personally for Mr. Willoughby's life. Knowing you to be a man of honor, I agreed, trusting you—"

"This is madness!" exclaimed Harrison. "I didn't call you, or have anybody call you. *You*, or rather, one of your men, called me—"

"I did not!" Yarghouz was on his feet, his stocky body under the rippling black silk quivering with rage and suspicion. His eyes narrowed to slits, his wide mouth knotted viciously.

"You deny that you promised to give me Job Hopkins' tooth?"

"Sure I do!" snapped Harrison. "I haven't got it, and what's more, I'm not 'compromising' as you call it—"

"Liar!" Yarghouz spat the epithet like a snake hissing. "You have tricked—betrayed me—used my trust in your blackened honor to dupe me—"

"Keep cool," advised Harrison. "Remember, I've got a Colt .45 trained on you."

"Shoot and die!" retorted Yarghouz. "I do not know what your game is, but I know that if you shoot me, we will fall together. Fool, do you think I would keep my promise to a barbarian dog? Behind this hanging is the entrance to a tunnel through which I can escape before any of your stupid police, if you have brought any with you, can enter this room. You have been covered since you came through that door, by a man hiding behind the tapestry. Try to stop me, and you die!"

"I believe you're telling the truth about not calling me," said Harrison slowly. "I believe somebody tricked us both, for some reason. You were called, in my name, and I was called, in yours."

Yarghouz halted short in some hissing tirade. His eyes were like black evil jewels in the lamplight.

"More lies?" he demanded uncertainly.

"No; I think somebody in your gang is double-crossing you. Now easy, I'm not pulling a gun. I'm just going to show you the knife that I found sticking in the back of the fellow you seem to think I killed."

He drew it from his coat-pocket with his left hand—his right still gripped his gun beneath the garment—and tossed it on the divan.

Yarghouz pounced on it. His slit eyes flared wide with a terrible light; his yellow skin went ashen. He cried out something in his own tongue, which Harrison did not understand.

In a torrent of hissing sibilances, he lapsed briefly into English: "I see it all now! This was too subtle for a barbarian! Death to them all!" Wheeling toward the tapestry behind the divan he shrieked: "Gutchluk!"

There was no answer, but Harrison thought he saw the black velvety expanse billow slightly. With his skin the color of old ashes, Yarghouz Barolass ran at the hanging, ignoring Harrison's order to halt, seized the tapestries, tore them aside—something flashed between them like a beam of white hot light. Yarghouz's scream broke in a ghastly gurgle. His head pitched forward, then his whole body swayed backward, and he fell heavily among the cushions, clutching at the hilt of a skewer-like dagger that quivered upright in his breast. The Mongol's yellow claw-like hands fell away from the crimsoned hilt, spread wide, clutching at the thick carpet; a convulsive spasm ran through his frame, and those taloned yellow fingers went limp.

Gun in hand, Harrison took a single stride toward the tapestries—then halted short, staring at the figure which moved imperturbably through them: a tall yellow man in the robes of a mandarin, who smiled and bowed, his hands hidden in his wide sleeves.

"You killed Yarghouz Barolass!" accused the detective.

"The evil one indeed has been dispatched to join his ancestors by my hand," agreed the mandarin. "Be not afraid. The Mongol who covered you through a peep-hole with an abbreviated shotgun has likewise departed this uncertain life, suddenly and silently, and my own people hold supreme in the House of Dreams this night. All that we ask is that you make no attempt to stay our departure."

"Who are you?" demanded Harrison.

"But a humble servant of Fang Yin, lord of Peking. When it was learned that these unworthy ones sought a formula in America which might enable the upstart Yah Lai to overthrow the government of China, word was sent in haste to me—almost too late. Two men had already died. The third was menaced.

"I sent my servants instantly to intercept the evil Sons of Erlik at the vaults they desecrated. But for your appearance, frightening the Mongols into flight, before the trap could be sprang, my servants would have caught them all in ambush. As it was, they did manage to slay he who carried the relic Yarghouz sought, and this they brought to me.

"I took the liberty of impersonating a servant of the Mongol in my speech with you, and of pretending to be a Chinese agent of yours, while speaking with Yarghouz. All worked out as I wished. Lured by the thought of the tooth, at the loss of which he was maddened, Yarghouz came from his secret, well-guarded lair, and fell into my hands. I brought you here to witness his execution, so that you might realize that Mr. Willoughby is no longer in danger. Fang Yin has no ambitions for world empire; he wishes but to hold what is his. That he is well able to do, now that the threat of the devil-gas is lifted. And now I must be gone. Yarghouz had laid careful plans for his flight out of the country. I will take advantage of his preparations."

"Wait a minute!" exclaimed Harrison. "I've got to arrest you for the murder of this rat."

"I am sorry," murmured the mandarin. "I am in much haste. No need to lift your revolver. I swore that you would not be injured and I keep my word."

As he spoke, the light went suddenly out. Harrison sprang forward, cursing, fumbling at the tapestries, which had swished in the darkness as if from the passing of a large body between them. His fingers met only solid walls, and when at last the light came on again, he was alone in the room, and behind the hangings a heavy door had been slid shut. On the divan lay something that glinted in the lamplight, and Harrison looked down on a curiously carven gold tooth.

The Black Moon

"And that, my honorable friend," intoned old Wang Yun, folding lean hands over his embroidered silk jacket, "is the legend of the White Fox Spirit, as the Sons of Han tell it. And now I must feed the Ancient One."

Steve Harrison, massive, dark, incongruous beside the frail delicacy of the Oriental porcelains and jades that filled the little shop, propped his aggressive jaw on his hammer-like fist and watched his host with a peculiar fascination, as the old Chinaman shuffled over to a long narrow bamboo cage which rested on the lap of a big green Buddha squatting against the wall among Ming vases and carpets from Eastern Turkestan. Wang Yun blinked his weak eyes and crooned a curious chant as he drew a milk bottle and a tiny jade saucer from some obscure recess. Harrison involuntarily shuddered.

"I've seen some queer pets in River Street joints," said the detective. "Chow dogs, Persian cats and fighting quails and white peacocks and baby alligators; but I'll be hanged if I ever before saw a man whose idea of a household companion was a king Cobra!"

"Pan Chau is very ancient and very wise," smiled Wang Yun. "He is named for a great warrior who would have destroyed the empire of Rome, had he lived another year. I keep the fangs of the Ancient One drawn, lest he harm me by mistake in his age and blindness."

"You're a strange man, Wang Yun," grunted Harrison.

"Life is full of strangeness," answered the old Chinaman, leisurely working the intricate gold catch of the cage-door; inside began a dry rustling that made Harrison's flesh crawl. "An hour perhaps before you dropped in to talk with me, a strange thing happened. My telephone, which seldom rings," he nodded toward a curtain at the back of the shop, "rang loudly, and when I answered

89

it, an unknown voice bade me remain at the machine until one came who would speak with me. I waited patiently for many minutes, but in vain. None ever came. Who would jest with Wang Yun? And perhaps I lost a sale, for while I waited at the telephone, I heard someone enter the door, though who it was I do not know, because I can not see into the shop from my telephone. I called to him that I would attend his pleasure in an instant, but after a few moments I heard him leave the shop. I hurried from the telephone, but the shop was empty."

"Did you miss anything?" asked the detective.

"I thought of theft," answered Wang Yun, thrusting his hand into the cage, "but I looked over my stock, and found nothing missing, and—" He stiffened with a wild, inarticulate cry, and reeled back, tearing his hand from the cage. From his wrist trailed a glistening, writhing horror that whipped and lashed—

The old Chinaman fell headlong, screaming in a ghastly whisper, and Harrison, cursing horrifiedly, smashed his heavy heel down on that awful hooded head, before the reptile could draw its long weaving loops into a coil. Kicking aside the looping, knotting length, he bent over Wang Yun. The old Chinaman was not yet dead, but his eyes were glazed. A claw-like convulsive hand clutched Harrison's wrist like steel hooks. There was awful meaning in the distended eyes.

"Not—mine!" The knotted lips forced out a spasmodic whisper. "Another—ebony ball—seventh—seventh—"

Froth and blood burst horribly from those straining lips, as an awful convulsion ruptured inner veins. Then the writhing form went limp under Harrison's hands.

"Damn!" muttered the detective, somewhat shaken. "I didn't know a cobra's bite killed that quick. But he was old and his heart was weak. The devil's fangs must have grown back—"

He paused, glaring down at the snaky abomination which lay still twisting and writhing on the floor.

"Not mine!" he repeated. "No, and by thunder, that's not Pan Chau. I've seen him hold up the old devil when he was feeding him. His snake was blind, and his scales were nearly white with old age."

The monster on the floor was iridescent, even in death, full-bodied, packed with lethal power.

"Did this devil get away from some zoo and crawl in with Pan Chau?" quested the detective. Setting his teeth, he squinted into the bamboo cage. It was empty. A shadow crossed Harrison's face, making it darker and grimmer than usual.

"I don't know who you were, or what you did before you came here," he muttered, scowling down at the dead Chinaman. "But you've always been a square-shooter here, and a friend of mine. This business isn't going to end here."

He went to the back of the shop and pulled aside the curtain, revealing a short corridor, littered with junk, which opened on a narrow, dark alley. Old Wang Yun had lived alone in a tiny apartment above the shop. But the stair letting to the rooms above did not descend into the corridor. It gave directly onto the shop, and was likewise concealed by a curtain, flanked on either hand by a grinning grotesque idol. Harrison found the telephone tucked away in a tiny alcove which would hardly admit his huge shoulders.

"Say, listen, Hoolihan," said Harrison into the phone. "Old Wang Yun's been croaked—I know you don't know him! What's that got to do with it? Send a man around—and say, have you had any reports of snakes missing from any of the zoos? Wang Yun was bitten by a cobra that I believe was planted purposely, and those things don't grow on trees."

"Well," came back over the wires, "a fellow over on Levant Street was raising merry hell this mornin' because somebody, he swore, had swiped a valuable reptile from him. Here's the address: William D. Feodor, 481 Levant Street—he's a scientist or something; has a laboratory there, and says he's conductin' experiments to find an antidote for snake poison—"

"All right," snapped Harrison, clicking the receiver back on the hook. Returning through the curtain, he stared at the vessels and images ranged along the shelves, until his gaze rested on a row of small objects, almost hidden by a bolt of watered Manchu silk.

"Ebony ball!" muttered the detective. "He was trying to tell me something—the seventh—"

He counted the small, highly polished spheres. There were thirteen. Taking up the middle one, he turned it in his hand, in bafflement. It was merely a small, shining ball of ebony, the use of which he was ignorant. Possibly it was a Chinese toy of some sort. Dropping it into his pocket, he went to the door and shrilled on his police whistle, grimly noting how many passers-by started and stared, and some slunk more hurriedly on their way. This was River Street, the mysterious Oriental quarter where anything could happen, and whose denizens had little love for the law; for white man's law, at least, though they had a strange and often ghastly code of their own.

A big policeman came on the run, and Harrison jerked a thumb at the crumpled form on the floor.

"Stay here until the boys come after him; don't let anybody in. Then lock up the joint and keep an eye on it. Here's the key."

"Murder?" inquired the cop.

"Maybe." Harrison's instincts were noncommittal. He had worked alone until taciturnity had become second nature.

Gingerly scooping up the limp shape of the cobra with a jeweled spearhead, he dumped it into a cardboard box, and carrying it under his arm, left the shop, cursing his imagination for conjuring up visions of the dead snake coming to life again and biting him through the cardboard.

He found 481 Levant without trouble, climbed three rickety flights of stairs, and knocked at a door whence issued unsavory and chemical odors. There was a fretful mutter inside, a hurrying clump of feet, and the door was jerked open abruptly, revealing a tall, erect figure, a middle-aged man with unkempt hair, horn-rimmed glasses, and slouchy, stained garments. His manner was distinctly irascible, as if he begrudged time wasted from whatever noisome task he was employed in.

"Well, well!" he jerked out before Harrison could speak. "What is it?"

"Are you William D. Feodor?" inquired the detective.

"Yes; what about it?"

"Did you lose a snake?"

The other started slightly and showed more interest in his visitor.

"I certainly did! Have you—"

"Is this it?" Harrison threw back the lid of the box.

Feodor's profanity was instant and fervent. He asked of high heaven who could have been such a monumental fool as to have reduced the head of that expensive specimen of the *cobra de capello* to a pulp utterly useless to science.

"Where will I get another?" he demanded of the world at large. "My experiments! Almost completed! Oh, the fool! The brainless, unconscious—"

"Now you wait!" Harrison objected, rebelling at last. "I killed this devil, if you want to know. You had no business bringing the brute into the city, if you had no way of keeping him confined. I smashed its head just after it had bitten poor old Wang Yun—"

"Eh?" The other ceased his tirade suddenly, and blinked at the detective from behind his thick-lensed glasses. "You mean the old Chinaman who runs the antique shop over on River Street?"

"The one that *did* run it," grunted Harrison. "Your infernal snake killed him."

"My God, that's terrible!" exclaimed Feodor, his manner changing instantly. "Come in, Mister—?"

"Harrison." The detective displayed his badge.

"Mr. Harrison," added the other, opening the door. "Sorry for my outbreak just now. My nerves are rather on edge—been working too hard lately."

Harrison entered a big room made up into a laboratory. He saw a small sink, stained with many colors, a Bunsen burner, glass tubes and retorts in racks, bottles filled with venomous looking liquids, and over in a corner a dejected white rabbit occupied a compartment in a wire cage which contained, in other cells, a guinea pig, a hairy tarantula, and a big blunt-headed snake of some harmless breed.

"I kept the cobra in a cage to itself," said Feodor, following the detective's gaze. "This morning when I came into the laboratory—I sleep in a bedroom across the hall—cage, cobra and all were gone. I distinctly remember locking the door last night."

"That wouldn't stop a thief," grunted Harrison. "These boarding house locks are a joke. I could pick that one myself with a knife point or a piece of wire in fifteen seconds. Or somebody could have come in through a window. I notice there's a fire escape within reach. And the catches on the windows are no better than the locks on the doors. Mr. Feodor, have you any idea as to who stole that snake?"

"I hesitate to accuse anybody," said Feodor slowly. "I know very few people in the city, and have been here only a short time. I have few guests, and those only in a business way. But day before yesterday, I did have a visitor who wanted to buy that very snake."

"Yeah? What kind of a looking fellow?"

"He was a Chinaman," answered Feodor. Harrison leaned forward, eyes blazing.

"Could you describe him?"

"Only in a general way," confessed Feodor. "He was tall and very stooped—almost hunch-backed; dressed rather more Oriental than most of the Chinese do nowadays—wore a close-fitting silk jacket, velvet cap, and a pigtail. I noticed the pigtail especially, as a rather uncommon feature.

"He was rather persistent that I sell him the cobra—said it would bring him good luck, or something of the sort. But he was courteous enough, and when he saw I wasn't to be moved, he bobbed his head, stuck his hands in his sleeves, and bowed himself out."

"So!" muttered Harrison. "And suppose this Chinaman—or whoever really stole your snake—suppose he wanted to shift it from one cage to another, how the devil would he keep it from biting him?"

"He could drug it," suggested the scientist. "Or he could have slipped a hood over its head, with air holes in it. He could have handled it like I always did, with wire tongs."

"And a string on the hood to pull it off after it was in the other cage," mused the detective. "He could have carried it that way under his clothes, without the original cage. You knew Wang Yun well?"

"Fairly well. I used to drop in and chat with him occasionally. I liked the old fellow."

"So did I. Did you ever see the Chinaman who tried to buy your snake hanging around his shop?"

"Not that I remember. However, I've been so busy I haven't been in Wang Yun's shop for three weeks. But you haven't told me how the snake came to bite the poor old devil."

"Somebody planted it in Pan Chau's cage," grunted Harrison. "You've seen old Pan Chau?"

"The snake Wang Yun kept in a cage on the lap of the green Buddha? Yes. I especially noticed him, because of my experiments with snakes. Old Wang took him out of his cage once and showed him to me. He must have been a hundred years old."

"Yeah." Harrison rose, after a few minutes silent cogitation. "I'll probably need you as a witness, if I succeed in what I'm going to try to do—find that hump-backed Chinaman. Can I reach you here, Mr. Feodor?"

"Night or day," declared the scientist. "Here's my phone number." He scribbled briefly on a piece of paper and proffered it to the detective.

"Thanks." Harrison folded it and thrust it into his pocket. "I'm hoping you'll get a call from me soon."

"So am I," was the fervent reply, as the detective swung down the ramshackle stairs.

Hoolihan, the chief of police, desired the same thing, for he recognized some peculiar phases in the affair, by the remains in the antique shop, and he greatly desired to hear a firsthand account from Harrison. But that individual had vanished from view; mysterious River Street had swallowed him up, as it had so often in the past. Cryptic, aloof, obsessed with the desire to work utterly alone, Harrison had a way of disappearing after a crime without a word, to reappear hours, days, or even weeks later with a prisoner— dead or alive—and a laconic report. Hoolihan, while recognizing his merit as a man-hunter in his peculiar domain, cursed him long, loud and fervently.

But this time his absence was not so lengthy. With the first flush of dawn he appeared to the policeman whose beat included the antique shop, and demanded news, if any.

"Somebody tried to bust into Wang Yun's shop last night," he was informed. "In fact, somebody *did*. I came past on my usual round a little after midnight, and I just got the gleam of a light playing around over the shelves. I had the key, so in I went—and out *he* went!"

"Who?"

"How should I know? He bolted out the back way and down the alley, with me throwin' lead at his heels and yellin' for him to stop. He seemed to know where all the ash cans were in that alley. I didn't. Look at this ear—that's what I lit on. All I know is, he was a Chinaman; I got a glimpse of his dinky cap and pigtail."

"Hmmmmm!" commented Harrison.

"I don't know if he got anything or not," continued the policeman. "All the damage I could figure out was the lock he'd pried off the alley door. Don't you want to go in and look around? You know pretty well what's in the shop, and—"

"I don't have to," grunted Harrison. "I know what he was after."

A short time later he was climbing the creaking stairs of 481 Levant.

Feodor, busy at his everlasting fumes and stenches, was nevertheless ready with a quick welcome.

"Last night somebody tried to burglarize Wang Yun's joint," said the detective bluntly. "Apparently it was that same Chinaman who stole your snake."

"Then you've found him?" exclaimed Feodor.

"Not yet," grunted Harrison. "I was lucky enough to trace that call; it came from a public pay-booth in a drug store right across the street from the antique shop. Wang Yun had told me about that call, so I knew approximately when it had been put in.

"The girl at the cashier's counter had a hazy recollection of a stoop-shouldered Chinaman corning in the drugstore about that time of day—but, like most eye-witnesses, she couldn't remember whether he went into a phone booth, or whether it wasn't day before yesterday, instead of yesterday, or whether he was a Chinaman after all, or a Jap. Eyes and memories are damned poor things to rely on.

"But I forgot; you don't know what I'm talking about. It was a phone call made to old Wang Yun an hour or so before his murder, and obviously connected with it. This case presents itself like this: this Chinaman stole your snake, and evidently drugged or hooded it, so he could carry it concealed on him; the cage would have attracted attention, even on River Street. He went into that booth across the street from the antique shop, phoned old Wang Yun and told him to hold the phone. Obviously knew that Wang couldn't see in the interior of the shop from his phone. Then he beat it across the street and shifted snakes, taking Wang Yun's with him. Probably dropped poor old Pan Chau down a sewer. All that wouldn't have taken five minutes. The chances were all for people thinking Wang had got bitten by his own snake—if I hadn't happened to be there."

"But what was his motive?" wondered Feodor.

"He wanted something in that shop." Harrison reached a hand into his coat pocket.

"Old Wang Yun tried to tell me something before he died. He recognized the snake that killed him wasn't *his* snake. And whether he realized that somebody had put the finger on him, and *why*, or just wanted to tell me about his secret, I don't know. Anyway, he gasped something about an ebony ball.

"I found it, alright, and last night I split it open, and then spent several hours trying to find out just what it was I'd found. I learned, by virtue of a certain Chinese friend who's a scholar as well as a gentleman."

Withdrawing his hand from his pocket, Harrison displayed something that winked and glowed like a round pool of iridescent blackness in his palm.

"A pearl!" exclaimed Feodor.

"More than *a* pearl!" answered Harrison. "*The* pearl. The biggest, most perfect black pearl in the world! Worn by the Empress Wu-hou, 684 A.D., and was the prize of the crown jewels of China until the early part of the thirteenth century, when the Mongols conquered the Chinese and carried it, with other plunder, to their royal city of Karakorum. Eventually it found its way into a Taoist temple in Korea, from which it was looted by Japanese soldiers during the fighting there in 1894. Then it disappeared; vanished utterly. Rumor said a Chinese soldier discovered it in the possession of a Japanese prisoner, murdered the fellow, and deserted, taking it with him."

"I believe that the story is true, and that old Wang Yun was that Chinese soldier. His love of the beautiful was an obsession; he would have starved with such a trinket in his hand, rather than part with it. 'Like a gem cut out of the iridescent bowl of the night, glowing with black stars that beat like a heart within'—that's the way the Chinese describe it. The Black Moon, they call it.

"Old Wang Yun cared nothing for money; he made little profit from his antiques; but he loved to handle beautiful things; he'd commit murder for a thing like the Black Moon.

"But I've got an idea that the fellow who's after it now cares little about its beauty. It's worth a fortune. Of course, I don't know how he learned of it. Maybe he spied on old Wang; the old man wouldn't keep it locked up in an ebony ball all the time. He'd take it out and sing to it, and fondle it, and chant songs in praise of its beauty—I've seen him do the same with things a hundred times less lovely than that.

"Well, the fellow who killed old Wang doesn't know I've found the pearl. He couldn't have known just where Wang kept it, or he'd have taken it just as easy as he shifted the snakes. He had to have time to hunt for it; that's why he killed old Wang—to get him out of the way, and give himself plenty of time to hunt.

"And I'm going to use it as bait. He came last night; he may not risk coming back tonight, but I believe he will; I believe he means to keep on coming and ransacking the shop until he finds the pearl. I'm going to be in that shop tonight, laying for him."

"You're taking an awful risk," objected Feodor.

"Not so much. The only way he can come in is the back way. He'd never dare come in by the front door. He'll sneak up the alley and pry the lock off the alley door again. I'll be waiting in the dark for him, just inside the curtain that covers the entrance of the corridor. It's too dark in that corridor for him to see me as he comes in. Then, if he goes past and looks in the front window first, he won't see anybody, because I'll be behind the curtain.

"The reason I came by here is to ask you to stay up and dressed until I call you. I'll want you to rush right over and identify the man—or corpse. And say, would you mind keeping this pearl for me?"

"Excuse *me!*" exclaimed the scientist, recoiling. "I'll help you any way I can, but not with that thing! It's evil! I wouldn't touch it for any amount of money. Pearls like that cause more murder than women do."

"All right." Harrison dropped it back in his pocket. "I'll take it with me, then, and keep it on me till this business is settled. I don't trust safety vaults. So long; be listening for my call."

"I will," assured Feodor, watching the hard, square-set figure swing down the narrow stair.

None of the curiously carven clocks in Wang Yun's antique shop was running, but up in the rooms he had occupied, another clock tolled twelve, with a clear, gong-like note. And on the heels of that sound came another, so faint it was like the groaning of settling house timbers, or the rustling of mice. There was no light in the shop below. Only the street lamps cast a certain radiance through the window, making a place of fantastic shadow, in which only the features of the carven green Buddha stood out with any distinctness.

But the curtain over the stair rippled. It moved. A hand—yellow and long-nailed had there been light enough to see—drew aside the curtain, and a dim face was thrust through. The eyes that burned there centered on the other curtain that, masking the corridor leading to the alley, hung somewhat lower and at right angles to the curtain of the stair. It was dark, but not too dark for those eyes to discern a distinct bulge in that curtain. Thin lips coiled in a mirthless grin.

The figure glided noiselessly out from the stair curtain—a tall, stooped figure, clad in a dark close-fitting jacket, and a velvet cap, from beneath which depended a pigtail. One hand gripped a blackjack, as the man stepped soundlessly down onto the shop floor, between the flanking, grinning idols, and leaned toward the curtain that covered the corridor.

He drew a long breath, lifted the blackjack—with the suddenness of doom, a bulky form heaved up from behind one of the idols at his back, and there was the crushing impact of a savage blow.

The next instant there was the click of a light-button, and the shop was flooded with light.

"Hit first and investigate later," grunted Steve Harrison, bending over the motionless shape on the floor; "and a .45 barrel is better than a blackjack, any time."

Even under the impact of the blow, the velvet cap had not come off. It was tied under the wearer's chin with a cord. Harrison gripped the crumpled head-piece and tore it away; the pigtail came with it, revealing unkempt reddish hair beneath.

"A hell of a Chinaman," commented Harrison; "stained skin; hmmmm! Must be something that washes off pretty quick and easy. The things real are the long finger nails."

The victim stirred dazedly and sat up, swearing incoherently.

"Well, Mr. William D. Feodor," greeted Harrison, "we meet again—just as I thought!"

Grotesque under its yellow paint, the prisoner's face reflected his bewilderment.

"You damned gorilla!" he muttered, in a voice not at all typical of an eminent scientist. "I thought you were behind that curtain—"

"I wanted you to think it," grinned Harrison. "That's why I went to the trouble of telling you I'd be there. That bulge is a pile of old rugs, and not me. I've been squatting behind this infernal idol all night, waiting for you to come down those stairs. Trouble with you crooks, you think all cops are saps. I knew you could get into the rooms upstairs from the outside, by climbing a fire escape in the adjoining building, and hopping across from the roof to a window ledge. I could do it myself. And with you knowing—or thinking—I was watching the alley door, that was the only way for you to come. And I knew you *would* come; why else do you think I let you know I'd be here alone with the pearl?

"You were pretty slick, refusing to take care of the pearl—but that was obvious; it was as the mysterious Chinaman you wanted to grab it—not as William D. Feodor who was too well known to get away with it.

"All I want to know is how you knew old Wang Yun had it?"

Feodor gave a gesture of surrender.

"All right. You've got me. A nigger who used to do odd jobs for Wang Yun saw him playing with the pearl. He's doing a stretch for theft now. I was in his cell for a while, doing a short one myself. He was a hop-head, and sold me the information for dope. He'd lacked the nerve to kill old Wang himself. But he didn't know where the pearl was kept; just knew the Chinee had it. And of course, he didn't know anything about its history—just knew it must be worth a lot from the looks.

"I've used that scientist's racket as a blind before. I stole the cobra out of a zoo in Chicago. The nigger had told me about Wang Yun's snake. The rest was a cinch.

"What I want to know is how did you get on to me?"

"That story about the Chinaman sounded fishy," answered the detective. "I couldn't see why a man would openly try to buy something he was going to commit murder with. But Chinese do crazy things, according to our way of thinking. What gave you away was when you spoke of the cobra cage and mentioned that it rested on a *green* Buddha."

"Well, doesn't it?" demanded Feodor.

"It does now. But until the morning of the murder, Wang Yun had always kept it on a *blue* Buddha. He sold the blue image that morning, and put the cage on the green one. You'd already said you hadn't been in the shop for three weeks. Yet you knew the cage was on a green Buddha. It was evident that you were lying about not having been in the shop recently. You'd been in there the morning of the murder, or you wouldn't have known about the green Buddha. There was only one reason why you'd lie. I decided that either the tall, stooped Chinaman was your partner, or else you yourself in disguise. The conclusion was obvious."

"But damn it all!" exclaimed Feodor. "That Buddha *was* green! It's always been green! There's never been a blue Buddha in this shop, since I've been visiting it!"

Harrison stared intently at him an instant, then picked up a bright blue porcelain wine jug.

"What color is this?" he demanded.

"Green, of course," was the prompt reply.

Harrison shook his head in wonder.

"Well, I'll be damned! *Color blind!* You didn't even know the Buddhas had been changed. They all looked green to you!

If the green one had looked blue to you, instead of the blue one looking green, I'd still be hunting for an imaginary hump-backed Chinaman!"

"So you're not so blamed smart after all!" jeered the other.

"I never said I was," Harrison tranquilly replied. "I leave that for wise guys like you!" And he grinned as he clamped the handcuffs onto his captive's wrists.

The Voice of Death

A scream, the heart-stopping screech of tortured brakes, and the figure on the sidewalk leaped desperately aside just as the speeding automobile crashed the curb with a jangle of breaking glass and crumpled steel. The man at the wheel, hurled out of the seat and half over the door by the impact, made no effort to extricate himself. He covered his face with his hands whimpering: "I've done it! I've done it! Oh my God, I've done it, in spite of myself!"

Steve Harrison caught that frantic whimper as he leaped out of his own car which he had wrenched to a halt alongside the wrecked machine. Even as he reached the latter car, the man who had leaped out of its way was on its buckled running board, switching off the ignition, and seizing the trembling driver by the shoulders.

"Edward!" he exclaimed. "Are you hurt?"

The one so addressed lifted a haggard, incredulous face, and with an inarticulate cry, caught the other's wrists in thin nervous fingers.

"Jim! You're not dead! I didn't hit you!" He was clawing all over the young fellow's arms as if he could not believe the truth of what he saw.

"Not me!" the latter laughed. He was a well built youngster, with a frank, intelligent face. "I looked up when your brakes squealed, and I jumped just in time. Wonder you weren't killed, though. What happened?"

Harrison, standing silently by, saw a shadow cross the fine sensitive features of the youth called Edward; he seemed to blench, to shrink from his friend.

"I don't know," he muttered. "I must have lost control of the car. I started to hail you—the next thing I knew something snapped and all I could see was you standing right in the path— God!" Again he bowed his head and his thin shoulders shook.

"Snap out of it!" The other slapped his back sympathetically. "Climb out and let me see if you're hurt. No," as the other shakily obeyed, "you're okay, as far as I can see, but the boat's pretty well smashed. Wait here while I run into this house and phone for a wrecker—" and "Jim," who seemed to overflow with an abundance of energy, darted into a nearby yard and knocked on the door.

The one called Edward followed him with somber eyes, sighed, shook his head—and apparently saw Harrison for the first time. The young man started back with an exclamation; obviously his nerves were in a bad way.

"Oh, excuse me!" he ejaculated. "I didn't see you—"

On that quiet, tree-lined suburban street there were no curious crowds to gather. Harrison, without comment, bent over the machine. From within the house came the faint jingling of a phone.

"I can't imagine why—" began Edward without conviction, as if moved to speech beyond his will.

"I can." Harrison straightened, big, dark, almost brutally muscular in contrast to the shivering youth with his thin light hair and slight frame. The latter started as if stung, avidly scanning the other's dark inscrutable countenance.

"Who—who are you?" he stuttered.

"Name's Harrison. I'm a detective," grunted the big man. All the color went out of the youth's face and he slumped back against the car, almost in collapse.

"Then you know!" he whispered. "But how could you? I didn't mean to do it—not consciously! I swear I didn't! Something snapped—"

"Sure it did," growled Harrison, working the wheel. "Something in the steering gear went haywire; hell, kid, it could have happened to anybody."

"Oh!" The youngster wavered and slipped to the pavement in a dead faint. At that instant Jim came running from the house, shouting cheerily until he saw Harrison working over his friend. Then he yelped explosively and knelt down, pale with anxiety.

"Just fainted," grunted Harrison, with his usual economy of words. "I'll take him home. Where's he live?"

Jim gave directions, and Harrison nodded.

"Alright. You stay here and see about his bus. He'll be all right." And lifting the limp youth in his arms with an ease that made the other youngster stare, the big detective carried him to his own small roadster. Edward was regaining consciousness when the detective propped him in the seat and climbed in beside him. He groaned, stirred, raked a hand over his eyes, then seemed to remember. His first words were: "Then it *was* an accident?"

"What else?" The detective cast him a side-long slit-eyed glance. Harrison was taking one of his rare vacations in this quiet old town, but the instincts of his profession were too strong in him not to respond to the slightest stimulus.

"Nothing," muttered Edward, greying.

"Listen, kid," said the big detective abruptly. "I can't figure you out. An ordinary accident *might* shake you up like this, but there's something deeper than ordinary hysteria. You're scared stiff. I heard you talking to yourself right after the crash, and you talked queer. You've acted queer since. Now, I know you didn't deliberately wreck your car trying to kill that kid back there—Jim, you called him—"

"Clanton," muttered the youth mechanically. "James Clanton. I'm Edward Willington."

"All right. There's something weighing on you. Why don't you spill it to me? It's none of my business, of course, but I might be able to help you. Anyway, I'd like to try. It gets in the blood," meditated Harrison, more to himself than to his companion. "Here I've looked forward to this vacation for three years, and come all the way up here where I didn't know a soul, just to get away from tong wars and hatchet murders, and already I'm getting the jitters because something isn't popping under my nose every hour or so.

"Something's worrying you, kid. You act like I've seen men act who were being forced into a crime they didn't want to commit."

"That's it!" muttered young Willington, his fists clenching and his face grimmer than Harrison had thought possible. "Forced into something—I'm going to tell you. Maybe you'll throw me into jail or the insane asylum, but I can't stand this much longer."

"I'm on vacation," Harrison reminded him. "I'm not speaking in any official capacity."

"Well," began Wellington abruptly, "something *is* preying on my mind—something psychic—or worse. For more than a month I've had a vague, uneasy feeling of impending peril that I couldn't define. Lately it's been stronger—as if something *outside* were whispering to me—whispering!" Again he shuddered.

"I've been having all sorts of bad dreams and nightmares—and they seem to center about my best friend, James Clanton. Why, I wouldn't purposely hurt him for anything. Yet lately I've felt that same dim inexorable power was driving me to harm him—at least, urging me to. I've begun to realize that was what the whispering meant—"

"What do you mean, whispering?" Harrison demanded.

Willington made a helpless gesture.

"It was like something outside me urging me, driving me, repeating the same command over and over, filling my mind until I could think of nothing else. *And last night I heard it!* In my room, while I slept—or lay half asleep—a sinister soft whispering. It said: 'Kill James Clanton!'"

Harrison grunted, suppressing his incredulity.

"It was so tangible it was like an actual voice," continued Willington. "I jumped up and snapped on the light. Of course no one was there. Then I realized that it wasn't an actual human whisper—it was some mad or evil prompting in my own soul! It was the voice of insanity whispering in my own brain, so loudly that my physical ear seemed to hear it. Oh God, am I going mad?" It was a cry from a tortured soul.

"Sure no one was hiding in your room?" asked Harrison.

"My door was locked. All other rooms on that floor are unoccupied, and kept locked. No, it was no one. It was in my own brain. I've been avoiding Jim lately, because I've never known when my obsession would overpower me and make me kill him. They say lunatics always kill those who mean most to them. When I saw him on the curb awhile ago I thoughtlessly hailed him, then the crash came—I was dazed—bewildered. I thought I'd done it deliberately." Again Willington sank his face in his hands. His voice came muffled. "I'd kill myself before I'd injure Jim Clanton; and I'd rather die than go to an insane asylum."

"Buck up, kid," advised the big detective. "If you'd haunted the Oriental quarters in the big cities as much as I have, nothing would surprise you, or bother you very much. You're not crazy," he voiced a conviction he was far from feeling. "This your house?"

Willington nodded, and Harrison pulled up before a large, rather ancient house, the cracked paint of which showed it had seen better days. On the wide, pillared veranda sat an old man, half hidden by a newspaper. He glanced casually at them, nodded, and went on reading.

"Who's that?" grunted Harrison.

"My uncle, Abner Jeppard," replied the youth. "He's my guardian. Won't you come in?"

"No. You and he live here alone?"

"Not exactly alone. There are a couple of servants; they live out in a servant house in the back yard. I wish you'd—"

"You told your uncle about this business?" demanded Harrison.

"No. No use to worry him. He has a weak heart, and he's easily upset. Besides, we have so little in common that I've never made what you'd call a confidant of him. We live pretty much our own lives."

"Can you smuggle me into the house tonight?" abruptly asked the detective. "Can you get me into your room so that no one, not even your uncle nor the servants will know?"

"Why—" bewilderedly began Willington, when he was interrupted by his companion.

"Which room is yours?"

"That one, on the side, in the left wing, upstairs. You can just see one of the windows from here."

"Good!" snapped Harrison. "Quite a lot of shrubs and trees underneath. Contrive to leave a ladder leaning against the house there below your window, and leave the window unfastened. And say, go through all the upstairs rooms before you go to bed, and tie a thread across the head of the stairs, a black thread, about the height of a man's ankles. I'll be watching your window. When I see your light go out, I'll sneak up into your room. Be expecting me and don't say anything about it, not even to your uncle."

The conversation had been carried on in a voice too low to reach the ears of the old man on the veranda, or anyone in the house.

"All right. The servants can't see what goes on about the left wing, from their quarters, and my uncle will be sound asleep downstairs on the other side of the house. But I can't figure—"

"You don't have to," grunted Harrison. "Leave that to me."

WATCHING from among the shrubs into which he had glided like a bulky shadow, Harrison watched young Willington's window. It was nearly midnight. Few lights shone in the widely spaced neighborhood houses; even the distant street lamp seemed to flicker, as if threatened by the surrounding darkness which was emphasized rather than illumined by the winking stars. A light breeze muttered through the leaves where Harrison crouched. Repeatedly he had seen Willington's shadow cross the window as if the young man were restlessly pacing his room. Harrison shook his head. Far from the rat-haunted mazes and devious purple corridors of Oriental River Street he had stumbled upon fantastic mystery amid prosaic surroundings—if, indeed, the whole episode were not the phantom of brain-sickness. Yet even so, on what stage have more ghastly and terrible dramas been enacted than the human mind?

The light went out. In the whispering darkness Harrison stole forward, feeling tips of leaves fumble at his face like blind ghost hands in the dark. He found the ladder and went up it, silently for all his muscular weight, with the stealth acquired by many nocturnal ventures in more exotic surroundings.

He hissed a soft query into blank darkness, and was answered with equal caution from within the room. Harrison levered his bulk over the window sill, noiselessly, but with haste, instinctively wincing as he realized the target he made framed against the stars. His eyes accustomed themselves to the thicker dark, recognizing articles of furniture.

"Did you do as I said before you turned off the light?" he murmured, his lips close to the ear of Edward Willington who sat in his pajamas on the edge of the bed.

"Yes. The upstairs part of the house is empty except for us. All windows but this one are locked. I tell you, it's inside my mind, not outside, and—"

"Shut up!" muttered Harrison. "Sit still."

Somewhere a clock ticked away with maddening monotony. Somewhere a night bird shrilled. The old house creaked with settling timbers, but there was no sound to suggest anything stealthily ascending the stairs. Time dragged by; an hour—Harrison sat motionless, like a carven statue. The bed springs creaked as Willington moved wearily and uneasily. And then somewhere there sounded a low eery whirring and scratching. Harrison stiffened; there was a gasping intake of breath from young Willington. And out of the darkness, softly, venomously, came an uncanny voice: "Kill James Clanton!" it whispered. "Kill James Clanton! Kill James Clanton!"

With a choking cry Willington sprang from his bed. Harrison snapped on the light, and as he did the voice cut short. Willington stared wild-eyed at his companion, perspiration beading his grey face.

"The whisper!" he choked. "I heard it again! I *am* mad!"

"Then I am, too," snarled Harrison, bending to shoot a glance under the bed. "Because I heard it, too."

"*You* heard it? Then it *is* from Outside. It isn't in my brain!"

"Wait here!" snapped the detective.

He went hurriedly into the unlighted corridor, flashing his electric torch ahead of him. The thread was still stretched unbroken across the stair head. The doors of the adjacent rooms were locked, but their old-fashioned locks gave way to his skeleton key. From room to room he went, quickly and thoroughly. All were empty except for unused and obsolete furniture, coated with dust. The windows were all fastened down on the inside. Baffled, he returned to the room where young Willington sat shuddering on the side of his bed, casting fearful glances about him as if he expected a phantom to rise up at his side.

"Nothing's come into this floor except me, and nothing's left it," growled Harrison. "But I know I heard a human voice in the darkness. It came from somewhere in this room."

"But there's nowhere anyone could hide!" protested Willington. "You see—there's only the bed, chairs, that bookcase, my desk, that big cabinet—and even those drawers aren't big enough to hold a man, not even that bottom one which I don't use. Lost the key to it, and can't open it, but there's nothing in it."

Harrison tested the walls. They sounded solid; besides they were too thin to conceal anything. He looked up at the ceiling.

"How can I get up in the roof?" he asked. Willington took up a flashlight and led him into the hall again, where he showed him a trap door in the ceiling. Trap and ceiling were dingy and unswept, clustered with weeks-old cobwebs.

"This the only way into the roof?"

"I can swear to it," confidently Willington replied.

"The voice didn't come from above, anyway," muttered Harrison. "But I'm going up. Hand me a chair."

The detective vanished into the blackness above, while young Willington stood in the unlighted hallway waiting and listening, nervously playing his own light about the corners where the shadows lurked thickest. He heard few noises above to advertise the detective's presence. The big man moved with the ease of a huge cat.

Presently Harrison came down, scowling.

"Nothing up there but the wiring system. Say, is there a radio in this house?" At a negative answer he frowned slightly, but said nothing. They re-entered Willington's room, and Harrison sat down on the bed, his chin on his massive fist.

Suddenly he reached a hand toward the light switch, but with an inarticulate cry, Willington caught his wrist with fingers that were like steel claws in their desperate strength.

"Don't turn out the light! *It* speaks only in the dark—I never want to be in darkness again. I'm haunted!"

"Don't be a sap, kid," grunted Harrison.

"How can you deny it, after hearing it yourself? I tell you I'm being possessed by some demon that won't cease tormenting me until I do as it commands—or die! It's a bodiless phantom—an evil visitant from the *outer* dark. Something that manifests itself only in darkness!" His voice sank to a fearsome whisper. "It's here now, in this room, with us, only we can't see it!"

Harrison eyed his companion narrowly. There was an unnatural tinge beneath the youth's skin, an unnatural light in his eyes. The detective realized that young Willington was indeed hovering on the very borderline of sanity. A slight push might suffice to topple him over.

"All right, kid," muttered Harrison. "We'll leave the light on, and I'll stay here with you till daylight. But I want to get out before people start stirring; don't want anybody to know I'm working on this case—yet."

A DAY HAD come and gone, and another night folded its dusky wings over the dreamy old town. Plodding grimly through the starlit darkness, his fists shoved deep in his pockets, Harrison suddenly stopped and swore.

"Why the hell didn't I think of it before?"

A short time later he was standing beneath young Willington's window, now dark and silent. The big detective shook his head, muttering between his teeth: "Poor devil!"

The ladder still leaned against the house. The window, when he reached it, was closed but not locked. A few seconds later he was in the dark room, bending down beside the huge antique cabinet. He laid his electric torch on the floor so that its beam was directed on the lock of the lower drawer, and set to work with a jimmy. In a few moments he grunted in wrathful satisfaction.

After a few minutes' scrutiny on what he had found, he rose, left the room, and descended the stairs. A light burned through the curtain that masked the door of the study, and he avoided it. Gliding along the lower hallway he entered a bedroom where he was employed for a few minutes. No noise disturbed the house; the servants had retired, and the detective's soft-footed prowling, trained to cope with the faculties of cat-eared Orientals, did not arouse the solitary occupant of the house, immersed as he was in his own occupation.

Leaving the bedroom, Harrison went down the hall and halted at the curtained door of the study, staring somberly at the bent and withered figure stooping over a thick volume in a huge arm chair. This man was so engrossed in his study that it was not until the detective spoke that he sprang up and turned.

Abner Jeppard was the picture of what his nephew would some day be—a thin, frail figure with wispy white hair, sensitive withered features, and dark expressive eyes peering from behind horn-rimmed spectacles.

"Why—what—" he sputtered, evincing the fact that uneven nerves ran in the family. "Where—who are you, sir?"

"Name's Harrison," answered the detective. "Pardon me for butting in so unceremoniously." He strolled over and seated himself opposite the old man. Resting his chin on one hammer-like fist, he stared fixedly at his host, who naturally seemed somewhat nervous under this unwinking scrutiny, and perplexed at his uninvited visitor's manner.

"You know where your nephew Edward is?" Harrison demanded suddenly.

Jeppard shook his head.

"He left the house early this morning. We see little of one another except at mealtimes. I suppose he is with some friend."

"He's a jumpy, excitable young fellow," said Harrison. "Now a fellow like me, for instance, is healthy as a bull, and about as easy to upset. But Edward's nerves are set on hair triggers."

"Admittedly, sir; but I don't see why—"

"Did you ever hear of the power of suggestion?" Before Jeppard, an expression of growing bewilderment on his face, could answer, Harrison went on: "Some research workers in psychic science believe that the subconscious mind records every suggestion made to it, waking or sleeping, and passes it on in one form or another to the higher, or conscious mind. If an impulse grows strong enough in the subconscious, eventually it'll push its way into the higher mind, and result in action of some sort. Do you follow me?"

A nod answered him, and he continued: "Since the subconscious mind never sleeps, then the best time to work on it is when its possessor is asleep—because then the conscious mind isn't in control of the subconscious. That's according to the old idea of hypnotism."

"Well?"

"Well, suppose somebody wanted to persuade somebody else—say your nephew Edward, for instance—to commit a crime, like killing his best friend, we'll say. If he could whisper the suggestion continually into his sleeping ear, according to this theory Edward would eventually commit the murder, in spite of himself."

"The difficulties are obvious," objected Jeppard.

"Sure. But they could be overcome by a knowledge of mechanics and electricity. You ought to know that; I understand you're something of an inventor yourself.

"Edward's neurotic; it wouldn't take much to drive him completely out of his head. Continual suggestion might provoke an obsession and actually cause him to kill his friend. Still, that was a remote possibility. The greatest danger was that Edward would either go mad, or believe that he was going crazy, and kill himself."

"But you were only using him as an example," protested Jeppard, moistening his lips. "You speak as if this fantastic supposition were an actual reality."

"It is!" snarled Harrison, dropping his mask of pretense. His heavy hand shot out and gripped Abner Jeppard's shoulder with brutal power. "I don't know what your game is, but I know how you did it. Never thought anybody would think to look in the bottom drawer of his cabinet, did you? Well, most people wouldn't bother to burst open what they thought was an empty drawer. But I'm a man-hunter by profession, and we have our instincts.

"You were damned clever in keeping Edward from suspecting you. You were always in your room at night, never prowling around or doing anything that might get him to thinking. Well, if you'd been prowling last night you'd have known that I was in Edward's room when you started the whispering. I'll admit it had me fooled. Even when I went up in the roof and found a lot of wires that didn't seem part of an ordinary light wiring system, it didn't mean anything to me.

"But tonight my brain finally got to working, and I came back and broke open that bottom drawer—the one that wasn't supposed to have a key. I found your electric phonograph, and the record on it. I didn't play the record. I knew what it was."

Jeppard lay limply back in his great armchair; his skin was a sickly green; he tugged at his wilted collar as if it were a noose about his neck.

"I came down and sneaked into your bedroom," Harrison continued remorselessly. "Careless of you to leave it unlocked. But who'd ever think of investigating that little wall cabinet by your bed? That dinky lock on it didn't stop me three seconds. It wasn't hard to guess the use of all those bulbs and buttons and switches. Pity an electrical genius like you had to be a criminal, Jeppard. Obviously you planted that phonograph in Edward's cabinet when he was out. The wires run through the back of the cabinet, up the wall into the roof and down again into your bedroom. You haunted him while lying in your own bed. An electrical signal told you when he snapped his light on or off. When you thought he'd had time to get to sleep, you pushed a button and started that infernal phonograph to going. When his light came on, showing he was getting up to investigate, you switched it off. Of course you'd made the record, yourself.

"Edward got the suggestion, all right. It was calculated either to make a murderer or a maniac out of him, according to your theory."

"You're insane yourself!" Jeppard was recovering some of his composure. "What if I did put a phonograph in his room? You can't prove it was anything but a practical joke. No harm has come of it—"

"No?" Harrison's laugh was the snarl of a hunting tiger. "Don't know where Edward is, eh? I'll tell you. He's in the county jail. *He killed James Clanton an hour ago!*"

"My God!" It was a strangled cry from Abner Jeppard. The man half rose, then sank back as if his legs were paralyzed.

"What are you yelling about?" asked the big detective sardonically. "Wasn't that what you were working for? But now that your secret's out, it makes a lot of difference, doesn't it? What did you have against Clanton? Or were you just trying to drive Edward crazy?

"Well, no matter. Edward's raving mad. When I present my evidence, he'll go to the madhouse, just as you planned—*but you'll go to the chair!*"

A wild hunted cry burst from Jeppard's grey lips. He lurched up, clawing at the detective's lapels. In his extremity he was a soul-sickened spectacle of stark animal terror, naked and unashamed, a sight to have revolted a less rugged nature than Harrison's.

"Not the chair! I'll confess! Help me! Swear you'll help me! Send me to prison if you will, but not the chair! What you say is true. I did plan to destroy Edward—I have nothing against James Clanton, but he was the most logical victim. Edward was with him continually. Nor did I have any spite toward Edward. The money—Edward's legacy. I lost all mine on an invention that failed to work. With Edward's money I could go on and perfect it; but his money was tied up so I couldn't handle it unless he died or was declared mentally unsound—"

Harrison heard a door open softly, but he was spellbound by the desperation of the frantic countenance so close to his. Then the yammering wretch stumbled in his headlong speech, as his gaze went past Harrison to the curtained door.

With a horrible scream he recoiled, sending the big detective staggering from the violent suddenness of his movement. Harrison, wheeling, saw a figure standing in the shadowed doorway. It spoke: "Where is Edward?"

"James Clanton!" screamed Abner Jeppard. "Have you come up from hell to haunt me?" He caught at his breast and pitched down across his desk.

Harrison bent over him, then straightened with a grunt and a shake of his head to face young Clanton, who came forward, white with horror.

"What's happened?" he whispered. "I came to see Edward. I knocked but nobody opened the door, so I came on in, as I'm in the habit of doing. What—"

"Fate," grunted Harrison cryptically. Then he qualified it: "The old fellow's heart was weak, and he suffered under the illusion that you were a ghost. As for Edward, he's up in my rooms at the hotel. Been up there all day. In the state his nerves are, I wanted him where I knew he'd be safe. He'll be all right now, though." He muttered under his breath: "It's as well it happened this way; never heard of a law governing this particular kind of crime."

"What did you say?" inquired Clanton.

"Don't pay attention to me. I've got a habit of talking to myself," grunted Harrison. "I was just meditating on the efficacy of a lie, when dealing with criminals. Lying's a bad habit, but sometimes it's the best way to get a confession. The lie was my idea—don't stare so; I'll explain in good time—but you walking in here just at the moment you did was fate, which nobody can figure upon any time."

The House of Suspicion

Steve Harrison drew a folded square of paper from an inside pocket and scanned it again in the light of the sunset that was sinking over the pinelands. He read, as he had read a score of times before, the message printed there.

> I can show you Richard Stanton, the man you want. Come to Storley Manor, near Crescentville. But for God's sake come alone, tell no one of your plans, and do not reveal your identity until I make myself known to you.
>
> The One Alone

Harrison looked again at that cryptic signature. Like the rest of the message, it had been written on a typewriter. There was no way of knowing whether the writer was a man or a woman. The envelope which had contained it had borne the postmark of Crescentville.

With a shrug he folded the note, replaced it in his pocket and strode along the dim road which wound through the pines. He might be taking a long chance, blindly following a tip like that, but the big detective was accustomed to taking long chances. This was a lead, at least, though it might be a false one, the only opening in the otherwise blank wall which confronted him.

In the silence which brooded over the pinelands, he thought he could catch the faint and far away rattle of wheels that told him the buggy which had brought him to the point where this dim path cut the main road, was on its way back to Crescentville. There was a peculiar sense of isolation with the fading of the sound. On both sides of the road the pines rose about him, forming labyrinths which the sight penetrated only a few yards. Somewhere behind them the sun was setting, and night would soon be stealing across the woodlands—

Something whined venomously past Harrison's ear and *chunked* solidly into a tree. Whirling, crouched, a big .45 springing into his fist, the detective saw the limbs of a sapling quivering some yards away.

"Come out of there!" he commanded. Only the silence answered him. A few strides carried him to the spot. No one stood behind the tree; the leaf-padded mold showed no footprints. But yonder in a big loblolly pine beside the road was stuck a knife that had not flown through the air at him of its own accord. Realizing the uselessness of plunging blindly into the woods in an effort to find the would-be killer, Harrison backed into the road again and examined the knife with interest. It was big, crude and deadly, obviously home-made; the blade had been made out of a big file, and the wooden hilt carved out by hand and wrapped with wire. Such knives were common enough in the rural districts of the South.

He left it sticking in the tree. It was too big and too razor-sharp for him to carry concealed about him. He went on more hurriedly, and with a peculiar crawling sensation between his shoulder blades. If another missile came humming out of the woods it might not miss. Besides, he was disturbed. That attempt suggested knowledge of his identity and mission. The man for whom he was searching was not a murderer, but men have become murderers under compulsion of fear.

The road wound tortuously on, over stumps that would never allow the passage of a motor vehicle, and out in the growing dimness under the trees he once caught a shuffling among the fallen pine needles that might have been a razorback rooting, or that might have been a skulking human. He was aware of a distinct feeling of relief when a big rambling house loomed through the trees ahead of him. The road ran up to it and stopped. Pines marched in solid ramparts about the clearing. Even in the gathering dusk the age and dilapidation of the house was evident, and behind it a ramshackle array of barns, sheds, rail-fenced lots and outhouses showed the same disintegration. Young forest growth encroached on what had once been gardens and yards. One faint light flickered in the back part of the big house. The man who had driven Harrison out from Crescentville had told the detective that Storley Manor had seen better days. In the gathering darkness, with a faint wind moaning through the pines, it was ominous and depressing in its loneliness and desolation.

Mounting the wide porch with its warped pillars, Harrison knocked at the door, starting at the sound which boomed unnaturally loud in the brooding stillness. After a moment a step sounded within, the door opened and the pale oval of a face was framed in the gloom.

"Yes, sir?" The simple phrase was an interrogation in itself.

"My name is Buckner," Harrison said. "I was driving from Crescentville to Vendison when my car broke down on the main road, just about where your road turns off. Knowing I couldn't walk back to Crescentville before night fell, I followed this path, hoping I'd come to a house where I could spend the night. If you could put me up—"

"Certainly, certainly! Come in, Mr. Buckner!" The invitation was hearty and given without hesitation. Harrison stepped into the gloom of a broad hallway, and the other shouted, "Rachel, bring a lamp!" To Harrison he said apologetically: "We're so used to the old house that we find our way around in the darkness, mostly; we don't have electricity this far from town."

A kerosene lamp glowed in a doorway, in the hand of a mulatto woman. Its yellow glow illumined her brown face, framed in a cluster of black hair, and the whites of her eyes. Harrison saw his host more distinctly—a tall, slight figure of a man, with a sensitive, intellectual countenance, a high brow crowned by a greying mane of hair.

"I am John Storley, sir," the man was saying. "You are welcome to Storley Manor—or to such of it as time and adverse circumstances have left. I was just sitting down to supper. Will you not join me?"

Harrison assented, and was escorted through the broad hall and into a large room which adjoined the kitchen. There was a broad table there, but only one place was set. Over in a corner another figure sat in a great armchair. It was a man who seemed asleep, his features almost hidden in an unkempt tangle of grey beard and hair.

"My uncle, William Blaine," said Storley. "He is blind, deaf, and dumb."

Harrison glanced anew at the man with the morbid fascination that normal people feel toward the abnormal. The shabby, patched coat did not conceal the broad shoulders, the lines of strength in the supine figure.

"He was a powerful man in his prime," said Storley, as if reading Harrison's thoughts. "Disease brought on by dissipation has reduced him to his present plight. He has no one but myself to look to."

The mulatto woman, Rachel, had set a plate for Harrison, and the detective seated himself at Storley's invitation. As he began with unfeigned relish on the boiled corn, fried ham, eggs, corn pone and butter-milk, he asked casually: "You have no family, Mr. Storley?"

"The household consists of those you see now, Mr. Buckner," answered the other, including in his gesture a big negro man who at that moment tramped into the kitchen from the outside porch with an armload of stove wood. "That is Joab, who does the heavy work of the place. Rachel attends to the duties of the house. They are light enough, with only myself and my Uncle William to care for. Thirty, forty, fifty years ago, before the wreckage of the family fortune, this old house indeed deserved the title of Storley Manor, which still clings to it, despite its present sorry condition."

Then one of these four people sent that message, thought Harrison as he ate. But which one? He stared furtively at Storley, eating fastidiously at the other end of the big table; at William Blaine, sitting motionless in his big chair and being fed like a baby by the woman Rachel; at Rachel herself; and at the giant Joab who appeared momentarily in the kitchen door. And he stiffened as he surprised a murky gleam in the negro's eyes as they rested on him with strained intensity. But when the big black man saw the detective was observing him, he bobbed his bullet head in a grotesque curtsey, and shambled out of sight.

Had he sent that message? Would he know how to use the old-fashioned typewriter on which the letter had been written? Well, he might, with the attention that was being given to the education of colored people these days. The woman Rachel seemed to have more than average intelligence; when she spoke, it was not in the corn-field patois of the average darky. Harrison hated working blindly in the dark, but until the unknown writer revealed himself, or herself, he could make no move. He dared not test either of these people for fear it might be the wrong one. He sensed an undercurrent of some sort. There was fear and suspicion in this house, and duplicity. His gaze kept wandering to the expressionless features of the deaf mute. Such a man might use a typewriter.

Rachel came from the kitchen, took Harrison's empty coffee cup and returned to the kitchen. Presently she came back, preceded by the fragrant aroma of the brimming cup. As she set it down by the detective's plate, the faint tinkle of the spoon against the rim arrested his trained attention. He saw the brown hand that held the cup was trembling violently. As if casually he glanced up into her face, and what he saw there galvanized him, though his expression remained unchanged. Her dusky skin was grey; perspiration stood on her ashy cheeks and stark fear shone out of her eyes. Hastily she turned away.

Stirring his coffee absently, appearing to listen to his host's small talk, Harrison mused over the mulatto's behavior. Why had she taken his cup to the kitchen to be refilled? Twice she had refilled John Storley's cup, and each time she had brought the coffee pot to the table. Harrison lifted the cup to his lips, naturally raising his eyes as he did so, and he saw her face staring at him from the doorway. Her lip was caught between her teeth, and her distended eyes reflected tension and awful fascination. As she felt Harrison's stare upon her, she ducked back out of sight. The detective set down the cup untasted. What was in it he could not know, but he was as sure that an attempt had been made to poison him as he was sure that there was a knife sticking in a pine tree back there in the woods.

The person who had thrown that knife could have reached the Manor before him, but he doubted the woman's ability to throw the heavy weapon with force enough to drive it so deeply into the wood. A strong man had thrown that knife. But why? Evidently he had been recognized, and someone did not intend that he should take Richard Stanton back with him. His jaw set. He was just as determined that Stanton should accompany him when—*or if*—he returned. If Stanton were behind these murderous attempts, *why?* He was not trying to drag the man back to prison; he merely wished him to testify in a trial which would send a brutal murderer to the gallows.

Harrison leaned back in his chair, determined to eat or drink nothing more in that house, and Storley, seeing that his guest had apparently satisfied his hunger, likewise pushed back his plate.

"I must apologize for the fare," he said. "Its coarseness is in keeping with the fortunes of the Storley name. But there was a time, Mr. Buckner—"

Harrison listened patiently to the past glories of Storley Manor; a Southerner himself, he understood the psychology of the decayed gentlefolk living in the ruins of their past.

"There is one consolation," Storley was saying. "I have no son to bequeath my legacy of poverty. I am the last of my line." He paused, then said in a subtly changed voice: "Yes, I am indeed *the one alone.*"

Harrison's start was almost perceptible in spite of himself; his eyes locked with Storley's and an electric spark of understanding flashed between them. Then Storley glanced toward the silent figure in the corner; the motion was furtive, almost imperceptible, but it carried a tense warning, a message that Harrison could understand only as a warning of danger. The detective said nothing, but covered his tenseness by rolling and lighting a cigarette. The one alone; he had supposed it to mean—if it had any meaning—that the unknown writer of the message lived alone. Now he took it to mean that the writer was one alone in a hostile group. Joab, Rachel, were they in on a plot? What part was played by the silent figure in the corner? In the detective's awakened tension the deaf mute seemed almost sinister.

"You are tired, Mr. Buckner," said Storley. "You will be wishing to retire." It was a statement rather than a question, and Harrison followed what seemed like a lead.

"Yes, I believe I do," he answered.

"I'll show you to your room!" Storley rose with alacrity and fairly snatched a lamp out of the hand of Rachel, who was already moving as if to escort their guest. As he followed his host out of the room, Harrison felt the glare of fierce eyes boring into his back. He dared not turn and look: the eyes of negroes, or eyes that feigned blindness?

Storley mounted a broad stair, went down a wide dim hall and opened a door. The room, like the hall, had a musty scent. Harrison did not believe the room had been occupied for years. Storley set the lamp on a small table, and turning, caught Harrison's lapel in a grasp that quivered with intensity. Storley's eyes were wild in the lamplight, and perspiration shone on his cheeks. His fear or excitement seemed as intense as the fear Rachel had exhibited.

"Talk softly!" he whispered urgently. "The very walls in this house have ears. I must be back before *he* grows suspicious. You are Detective Stephen Harrison. You can be no other person. You came in response to my letter!"

"That's right," muttered Harrison, "and—"

"Shhh! You have played your part well, but we must be cautious. One slip means death for us both. Secrecy has been, and will be, our only salvation. Let us reach a perfect understanding. You are looking for Richard Stanton, on whose testimony the state depends to convict Edward Stark of murder?"

"That's right," answered Harrison. "The trial's set for next week. But a week ago Stanton just dropped out of sight. I traced him to the state line, and then—"

"Yes, yes, I know. You lost all trace of him. Richard Stanton is hiding almost within a stone's throw of this house!"

"Then why don't you—" began the detective, but the frenzied grasp of his companion silenced him. Storley shook as with an ague.

"Not so loud, in God's name. We are dealing with a man who is the devil incarnate. I can tell you no more. I must give you my message and hasten back before I am discovered. To loiter will cost me my life.

"Bolt your door and put out the light, but do not sleep. Do not dare to move out of your room until midnight, when the coast will be clear. Steal down the stair and out of a door I will leave open in the hall, and follow the trail you will find leading into the pines behind the sheds, until you come to a small log hut which once was used for smoking meat. Go in and wait for me. I will come to you within a few minutes and lead you to Richard Stanton's hiding place. And now I must go."

"But tell me first who is this fellow you fear so?" urged Harrison.

"You have seen him," Storley shuddered. "He poses as a deaf mute. The man we have to fear is William Blaine, who is neither blind nor deaf nor dumb, but a fiend incarnate—devil or madman, God only knows."

"But why is he hiding Richard Stanton?" persisted Harrison. "Why doesn't Stanton want to testify?"

"I can't stop to explain," panted Storley. "I must go!"

"But there's something you've got to know," expostulated Harrison. "Somebody in this house knows who I am. They tried to—"

"Mistah Storleh!" the rich musical call of Rachel floated up the stair. "Oh, Mistah Storleh!"

Storley started violently and jerked away from Harrison's detaining hand. "I can't linger!" he hissed urgently. "I've *got* to go! Trust me! Do as I say and all will be well."

Then quickly he glided out of the door and was gone, before Harrison could tell him of the two attempts that had been made upon his life.

With a helpless shrug of his shoulders, Harrison turned and glanced over his room. There was an old-fashioned bed, a few chairs, a table. That was all. There was but the one door, and a screenless, wood-barred window which looked out over the black pine woods. The door had no lock, only a bolt which was fastened with a pivot-pin to the door and lowered into a bracket on the jamb. Harrison scowled. The door was warped and did not fit closely; a knife blade thrust through the crack would lift that bar.

But the sight of a thick stick used to prop the window cheered him somewhat. In the dark a cudgel was better than a gun. He laid it beside him on the bed and blew out the light. It was several hours until midnight.

He lay there in the darkness brooding over Richard Stanton. Why had he ducked out in the first place? He was no friend of

Edward Stark's. He had expressed perfect willingness to give the testimony that would send Stark to the gallows for murdering his fiancée. Then without warning he had dropped out of sight. And without his testimony, the state's case would be crippled. Harrison himself was the only other important witness. If neither he nor Stanton showed up at the trial, he reflected wryly, all the work he had done in running Stark to earth would come to naught.

Suddenly he stiffened as something clinked through the window bars and fell with a clatter on the floor. In an instant he was up and glaring down into the shadowed yard. He saw a figure just darting around the corner of the house and knew it was a woman. Turning back into the room he snapped on his electric torch and saw a white cylinder bound with string to a rusty bolt. The cylinder was a rolled up piece of paper and on it was scrawled with a pencil: "Pleese go befor you are kild." There was no signature.

Well, this tangled things more than ever. First the mulatto Rachel tried to poison him, and now she sent him a warning. Was she trying to frighten him away, having failed to murder him? Storley did not seem to believe that Harrison had been recognized; had warned him against no one except Blaine. Yet surely the woman had been acting under orders from Blaine; probably had received them while she pretended to be feeding him his supper. But if so, why now this warning? And how had Blaine guessed his identity? If Blaine knew of Storley's hand in bringing him, there was no telling what the man might do to Storley, if he was as devilish as the master of Storley Manor said. Storley might be in danger that very minute; but to rush downstairs on that supposition would be to give the whole game away.

With a muttered oath Harrison lay back on the bed, caressing the thick window stick. His stock of patience in such matters was short. He hated groping in the dark, and yearned for a bit of violent physical action to clear the atmosphere.

Time passed slowly. The old house creaked as the timbers settled. Somewhere sounded the squealing and scampering of mice; out in the woods a hoot owl lifted his ghostly voice; further off there came the croaking of a bullfrog. Harrison glanced out of the window which he had propped with a shoe. There was no moon and in the starlight the pines presented a shapeless black block in which no single trunk was apparent.

In spite of himself he was beginning to doze when a sudden sound brought him tensely awake.

It was the soft but heavy tread of bare feet in the hallway. They stopped outside his door, and Harrison reached for flashlight and pistol as he heard the gentle lifting of the bar. He could see nothing in the darkness, but he heard the door begin to open stealthily. Then as he gathered himself for action, it closed again, the bar settled softly in place, and the dim footsteps padded away.

Harrison sat up on his bed, scowling. What was the purpose of that invasion—to see if he was still in his room? As he meditated he heard another noise, this time inside the room—a curious faint scruffing he could not classify. Simultaneously he was aware of a peculiar odor, faint, almost vegetable in its nature. He frowned in perplexity, groping for the explanation, which was in the back of his mind—then suddenly his breath hissed explosively from his teeth, and he grabbed the flashlight, feeling beads of cold sweat break out on his skin.

The click of the snap was answered by a chilling hiss. The beam of light stabbed through the dark and limned a swaying, wedge-shaped head that lifted on a thick mottled trunk that glistened darkly in the light. A forked tongue licked in and out and two eyes glittered redly. Then the monster came gliding toward the source of the light, as a water-moccasin always will, its thick length oozing swiftly over the floor.

Harrison dared not fire and rouse the house. Setting his teeth he grasped his stick and waited until the hideous head was almost within arm's length, rearing up toward the bed. Then the stick flailed unerringly down, and crushed that grisly death-laden wedge. The reptile flopped and knotted in its death-throes, and Harrison almost vomited with repulsion, and the thought of what would have happened had he risen in his bare feet to investigate the sound in the dark.

He played his light all over the room, sighing with relief when he saw that only one monster had been loosed upon him. And he sat up and pulled on his shoes. It lacked some time until midnight, but he was not going to lie helplessly in the dark while his enemies thought up some other hellish strategy. He wondered wrathfully when they'd start shooting at him. Harrison was ready to take the bit in his teeth. It galled him intensely to think that he had done nothing on his own initiative since coming to Storley Manor. Knife, poison and a snake had been loosed on him while he sat meekly, following John Storley's lead. Maybe Storley was lying out in the woods with his throat cut right now. Anyway, Harrison was tired of moving blindly. He intended to force a showdown and let things work out as Fate intended. Harrison had little faith in Fate, but he had a great deal in his own iron muscles.

Going to the door he opened it and played his light down the hall. It was empty, and so was the stair. As he moved down the steps, the whole house was wrapped in silence, which to Harrison seemed tense. The whole night had an air of waiting, of expectancy. The stage was set for some grim drama, he knew not what.

In the silence he heard a man's even breathing; one slumbered or feigned to slumber. Opening the door beyond which that sound came, he directed his light suddenly into the room. It shone on a bed and on a hairy, bearded visage. This Harrison eyed grimly, covering the recumbent form with his .45.

"Come out of it, Blaine," he ordered. "Quit stalling. I'm on to you."

There was no answer, but there was a change in the rhythmical breathing, and the man stirred and groped to a sitting posture, just as, Harrison reflected sardonically, a blind and deaf man might waken and move, sensing something his dead faculties did not record.

"Quit acting, Blaine," requested Harrison. "I know you're not what you pretend to be. Guess that beard's phony, too. I wonder if *you're* Dick Stanton, yourself—"

It was a movement by the open door behind him that caused him to whirl, despite the danger he might be turning his back on. And as he turned something that whirred through the air knocked the flashlight out of his hand; he felt the missile glance away, heard a thudding impact, and a whistling intake of breath. Then a hurtling; body smashed against his breast in the sudden darkness, knocking him to the floor. He dropped the gun, useless at such close range, and tore loose the hands that had locked frenziedly on his throat.

Something was crouching on him, clawing at his throat and mouthing gibberish. He knew his assailant was a negro, by the smell that was in his nostrils, and by the senseless ape-like gibbering. Still fending the clutching hands from his jugular, he threw up his legs, hooked a heel under an unseen chin, and then, exercising irresistible leverage, tumbled the man backward and over. In an instant their positions were reversed and it was Harrison who was on top.

But the man under him was as big as himself, and his bulging muscles were hard as oak. He fought fiercely and he fought foully, and Harrison kept wondering when Blaine would come to the aid of his ally or servant. A savage drive of a knee to Harrison's groin doubled the detective with racking pain and weakened his hold. The negro tore away and scrambled up, but Harrison, swearing sickly, was after him, not daring to lose contact for an instant. He lashed out blindly in the dark; his left glanced harmlessly from a muscular shoulder, and a wild blow cut his lips and filled the darkness with sparks of fire, but the next instant his savagely driven right sank to the wrist in his enemy's belly and the black man's breath went out of him in an explosive gasp. He folded up on the floor and Harrison began groping for a match. He did not need to investigate to see if the negro were really out. He knew his own power. He struck the match and its glow showed him a kerosene lamp on a table. He lighted it and glared down at the man on the floor. It was Joab, bent in a tortured knot, his white eyeballs rolled up at his conqueror.

Harrison resisted an impulse to employ his boot heels on the prostrate figure. Instead he found his flashlight and picked up his gun. He was fumbling for his handcuffs as he turned toward the bed where William Blaine had lain, and then he halted. Blaine still lay there; a wire-wrapped knife hilt stood up from his breast. Harrison needed no second glance to know that he was dead. And the knife which, glancing blindly in the dark, had found the fake deaf mute's heart, was the same one that had been thrown at Harrison in the woods.

Harrison turned again to Joab, gun in hand.

"Get up," he ordered, and the ashy-faced black hauled himself painfully to his feet. That body smash would have sickened a trained prizefighter. "Back up against the wall." Joab did so, or rather he backed up against a big old-fashioned chest of drawers which stood against the wall.

"So you were the one who threw that knife at me on the road," said Harrison. "Who told you to?"

Joab maintained a sullen silence.

"Did he tell you to?" Harrison nodded toward the dead Blaine. Surprize mingled with stubbornness on the sullen countenance.

"He couldn't tell nobody nothin'," muttered, Joab. "He couldn't talk at all."

"Is that a lie, or has he got you fooled, too?" Harrison wondered aloud. "Do you know who I am?"

"Policeman," mumbled Joab.

"Who told you?"

"Mistah Stohley."

"Eh?" Harrison was startled. "When?"

"Long time ago," muttered Joab. "He said some day he'd have a policeman to come git me. Otheth day he writ a letteh. Don' know I can read a little. I seen name of Steve Harrison on letteh. I knowed Mistah Stohley was sendin' for policeman. I done read 'bout you in newspapehs. I been watchin'. When I seen you comin' through the pines I knowed you 'uz comin' atter me."

"Why would a policeman be coming after you?" demanded Harrison.

Joab did not reply; his head was lowered on his great breast, and from under sunken lids his eyes flamed with the murk of hell's fire at the detective.

"Where's Richard Stanton?" suddenly rapped the detective.

"Neveh heered of him," answered Joab, and Harrison, wise in the ways of the colored folk, believed he was telling the truth.

"Well," Harrison admonished, "you stand still. The further I get into this business, the more tangled it gets. But I'm going to put the cuffs on you—"

Joab had never lifted his hands; they rested against the drawers upon which he was leaning. And now, as Harrison groped in his pocket, he saw Joab's eyes flash with a ferocious exultation. With a bestial cry he wheeled, ripping open the drawer on which his hands had been resting, and diving his hand into the drawer. It was the berserk madness of the primitive, but Harrison held his fire until Joab wheeled toward him, an old-fashioned pistol lifting in his hand. Then the detective's gun roared and Joab pitched backward against the drawers and then toppled to the floor to lie motionless in a slowly oozing red pool.

Harrison stood listening, the smoking gun in his hand. No sound broke the stillness. No one came to investigate the shot that had crashed deafeningly in the still house. Where in the devil were Storley and the mulatto woman? A brief investigation showed him that Joab was dead. Then he turned to the man on the bed. A quick tug assured him that the hair and beard were real enough. Then he turned back the lids and grunted in surprise. Even in death the eyes were those of a blind man, a confusion of dimmed colors, glazed like agates. Then the man had been blind, at least, despite John Storley's assertions to the contrary. But why should Storley lie about it?

The detective crossed over to the other sprawling body, stooped and lifted the fallen pistol. Then he saw something else. The drawer which had contained the weapon had been jerked out of its place when Joab fell, and had burst on the floor, spilling its contents. Among these were a number of old-fashioned photographs. One of these, lying face up, caught Harrison's attention. He took it up and gazed long at it. Then he put it in his pocket and sat down on the side of the bed, resting his chin on his massive fist.

The realization kept occurring to him that besides Richard Stanton, he, Steve Harrison, was the only other important witness against Edward Stark.

With sudden determination he rose, glanced at his watch and blew out the light. It lacked a few minutes of twelve. John Storley would be expecting him in the log hut back in the pines presently, and Harrison did not intend to disappoint him.

It was obvious that there was no one in the house except himself and the dead men. Where Storley and Rachel were, Harrison had no idea, but they were not in the house.

He went out into the hall and his flashlight showed him a door standing open, as Storley had promised. He emerged into the starlight and stood straining his ears for some sound in the shadows about him. Utter silence reigned except for the weird whimpering of the wind in the pines.

He made his way to the sheds, passed around them, and saw a dim opening in the black bulwark of the pines. Gun in hand, he entered the path, guided mainly by the stars that shown unobstructed above him.

It was dark as only the piney woods can be. The blackness was almost tangible; Harrison felt it could be cut with a knife. He went slowly, groping with his feet and his free hand. He did not fear a shot or a knife-cast in that darkness. But a trap is not always fanged with lead or steel.

However, nothing struck at him from the dark, and presently he came to the edge of a clearing and saw a small square building looming before him—one of the one-room log huts so common in the pine woods country. He crouched, watching it. And his fingers involuntarily closed on the photograph in his pocket. What lurked inside that black cabin he could not know; but he did know that nothing on earth could tempt him into it before daylight. He settled himself for a patient wait. The man he was hunting now would be coming soon, according to previous agreement. Then he heard it.

At first he thought it was an owl moaning away off in the woods. Then he heard it again, and the hair prickled at the base of his skull. That was no owl. Again it came. Turning into the dense woods, he groped his way among the trunks, his feet making little sound on the thick-leafed mold. He headed unerringly toward the noise, and as he approached it he recognized it as a human in dire anguish. Presently he stumbled over something soft and yielding, and the low groan rose from his feet.

His flashlight showed him the form of a woman. It was the mulatto Rachel, her thick wavy hair clotted with blood. Her eyes shone glazed in the light, and she moaned like an animal in pain. Swearing in bewilderment, Harrison knelt beside her, running practiced hands over her head. They came away bloody. She had been cruelly beaten, but he discovered no fracture in her skull.

Pondering a moment, he lifted her and groped his way back to the path that led to the hut. Following this, he came out behind the sheds again, and went straight to the house. He might be signing his own death-warrant, but he could not allow a woman, even a black woman, to die without attention.

His flesh crawled as he approached that dark, silent house where two dead men lay staring at nothing, but he entered without hesitation, and no silent death struck at him out of the shadows. Then at the very threshold he stopped short. Far back in the woods there had come the unmistakable boom of a revolver. What did that portend? He listened intently for a few moments, but heard nothing more. He went in then, found and lighted a kerosene lamp in the dining room, and laying the woman on the floor, procured water and clean rags from a cupboard and set to work dressing her head. The wounds were ragged and ugly, but not as dangerous as they looked. He found a jug of whiskey and placed it to her lips, and presently a dazed intelligence seeped into her glazed eyes.

"Who did this?" he demanded.

"Mistah Storleh," she faltered, still dazed and partly incoherent.

"What for?" he demanded, but she was too groggy to reply. She only groaned and held her head.

"Why did you throw me that note?" he tried another tack.

That roused a spark of intelligence.

"I didn't want him to kill you," she whimpered. "Too much killin' goin' on 'round hyuh."

"Didn't want who to kill me?"

"I cain't tell," she moaned. "He'd kill me. He said so."

"Who? Mister Storley?"

She shook her head.

"Then who, confound it? If it's Blaine you're afraid of, he's dead. Joab killed him, and I killed Joab."

"Joab—daid?" she exclaimed. "Oh, praise Gawd!" Her dazed exultation was terrible to see. "Joab was goin' to kill you," she whispered. "He put rat-pizen in the coffee and made me take it to you. He'd killed me if I hadn't."

"Why did Joab want to kill me?" he asked.

"Joab killed a man long time ago," she answered, growing stronger in her excitement. "He come and hid with Mistah Storleh. Mistah Storleh knowed he'd killed that man, and he use to tell Joab that if Joab didn't do like he wanted him to, he'd send for a policeman to take Joab to the death-house. Joab thought you was a policeman. If you ain't, what you doin' hyuh?"

"And I reckon it was Joab who put the snake in my room," muttered the white man. "Tell me this: was Mister Blaine a bad man?"

"Him? What you talkin' about? Po' Mistah Blaine, he was so blin' and deef and dumb he couldn't do nothin' but just set. I had to feed him like a baby."

"I thought so," growled Harrison. "Why did Storley beat you up?"

"He cotch me takin' grub to the young man he killed," she whispered fearsomely.

"What the devil are you talking about?" demanded Harrison testily. "What young man?"

"I dunno," she whimpered. "A week ago Mistah Storleh told us—me and Joab—to go and spend the night somewhere else. We went, and I stayed with my frien' Ellen Jackson what lives on the Crescentville road, but about midnight her man come in drunk, and they got to fightin', and I got scared and run out and run home. Then I got afraid to come in, too, because Mistah Storley had told me not to come home till good mornin'.

"They was a light in the house, and I crope up to the window and looked in and Mistah Storley was talkin' to a young white man. I couldn't understand what they said, but all at once Mistah Storley hit him an awful lick with a axe handle, and he fell down with the blood runnin' out of his head. Then Mistah Storley took a pistol-gun and shot him in the head, and then he dragged him out of the house, and lifted him on a skid with a horse hitched to it, and dragged him off down in the woods. I followed after, but I was awful scared and kept in the shadows. Mistah Storley took the young man to the creek and threw him in; water's awful fast there and runs into a big hole a little further down. Don't no body ever come up again when it gits sucked in there.

"Then Mistah Storley went back to the house, and I crope down to the shore and saw the young man's sleeve had caught on a snag, and he wasn't dead, because he was movin' and groanin'. So after a while I managed to git him up on the bank, and after so long a time I got him into a old cabin near the creek where nobody ain't lived for a long time, and I been takin' kyere of him every since. I been slippin' out at night with grub—"

"Did he tell you his name?" broke in Harrison.

"No, sah. Seem like he cain't remember his name nor nothin' since Mistah Storley done hit him so hard."

"Is he about my height, but slimmer?" demanded Harrison. "With light hair and brown eyes, and a scar on his ear?"

"Yes, sah. He's mighty nice spoken. Tonight when I was slippin' out with the grub, Mistah Storley catched me and suspicioned me, and dragged me off in the woods, and beat me till I told him all about it." She began to weep loudly. "Then he hit me on the head, and I reckon he's done gone to kill de po' young man again."

"Damn!" Harrison swore fervently. "Stanton, sure as the devil! I never expected to hear of him alive, after finding that picture— and now Storley's after him! That pistol-shot—where did you have him hidden? Tell me, quick!"

"In a cabin close to the creek. You follow the path behind the sheds, past the old meat hut, till the trail forks. Take the left hand—"

Harrison was already gone. He dived behind the sheds, raced recklessly down the path. He passed the meat hut, swinging wide of it, and plunged on down the trail. He played his light recklessly before him, but he almost missed the forking of the narrow trail in the shadows. He turned to the left and presently he saw another cabin ahead of him. It was dark and silent. He slid up to it with his flash extinguished, gun in hand. A presentiment of evil gripped him as he saw the door sagging open on its ancient hinges. He called, "Stanton!" in a low voice. The owls and the frogs mocked him from the creek. He shot a beam through the door. It played on a pallet of rags, a broken box, a darkly stained coat thrown carelessly on the floor. That was all.

Harrison snapped off his light, pervaded by a feeling of furious helplessness. He had failed. That distant shot had been Richard Stanton's knell, and now undoubtedly the creek had claimed the body chance had robbed it of before. To go searching for John Storley in that Stygian blackness would be worse than useless. Harrison knew he would be lucky to escape alive himself. The trap had been baited and cleverly hidden. Storley knew Harrison was a dangerous man to deal with. The web of lies he had spun had all been intended to throw the detective off his guard. He had known that he was no match for Harrison's courage and brute strength. Evidently he had not let the negroes into the plot because he did not wish to give them a hold over him. If he had known that Joab desired Harrison's death, it would have simplified matters a great deal for Storley.

Suddenly Harrison started as a reverberation echoed through the pines. Another shot! Not so far away this time. Galvanized by a sudden conjecture, the detective sprang toward the direction of the sound. In the silence that followed the shot he heard the tense beating of his own heart. Sweat kept running into his eyes and when he stumbled over projecting roots it sounded to him like the crashing of a bull through the timber. But he was not making nearly so much noise as he thought, for presently he heard, above the sounds of his own progress, the panting gasps of a man.

Somebody caromed heavily into a tree, whimpered an oath. Further back in the woods a twig cracked loudly. Stealing forward toward the sounds, Harrison's groping fingers closed on a human shoulder, and there sounded a shriek of overwrought nerves, and a wild plunge. Twisting from Harrison's grasp, the man blundered into a tree and fell sprawling, and at that instant, further back among the black trees, an orange jet stabbed the night and a bullet smashed through the branches close by. Harrison fired at the flash, and dropped to the earth, almost on top of the unseen man.

In the silence that followed the latter whispered gaspingly: "Shoot and get it over with!"

"*Stanton!*" hissed Harrison. "I thought you were dead."

"Who in the devil are you?" sputtered the other. "Your voice is familiar, but I'm too addled to recognize it."

"Steve Harrison," grunted the detective, his ears alert for any sounds in the darkness about them. "Is that John Storley out there?"

"Yes. I woke up an hour or so ago and heard somebody fumbling at the door. I looked out a crack and saw a man strike a match to examine the door. Then I recognized him as Storley and it all came back. He was the one that slugged me. I've been in a daze for days. I sneaked out the window as he was getting in at the door—he had a gun a yard long. But he heard me and was right after me. My God, I've been playing hide-and-seek with him for the last hour. Every time I thought I had shaken him off, he bobbed up and took a shot at me. He's out there now, sneaking up on us!"

Stanton's nerves were in a bad way. He shook as with an ague. Harrison rose cautiously to his knee. He heard no sound. It was logical to suppose that his unexpected shot had given Storley pause, made him more wary. But the man had a terrific advantage in his familiarity with the woods.

"We've got to get out of here and into the open where we stand an even chance," muttered the detective.

"But how?" demanded Stanton. "I've lost all sense of direction; been going in circles, I imagine. Besides, I don't even know where we are."

"I do," grunted Harrison. "Follow me. Keep hold of my coat, and keep your head down."

They began to move away in the direction in which Harrison knew lay the path from the creek to the house. Harrison did not wonder that Stanton had been unable to elude Storley; the man blundered and floundered even with his guidance. The only wonder was that he had been able to keep out of Storley's hands as long as he had. Harrison cursed the noise they were making, momentarily expecting a shot in the dark, but they reached the path without molestation.

"Where now?" whispered Stanton, still grasping Harrison's coat with a sweating hand.

"Up the trail—*no, down!*" Harrison threw Stanton bodily and fell on him, just as a gun cracked up the path. The bullet hummed over their heads, and Harrison returned the fire from the ground. He rolled into the thicker dark beside the trail, dragging the bewildered Stanton with him.

"Might have known he'd figure we'd make for the trail," he snarled. "He knows it's me with you; knows it couldn't be anybody else. That's why he didn't come after us. He made for the path and is laying for us up there. We can't get back to the house, and I'm not going to try to grope through these woods. Best thing is to lay still and make him come to us."

There ensued a tense period of waiting. Harrison, listening intently for a sound to tell him that Storley was creeping up on them, muttered: "What I want to know is, why did you drop out of sight? What reason did you have for not wanting to testify against Stark?"

"No reason at all," answered Stanton. "I got a letter that purported to come from a lawyer in Vendison, saying that he had charge of a large estate, and was trying to find missing heirs. He said he'd seen my picture in the papers in regard to the Stark trial, and believed I was distantly related to the family he represented. He enclosed some money for expenses, and asked me to run down to Vendison and talk to him. Maybe I was a sap for falling for such a thing, but it seemed on the level, and a fellow as broke as I am is ready to grab at anything that promises money. He asked me to keep it a secret and say nothing of my plans to anyone, because he said some of the people trying to grab this fortune were pretty unscrupulous. He said I'd get back in plenty of time for the trial. So I came under an assumed name. Storley met me at Vendison, and drove me right out here. We got in late, went into the house—and that's all I remember until I came to in that cabin with a black woman bandaging my head.

"She said Storley had tried to kill me, but she didn't know why. He'd shot me, but the bullet just ripped along the scalp. She's been feeding me and taking care of me, just out of the kindness of her heart. I've been too weak to make a getaway, but I was planning on trying tomorrow night. What is all this anyway?"

"Storley didn't want you to appear at the trail," grunted Harrison. "He got you, and then he used you as a decoy to get me down there, so he could bump me off too."

"What are we going to do now? Wait here until he sneaks up and blows our brains out?"

"He can't sneak up without us hearing him, and we've got as good a chance then as he has. He'll get us sure if we go blundering through the woods. We'll wait here until morning. In the daylight we'll have an even chance."

"It's getting day now," muttered Stanton, but Harrison suddenly cursed softly. It was not the light of day which was tinging the sky; a moon was coming up, a late, dim, crescent which gave no real illumination, only a vague illusive half-light which was in some ways worse than utter darkness.

But it was this light that was their salvation. How Storley located their exact position, and how he stole upon them so silently, Harrison never knew, unless it was the instinct of the life-long pineland dweller; but he wheeled suddenly at Stanton's wild cry, to see a dim figure looming almost over them. Their guns cracked simultaneously. A bullet fanned Harrison's ear, and from the shadowy figure which staggered drunkenly came a screech of pain and fury. Then the figure lunged forward recklessly. Harrison, seeing the right arm flapping uselessly, held his fire until he realized that steel gleamed in the other hand. Then it was too late.

He caught the descending knife on his lifted revolver, and grappled with the panting, gasping wild man, finding that slim frame a knitted mass of steel wires. He dared not shoot for fear of hitting Stanton, who was blundering wildly about the battlers; and despite the other's broken arm, he was hard put to it to fend that lunging knife from his breast.

Storley was fighting with the fury of madness; his eyes blazed in the dim light like those of a mad dog, and foam dripped from his bared teeth. But Harrison's superior strength told. Dropping his revolver, he caught Storley's left arm in both his hands, and twisted it until it seemed ready to start from its socket.

Gibbering curses Storley slowly relaxed his grip on the knife, and the weapon fell to the ground.

"Take it easy, Storley," snarled Harrison. "I don't want to kill you."

"You'll never take me alive!" shrieked Storley, and then Stanton, who in his bewilderment did not realize that the fight was practically won, and was obsessed with the idea of helping his ally, picked up Harrison's pistol by the barrel and swung it with a hearty good will. And as he struck a violent heave of Storley's changed the position of the fighters. The gun butt *chunked* solidly against Harrison's skull.

With a grunt the detective staggered, relaxing his grip. Storley shrieked, smashed his left full into Harrison's face, and breaking free, darted down the path.

"Oh, you condemned fool!" moaned the detective, wrenching the gun from Stanton's dazed hands. He staggered in pursuit, and the growing light showed him Storley running down the path ahead of him. Storley, too, was crippled; he reeled in his stride. The meat hut where he had told Harrison to meet him loomed just ahead.

"Stop, or I'll shoot, Storley!" yelled Harrison.

"Shoot and be damned!" came back the wild cry. "You'll never take me alive!"

"I'll shoot you in the leg!" roared the detective, cursing the dizzy swimming of his throbbing head and the lights that kept dancing before his eyes.

He leveled the wobbling gun and fired, and Storley flinched aside as the bullet ripped the earth near his foot. He was plunging toward the hut, not trying to duck into the woods, seemingly quite mad. Harrison's next bullet clipped his leg in mid-stride, but his momentum carried him staggering on, to lunge against the door of the cabin with outthrust hands as he fell. And as the door crashed open under the impact, man, cabin and moonlight were blotted out by a gigantic blinding flash, and the pines reeled with a cataclysmic explosion. Harrison was knocked flat by the concussion, and when he rose dazedly, he stared in awe. There was no sign of the hut: only a few twisted shreds of wood, among which lay bits of tattered clothing.

"That was the trap he set for me," muttered Harrison. "Dynamite! Set off by opening the door. Good God, how much did he have in there? *Corpus delicti* with a vengeance. I'd have simply vanished into thin air. He could have always claimed I got blown up accidentally if it had been traced to him. He didn't have to let the niggers in on the scheme, or even send them off tonight. If I walked into a hut full of dynamite and got blown up, people couldn't blame him."

Stanton was coming up the path, a wild disheveled figure in his torn shirt-sleeves, and the bandage about his head.

"He did it on purpose," he kept repeating. "He must have known that hut had dynamite in it—he said he wouldn't be taken alive."

"He meant that for me," grunted Harrison. "He had you out of the way, or thought he had. He didn't count on human nature. Some people kill, others save. It was as natural for Rachel to haul you out of the water and feed you as it was for him to crack you on the head."

"But it was me he wanted to kill, not you. That fortune—"

"But why did Storley want to keep me from testifying? Gangsters kill witnesses, I know, but Storley was no gangster, and neither is Stark—no regular criminal at all. He's just a cheap crook on his own, playing the society racket and pulling a sordid murder out of jealousy."

"Storley had a logical reason," answered Harrison, fumbling in his pocket. "I was puzzled too, until I found this picture. That's what made me realize that Storley was lying, that he'd brought me down here to kill me, just like he had you. That's why I didn't go into that cabin as he'd instructed me to." He produced the snapshot he had found in the broken drawer.

It portrayed two young men, one a mere boy in knee pants. In spite of their youth, their faces were instantly recognizable. The older man was John Storley; the other was a face familiar to every reader of newspapers in the United States, the face of the man whom Richard Stanton's testimony was to hang. On the back was written in a fine flowing hand: "John and Edward Storley, 1916."

"Brothers!" exclaimed Stanton. "But—"

"Edward Storley changed his name when he went out to rebuild the family fortunes, evidently" grunted Harrison. "It's been done before—didn't care to have a connection with a broken-down, gone-to-seed family. But the family loyalty still burned strong enough in John Storley. Pity such fidelity as his had to be wasted in such a cause."

The Names in the Black Book

"Three unsolved murders in a week are not so unusual—for River Street," grunted Steve Harrison, shifting his muscular bulk restlessly in his chair.

His companion lighted a cigarette and Harrison observed that her slim hand was none too steady. She was exotically beautiful, a dark, supple figure, with the rich colors of purple Eastern nights and crimson dawns in her dusky hair and red lips. But in her dark eyes Harrison glimpsed the shadow of fear. Only once before had he seen fear in those marvelous eyes, and the memory made him vaguely uneasy.

"It's your business to solve murders," she said.

"Give me a little time. You can't rush things, when you're dealing with the people of the Oriental quarter."

"You have less time than you think," she answered cryptically. "If you do not listen to me, you'll never solve these killings."

"I'm listening."

"But you won't believe. You'll say I'm hysterical—seeing ghosts and shying at shadows."

"Look here, Joan," he exclaimed impatiently. "Come to the point. You called me to your apartment and I came because you said you were in deadly danger. But now you're talking riddles about those three men who were killed last week. Spill it plain, won't you?"

"Do you remember Erlik Khan?" she asked abruptly.

Involuntarily his hand sought his face, where a thin scar ran from temple to jaw-rim.

"I'm not likely to forget him," he grunted. "A Mongol who called himself Lord of the Dead. His idea was to combine all the Oriental criminal societies in America in one big organization, with himself at the head. He might have done it, too, if his own men hadn't turned on him."

"Erlik Khan has returned," she said.

"What!" His head jerked up and he glared at her incredulously. "What are you talking about? I saw him die, and so did you!"

"I saw his hood fall apart as Ali ibn Suleyman struck with his keen-edged scimitar," she answered. "I saw him roll to the floor and lie still. And then the house went up in flames, and the roof fell in, and only charred bones were ever found among the ashes. Nevertheless, Erlik Khan has returned."

Harrison did not reply, but sat waiting for further disclosures, sure they would come in an indirect way. Joan La Tour was half Oriental, and partook of many of the characteristics of her subtle kin.

"How did those three men die?" she asked, though he was aware that she knew as well as he.

"Li-chin, the Chinese merchant, fell from his own roof," he grunted. "People on the street heard him scream and then saw him come hurtling down. Might have been an accident—but middle-aged Chinese merchants don't go climbing around on roofs at midnight.

"Ibrahim ibn Achmet, the Syrian curio dealer, was bitten by a cobra. That might have been an accident, too, only I know somebody dropped the snake on him through his skylight.

"Jacob Kossova, the Levantine exporter, was simply knifed in a back alley. Dirty jobs, all of them, and no apparent motive on the surface. But motives are hidden deep, in River Street. When I find the guilty parties I'll uncover the motives."

"And these murders suggest nothing to you?" exclaimed the girl, tense with suppressed excitement. "You do not see the link that connects them? You do not grasp the one point they all have in common? Listen—all these men formerly associated in one way or another with Erlik Khan!"

"Well?" he demanded. "That doesn't mean that the Khan's spook killed them! We found plenty of bones in the ashes of the house, but there were members of his gang in other parts of the city. His gigantic organization went to pieces, after his death, for lack of a leader, but the survivors were never uncovered. Some of these may be paying off old grudges."

"Then why did they wait so long to strike? It's been a year since we saw Erlik Khan die. I tell you, the Lord of the Dead himself, alive or *dead*, has returned and is striking down these men for one reason or another. Perhaps they refuse to do his bidding once more. Five were marked for death. Three have fallen."

"How do you know that?" demanded Harrison.

"Look!" From beneath the cushions of the divan on which she sat she drew something, and rising, came and bent beside him while she unfolded it.

It was a square piece of parchment-like substance, black and glossy. On it were written five names, one below the other, in a bold flowing hand—and in crimson, like spilled blood. Through the first three names a crimson bar had been drawn. They were the names of Li-chin, Ibrahim ibn Achmet, and Jacob Kossova. Harrison grunted explosively. The last two names, yet unmarred, were those of Joan La Tour and Stephen Harrison.

"Where did you get this?" he demanded.

"It was shoved under my door last night, while I slept. If all the doors and windows had not been locked, the police would have found it pinned to my corpse this morning."

"But still I don't see what connection—"

"It is a page from the Black Book of Erlik Khan!" she cried. "The book of the dead! I have seen it, when I was a subject of his in the old days. There he kept accounts of his enemies, alive and dead. I saw that book, open, the very day of the night Ali ibn Suleyman killed him—a big book with jade-hinged ebony covers and glossy black parchment pages. Those names were not in it then; they have been written in since Erlik Khan died—and that is Erlik Khan's handwriting!"

If Harrison was impressed he failed to show it.

"Does he keep his books in English?"

"No, in a Mongolian script. This is for our benefit. And I know we are hopelessly doomed. Erlik Khan never warned his victims unless he was sure of them."

"Might be a forgery," grunted the detective.

"No! No man could imitate Erlik Khan's hand. He wrote those names himself. He has come back from the dead! Hell could not hold a devil as black as he!" Joan was losing some of her poise in her fear and excitement. She ground out the half-consumed cigarette and broke the cover of a fresh carton. She drew forth a slim white cylinder and tossed the package on the table. Harrison took it up and absently extracted one for himself.

"Our names are in the Black Book! It is a sentence of death from which there is no appeal!" She struck a match and was lifting it, when Harrison struck the cigarette from her hand with a startled oath. She fell back on the divan, bewildered at the violence of his action, and he caught up the package and began gingerly to remove the contents.

"Where'd you get these things?"

"Why, down at the corner drug store, I guess," she stammered. "That's where I usually—"

"Not these, you didn't," he grunted. "These fags have been specially treated. I don't know what it is, but I've seen one puff of the stuff knock a man stone dead. Some kind of a hellish Oriental drug mixed with the tobacco. You were out of your apartment while you were phoning me—"

"I was afraid my wire was tapped," she answered. "I went to a public booth down the street."

"And it's my guess somebody entered your apartment while you were gone and switched cigarettes on you. I got only a faint whiff of the stuff when I started to put that fag in my mouth, but it's unmistakable. Smell it yourself. Don't be afraid. It's deadly only when ignited."

She obeyed, and turned pale.

"I told you! We were the direct cause of Erlik Khan's overthrow! If you hadn't smelt that drug, we'd both be dead now, as he intended!"

"Well," he grunted, "it's a cinch somebody's after you, anyway. I still say it can't be Erlik Khan, because nobody could live after the lick on the head I saw Ali ibn Suleyman hand him, and I don't believe in ghosts. But you've got to be protected until I run down whoever is being so free with his poisoned cigarettes."

"What about yourself? Your name's in his book too."

"Never mind me," Harrison growled pugnaciously. "I reckon

I can take care of myself." He looked capable enough, with his cold blue eyes, and the muscles bulging in his coat. He had shoulders like a bull.

"This wing's practically isolated from the rest of the building," he said, "and you've got the third floor to yourself?"

"Not only the third floor of the wing," she answered. "There's no one else on the third floor anywhere in the building at present."

"That makes it fine!" he exclaimed irritably. "Somebody could sneak in and cut your throat without disturbing anyone. That's what they'll try, too, when they realize the cigarettes didn't finish you. You'd better move to a hotel."

"That wouldn't make any difference," she answered, trembling. Her nerves obviously were in a bad way. "Erlik Khan would find me, anywhere. In a hotel, with people coming and going all the time, and the rotten locks they have on the doors, with transoms and fire escapes and everything, it would just be that much easier for him."

"Well, then, I'll plant a bunch of cops around here."

"That wouldn't do any good, either. Erlik Khan has killed again and again in spite of the police. They do not understand his ways."

"That's right," he muttered, uncomfortably aware of a conviction that to summon men from headquarters would merely be signing those men's death warrants, without accomplishing anything else. It was absurd to suppose that the dead Mongol fiend was behind these murderous attacks, yet—Harrison's flesh crawled along his spine at the memory of things that had taken place in River Street—things he had never reported, because he did not wish to be thought either a liar or a madman. The dead do not return—but what seems absurd on Thirty-ninth Boulevard takes on a different aspect among the haunted labyrinths of the Oriental quarter.

"Stay with me!" Joan's eyes were dilated, and she caught Harrison's arm with hands that shook violently. "We can defend these rooms! While one sleeps the other can watch! Do not call the police; their blunders would doom us. You have worked in the quarters for years, and are worth more than the whole police force.

The mysterious instincts that are part of my Eastern heritage are alert to danger. I feel peril for us both, near, creeping closer, gliding around us like serpents in the darkness!"

"But I can't stay here," he scowled worriedly. "We can't barricade ourselves and wait for them to starve us out. I've got to hit back—find out who's behind all this. The best defense is a good offense. But I can't leave you here unguarded, either. Damn!" He clenched his big fists and shook his head like a baffled bull in his perplexity.

"There is one man in the city besides yourself I could trust," she said suddenly. "One worth more than all the police. With him guarding me I could sleep safely."

"Who is he?"

"Khoda Khan."

"That fellow? Why, I thought he'd skipped months ago."

"No; he's been hiding in Levant Street."

"But he's a confounded killer himself!"

"No, he isn't; not according to his standards, which mean as much to him as yours do to you. He's an Afghan who was raised in a code of blood-feud and vengeance. He's as honorable according to his creed of life as you or I. And he's my friend. He'd die for me."

"I reckon that means you've been hiding him from the law," said Harrison with a searching glance which she did not seek to evade. He made no further comment. River Street is not South Park Avenue. Harrison's own methods were not always orthodox, but they generally got results.

"Can you reach him?" he asked abruptly. She nodded.

"All right. Call him and tell him to beat it up here. Tell him he won't be molested by the police, and after the brawl's over, he can go back into hiding. But after that it's open season if I catch him. Use your phone. Wire may be tapped, but we'll have to take the chance. I'll go downstairs and use the booth in the office. Lock the door, and don't open it to anybody until I get back."

When the bolts had clicked behind him, Harrison turned down the lighted corridor toward the stairs. The apartment house boasted no elevator. He watched all sides warily as he went. A peculiarity of architecture had, indeed, practically isolated that wing. The wall opposite Joan's doors was blank. The only way to reach the other suites on that floor was to descend the stair and ascend another on the other side of the building.

As he reached the stair he swore softly; his heel had crunched a small vial on the first step. With some vague suspicion of a planted poison trap he stooped and gingerly investigated the splintered bits and the spilled contents. There was a small pool of colorless liquid which gave off a pungent, musky odor, but there seemed nothing lethal about it.

"Some damned Oriental perfume Joan dropped, I reckon," he decided. He descended the twisting stair without further delay and was presently in the booth in the office which opened on the street; a sleepy clerk dozed behind the desk.

Harrison got the chief of police on the wire and began abruptly.

"Say, Hoolihan, you remember that Afghan, Khoda Khan, who knifed a Chinaman about three months ago? Yes, that's the one. Well, listen: I'm using him on a job for a while, so tell your men to lay off, if they see him. Pass the word along pronto. Yes, I know it's very irregular; so's the job I hold down. In this case it's the choice of using a fugitive from the law, or seeing a law-abiding citizen murdered. Never mind what it's all about. This is my job, and I've got to handle it my own way. All right; thanks."

He hung up the receiver, thought vigorously for a few minutes, and then dialed another number that was definitely not related to the police station. In place of the chief's booming voice there sounded at the other end of the wire a squeaky whine framed in the argot of the underworld.

"Listen, Johnny," said Harrison with his customary abruptness, "you told me you thought you had a lead on the Kossova murder. What about it?"

"It wasn't no lie, boss!" The voice at the other end trembled with excitement. "I got a tip, and it's big!—*big!* I can't spill it over the phone, and I don't dare stir out. But if you'll meet me at Shan Yang's hop joint, I'll give you the dope. It'll knock you loose from your props, believe me it will!"

"I'll be there in an hour," promised the detective. He left the booth and glanced briefly out into the street. It was a misty night, as so many River Street nights are. Traffic was only a dim echo from some distant, busier section. Drifting fog dimmed the street lamps, shrouding the forms of occasional passers-by. The stage was set for murder; it only awaited the appearance of the actors in the dark drama.

Harrison mounted the stair again. This stair wound up out of the office and up into the third floor of the wing without opening upon the second floor at all. The architecture, like much of it in or near the Oriental section, was rather unusual. People of that quarter were notoriously fond of privacy, and even apartment houses were built with this passion in mind. His feet made no sound on the thickly carpeted stairs, though a slight crunching at the top step reminded him of the broken vial again momentarily. He had stepped on the splinters.

He knocked at the locked door, answered Joan's tense challenge and was admitted. He found the girl more self-possessed.

"I talked with Khoda Khan. He's on his way here now. I warned him that the wire might be tapped—that our enemies might know as soon as I called him, and try to stop him on his way here."

"Good," grunted the detective. "While I'm waiting for him I'll have a look at your suite."

There were four rooms, drawing room in front, with a large bedroom behind it, and behind that two smaller rooms, the maid's bedroom and the bathroom. The maid was not there, because Joan had sent her away at the first intimation of danger threatening. The corridor ran parallel with the suite, and the drawing room, large bedroom and bathroom opened upon it. That made three doors to consider. The drawing room had one big east window, overlooking the street, and one on the south. The big bedroom had one south window, and the maid's room one south and one west window. The bathroom had one window, a small one in the west wall, overlooking a small court bounded by a tangle of alleys and board-fenced backyards.

"Three outside doors and six windows to be watched, and this top-story," muttered the detective. "I still think I ought to get some cops here." But he spoke without conviction. He was investigating the bathroom when Joan called him cautiously from the drawing room, telling him that she thought she heard a faint scratching outside the door. Gun in hand he opened the bathroom door and peered out into the corridor. It was empty. No shape of horror stood before the drawing room door. He closed the door, called reassuringly to the girl, and completed his tour of inspection, grunting approval. Joan La Tour was a true daughter of the Oriental quarter. Long ago she had provided against secret enemies as far as locks and bolts could provide. The windows were guarded with heavy iron-braced shutters, and there was no trapdoor, dumb waiter nor skylight anywhere in the suite.

"Looks like you're ready for a siege," he commented.

"I am. I have canned goods laid away to last for weeks. With Khoda Khan I can hold the fort indefinitely. If things get too hot for you, you'd better come back here yourself—if you can. It's safer than the police station—unless they burn the house down."

A soft rap on the door brought them both around.

"Who is it?" called Joan warily.

"I, Khoda Khan, *sahiba,*" came the answer in a low-pitched, but strong and resonant voice. Joan sighed deeply and unlocked the door. A tall figure bowed with a stately gesture and entered.

Khoda Khan was taller than Harrison, and though he lacked something of the American's sheer bulk, his shoulders were equally broad, and his garments could not conceal the hard lines of his limbs, the tigerish suppleness of his motions. His garb was a curious combination of costume, which is common in River Street. He wore a turban which well set off his hawk nose and black beard, and a long silk coat hung nearly to his knees. His trousers were conventional, but a silk sash girdled his lean waist, and his foot-gear was Turkish slippers.

In any costume it would have been equally evident that there was something wild and untamable about the man. His eyes blazed as no civilized man's ever did, and his sinews were like coiled springs under his coat. Harrison felt much as he would have felt if a panther had padded into the room, for the moment placid but ready at an instant's notice to go into flaming-eyed, red-taloned action.

"I thought you'd left the country," he said.

The Afghan smiled, a glimmer of white amidst the dark tangle of his beard.

"Nay, *sahib*. That son of a dog I knifed did not die."

"You're lucky he didn't," commented Harrison. "If you kill him you'll hang, sure."

"*Inshallah,*" agreed Khoda Khan cheerfully. "But it was a matter of *izzat*—honor. The dog fed me swine's flesh. But no matter. The *memsahib* called me and I came."

"Alright. As long as she needs your protection the police won't arrest you. But when this matter's finished, things stand as they were. I'll give you time to hide again, if you wish, and then I'll try to catch you as I have in the past. Or if you want to surrender and stand trial, I'll promise you as much leniency as possible."

"You speak fairly," answered Khoda Khan. "I will protect the *memsahib*, and when our enemies are dead, you and I will begin our feud anew."

"Do you know anything about these murders?"

"Nay, *sahib*. The *memsahib* called me, saying Mongol dogs threatened her. I came swiftly, over the roofs, lest they seek to ambush me. None molested me. But here is something I found outside the door."

He opened his hairy hand and exhibited a bit of silk, evidently torn from his sash. On it lay a crushed object that Harrison did not recognize. But Joan recoiled with a low cry.

"God! A black scorpion of Assam!"

"Aye—whose sting is death. I saw it running up and down before the door, seeking entrance. Another man might have stepped upon it without seeing it, but I was on my guard, for I smelled the Flower of Death as I came up the stair. I saw the thing at the door and crushed it before it could sting me."

"What do you mean by the Flower of Death?" demanded Harrison.

"It grows in the jungles where these vermin abide. Its scent attracts them as wine draws a drunkard. A trail of the juice had somehow been laid to this door. Had the door been opened before I slew it, it would have darted in and struck whoever happened to be in its way."

Harrison swore under his breath, remembering the faint scratching noise Joan had heard outside the door.

"I get it now! They put a bottle of that juice on the stairs where it was sure to be stepped on. I did step on it, and broke it, and got the liquid on my shoe. Then I tracked it down the stair, leaving the scent wherever I stepped. Came back upstairs, stepped in the stuff again and tracked it on through the door. Then somebody downstairs turned that scorpion loose—the devil! That means they've been in this house since I was downstairs!—may be hiding somewhere here now! But somebody had to come into the office to put that scorpion on the trail—I'll ask the clerk—"

"He sleeps like the dead," said Khoda Khan. "He did not waken when I entered and mounted the stairs. What matter if the house be full of Mongols? These doors are strong, and I am alert!" From beneath his coat he drew the terrible Khyber knife—a yard long, with an edge like a razor. "I have slain men with this," he announced, grinning like a bearded mountain devil. "Pathans, Indians, a Russian or so. These Mongols are dogs on whom the good steel will be shamed."

"Well," grunted Harrison. "I've got an appointment that's overdue now. I feel queer walking out and leaving you two to fight these devils alone. But there'll be no safety for us until I've smashed this gang at its root, and that's what I'm out to do."

"They'll kill you as you leave the building," said Joan with conviction.

"Well, I've got to risk it. If you're attacked call the police, anyway, and call me, at Shan Yang's joint. I'll come back here some time before dawn. But I'm hoping the tip I expect to get will enable me to hit straight at whoever's after us."

He went down the hallway with an eerie feeling of being watched, and scanned the stairs as if he expected to see it swarming with black scorpions, and he shied wide of the broken glass on the step. He had an uncomfortable sensation of duty ignored, in spite of himself, though he knew that his two companions did not want the police, and that in dealing with the East it is better to heed the advice of the East.

The clerk still sagged behind his desk. Harrison shook him without avail. The man was not asleep; he was drugged. But his heartbeat was regular, and the detective believed he was in no danger. Anyway, Harrison had no more time to waste. If he kept Johnny Kleck waiting too long, the fellow might become panicky and bolt, to hide in some rat-run for weeks.

He went into the street, where the lamps gleamed luridly through the drifting river mist, half expecting a knife to be thrown at him, or to find a cobra coiled on the seat of his automobile. But he found nothing his suspicion anticipated, even though he lifted the hood and the rumble-seat to see if a bomb had been planted. Satisfying himself at last, he climbed in and the girl watching him through the slits of a third-story shutter sighed relievedly to see him roar away unmolested.

.2.

Khoda Khan had gone through the rooms, murmuring approval in his beard of the locks, and having extinguished the lights in the other chambers he returned to the drawing room, where he turned out all lights there except one small desk lamp. It shed a pool of light in the center of the room, leaving the rest in shadowy vagueness.

"Darkness baffles rogues as well as honest men," he said sagely, "and I see like a cat in the dark."

He sat cross-legged near the door that let into the bedroom, which he left partly open. He merged with the shadows so that all of him Joan could make out with any distinctness was his turban and the glimmer of his eyes as he turned his head.

"We will remain in this room, *sahiba*," he said. "Having failed with poison and reptile, it is certain that men will next be sent. Lie down on that divan and sleep, if you can. I will keep watch."

Joan obeyed, but she did not sleep. Her nerves seemed to thrum with tautness. The silence of the house oppressed her, and the few noises of the street made her start.

Khoda Khan sat motionless as a statue, imbued with the savage patience and immobility of the hills that bred him. Grown to manhood on the raw barbaric edge of the world, where survival depended on personal ability, his senses were whetted keener than is possible for civilized men. Even Harrison's trained faculties were blunt in comparison. Khoda Khan could still smell the faint aroma of the Flower of Death, mingled with the acrid odor of the crushed scorpion. He heard and identified every sound in or outside the house—knew which were natural, and which were not.

He heard the sounds on the roof long before his warning hiss brought Joan upright on the divan. The Afghan's eyes glowed like phosphorus in the shadows and his teeth glimmered dimly in a savage grin. Joan looked at him inquiringly. Her civilized ears heard nothing. But he heard, and with his ears followed the sounds accurately and located the place where they halted. Joan heard something then, a faint scratching somewhere in the building, but she did not identify it—as Khoda Khan did—as the forcing of the shutters on the bathroom window.

With a quick reassuring gesture to her, Khoda Khan rose and melted like a slinking leopard into the darkness of the bedroom. She took up a blunt-nosed automatic, with no great conviction of reliance upon it, and groped on the table for a bottle of wine, feeling an intense need of stimulants. She was shaking in every limb and cold sweat was gathering on her flesh. She remembered the cigarettes, but the unbroken seal on the bottle reassured her. Even the wisest have their thoughtless moments. It was not until she had begun to drink that the peculiar flavor made her realize that the man who had shifted the cigarettes might just as easily have taken a bottle of wine and left another in its place, a facsimile that included an unbroken seal. She fell back on the divan, gagging.

Khoda Khan wasted no time, because he heard other sounds, out in the hall. His ears told him, as he crouched by the bathroom door, that the shutters had been forced—done almost in silence, a job that a white man would have made sound like an explosion in an iron foundry—and now the window was being jimmied. Then he heard something stealthy and bulky drop into the room. Then it was that he threw open the door and charged in like a typhoon, his long knife held low.

Enough light filtered into the room from outside to limn a powerful, crouching figure, with dim snarling yellow features. The intruder yelped explosively, started a motion—and then the long Khyber knife, driven by an arm nerved to the fury of the Himalayas, ripped him open from groin to breastbone.

Khoda Khan did not pause. He knew there was only one man in the room, but through the open window he saw a thick rope dangling from above. He sprang forward, grasped it with both hands and heaved backward like a bull. The men on the roof holding it released it to keep from being jerked headlong over the edge, and he tumbled backward, sprawling over the corpse, the loose rope in his hands. He yelped exultantly, then sprang up and glided to the door that opened into the corridor. Unless they had another rope, which was unlikely, the men on the roof were temporarily out of the fight.

He flung open the door and ducked deeply. A hatchet cut a great chip out of the jamb, and he stabbed upward once, then sprang over a writhing body into the corridor, jerking a big pistol from its hidden scabbard.

The bright light of the corridor did not blind him. He saw a second hatchet-man crouching by the bedroom door, and a man in the silk robes of a mandarin working at the lock of the drawing room door. He was between them and the stairs. As they wheeled toward him he shot the hatchet-man in the belly. An automatic spat in the hand of the mandarin, and Khoda Khan felt the wind of the bullet. The next instant his own gun roared again and the Manchu staggered, the pistol flying from a hand that was suddenly a dripping red pulp. Then he whipped a long knife from his robes with his left hand and came along the corridor like a typhoon, his eyes glaring and his silk garments whipping about him.

Khoda Khan shot him through the head and the mandarin fell so near his feet that the long knife stuck into the floor and quivered a matter of inches from the Afghan's slipper.

But Khoda Khan paused only long enough to pass his knife through the hatchet-man he had shot in the belly—for his fighting ethics were those of the savage Hills—and then he turned and ran back into the bathroom. He fired a shot through the window, though the men on the roof were making no further demonstration, and then ran through the bedroom, snapping on lights as he went.

"I have slain the dogs, *sahiba!*" he exclaimed. "By Allah, they have tasted lead and steel! Others are on the roof but they are helpless for the moment. But men will come to investigate the shots, that being the custom of the *sahibs*, so it is expedient that we decide on our further actions, and the proper lies to tell—*Allah!*"

Joan La Tour stood bolt upright, clutching the back of the divan. Her face was the color of marble, and the expression was rigid too, like a mask of horror carved in stone. Her dilated eyes blazed like weird black fire.

"Allah shield us against Shaitan the Damned!" ejaculated Khoda Khan, making a sign with his fingers that antedated Islam by some thousands of years. "What has happened to you, *sahiba?*"

He moved toward her to be met by a scream that sent him cowering back, cold sweat starting out on his flesh.

"Keep back!" she cried in a voice he did not recognize. "You are a demon! You are all demons! I see you! I hear your cloven feet padding in the night! I see your eyes blazing from the shadows! Keep your taloned hands from me! *Aie!*" Foam flecked her lips as she screamed blasphemies in English and Arabic that made Khoda Khan's hair stand stiffly on end.

"*Sahiba!*" he begged, trembling like a leaf. "I am no demon! I am Khoda Khan! I—" His outstretched hand touched her, and with an awful shriek she tore away and darted for the door, tearing at the bolts. He sprang to stop her, but in her frenzy she was even quicker than he. She tore the door open, eluded his grasping hand and fled down the corridor, deaf to his anguished yells.

.3.

When Harrison left Joan's apartment he drove straight to Shan Yang's dive, which, in the heart of River Street, masqueraded as a low-grade drinking joint. It was late. Only a few derelicts huddled about the bar, and he noticed that the barman was a Chinaman he had never seen before. He stared impassively at

Harrison, but jerked a thumb toward the back door, masked by dingy curtains, when the detective asked abruptly: "Johnny Kleck here?"

Harrison passed through the door, traversed a short dimly-lighted hallway and rapped authoritatively on the door at the other end. In the silence he heard the rats scampering. A steel disk in the center of the door shifted and a slanted black eye glittered in the opening.

"Open the door, Shan Yang," ordered Harrison impatiently, and the eye was withdrawn, accompanied by the rattling of bolts and chains.

He pushed open the door and entered a room whose illumination was scarcely better than that of the corridor. It was a large, dingy, drab affair, lined with bunks. Fires sputtered in braziers, and Shan Yang was making his way to his accustomed seat behind a low counter near the wall. Harrison spent but a single casual glance on the familiar figure, the well-known dingy silk jacket worked in gilt dragons. Then he strode across the room to a door in the wall opposite the counter to which Shan Yang was making his way. This was an opium joint and Harrison knew it—knew those figures in the bunks were Chinamen sleeping the sleep of the smoke. Why he had not raided it, as he had raided and destroyed other opium-dens, only Harrison could have said. But law-enforcing in River Street is not the orthodox routine it is on Baskerville Avenue, for instance. Harrison's reasons were those of expediency and necessity. Sometimes certain conventions have to be sacrificed for the sake of more important gains—especially when the law-enforcement of a whole district (and in the Oriental quarter) rests on one's shoulders.

A characteristic smell pervaded the dense atmosphere, in spite of the reek of dope and unwashed bodies—the dank odor of the river, which hangs over the River Street dives or wells up from their floors like the black intangible spirit of the quarter itself. Shan Yang's dive, like many others, was built on the very bank of the river. The back room projected out over the water on rotting piles, at which the black water lapped suckingly.

Harrison opened the door, entered and pushed it to behind

him, his lips framing a greeting that was never uttered. He stood dumbly, glaring.

He was in a small dingy room, bare except for a crude table and some chairs. An oil lamp on the table cast a smoky light. And in that light he saw Johnny Kleck. The man stood bolt upright against the far wall, his arms spread like a crucifix, rigid, his eyes glassy and staring, his mean, ratty features twisted in a frozen grin. He did not speak, and Harrison's gaze, traveling down him, halted with a shock. Johnny's feet did not touch the floor by several inches—

Harrison's big blue pistol jumped into his hand. Johnny Kleck was dead, that grin was a contortion of horror and agony. He was crucified to the wall by skewer-like dagger blades through his wrists and ankles, his ears wired to the wall to keep his head upright. But that was not what had killed him. The bosom of Johnny's shirt was charred, and there was a round, blackened hole.

Feeling suddenly sick the detective wheeled, opened the door and stepped back into the larger room. The light seemed dimmer, the smoke thicker than ever. No mumblings came from the bunks; the fires in the braziers burned blue, with weird sputterings. Shan Yang crouched behind the counter. His shoulders moved as if he were tallying beads on an abacus.

"Shan Yang!" the detective's voice grated harshly in the murky silence. "Who's been in that room tonight besides Johnny Kleck?"

The man behind the counter straightened and looked full at him, and Harrison felt his skin crawl. Above the gilt-worked jacket an unfamiliar face returned his gaze. That was not Shan Yang; it was a man he had never seen—it was a Mongol. He started and stared about him as the men in the bunks rose with supple ease. They were not Chinese; they were Mongols to a man, and their slanted black eyes were not clouded by drugs.

With a curse Harrison sprang toward the outer door and with a rush they were on him. His gun crashed and a man staggered in mid-stride. Then the lights went out, the braziers were overturned, and in the Stygian blackness hard bodies caromed against the detective. Long-nailed fingers clawed at his throat, thick arms locked about his waist and legs. Somewhere a sibilant voice was hissing orders.

Harrison's mauling left worked like a piston, crushing flesh and bone; his right wielded the gun barrel like a club. He forged toward the unseen door blindly, dragging his assailants by sheer strength. He seemed to be wading through a solid mass, as if the darkness had turned to bone and muscle about him. A knife licked through his coat, stinging his skin, and then he gasped as a silk cord looped about his neck, shutting off his wind, sinking deeper and deeper into the straining flesh. Blindly he jammed the muzzle against the nearest body and pulled the trigger. At the muffled concussion something fell away from him and the strangling agony lessened. Gasping for breath he groped and tore the cord away—then he was borne down under a rush of heavy bodies and something smashed savagely against his head. The darkness exploded in a shower of sparks that were instantly quenched in Stygian blackness.

The smell of the river was in Steve Harrison's nostrils as he regained his addled senses, river-scent mingled with the odor of stale blood. The blood, he realized, when he had sense enough to realize anything, was clotted on his own scalp. His head swam and he tried to raise a hand to it, thereby discovering that he was bound hand and foot with cords that cut into the flesh. A candle was dazzling his eyes, and for awhile he could see nothing else. Then things began to assume their proper proportions, and objects grew out of nothing and became identifiable.

He was lying on a bare floor of new, unpainted wood, in a large square chamber, the walls of which were of stone, without paint or plaster. The ceiling was likewise of stone, with heavy, bare beams, and there was an open trap door almost directly above him, through which, in spite of the candle, he got a glimpse of stars. Fresh air flowed through that trap, bearing with it the river-smell stronger than ever. The chamber was bare of furniture, the candle stuck in a niche in the wall. Harrison swore, wondering if he was delirious. This was like an experience in a dream, with everything unreal and distorted.

He tried to struggle to a sitting position, but that made his head swim so that he lay back and swore fervently. He yelled wrathfully, and a face peered down at him through the trap—a square, yellow face with beady slant eyes. He cursed the face and it mocked him and was withdrawn. The noise of a door softly opening checked Harrison's profanity and he wriggled around to glare at the intruder.

And he glared in silence, feeling an icy prickling up and down his spine. Once before he had lain bound and helpless, staring up at a tall black-robed figure whose yellow eyes glimmered from the shadow of a dusky hood. But that man was dead; Harrison had seen him cut down by the scimitar of a maddened Druse.

"Erlik Khan!" The words were forced out of him. He licked lips suddenly dry.

"Aye!" It was the same strange, hollow, ghostly voice that had chilled him in the old days. "Erlik Khan, the Lord of the Dead."

"Are you a man or a ghost?" demanded Harrison.

"I live."

"But I saw Ali ibn Suleyman kill you!" exclaimed the detective. "He slashed you across the head with a heavy sword that was sharp as a razor. He was a stronger man than I am. He struck with the full power of his arm. Your hood fell in two pieces—"

"And I fell like a dead man in my own blood," finished Erlik Khan. "But the steel cap I wore—as I wear now—under my hood saved my life as it has more than once. The terrible stroke cracked it across the top and cut my scalp, fracturing my skull and causing concussion of the brain. But I lived, and some of my faithful followers, who escaped the sword of the Druse, carried me down through the subterranean tunnels which led from my house, and so I escaped the burning building. But I lay like a dead man for weeks, and it was not until a very wise man was brought from Mongolia that I recovered my senses, and sanity.

"But now I am ready to take up my work where I left off, though I must rebuild much. Many of my former followers had forgotten my authority. Some required to be taught anew who was master."

"And you've been teaching them," grunted Harrison, recovering his pugnacious composure.

"True. Some examples had to be made. One man fell from a roof, a snake bit another, yet another ran into knives in a dark alley. Then there was another matter. Joan La Tour betrayed me in the old days. She knows too many secrets. She had to die. So that she might taste agony in anticipation, I sent her a page from my book of the dead."

"Your devils killed Kleck," accused Harrison.

"Of course. All wires leading from the girl's apartment house are tapped. I myself heard your conversation with Kleck. That is why you were not attacked when you left the building. I saw you were playing into my hands. I sent my men to take possession of Shan Yang's dive. He had no more use for his jacket, presently, so one donned it to deceive you. Kleck had somehow learned of my return; these stool-pigeons are clever. But he had time to regret. A man dies hard with a white-hot point of iron bored through his breast."

Harrison said nothing, and presently the Mongol continued.

"I wrote your name in my book because I recognized you as my most dangerous opponent. It was because of you that Ali ibn Suleyman turned against me.

"I am rebuilding my empire again, but more solidly. First I shall consolidate River Street, and create a political machine to rule the city. The men in office now do not suspect my existence. If all were to die, it would not be hard to find others to fill their places— men who are not indifferent to the clink of gold."

"You're mad," growled Harrison. "Control a whole city government from a dive in River Street?"

"It has been done," answered the Mongol tranquilly. "I will strike like a cobra from the dark. Only the men who obey my agent will live. He will be a white man, a figurehead whom men will think the real power, while I remain unseen. You might have been he, if you had a little more intelligence."

He took a bulky object from under his arm, a thick book with glossy black covers—ebony with black jade hinges. He riffled the night-hued pages and Harrison saw they were covered with crimson characters.

"My book of the dead," said Erlik Khan. "Many names have been crossed out. Many more have been added since I recovered my sanity. Some of them would interest you; they include names of the mayor, the chief of police, the district attorney, a number of aldermen—"

"That lick must have addled your brains permanently," snarled Harrison. "Do you think you can substitute a whole city government and get away with it?"

"I can and will. These men will die in various ways, and men of my own choice will succeed them in office. Within a year I will hold this city in the palm of my hand, and there will be none to interfere with me."

Lying staring up at the bizarre figure, whose features were, as always, shadowed beyond recognition by the hood, Harrison's flesh crawled with the conviction that the Mongol was indeed mad. His crimson dreams, always ghastly, were too grotesque and incredible for the visions of a wholly sane man. Yet he was dangerous as a maddened cobra. His monstrous plot must ultimately fail, yet he held the lives of many men in his hand. And Harrison, on whom the city relied for protection from whatever menace the teeming Oriental quarter might spawn, lay bound and helpless before him. The detective cursed in a paroxysm of fury.

"Always the man of violence," mocked Erlik Khan, with the suggestion of scorn in his voice. "Barbarian! Who lays his trust in guns and blades, who would check the stride of imperial power with blows of the naked fists! Brainless arm striking blind blows! Well, you have struck your last. Smell the river damp that creeps in through the ceiling? Soon it shall enfold you utterly and your dreams and aspirations will be one with the mist of the river."

"Where are we?" demanded Harrison.

"On an island below the city, where the marshes begin. Once there were warehouses here, and a factory, but they were abandoned as the city grew in the other direction, and have been crumbling into ruin for twenty years. I purchased the entire island through one of my agents, and am rebuilding to suit my own purposes an old stone mansion which stood here before the factory was built. None notices, because my own henchmen are the workmen, and no one ever comes to this marshy island. The house is invisible from the river, hidden as it is among the tangle of old rotting warehouses. You came here in a motorboat which was anchored beneath the rotting wharves behind Shan Yang's dive. Another boat will presently fetch my men who were sent to dispose of Joan La Tour."

"They may not find that so easy," commented the detective.

"Never fear. I know she summoned that hairy wolf, Khoda Khan, to her aid, and it's true that my men failed to slay him before he reached her. But I suppose it was a false sense of trust in the Afghan that caused you to make your appointment with Kleck. I rather expected you to remain with the foolish girl and try to protect her in your puny way."

Somewhere below them a gong sounded. Erlik Khan did not start, but there was a surprise in the lift of his head. He closed the black book.

"I have wasted enough time on you," he said. "Once before I bade you farewell in one of my dungeons. Then the fanaticism of a crazy Druse saved you. This time there will be no upset of my plans. The only men in this house are Mongols, who know no law but my will. I go, but you will not be lonely. Soon one will come to you."

And with a low, chilling laugh the dark phantom-like figure moved through the door and disappeared. Outside a lock clicked, and then there was stillness.

.4.

The silence was broken suddenly by a muffled scream. It came from somewhere below and was repeated half a dozen times. Harrison shuddered. No one who has ever visited an insane asylum could fail to recognize that sound. It was the shrieking of a mad woman. After these cries the silence seemed even more stifling and menacing.

Harrison swore to quiet his feelings, and again the velvet-capped head of the Mongol leered down at him through the trap.

"Grin, you yellow-bellied ape!" roared Harrison, tugging at his cords until the veins stood out on his temples. "If I could break these damned ropes I'd knock that grin around where your pigtail ought to be, you—" He went into minute details of the Mongol's ancestry, dwelling at length on the more scandalous phases of it, and in the midst of his noisy tirade he saw the leer change suddenly to a startled snarl. The head vanished from the trap and there came a sound like the blow of a butcher's cleaver.

Then another face was poked into the trap—a wild, bearded face, with blazing, bloodshot eyes, and surmounted by a disheveled turban.

"*Sahib!*" hissed the apparition.

"Khoda Khan!" ejaculated the detective, galvanized. "What the devil are you doing here?"

"Softly!" muttered the Afghan. "Let not the accursed ones hear!"

He tossed the loose end of a rope ladder down through the trap and came down in a rush, his bare feet making no sound as he hit the floor. He held his long knife in his teeth, and blood dripped from the point.

Squatting beside the detective he cut him free with reckless slashes that threatened to slice flesh as well as hemp. The Afghan was quivering with half-controlled passion. His teeth gleamed like a wolf's fangs amidst the tangle of his beard.

Harrison sat up, chafing his swollen wrists.

"Where's Joan? Quick, man, where is she?"

"Here! In this accursed den!"

"But—"

"That was she screaming a few minutes ago," broke in the Afghan, and Harrison's flesh crawled with a vague monstrous premonition.

"But that was a mad woman!" he almost whispered.

"The *sahiba* is mad," said Khoda Khan somberly. "Hearken, *sahib*, and then judge if the fault is altogether mine.

"After you left, the accursed ones let down a man from the roof on a rope. Him I knifed, and I slew three more who sought to force the doors. But when I returned to the *sahiba*, she knew me not. She fled from me into the street, and other devils must have been lurking nearby, because as she ran shrieking along the sidewalk, a big automobile loomed out of the fog and a Mongol stretched forth an arm and dragged her into the car, from under my very fingers. I saw his accursed yellow face by the light of a street lamp.

"Knowing she were better dead by a bullet than in their hands, I emptied my pistol after the car, but it fled like Shaitan the Damned from the face of Allah, and if I hit anyone in it, I know not. Then as I rent my garments and cursed the day of my birth—for I could not pursue it on foot—Allah willed that another automobile should appear. It was driven by a young man in evening clothes, returning from a revel, no doubt, and being cursed with curiosity he slowed down near the curb to observe my grief.

"So, praising Allah, I sprang in beside him and placing my knife point against his ribs bade him go with speed and he obeyed in great fear. The car of the damned ones was out of sight, but presently I glimpsed it again, and exhorted the youth to greater speed, so the machine seemed to fly like the steed of the Prophet. So, presently I saw the car halt at the river bank. I made the youth halt likewise, and he sprang out and fled in the other direction in terror.

"I ran through the darkness, hot for the blood of the accursed ones, but before I could reach the bank I saw four Mongols leave the car, carrying the *memsahib* who was bound and gagged, and they entered a motorboat and headed out into the river toward an island which lay on the breast of the water like a dark cloud.

"I cast up and down the shore like a madman, and was about to leap in and swim, though the distance was great, when I came upon a boat chained to a pile—not a motorboat, but one driven by oars. I gave praise to Allah and cut the chain with my knife— see the nick in the edge?—and rowed after the accursed ones with great speed.

"They were far ahead of me, but Allah willed it that their engine should sputter and cease when they had almost reached the island. So I took heart, hearing them cursing in their heathen tongue, and hoped to draw alongside and slay them all before they were aware of me. They saw me not in the darkness, nor heard my oars because of their own noises, but before I could reach them the accursed engine began again. So they reached a wharf on the marshy shore ahead of me, but they lingered to make the boat fast, so I was not too far behind them as they bore the *memsahib* through the shadows of the crumbling shacks which stood all about.

"Then I was hot to overtake and slay them, but before I could come up with them they had reached the door of a great stone house—this one, *sahib*—set in a tangle of rotting buildings. A steel fence surrounded it, with razor-edged spearheads set along the top but by Allah, that could not hinder a *lifter* of the Khyber! I went over it without so much as tearing my garments. Inside was a second wall of stone, but it stood in ruins.

"I crouched in the shadows near the house and saw that the windows were heavily barred and the doors strong. Moreover, the lower part of the house is full of armed men. So I climbed a corner of the wall, and it was not easy, but presently I reached the roof which at that part is flat, with a parapet. I expected a watcher, and so there was, but he was too busy taunting his captive to see or hear me until my knife sent him to hell. Here is his dagger; he bore no gun."

Harrison mechanically took the wicked, lean-bladed poniard.

"But what caused Joan to go mad?"

"*Sahib*, there was a broken wine bottle on the floor, and a goblet. I had no time to investigate it, but I know that wine must have been poisoned with the juice of the fruit called the black pomegranate. She can not have drunk much, or she would have died frothing and champing like a mad dog. But only a little will rob one of sanity. It grows in the jungles of Indo-China, and white men say it is a lie. But it is no lie; thrice I have seen men die after having drunk its juice, and more than once I have seen men and women, too, turn mad because of it. I have traveled in that hellish country where it grows."

"God!" Harrison's foundations were shaken by nausea. Then his big hands clenched into chunks of iron and bale-fire glimmered in his savage blue eyes. The weakness of horror and revulsion was followed by cold fury dangerous as the blood-hunger of a timber wolf.

"She may be already dead," he muttered thickly. "But dead or alive we'll send Erlik Khan to hell. Try that door."

It was of heavy teak, braced with bronze straps.

"It is locked," muttered the Afghan. "We will burst it."

He was about to launch his shoulder against it when he stopped short, the long Khyber knife jumping into his fist like a beam of light.

"Someone approaches!" he whispered, and a second later Harrison's more civilized—and therefore duller—ears caught a cat-like tread.

Instantly he acted. He shoved the Afghan behind the door and sat down quickly in the center of the room, wrapped a piece of rope about his ankles and then lay full length, his arms behind and under him. He was lying on the other pieces of severed cord, concealing them, and to the casual glance he resembled a man lying bound hand and foot. The Afghan understood and grinned hugely.

Harrison worked with the celerity of trained mind and muscles that eliminates fumbling delay and bungling. He accomplished his purpose in a matter of seconds and without undue noise. A key grated in the lock as he settled himself, and then the door swung open. A giant Mongol stood limned in the opening. His head was shaven, his square features passionless as the face of a copper idol. In one hand he carried a curiously shaped ebony block, in the other a mace such as was borne by the horsemen of Ghengis Khan—a straight-hafted iron bludgeon with a round head covered with steel points, and a knob on the other end to keep the hand from slipping.

He did not see Khoda Khan because when he threw back the door, the Afghan was hidden behind it. Khoda Khan did not stab him as he entered because the Afghan could not see into the outer corridor, and had no way of knowing how many men were following the first. But the Mongol was alone, and he did not bother to shut the door. He went straight to the man lying on the floor, scowling slightly to see the rope ladder hanging down through the trap, as if it was not usual to leave it that way, but he did not show any suspicion or call to the man on the roof.

He did not examine Harrison's cords. The detective presented the appearance the Mongol had expected, and this fact blunted his faculties as anything taken for granted is likely to do. As he bent down, over his shoulder Harrison saw Khoda Khan glide from behind the door as silently as a panther.

Leaning his mace against his leg, spiked head on the floor, the Mongol grasped Harrison's shirt bosom with one hand, lifted his head and shoulders clear of the floor while he shoved the block under his head—like twin striking snakes the detective's hands whipped from behind him and locked on the Mongol's bull throat.

There was no cry; instantly the Mongol's slant eyes distended and his lips parted in a grin of strangulation. With a terrific heave he reared upright, dragging Harrison with him, but not breaking his hold, and the weight of the big American pulled them both down again. Both yellow hands tore frantically at Harrison's iron wrists; then the giant stiffened convulsively and brief agony reddened his black eyes. Khoda Khan had driven his knife between the Mongol's shoulders so that the point cut through the silk over the man's breastbone.

Harrison threw aside the corpse and rose. He saw Khoda Khan shaking the red drops from his blade, and he did not hand out any platitudes about sportsmanship and knifing in the back. They were not dealing with any sort of sportsman, but with human snakes who despised any sort of ethics as contemptible weakness.

Harrison caught up the mace, grunting with savage satisfaction. It was a weapon more suited to his temperament than the dagger Khoda Khan had given him. No need to ask its use; if he had been bound and alone when the executioner entered, his brains would now have been clotting its spiked ball and the hollowed ebon block which so nicely accommodated a human head. Erlik Khan's executions varied along the whole gamut from the exquisitely subtle to the crudely bestial.

"The door's open," said Harrison. "Let's go!"

.5.

There were no keys on the body. Harrison doubted if the key in the door would fit any other in the building, but he locked the door and pocketed the key, hoping that would prevent the body from being soon discovered.

They emerged into a dim-lit corridor which presented the same unfinished appearance as the room they had just left. At the other end a stair wound down into shadowy gloom, and they descended warily, Harrison feeling along the wall to guide his steps. Khoda Khan seemed to see like a cat in the dark; he went down silently and surely. But it was Harrison who discovered the door. His hand, moving along the convex surface, felt the smooth stone give way to wood—a short narrow panel, through which a man could just squeeze. When the wall was covered with tapestry—as he knew it would be when Erlik Khan had completed his house—it would be sufficiently hidden for a secret entrance.

Khoda Khan, behind him, was growing impatient at the delay, when somewhere below them both heard a noise simultaneously. It might have been a man ascending the winding stairs and it might not, but Harrison acted instinctively. He pushed and the door opened inward on noiseless oiled springs. A groping foot discovered narrow steps inside. With a whispered word to the Afghan he stepped through and Khoda Khan followed. He pulled the door shut again and they stood in total blackness with a curving wall on either hand. Harrison struck a match and a narrow stair was revealed, winding down.

"This place must be built like a castle," Harrison muttered, wondering at the thickness of the walls. The match went out and they groped downward in darkness too thick for even the Afghan to pierce. And suddenly both halted in their tracks. Harrison estimated that they had reached the level of the second floor, and through the inner wall came a mutter of voices. Harrison groped for another door, or a peep-hole for spying, but he found nothing of the sort. But straining his ear close to the stone, he began to understand what was being said beyond the wall, and a long-drawn hiss between clenched teeth told him that Khoda Khan likewise understood.

The first voice was Erlik Khan's; there was no mistaking that hollow reverberance. It was answered by a piteous, incoherent whimpering that brought sweat suddenly out on Harrison's flesh.

"No," the Mongol was saying. "I have come back, not from hell as your barbarian superstitions suggest, but from a refuge unknown to your stupid police. I was saved from death by the steel cap I always wear beneath my coif. You are at a loss as to how you got here?"

"I don't understand!" It was the voice of Joan La Tour, half-hysterical, but undeniably sane. "I remember opening a bottle of wine, and as soon as I drank I knew it was drugged. Then everything faded out—I don't remember anything except great black walls, and awful shapes skulking through the darkness. I ran through gigantic shadowy halls for a thousand years—"

"They were hallucinations of madness, of the juice of the black pomegranate," answered Erlik Khan. Khoda Khan was muttering blasphemously in his beard until Harrison admonished him to silence with a fierce dig of his elbow. "If you had drunk more you would have died like a rabid dog. As it was, you went insane. But I knew the antidote—possessed the drug that restored your sanity."

"Why?" the girl whimpered bewilderedly.

"Because I did not wish you to die like a candle blown out in the dark, my beautiful white orchid. I wish you to be fully sane so as to taste to the last dregs the shame and agony of death, subtle and prolonged. For the exquisite, an exquisite death. For the coarse-fibered, the death of an ox, such as I have decreed for your friend Harrison."

"That will be more easily decreed than executed," she retorted with a flash of spirit.

"It is already accomplished," the Mongol asserted imperturbably. "The executioner has gone to him, and by this time Mr. Harrison's head resembles a crushed egg."

"Oh, God!" At the sick grief and pain in that moan Harrison winced and fought a frantic desire to shout out denial and reassurance.

Then she remembered something else to torture her.

"Khoda Khan! What have you done with Khoda Khan?"

The Afghan's fingers clamped like iron on Harrison's arm at the sound of his name.

"When my men brought you away they did not take time to deal with him," replied the Mongol. "They had not expected to take you alive, and when fate cast you into their hands, they came away in haste. He matters little. True, he killed four of my best men, but that was merely the deed of a wolf. He has no mentality. He and the detective were much alike—mere masses of brawn, brainless, helpless against intellect like mine. Presently I shall attend to him. His corpse shall be thrown on a dung-heap with a dead pig."

"Allah!" Harrison felt Khoda Khan trembling with fury. "Liar! I will feed his yellow guts to the rats!"

Only Harrison's grip on his arm kept the maddened Moslem from attacking the stone wall in an effort to burst through to his enemy. The detective was running his hand over the surface, seeking a door, but only blank stone rewarded him. Erlik Khan had not had time to provide his unfinished house with as many secrets as his rat-runs usually possessed.

They heard the Mongol clap his hands authoritatively, and they sensed the entrance of men into the room. Staccato commands followed in Mongolian, there was a sharp cry of pain or fear, and then silence followed the soft closing of a door. Though they could not see, both men instinctively knew that the chamber on the other side of the wall was empty. Harrison almost strangled with a panic of helpless rage. He was penned in these infernal walls and Joan La Tour was being borne away to some abominable doom.

"*Wallah!*" the Afghan was raving. "They have taken her away to slay her! Her life and our *izzat* is at stake! By the Prophet's beard and my feet! I will burn this accursed house! I will slake the fire with Mongol blood! In Allah's name, *sahib*, let us do *something!*"

"Come on!" snarled Harrison. "There *must* be another door somewhere!"

Recklessly they plunged down the winding stair, and about the time they had reached the first floor level, Harrison's groping hand felt a door. Even as he found the catch, it moved under his fingers. Their noise must have been heard through the wall, for the panel opened, and a shaven head was poked in, framed in the square of light. The Mongol blinked in the darkness, and Harrison brought the mace down on his head, experiencing a vengeful satisfaction as he felt the skull give way beneath the iron spikes. The man fell face down in the narrow opening and Harrison sprang over his body into the outer room before he took time to learn if there were others. But the chamber was empty.

The lower part of the house was complete. This chamber was thickly carpeted, the walls hung with black velvet tapestries. The doors were of bronze-bound teak, ornamented with gilt-worked arches. Khoda Khan presented an incongruous contrast, barefooted, with draggled turban and red-smeared knife.

But Harrison did not pause to philosophize. Ignorant as he was of the house, one way was as good as another. He chose a door at random and flung it open boldly, revealing a wide corridor carpeted and tapestried like the chamber. At the other end, through wide satin curtains that hung from roof to floor, a file of men was just disappearing—tall, black-silk clad Mongols, heads bent somberly, like a train of dusky ghosts. They did not look back.

"Follow them!" snapped Harrison. "They must be headed for the execution—"

Khoda Khan was already gone down the corridor like a vengeful whirlwind. The thick carpet deadened their footfalls, so even Harrison's big shoes made no noise. There was a distinct feeling of unreality, running silently down that fantastic hall—it was like a dream in which natural laws are suspended. Even in that moment Harrison had time to reflect that this whole night had been like a nightmare, possible only in the Oriental quarter, its violence and bloodshed like an evil dream. Erlik Khan had loosed the forces of chaos and insanity; murder had gone mad, and its frenzy was imparted to all actions and men caught in its maelstrom.

Khoda Khan would have burst headlong through the curtains—he was already drawing breath for a yell, and lifting his knife—when Harrison seized him. The Afghan's sinews were like cords under the detective's hands, and Harrison doubted his own ability to restrain him forcibly, but a vestige of sanity remained to the hillman.

Pushing him back, Harrison gazed between the curtains. There was a great double-valved door there, but it was partly open, and he looked into the room beyond. Khoda Khan's beard was jammed hard against his neck as the Afghan glared over his shoulder.

It was a large chamber, hung like the others with black velvet on which golden dragons writhed; there were thick rugs, and lanterns hanging from the ivory-inlaid ceiling cast a red glow that made for illusion. Black-robed men ranged along the wall might have been shadows but for their glittering eyes.

On a throne-like chair of ebony sat a grim figure, motionless as an image except when its loose robes stirred in the faintly moving air. Harrison felt the short hairs prickle at the back of his neck, just as a dog's hackles rise at the sight of an enemy. Khoda Khan muttered some incoherent blasphemy.

The Mongol's throne was set against a side wall. No one stood near him as he sat in solitary magnificence, like an idol brooding on human doom. In the center of the room stood what looked uncomfortably like a sacrificial altar—a curiously carved block of stone that might have come out of the heart of the Gobi. On that stone lay Joan La Tour, white as a marble statue, her arms outstretched like a crucifix, her hands and feet extending over the edges of the block. Her dilated eyes stared upward as one lost to hope, aware of doom and eager only for death to put an end to agony. The physical torture had not yet begun, but a gaunt half-naked brute squatted on his haunches at the end of the altar, heating the point of a bronze rod in a dish full of glowing coals.

"Damn!" It was half curse, half sob of fury, bursting from Harrison's lips. Then he was hurled aside and Khoda Khan burst into the room like a flying dervish, bristling beard, blazing eyes, knife and all. Erlik Khan came erect with a startled guttural as the Afghan came tearing down the room like a headlong hurricane of destruction. The torturer sprang up just in time to meet the yard-long knife lashing down, and it split his skull down through the teeth.

"*Aie!*" It was a howl from a score of Mongol throats.

"*Allaho akabar!*" yelled Khoda Khan, whirling the red knife about his head. He threw himself on the altar, slashing at Joan's bonds with a frenzy that threatened to dismember the girl.

Then from all sides the black-robed figures swarmed in, not noticing in their confusion that the Afghan had been followed by another grim figure who came with less abandon but with equal ferocity.

They were aware of Harrison only when he dealt a prodigious sweep of his mace, right and left, bowling men over like ten-pins, and reached the altar through the gap made in the bewildered throng. Khoda Khan had freed the girl and he wheeled, spitting like a cat, his bared teeth gleaming and each hair of his beard stiffly on end.

"Allah!" he yelled—spat in the faces of the oncoming Mongols—crouched as if to spring into the midst of them—then whirled and rushed headlong at the ebony throne.

The speed and unexpectedness of the move were stunning. With a choked cry Erlik Khan fired and missed at point-blank range—and then the breath burst from Khoda Khan in an ear-splitting yell as his knife plunged into the Mongol's breast and the point sprang a hand's breadth out of his black-clad back.

The impetus of his rush unchecked, Khoda Khan hurtled into the falling figure, crashing it back on to the ebony throne which splintered under the impact of the two heavy bodies. Bounding up, wrenching his dripping knife free, Khoda Khan whirled it high and howled like a wolf.

"*Ya Allah!* Wearer of steel caps! Carry the taste of my knife in your guts to hell with you!"

There was a long hissing intake of breath as the Mongols stared wide-eyed at the black-robed, red-smeared figure crumpled grotesquely among the ruins of the broken throne; and in the instant that they stood like frozen men, Harrison caught up Joan and ran for the nearest door, bellowing: "Khoda Khan! This way! Quick!"

With a howl and a whickering of blades the Mongols were at his heels. Fear of steel in his back winged Harrison's big feet, and Khoda Khan ran slantingly across the room to meet him at the door.

"Haste, *sahib!* Down the corridor! I will cover you retreat!"

"No! Take Joan and run!" Harrison literally threw her into the Afghan's arms and wheeled back in the doorway, lifting the mace. He was as berserk in his own way as was Khoda Khan, frantic with the madness that sometimes inspired men in the midst of combat.

The Mongols came on as if they, too, were blood-mad. They jammed the door with square snarling faces and squat silk-clad bodies before he could slam it shut. Knives licked at him, and gripping the mace with both hands he wielded it like a flail, working awful havoc among the shapes that strove in the doorway, wedged by the pressure from behind. The lights, the upturned snarling faces that dissolved in crimson ruin beneath his flailing, all swam in a red mist. He was not aware of his individual identity. He was only a man with a club, transported back fifty thousand years, a hairy-breasted, red-eyed primitive, wholly possessed by the crimson instinct for slaughter.

He felt like howling his incoherent exultation with each swing of his bludgeon that crushed skulls and spattered blood into his face. He did not feel the knives that found him, hardly realizing it when the men facing him gave back, daunted at the havoc he was wreaking. He did not close the door then; it was blocked and choked by a ghastly mass of crushed and red-dripping flesh—

He found himself running down the corridor, his breath coming in great gulping gasps, following some dim instinct of preservation or realization of duty that made itself heard amidst the red dizzy urge to grip his foes and strike, strike, strike! until he was himself engulfed in the crimson waves of death. In such moments the passion to die—die fighting—is almost equal to the will to live.

In a daze, staggering, bumping into walls and caroming off them, he reached the further end of the corridor where Khoda Khan was struggling with a lock. Joan was standing now, though she reeled on her feet, and seemed on the point of collapse. The mob was coming down the long corridor full cry behind them. Drunkenly Harrison thrust Khoda Khan aside and whirling the blood-fouled mace around his head, struck a stupendous blow that shattered the lock, burst the bolts out of their sockets and caved in the heavy panels as if they had been cardboard. The next instant they were through and Khoda Khan slammed the ruins of the door which sagged on its hinges, but somehow held together. There were heavy metal brackets on each jamb, and Khoda Khan found and dropped an iron bar in place just as the mob surged against it.

Through the shattered panels they howled and thrust their knives, but Harrison knew that until they hewed away enough wood to enable them to reach in and dislodge it, the bar across the door would hold the splintered barrier in place. Recovering some of his wits, and feeling rather sick, he herded his companions ahead of him with desperate haste. He noticed, briefly, that he was stabbed in the calf, thigh, arm and shoulder. Blood soaked his ribboned shirt and ran down his limbs in streams. The Mongols were hacking at the door, not yelling like Khoda Khan, but snarling like jackals over carrion.

The apertures were widening, and through them he saw other Mongols running down the corridor with rifles; just as he wondered why they did not shoot through the door, he saw the reason. They were in a chamber which had been converted into a magazine. Cartridge cases were piled high along the wall, and there was at least one box of dynamite. But he looked in vain for rifles or pistols. Evidently they were stored in another part of the building.

Khoda Khan was jerking the bolts on an opposite door, but he paused to glare about and yelping "Allah!" he pounced on an open case, snatched something out—wheeled, yelled a curse and threw back his arm, but Harrison grabbed his wrist.

"Don't throw that, you idiot! You'll blow us all to hell! They're afraid to shoot into this room, but they'll have that door down in a second or so, and finish us with their knives. Help Joan!"

It was a hand grenade Khoda Khan had found—the only one in an otherwise empty case, as a glance assured Harrison. The detective threw the door open, slammed it shut behind them as they plunged out into the starlight, Joan reeling, half carried by the Afghan. They seemed to have emerged somewhere at the back of the house. They ran across an open space, hunted creatures looking for a refuge. There was a crumbling stone wall, about breast-high to a man, and they ran through a wide gap in it, only to halt, a groan bursting from Harrison's lips. Thirty steps behind the ruined wall rose the steel fence of which Khoda Khan had spoken, a gleaming barrier ten feet high, topped with keen points. The door crashed open behind them and a gun spat venomously. They were in a trap. If they tried to climb the fence the Mongols had but to pick them off like monkeys shot off a ladder.

"Down behind the wall!" snarled Harrison, forcing Joan prostrate behind an uncrumbled section of the stone barrier. "We'll make 'em pay for it, before they take us!"

The door was crowded with snarling faces, now split in toothy leers of triumph. There were rifles in the hands of a dozen. They knew their victims had no firearms, and could not escape, and they themselves could use rifles without fear. Bullets began to splatter

on the stone, then with a long-drawn yell Khoda Khan bounded to
the top of the wall, ripping out the pin of the hand grenade with
his teeth.

"La illaha illulah; Muhammad rassoul ullah!" he yelled, and
hurled the bomb with a long over-hand swing—not at the group
which howled and ducked, but over their heads, into the magazine!

The next instant a rending crash tore the guts out of the night
and a blinding blaze of fire ripped the darkness apart. In that glare
Harrison had one stunned glimpse of Khoda Khan, etched against
the flame, hurtling backward, arms out-thrown—then there was
utter blackness in which roared the earthquake thunder of the fall
of the house of Erlik Khan as the shattered walls buckled, the beams
splintered, the roof fell in and story after story came crashing down
on the crumpled foundations.

How long Harrison lay like a dead man he never knew,
stunned, blinded, deafened and paralyzed, half-covered by falling
debris. His first realization was that there was something soft
under him, something that writhed and whimpered. He had a
vague feeling that he ought not to hurt this soft something, so he
began to shove the broken stones and pulverized mortar off him.
His right arm seemed dead, but eventually he excavated himself
and staggered up, looking like a scarecrow in his rags. He groped
among the rubble, grasped the girl and pulled her up.

"Joan!" His own voice seemed to come to him from a great
distance, or through closed doors, and he had to shout to make her
hear him. Their eardrums had been almost split by the concussion.

"Are you hurt?" He did not stand on ceremony, but ran his
one good hand over her to make sure.

"I don't think so," she faltered dazedly. "What—what
happened?"

"Khoda Khan's bomb exploded the dynamite. The house fell
in on the Mongols. We were sheltered by that wall; that's all that
saved us."

The wall was a shattered heap of broken stone, half covered by
rubble—a waste of shattered masonry with broken beams thrust up
through the litter, and shards of walls reeling drunkenly. Harrison
fingered his broken arm and tried to think, his head swimming.

"Where is Khoda Khan?" cried Joan, seeming finally to shake off her daze.

"I'll look for him." Harrison dreaded what he expected to find. "He was blown off the wall like a straw in a wind."

Stumbling over broken stones and bits of timber, he found the Afghan huddled grotesquely against the steel fence. His fumbling fingers told him of broken bones—but the man was still breathing. Joan came stumbling toward him, to fall beside Khoda Khan and flutter her quick fingers over him, sobbing hysterically.

"He's not like civilized man!" she exclaimed, tears running down her stained, scratched face. "Afghans are harder than cats to kill. If we could get him medical attention he'll live. Listen!" She caught Harrison's arm with galvanized fingers; but he had heard it too—the sputter of a motor that was probably a police launch, coming to investigate the explosion.

Joan was tearing her scanty garments to pieces to staunch the blood that seeped from the Afghan's wounds, when miraculously Khoda Khan's pulped lips moved. Harrison, bending close, caught fragments of words: "The curse of Allah—Chinese dog—swine's flesh—my *izzat.*"

"You needn't worry about your *izzat,*" grunted Harrison, glancing at the ruins which hid the mangled figures that had been Mongolian terrorists. "After this night's work you'll not go to jail— not for all the Chinamen in River Street."

The Silver Heel

Chapter .1.

Steve Harrison thrust his hands deep in his coat pockets, cursing the profession which dragged him out into deserted streets at ungodly hours. A faint mist was rising from the river which was at that point invisible. River Street stretched empty before him, except for the solitary figure of a man who tramped along half a block ahead of him. For three blocks Harrison had seen no other person except this wayfarer who trudged along, coat collar turned up against the dampness, hands thrust in his pockets.

Harrison drew forth a watch and scowled at it by the light which fell over his shoulder from a street lamp.

"Twelve o'clock, almost to the second," he muttered to himself. "If that tip wasn't a fake—"

"Help! Help! Ahhh—!" It was a scream of fright and agony from somewhere across the street, that broke short in a ghastly gurgle. Before it had died away Harrison was charging across the street, moving with a speed surprizing for one of his bulk. The man on the sidewalk ahead of him had started and turned at the cry, and now, after an instant's apparent indecision, followed the detective across the street.

The cry had come from behind a high board fence which, as Harrison knew, closed the mouth of a long unused alley. Without wasting time climbing the fence, he drove his heavy shoulder like a battering ram against the rotting boards, which splintered under the impact. He smashed through, scarcely checking his bull-like lunge.

Light from a lamp in the street outside streamed over the fence and revealed a huddled figure on the ground. The alley ran away from the street at right angles, and, a few yards away, made a bend around a sharp-angled corner. Harrison lunged around the bend, pistol in hand. It was darker there, but ahead of him he saw a dull glow limning the mouth where the alley came into Levant Street. He ran down it, glancing at the boarded-up doors and windows on either hand. The only way out of this lane, which was known as China Alley, was out of one mouth or the other. Doubtless a fleet-footed man could have escaped into Levant Street while Harrison was crashing into the alley at the other end.

The Levant Street end was also closed with a board fence, but a missing board formed a gap through which a man could squeeze. Harrison peered through. As far as he could see in either direction, Levant Street stretched empty and bare under the lamps that glowed redly through the mist. There were a score of places within reach, however, doorways and alleys, into which a fugitive could duck out of sight. Harrison strode back down the alley, swearing under his breath.

The man who had followed him across the street was leaning over the figure on the ground, staring down at it with morbid fascination. He looked up as Harrison approached—a blond young fellow, of athletic build.

"This fellow's been hurt!" he exclaimed. "There's blood on the ground—"

"I hope you haven't touched him," grunted Harrison.

"Not me. I know better than that. But what about you—"

"I'm a detective," answered Harrison. He drew forth an electric torch and directed it on the figure. "Hurt, hell! He's dead!"

The body was that of a man of medium height and early middle age, with black hair and a sallow complexion. It lay on its side, one arm outstretched, the fingers clawing at the dirt. From the back projected the curiously ornamented hilt of a dagger.

"Who is he?" asked the young man eagerly. "Do you know him?"

Harrison grunted noncommittally; he habitually worked alone, and he had a prejudice against making any disclosures concerning a crime. But after all, there was no harm in divulging the man's identity.

"Jelner Kratz. Lawyer. Of Kratz & Lepstein, River Street."

"A white man? He doesn't look exactly like—"

"He was born in Shanghai, I understand. Might have had some mixed blood in him."

Harrison did not add that the lawyer had been mixed up in or suspected of many shady transactions characteristic of River Street, which is the heart of the Oriental quarter. Kratz had served as a sort of sinister link between yellow and white, dwelling as he did in the shadowy borderline of the races.

There was no doubt that the man was dead, but Harrison ran expert hands over the body. And he paused a moment, his eyes narrowing in a peculiar manner. Then without comment he drew a pair of gloves from his pocket, donned them and pulled out the dagger.

"Do you suppose there'll be fingerprints?" asked the young man. "I thought crooks now-a-days were too smart to leave any."

"Not all River Street killers are up on modern crime detection methods," Harrison replied. "Some of them are newly come from the Orient."

"You think an Oriental killed him?"

"It's a Chinese dagger." Harrison displayed the weapon before he wrapped it in a handkerchief and deposited it in his inside coat pocket. It had a thin, skewer-like blade, a round guard, shaped like a coin, and a curiously-wrought bronze hilt, almost too small for a white man's hand. A carven dragon writhed about the hilt, its head serving as the pommel.

He began to go through the pockets with quick, deft hands, while the young man squatted beside him and watched each move with interest.

"Wristwatch intact," muttered Harrison to himself; "diamond ring on finger of left hand—billfold untouched. It wasn't robbery, then."

He opened the billfold and riffled the edges of the banknotes it contained. More than a hundred dollars was represented there. In one of the compartments there was a bit of paper folded. Harrison smoothed it out and glanced over it by the light of his electric torch. It was a faded newspaper clipping, with a Shanghai dateline, dated three months previous—a brief item relating the mysterious death of one Wu Shun, eldest son of the Mandarin Tang, of Shanghai.

"Wonder why he kept that?" remarked the young man, who, Harrison noted with annoyance, was peering over his shoulder. Harrison refolded the clipping and replaced it as he rose.

"How should I know? He was born and raised in Shanghai. Not strange he should get news from there. Maybe this Wu Shun was a friend of his."

"What's that on the ground?" The young man pointed, and Harrison picked up the object—an old-fashioned silver cigar-case, empty, and lying open a few feet from the body. Harrison put it in the pocket with the cloth-wrapped dagger. He stepped to the gap in the fence, thrust his head through and blew a shrill, far-carrying blast on a police whistle. The nearest policeman, O'Rourke, was not in sight, but he would hear that signal.

As Harrison turned back into the alley, the young stranger asked: "What do you think?"

"I don't think anything," answered Harrison, somewhat annoyed. "It's my business to find out. You'd better run along, hadn't you?"

"Where to?" retorted the other. "I've been pounding the pavements since sun-up, trying to land a job. I'm nearly broke. I bet I know you. You're Steve Harrison. You just about run River Street. You're a sort of combination of detective, unofficial judge, police court, state militia and what-not. Well, look—I'm a reporter. At least I am when I'm working. I came here from San Francisco, looking for a job. But these editors can't see me with a ten-foot pole. My name's Jack Bissett. Give me a break, will you?"

"What do you mean?"

"Let me tag around with you and get the inside dope on this job! I can make a story out of it that might mean a job for me. I know you're poison to reporters, but be human for once in your life!"

"I don't like publicity," growled Harrison. "It hinders my work. Enforcing white man's law in River Street is a tough enough job as it is."

"I know—and you've lived up to that conviction nobly. The public never gets anything but a smattering of what goes on in the

Oriental district. The newspapers never get any of the real dope on how you solve crimes. But just this once—man, I need a job!"

"All right—all right!" growled Harrison. "This job probably isn't important, anyway. But keep out from under my feet, will you? And don't bank too strong on any editor giving you a hand for this yarn, even if you get one. Murders are too common on River Street."

"Yes, but the inside dope on how Steve Harrison runs down a killer isn't common!"

"I haven't run him down yet."

"I can see the headlines now," went on Bissett, heedlessly. "'Lone Sleuth Tracks Down Mystery Killer! Harrison Breaks Long Silence To Reveal Methods—'"

"Can it, will you?" growled Harrison. "Don't you realize there's a man lying there dead?"

Even while he talked he had been going over the ground carefully with his flashlight. The hard-beaten earth and the broken paving which covered part of the alley revealed no track. The thud of feet sounded on the sidewalk and a policeman peered through the gap in the fence.

"What's up, Harrison?"

"Murder. Jelner Kratz. Call the station and then come back here."

"Okay." The cop vanished.

Harrison moved around the brick angle which bent the kink in the alley. As his light travelled along the ground something winked, wedged in a crack of the broken paving. He bent, wrenched it free and straightened, holding the light close to it. Bissett was beside him instantly, exclaiming eagerly: "What is it? What have you found? Is it a clue?"

Harrison glanced at him in irritation, then shrugged his shoulders and displayed his find.

"Why, that's the heel of a woman's slipper—looks like silver!"

"It is silver. Wedged in that crack and broken off. Recently, too. The luster hasn't had time to tarnish. The woman who wore that must have left in a hurry, or she'd have stopped to pick up a heel that expensive."

"A woman in the case!" ejaculated Bissett. His eyes snapped and he impulsively reached for the heel, being not at all abashed when Harrison repulsed him. "A society dame! Oh, boy! This is going to be a yarn yet! What do you think? Come on—you agreed to give me the dope as we went along."

"I don't remember any such damned agreement," snorted Harrison. "But I'll humor you. Think? What basis have I for thinking anything yet? I happen to know, though, that the only establishment in town that sells slippers with silver heels is The French Shop. As soon as O'Rourke gets back I'm going to roust out the manager and try to trace the owner of this heel."

"And I'm tagging right along with you!" announced Bissett. "Oh, boy! This has possibilities! 'Socialite Murders River Street Lawyer'—man, this may have tie-ups that'll shake this town right off its props!"

"How do you know a society dame wore that heel?" demanded Harrison.

"Who else would?"

"There are plenty of dancing girls right here on River Street that wear duds just as ritzy as that," grunted Harrison. "They make plenty of dough, and they put it all on their backs. And some of them have Oriental sports on their strings who make white boys look like pikers when it comes to spending. Hell's fire! Have I got to stand here and chin with you all night? That you, O'Rourke?"

The policeman crawled through the fence.

"Hoolihan's sending a wagon," he announced.

"All right. You stay here and watch the body. You might browse around the alley and see if you find anything while you're doing it. I'm going to call on the manager of The French Shop. Tell Hoolihan I'll drop in on the station later with a few things for the fingerprint department to work on.

"Come on, Bissett, if you must go. I've got my car parked a few blocks down the street."

Chapter .2.

The manager of The French Shop, the most exclusive and expensive shop in the city, was neither French nor exotic in appearance. He was short, stout, and far from artistic-looking in the dressing gown he had donned when roused protestingly from sleep. He yawned prodigiously and blinked as Harrison, without preamble, stuck the broken silver heel under his rubicund nose.

"Did that come off a slipper out of your shop?"

"How do I know? It looks like the brand we handle."

"How many women in this town own shoes with heels like that?"

"How the devil do I know? Some of them trade in other cities. Only three women have bought slippers like that from us, though. It's the latest fad; we just got them in a few days ago."

"Have you a list of those women at hand?"

"I don't have to have one. I know who they were: Miss Elizabeth Richards, 171 South Park Boulevard; Mrs. J.J. Gottschenger, Old Ridgely Place; and Zaida Lopez, from River Street."

"Who's Zaida Lopez?" demanded Bissett.

"A Eurasian dancer," answered Harrison. "Dances at Yun Wi's Shrine of Pleasure—sort of a Chinese nightclub. I'll bet this is her heel. Even if a society dowager or a debutante did sneak down a dark alley on River Street, she'd wear more sensible shoes than a pair of silver-heeled slippers. Zaida's the kind of dame who'd wear them on such an occasion."

"Well," yawned the manager, "I don't know what you're talking about, but Mrs. Gottschenger left for New York three days ago, and I happen to know that Miss Richards was giving a ball at her old man's house tonight."

"Well, that lets them out," Harrison rose. "Come on, Bissett."

Out on the street Harrison said: "I've got to draw a line somewhere. These River Street people are hard enough to deal with in private. I'm going to drop in on Zaida and have a talk with her, and I look for fireworks enough as it is. With a stranger, it would make it that much harder."

"Meaning what?"

"Meaning I can't let you go with me to Zaida's."

"But you promised—"

"I know, but this is business. I'll give you the dope afterwards."

"All right. I'll have to be content, I guess. Are you going straight there?"

"No, I'm going to stop off by the station and leave this cigar-case and dagger with the fingerprint expert. Then I'll go to Zaida's."

"She may skip while you're hanging around the station."

"If she meant to skip, she's skipped already. But it's my bet she hasn't."

"You think she killed Kratz?"

"It looks like it."

"Damn!" mourned Bissett. "Just my luck to be barred out of the interview. But I'll go back to my room and write up what's happened so far. You'll give me the dope, tomorrow, at the station?"

"Sure, sure. I promised, didn't I?" Harrison climbed into his coupe and roared off down the street, not glancing back at the dejected figure on the curb.

The street where lived the manager of the fashionable French Shop was not far from the edge of the Oriental district. The police station was further away. Harrison's stay there was brief.

"What have you got this time?" asked Chief Hoolihan as Harrison entered. The River Street detective was an enigma and a mystery even to his fellow officers. He always worked alone, and neither his methods nor his theories were generally open for public inspection. His methods were his own, and were frequently irregular and unorthodox, but they got results. As Bissett said, practically the whole responsibility for law-enforcement in the Oriental quarter rested on Harrison's brawny shoulders.

"Some work for the fingerprint department," answered Harrison, placing the dagger and cigar-case on the desk.

"Think you've got a lead?"

"Maybe. Not sure yet."

"Coincidence that you happened to be walking along the street just as the murder was committed."

"Coincidences don't happen that way," grunted Harrison. "I wasn't just happening along."

"You mean you knew something was going to break?"

"Look here." Harrison spread out a bit of paper before Hoolihan. On it was written in a flowing woman's hand:

Detective Harrison:

A murder will be committed tonight on River Street, somewhere between Ormond and Bridge Streets, at or about midnight.

It was unsigned.

"I got that this morning. It was mailed downtown somewhere. I'm always getting screwy tips that don't mean anything, but I don't pass up anything that isn't completely nutty. I left my car at the corner of Ormond and River Street at a few minutes until twelve and walked down River Street—and just at twelve I heard a howl and found Jelner Kratz in China Alley with this knife in him, and this heel wedged in the paving. It looks like the woman who wore this heel might have knifed Kratz, turned to run, and got the heel wedged in a crack and broke it off in her panic."

"And who was the woman?"

"It might have been Zaida Lopez. I'm going over and talk to her—if I can find her."

A few minutes later Harrison's coupe swung into River Street, and a little later he drew up to the curb in front of the apartment house in which lived the Eurasian dancer. A sleepy clerk yawned at the desk—a Jap or a Filipino. This was the Oriental quarter where the strains of a hundred exotic races mixed and mingled.

"Is Miss Lopez in her apartment?" asked Harrison.

"Yes, sir."

"When did she come in?"

"A few minutes after twelve, sir." He glanced at the clock which showed it to be five minutes after one. He did not ask if the detective wished to be announced. His manner was politely uninterested, but his eyes gleamed. All River Street knew Steve Harrison, the inexplicable white man who enforced his race's inexplicable laws among the quarter's alien inhabitants.

The elevator was not running at that hour. As Harrison mounted the stair, to the top floor, where he knew Zaida's apartment to be, he reflected that the dancer could easily have left it unbeknownst to the clerk. In both wings of the building, stairs led down to side-entrances. Anyone could enter or leave without passing through the lobby.

He reached the upper corridor and knocked on the door he knew opened into Zaida's drawing room. No one answered. No light streamed through the transom. He knocked louder and called. No one replied. He rattled the knob impatiently. The door was locked, but his trained eyes caught something that made him bend and examine the lock and the woodwork adjacent to it. The faint marks and scratches that showed were unmistakable; someone—and someone not too expert—had used or attempted to use a jimmy on that lock recently. He started at the sound of a stealthy footfall; it seemed to come from inside the room.

He remembered that Zaida's bedroom opened on the roof. He hurried down the hall, around an abrupt turn in the corridor, and came to a glass-paneled door which let onto the roof, and which, ordinarily, was not locked. It was not locked now. He came out onto a flat expanse where a few seats and a number of potted palms represented a former abortive attempt to create a roof-garden for dancing. Only one room opened on the roof, and that Harrison knew, was Zaida's bedroom. The door stood open. No light shone through.

Harrison remembered that stealthy padding step. He swept the roof with a narrow glance; it was shadowy in the starlight. But if anyone had been standing upright behind any of the palms, he would have seen him. There was a sinister aspect about that strip of darkness the doorway framed.

Harrison drew his pistol and advanced warily. Potted palms made a miniature jungle near the door, but a narrow glance revealed no figure crouching among or behind them. Unwilling to outline his bulk against the stars before the open door, Harrison moved along the wall until he could reach an arm around the jamb and feel for the light switch which he knew was near the door. He had been in Zaida's apartment before. His fingers found the switch, and in an instant the room was flooded with light. Harrison stopped short, staring grimly.

In the middle of a room appointed with the bizarre taste of a half-caste dancing girl, there sprawled the second body he had found that night.

It was Zaida Lopez and she was dead. There had been a struggle. The dancer had been as supple and strong as a she-panther, and Harrison could imagine her last, desperate fight for life. It must have been a powerful man who had overpowered her. Her dress was torn, exposing her bosom, and between her firm young breasts stood the bronze hilt of a dagger, with a carved dragon coiling about it, its head forming the pommel.

Harrison bent over her. She had not been dead long. The body was still warm. She wore boudoir slippers, and near a dressing table, as if flung carelessly aside, lay a pair of ballroom slippers that glimmered in the light. One showed a long slim silver heel; the heel of the other was missing, and Harrison did not bother to match it with the heel in his pocket.

"Where the devil's her maid, Selda?"

Zaida's bed had not been slept in. The adjoining room, he knew, was her maid's bedroom. He entered it, turning on the light. He went into the drawing room. But he found no skulking figure there. If he had heard a step inside the apartment, the skulker had made his escape before the detective entered. Harrison remembered the fire-escape that led down from the roof.

The maid's bed had been occupied. The pillow was still dented by the pressure of a human head. But the maid was gone. A quick survey showed him that every door—except the one opening on the roof—was locked, and every window securely fastened. There was a window opening on the roof, in the left-hand wall. The door opening on the roof had not been forced. There was a key in the lock, on the inside.

"She must have opened the door herself," muttered Harrison, bending over the body again, and noting the blue marks on the tawny throat. "Therefore the man who killed her was someone she knew—or was expecting. He strangled her— obviously to keep her from screaming. He must have been a powerful man. He came in by a side-entrance—or by way of the fire-escape."

He stepped to the door and stared out over the starlit roof. And he stiffened suddenly. The light from the doorway shone on the palms that clustered near the door, and something projected from behind one of the huge pots—a human foot. In an instant Harrison was bending over the man, and he grunted softly in recognition. It was an Arab, whom Harrison knew as Ahmed, a rug dealer. He was a young man, with a powerful, muscular frame; Harrison believed he had formerly been a wrestler. Such a man might easily overpower even such a supple tigress as Zaida Lopez. His eyes were closed and he lay limply. A round crimson gilt-worked skull-cap lay near him. Harrison ran his fingers expertly over the Arab's head and frowned in puzzlement as he discovered no bruise, lump or contusion. He picked up the cap, but it told him nothing. A blow upon it would not crush it and show upon it as in the case with a hat. He was unarmed.

"Doped?" wondered Harrison. Just then Ahmed groaned, moved and muttered incoherently. He opened his eyes and stared blankly at Harrison.

"*Wallah!* What happened?"

"That's what I'd like to know," retorted the detective. "What are you doing here? What's the matter with you?"

The Arab struggled to a sitting posture and pressed his hands to his temples.

"Somebody hit me—" he shook his head, with a grimace of pain. Then suddenly his head jerked up, and his gaze cleared. "The man behind the palms! Where is he?"

"There's nobody there." Harrison did not glance at the potted trees. His slit-eyed gaze was fixed on the Arab, who rose, weaving dizzily.

"He was there. He sprang out from behind the palms and struck me—just as Zaida opened the door—"

"So it was you she opened the door for?"

"Why, yes! I—" He was staring through the doorway, over Harrison's shoulder, and his eyes dilated, his swarthy skin went ashy.

"Zaida! She's dead!"

"Yes," said Harrison softly, watching him like a hawk. The Arab pushed past him and went into the room, to stare down wide-eyed at the murdered girl.

"The man behind the palms!" he muttered. "He did this! Allah!"

"Why did you kill her?" asked Harrison abruptly.

Ahmed lifted his head to stare at him.

"I? I kill Zaida Lopez? Are you mad, *sahib?* Zaida was my friend. I came here to protect her—"

"From whom?"

"I don't know. Her maid brought me a note—"

"Where is it?"

"I destroyed it."

"What did it say?"

Ahmed pressed his temples with his hands. "I can't remember, exactly. She mentioned no names. When I try to think my brain clouds over. The note said she was afraid—that she needed a man to protect her. She'd seen something that frightened her. We have been friends for a long time. I came."

"Who brought it?"

"Her maid, Selda."

"Where's the maid?"

"I don't know. I didn't see her. She gave the note to the clerk at the hotel where I live. He sent it up to my room. When I came down, she was gone."

"When did you receive it?"

"About twelve-thirty, I think. I don't know exactly."

"What then?"

"I came straight here, of course. I left my auto parked on the side street, entered by a side door and came up a stair from that entrance. I didn't come through the lobby. When I came up into the corridor I saw a man bending over the lock of Zaida's door—"

"What did he look like?"

"He had his back to me. I got only a glimpse, and then he darted around the bend in the hallway. I ran after him, and the door to the roof was open, but when I got on the roof, he was nowhere in sight. I thought he'd gone down by the fire-escape, but he must have been hiding on the roof. Before I had time to look for him, Zaida called out from her bedroom to know if it were I, and when she recognized my voice, she opened the door. As I started toward it she screamed, and I turned just as a man leaped out from behind the palms. He was swinging something at my head when I turned. I don't remember anything more."

"What did he look like?"

Ahmed shook his head helplessly.

"I don't remember. My brain gets cloudy when I try to think about it. I can't remember anything about him. Just a shadowy figure springing at me from behind the palms."

Harrison wheeled as a knock sounded on the drawing-room door that opened upon the corridor.

"Who's there?" he called.

"Me! Bissett! Let me in!"

"Sit down on that couch and stay there, Ahmed," ordered Harrison, and the Arab sank down on the divan and sank his head in his hands. Harrison started toward the door, watching the Arab from the corner of his eye, his pistol ready—if Ahmed made a break it would be a clear confession of guilt, and Harrison had acted as informal executioner before. But the bent figure sat motionless. Harrison turned the key and pulled the door partly open. Bissett's eager face was framed in the crack.

"What the hell are you doing here? I told you to scram."

"I got to thinking what a sap I'd be to mind you!" proclaimed Bissett. "My conscience wouldn't let me stay away! Come on—be a sport and let me in! Have you given the dame the third degree? Has she squawked yet?"

For answer Harrison threw open the door and gestured across the chamber into the bedroom and at the body that lay there. Bissett's eyes almost popped out of his head.

"Who's that?"

"Zaida Lopez!"

Bissett advanced and stared down at her.

"She's dead! Look there, Harrison!" he shrilled, pointing. "The same kind of knife that killed what's-his-name—Kratzie!"

"Do you think I hadn't noticed that?" snorted Harrison.

Bissett turned and stared at Ahmed.

"Is this the egg that did it?"

"Looks like it."

"I kill no one," muttered Ahmed. "Only a Turk, once, in Istanbul—I broke his neck in a wrestling bout. I never killed a woman in my life."

"Your yarn sounds fishy, Ahmed," said Harrison. "If somebody knocked you out, why isn't there a knot on your head? It would take a terrible lick to stiffen a fellow as powerful as you. Yet there's no sign of a bruise of any kind. Your cap isn't even dented."

Ahmed shook his head helplessly.

"I do not know. I only know I did not kill Zaida Lopez."

"I'm forced to believe you did," said Harrison. "Somebody's used a jimmy on the door out in the hall. I believe you first tried to force your way in, then somehow persuaded her to open the door. Then you choked her so she couldn't scream, and stabbed her with that dagger. You were in the apartment when I knocked on the drawing-room door. I heard you sneaking away. I suppose I got on the roof before you could make your getaway and you lay down behind those palms to hide until you had a chance to slip away. But I discovered you, and you made up this fantastic yarn."

Ahmed merely shook his head, unspeaking.

"Keep an eye on him, Bissett," Harrison ordered. "I'm going to look through the rooms a bit."

Bissett cast a dubious eye over the muscular proportions of the Arab, but he planted himself between the couch and the door that opened on the roof, and knotting a fist of generous size, blew gently on the knuckles with significant meaning. Ahmed did not show that he was even aware of the reporter's presence.

A brief but thorough search of the bedroom failed to reveal anything of importance. He took the maid's room next; went straight to a writing desk that stood there, and drew open drawer after drawer. At the bottom of the last drawer he opened he found a sheet of scented and tinted paper, carefully folded. He unfolded it and read, in Zaida's bold scrawl:

Kratz:

   I must see you. I have gone as far as I can. Meet me in the back room of The Purple Cat at eleven o'clock, if you value your filthy life.

It was not signed. He selected a piece of paper containing a list of articles written by the maid and put it in his pocket along with the note. The Purple Cat was a low-class cabaret on Levant Street, a few blocks from the mouth of China Alley.

He went to a telephone and called the desk of the hotel where he knew Ahmed lived. The clerk answered.

"This is Steve Harrison." That name would bring prompt answers, even though they might be lies. "How long have you been on duty?"

"Since ten o'clock, sir."

"What time did the Arab, Ahmed, leave the hotel?"

"About twelve-thirty-five, Mr. Harrison."

"Did a woman bring him a note?"

"Yes, Mr. Harrison. The maid of Zaida Lopez. She gave me the note and left. I sent it right up to him."

"Had he been up in his room all evening?"

"I really don't know, sir. So many people come and go, and he usually carries his key with him, all the time—"

"All right. Thanks."

He set down the phone and turned to meet Ahmed's haggard stare.

"It seems you're telling the truth about the maid bringing you the note, Ahmed," said Harrison. "Do you know whether Kratz was blackmailing Zaida or not?"

Ahmed's expression grew stubborn, and he did not reply.

"Well, I believe he was. Sometimes I think half of River Street is blackmailing the other half. He might have been blackmailing you, too—"

"Might have been?"

"In case you don't know," said Harrison sardonically, "Kratz was murdered in China Alley tonight, with a dagger like that one sticking in Zaida. Since I believe you killed her, I'm forced to believe you killed him. For some reason she was in the alley and saw you do it. But you didn't see her, or you'd have killed her there. She was foolish enough to send you a note asking you to come here—I don't know why, unless she wanted to blackmail you because of it—"

"You are mad, you Infidel dog!" Ahmed's temper got the best of his stoicism for an instant. Harrison showed no annoyance at the uncomplimentary term. He had been called worse names than that.

"She was playing with fire, and got burnt. You killed her, as you'd killed Kratz. Why did you kill Kratz? Was he blackmailing you, too?"

Ahmed did not reply; he was either crushed by the accusations, or had taken refuge in the stoic fatalism of the Oriental, a characteristic Harrison had encountered so many times before in his dealings with the inhabitants of River Street.

"Won't talk, eh? All right." Third degree methods found little favor with Harrison; besides, he knew the impossibility of breaking down that wall of silence.

Turning away, he began searching the drawing room. He noticed there was a stain of ink on Zaida's left hand, and remembered she was left-handed. There was a writing desk in the drawing room, much more elaborate than the one in the maid's room, and a pen lay upon it, the ink not yet dry on the point. An open inkwell stood nearby. He dumped the contents of the wastepaper basket on the floor, or started to, when he saw a crumpled sheet of tinted paper on top of the heap. He caught it up. It was a scented sheet similar to the one on which the other note had been written. On it was written in the same hand:

Ahmed:
    Come quickly.
    I am terribly afraid. Kratz is dead, and I saw Joseph Lepstein kill—

The line ceased in the middle of the sentence. For some reason Zaida had started to write a note on that sheet, then had crumpled it up and thrown it into the wastepaper basket. Ahmed swore the note he received named no names; had she been afraid that names mentioned were too indiscreet?

Harrison shrugged his shoulders; that put a new construction entirely upon the matter. He re-entered the bedroom with the paper in his hand.

"What have you found?" asked Bissett, instantly alert.

"Something that makes me think Ahmed might be telling the truth, after all," said the detective. "Evidence that throws a new light on the matter, entirely. Ahmed, can't you remember anything about the fellow you say jumped at you from behind the palms?"

"I can not think straight," muttered the Arab, caressing his head. "Sometimes I think I can almost remember what he looked like—then it is all gone from me. Perhaps if I ever see him again I will know him. Perhaps not. Only in Allah is there knowledge."

"Well," began Harrison, when he felt eyes boring into his back. He wheeled. "The devil!" A face was glaring in at the window that opened on the roof—a square, yellow face with glittering black slant eyes.

"Halt!" shouted the detective, springing toward the window—even then he realized his mistake and wheeled back toward the open door. But even as he wheeled, the room was plunged in darkness. Somebody cried out, and then an iron hand caught his wrist and he felt the paper wrenched from his fingers. He lunged forward, collided with a figure in the dark and grappled with it—only to sink to his knees under the impact of a terrific blow on his head. As he went down the wind of another stroke swished venomously past his ear, and wrenching out his .45 he fired blindly upward, three times, for he felt murder in the darkness about him. Something fell heavily. In the silence following the shots he shook his head groggily. Blood was stealing down his face. Somewhere a man was groaning and cursing, and something else was flopping convulsively, making a noise like a beheaded chicken.

Harrison groped for his flashlight, but it had fallen on the floor, and he could not find it. He rose gingerly and felt his way to the wall, poking his pistol ahead of him. His eyes had not accustomed themselves to the sudden darkness, and his head swam from the effects of that blow, but a faint light patch marked the window and he guided his steps by that. Presently his hand felt the switch. It had been thrown, and the door beside it was closed. He turned and placed his back to the wall, lifted his smoking gun, and turned on the switch.

He blinked as light flooded the room. No menacing figure skulked before him. But he was the only man on his feet. Three figures sprawled on the floor now instead of one. Ahmed lay beside the couch where he had been sitting, and Bissett sprawled across his legs. The Arab lay quite still, but the newspaper man was half supporting himself on his elbow; when he lifted his head, there was a trickle of blood down his face.

Crash! It was the shattering tinkle of the window pane which warned Harrison. He ducked, instinctively, and something whirred past his ear and thudded into the wall. He did not fire blindly at the broken window. Ripping the door open, he lunged out, gun lifted, his mood too berserk to care that he was outlined against the lighted doorway. He dashed around the corner of the bedroom, just in time to see something vague and shadowy vanish over the edge of the roof. He rushed over there, tripping over a pot that contained no palm tree, and sprawled headlong.

Hauling himself to his feet, he rushed to the parapet. From that point the fire-escape led down. But his fall had given the fugitive time to escape. The ladder descended into an alley, and just as he looked down, he saw the weighted end quivering upward. As he glared, undecided, three jets of flame spat up at him from the black shadows below; with the crash of the reports lead sang past his ears and splattered on the brick parapet. He gave back, suddenly. It would be suicide to try to descend that ladder with three gunmen potting at him from below. He fired back once and crouched down behind the parapet. When he raised his head, there was no sound or movement in the alley below.

He rose and strode back to the bedroom. Bissett was up, tottering dizzily, while he tried to wipe the blood off his face.

"What the devil happened?" he demanded groggily. "The lights went out—somebody started shooting—I'm shot! My head's bleeding!"

Harrison examined the wound. On his right temple, just at the line of the hair, was a short, shallow, ploughing cut.

"That's not a bullet wound," grunted the detective.

"Then somebody hit me with something!"

"Evidently."

"But why slug me?" clamored the reporter. "I wasn't doing anything—I was just an innocent bystander—"

"You were between me and the door," Harrison pointed out. "That fellow wanted the paper I'd found. He got it, too."

"What's the matter with Ahmed?" asked Bissett uneasily.

Harrison bent and investigated briefly.

"Shot through the heart." The telephone tinkled suddenly. Harrison picked it up. The quavering voice of the Japanese clerk timidly asked if all was well.

"Everything's okay," Harrison assured him. "That is, as far as you're concerned. If any of the people in the building ask what's going on, tell them Steve Harrison's up here."

He set the phone down, remarking: "That's the difference between white people and Orientals. In a white apartment house all this shooting would have that roof and corridor crowded by this time. Orientals lock their doors and stay close till they know what's going on."

He bent over Ahmed again, noting that the Arab's coat lapel was burned by the flash of the gun that had killed him.

"He must have been the one that slugged me," muttered Harrison. "You were watching him. Was it Ahmed who turned out the light?"

"I don't know. When you yelled and swung toward the window, I swung too. The next thing I knew the lights were out and something gave me a clip that made me see a million stars."

"Ahmed could have reached the light switch without getting up," said Harrison. "If he grabbed the note, he ought to have it in his hand."

But a thorough search failed to reveal the note, and Harrison noticed something else—a blue welt on the Arab's jaw that had not been there before.

"The devil! Did you hit out in the dark, Bissett?"

"Not me! I was down and out before I knew what hit me!" Harrison scratched his head angrily.

"Somebody might have reached in out of the dark and turned that light off, slugged you and Ahmed, and me, one after the other and grabbed that note out of my hand—but if that was so, how is it that Ahmed stopped one of my bullets? I held high. If he'd been on the floor the bullet would have passed over him. It must have been Ahmed who attacked me—but where's the note? Did that Chinaman duck in here and grab it? And if he did, how did he manage to get back to that window—"

Remembering something, Harrison turned and stepped over to the wall opposite the window. He wrenched something from the wall, and weighed it in his palm.

"What Chinaman?" demanded Bissett. "Where'd that knife come from?"

"It was thrown at me through the window," answered Harrison. "Didn't you see that Chinaman leering in, just before the lights went out?"

"No. Didn't have time to see anything. That another Chinese knife?"

Harrison nodded, laying the weapon on the writing desk. It was a heavy weapon, with a straight, double-edged blade and a weighted handle.

"The only thing I can see," said Harrison, "is that Ahmed jerked off the switch, slugged you, jerked the paper out of my hand, and got shot, and then somebody—a Chinaman maybe—ducked in here in the dark and snatched the note out of his hand. That's pretty farfetched. If that's so, how did he get that bruise on the jaw? He was shot before the unknown got the note. And even a Chinaman can't see in the dark."

"What was in the note?" asked Bissett.

"Zaida evidently started it, for Ahmed, then changed her mind and wrote something else. It implicates Joe Lepstein," said Harrison.

"Who the devil's that?"

"Kratz's partner." He took up the phone and dialed a number. "Mrs. De Kosa's boarding house," he explained. "Kratz and Lepstein both lived there."

"You know everything about everybody on River Street, don't you?" remarked Bissett curiously.

"Not by a hell of a lot. But I try to keep up with their surface movements, so to speak.

"This Mrs. De Kosa? Okay. This is Steve Harrison. I want to speak—yes, yes! I know it's an ungodly hour to drag an honest woman out of bed, but it can't be helped. I want to speak to Joe Lepstein. What? Oh, isn't there, eh? When did you see him last? When did you see Kratz last? Well, all right."

He set down the phone.

"The landlady says she hasn't seen Lepstein since dinner; says Kratz pulled out shortly after dinner, and Lepstein left soon after Kratz."

"What do you infer?"

"I don't know. We have these facts to go on: Kratz, Zaida and one other were in China Alley. Kratz was killed, and Zaida saw the murder done."

"Then you don't think Zaida did it?"

"No, I don't. The same man who killed her, killed Kratz."

"But I thought Ahmed—"

"Ahmed might have killed them both. But Zaida wouldn't have called on him for help if she'd known he was the murderer. Damn it, I'd believe Ahmed's yarn but for one thing: he was lying about having been knocked out. Then it must have been he who made the attack on me. How else did he get shot? The only thing I can see is that he and Lepstein, or whoever killed Kratz, were working together, and he killed Zaida to close her mouth."

"Maybe she killed Kratz, and Lepstein had her killed in revenge."

Harrison laughed. "You don't know Kratz. He and Lepstein were rogues of the same stripe, and they worked together. But there was no love lost between them. Well, I'm reserving judgment until I collect some more evidence."

"What are you going to do now?"

"Going to call up the station. Three corpses in a night. That's pretty bad, even for River Street. Then I'm going to drop in at the station and see what the fingerprint boys have found. Then I'm going to call at the offices of Kratz & Lepstein."

"And I'm going to get this gash sewed up and drink a gallon of coffee," announced Bissett. "Trailing you is a tough game. Man, don't you ever sleep?"

"Sometimes—when I get the time. You can get sewed up at the police station."

"Nix. I can't wait that long. I know a sawbones a few blocks down the street. Saw his sign today. You've got a sizable knot on your dome yourself, but I don't suppose a little thing like that bothers you."

"I've had worse knots," grunted Harrison, spinning the dial.

"I'm going," said Bissett, picking up his hat. "I'll come on to the station when I get through, and meet you there."

Chapter .3.

After Bissett's footsteps had faded down the corridor, Harrison began scanning the knife that had been hurled at him through the window. He had seen knives like those—imbedded in the bodies of men found dead under wharves and in winding back alleys. The weapon proclaimed the nature of its owner; a hatchet-man had flung that knife at him. He glanced at the skewer-like dagger he had pulled out of Zaida's breast and laid on the writing desk. He remembered the square, yellow face at the window. He sensed behind this mystery a yellow hand—the shadowy, mysterious hand of the cryptic Celestial. But who? He drew from an inner pocket the clipping he had found in the billfold of the dead Kratz, re-read it.

He laid it down suddenly, and as quickly he rose, drawing his pistol. He stood perfectly still, hardly breathing. He was not sure what he had heard, or that he had heard anything. But a man-hunter, like any beast of prey, develops certain instincts latent in the ordinary man; and his mysterious instincts warned him that peril was close about him, was creeping, slinking nearer on stealthy feet. The door to the roof was closed. He stepped back quickly to be out of range of the broken window, at the same time turning so he could watch the drawing-room door that opened on the corridor.

Then he heard a stealthy padding of feet on the roof. Harrison crouched, gun gleaming bluely in his big fist. A choking cry gurgled outside the door, and there was the sound of a heavy body falling. Something thrashed about, and then a strangled gasping began. Harrison stepped quickly to the door, switched off the light, and opened the door a crack. As soon as his eyes became accustomed to the starlight he saw a bulky figure lying before the door. Gradually this figure assumed the shape of a man, lying on his back; Harrison could make out that the arms were thrown back as if frozen in the throes of a convulsion, the head bent back at an unnatural angle.

"What the hell?" he muttered. The events of this night were turning into a nightmare. He scanned the potted palms. They were outlined against the stars, and if anyone was behind them, he was lying flat. With sudden decision he lifted his flashlight and directed a beam through the crack of the door, drawing aside out of line of a possible shot. No shot came. In the circle of light he saw the prostrate man was a Chinaman; his head was bent back so that his chin tilted upward; his lips were drawn back from fang-like teeth in a frozen snarl; his eyes were rolled back until only the whites were visible. The light played over the palms and disclosed no lurking foe. Harrison stepped to the broken window and flashed his light through it. That side of the roof was empty of human occupancy.

He stepped back to the door, turned off the light and stepped out, gun ready. Only the motionless figure on the roof met his sight.

"Now who in the hell killed him?" he wondered, turning on the light again and bending down toward the figure—the sudden roll of the eyes and the flame in them did not warn him in time, for simultaneously the gun was knocked from his hand and before he could move, ten iron fingers locked crushingly on his throat.

The flashlight flew from his hands as he caught at the great wrists, and went out as the men rolled over and over on the roof, caroming into the palm-pots.

Lights were flashing before Harrison's eyes; the stars, which he glimpsed dizzily in his revolutions, were dim and red as blood. That iron grip, the grip of the Chinese strangler, had come so near to killing him with the first clutch, that for a moment he could only tear blindly at the huge wrists, thick with corded muscles. Only his powerful neck muscles saved him. And then, even as he was slipping into unconsciousness, he released the wrists, groped for and found the little finger of each crushing hand. Each finger was sunk deeply into his neck, but he thrust the index finger of each hand under the little finger, and bent it fiercely backward. It was like tearing away the deeply imbedded talons of a grizzly. Slowly, reluctantly they came away—and then Harrison was free, and wind rushed back into his tortured gullet as he gulped deep.

He whirled over on his back as the strangler lunged for a fresh hold, and met the hurtling bulk with both legs lashing out. His heels rammed hard into the barrel-like breast, and the giant Chinaman reeled backward. Harrison, rising slowly, was coming up from his knee as the Chinaman charged in again. Harrison saw the gigantic brute looming over him, eyes and teeth gleaming in the starlight, great arms spread wide—and between those arms Harrison lunged, driving his heavy fist with all the power of his thick forearm and corded triceps and brawny shoulder, and backed by the lifting lunge of his thighs and knotted calves. Full beneath that jutting jaw Harrison's great fist crashed. The blow might have felled an ox; the giant was lifted clear of the roof, shot backward half a dozen feet and measured his length with an impact which seemed to shake the building.

Harrison himself staggered and went to his knees from the force of that terrible blow. To his amazement, the Chinaman staggered slowly to his feet. His jaw hung broken, and foam dripped from his lips; he rocked drunkenly.

"Hell's fire!" Harrison swore thickly. "The brute's not human!"

He rose stiffly, feeling as if his limbs were weighted with lead. Blood was streaming down his breast from his torn throat.

"One more ought to do the job," he muttered, and moved toward his antagonist, head sunk, fists clenched, unconsciously assuming a boxer's pose. With an incoherent cry the Chinaman gave back; he turned suddenly and fled toward the fire escape. Harrison plunged after him, but the manhandling he had received had taken more out of him than he realized. Before he could reach the wall, the Chinaman was fleeing down the escape, and when

Harrison looked down, it was to see him dropping from tier to tier like a great ape. He dropped a full ten feet into the alley and vanished. Somewhere a police siren was screaming.

Harrison turned and groped his way back to the room. He turned on the light, and when it streamed through the door onto the roof, he found his flashlight and pistol. A few moments later feet stormed up the stairs, and Hoolihan banged on the drawing-room door.

"Harrison! Are you in there? Harrison—" he ceased as the door opened and Harrison stood before them, hatless, disheveled, blood dried on his face, and oozing from cuts made by talon-like fingernails on his neck. Beyond them the police saw the corpses of Zaida and Ahmed where they lay.

Hoolihan swore.

"By the Saints, when a call comes from River Street, I know it'll be something bloody and grisly! And only on River Street would you be seein' a picture like this! What's happened? The clerk below is in fear of his life. He swears you've been up here all night, fighting and shooting and killing each other."

"Nothing much," said Harrison, his reticence upon him. "I'm up to my neck in a mystery I can't make heads nor tails of—but that's nothing new."

During the ride to the station—which he made in his own car—Harrison spoke little to Hoolihan who rode with him. He was still smarting from remembering how easily he had been taken in by that oldest trick of the hatchet-men.

"What did the fingerprint men find?" he asked presently.

"No prints on the dagger hilt. Evidently the killer wore gloves. Prints on the cigar-case, though. We compared them with all the prints you've given us of River Street characters—how the devil do you get all those prints from people who have no police record?"

"You'd be surprised to find out—and so would they," was Harrison's cryptic reply. "Well, did they match?"

"Yes. The fingerprints on the cigar-case were those of Joseph Lepstein, Jelner Kratz' partner."

Bissett met them at the station, and he stared at Harrison's appearance.

"What the devil happened to you?"

"One of our Chinese friends came back after you left. How long have you been here?"

"Just a little while. It took longer to sew up that gash than I thought. What are you going to do now?"

"Go home and change my clothes, and get a little sleep. If you want more dope, meet me at Kratz & Lepstein's offices in the morning—hell, it's nearly morning now. Well, meet me there at nine o'clock."

Chapter .4.

As Harrison met Bissett at the appointed time, the reporter hailed him with: "Before we go up there, tell me: who do you think killed Kratz?"

"I know it wasn't Ahmed," replied Harrison. "At least, Ahmed didn't kill Zaida. And I didn't kill Ahmed. The autopsy showed he'd been slugged with a sandbag; that leaves no external bruises, but causes concussion of the brain. And the slug in his heart was a .44. I pack a .45. I was back over at Zaida's apartment this morning, and found three holes in the walls where my bullets went. I'm glad I didn't kill him, now that I know he was telling the truth all the time."

The reporter's eyes gleamed.

"Well, say! The chief told me Lepstein's fingerprints were on the cigar-case. And Zaida mentioned Lepstein in the note, you said. That just about proves Lepstein did the killing, doesn't it?"

"Looks that way," admitted Harrison. "But the Chinese fit in somewhere."

"Well, listen!" exclaimed Bissett. "Maybe this Lepstein egg hired them! Maybe a Chinaman did the killing—gloves on his hands—and Lepstein picked up the cigar-case—why, God knows—and left his prints on it. Then for some reason he learned that Zaida had seen the murder, and sent a man to do for her— maybe he did it himself! Like Ahmed said! They were hiding all around that bedroom, and when you found that note implicating

Lepstein, they heard you talking about it—reached in at the door when we were all looking toward the window—snapped off the light—slugged me—shot Ahmed—grabbed the note from you—and beat it."

"That sounds reasonable," admitted Harrison. "But why did one of them come back and try for me later?"

"Something in the apartment he wanted, maybe."

"I don't think so. I got this in the morning's mail." He displayed it—a square of parchment with a curious symbol upon it. "The envelope had a River Street station postmark."

"But what does it mean?"

"It's the Flower of Death. A number of tongs use it, so there's no tracing it down to any one tong. It means some gang of Chinese are out to get me."

"The hell you say!" Bissett's eyes were wide and he was rather pale. "Say, this will make a story, if I ever live to write it! 'Sleuth Menaced By Celestial Murder Society While On Trail Of Triple-Killer'! What are you going to do now?"

"Let's have a look at the offices of Messrs. Kratz & Lepstein," answered Harrison.

The office girl who presided over the dingy outer office of Kratz & Lepstein, Attorneys at Law, stared at Harrison with apprehension. The mere sight of the detective was enough to rouse uneasy speculation in River Street consciences.

"No, Mr. Harrison, Mr. Lepstein isn't down yet. I haven't seen him or Mr. Kratz either since we shut up the offices yesterday evening at six o'clock, like always. They're usually down earlier than this."

"Mr. Kratz won't be down," grunted Harrison. "Somebody knifed him in China Alley last night. And I've got a hunch Mr. Lepstein won't be down either. We've got to look through their offices, Miss Pulisky."

"Am I saying no, Mr. Harrison?" Miss Pulisky's English skidded slightly in her perturbation. "Going right ahead, Mr. Harrison. But I ain't got no keys for the desks."

"I'll attend to that." Harrison strode into the inner room which had served as sanctum for Messrs. Kratz and Lepstein. Two huge roll-top desks stood on opposite sides of the room from each other, and a squat iron safe sat against the wall between them. Miss Pulisky voiced a harried yelp.

"We've been robbed!" she shrilled. "Look at the papers—all over the floor!"

The safe stood open, and the desks were in a similar condition. The floor was littered with papers, and bits of papers, and a coal scuttle was partly filled with charred fragments.

"Call a cop!" said Miss Pulisky wildly. "I just got here! I'd just hung up my hat when you gents came in—I hadn't been in here at all—"

"Which desk was Lepstein's?" Harrison demanded. When Miss Pulisky designated the one, he ran an expert hand over the lock; then stepped over to the other desk and duplicated the feat.

"Did anybody have the keys to these desks except Kratz and Lepstein?"

"No, Mr. Harrison. Each one had his key to his own desk, and I don't believe there were any more keys."

"And Lepstein's desk was unlocked, while Kratz's was forced."

He made a quick circuit of the doors and windows, while Miss Pulisky stood in nervous demoralization in the middle of the floor, and Bissett rummaged vaguely through the debris on the floor.

Harrison returned, and said: "No locks have been forced. That safe was blown. This is bound to be Lepstein's work. Whoever made this mess had a key that would let him into the offices, and one that let him into Lepstein's desk, and the combination of the safe, but he had to force Kratz's desk. Who could that have been but Lepstein?"

"But why?" asked Bissett.

"Suppose he'd done something that made him want to duck? Suppose he came here and—was there any money in the safe, Miss Pulisky?"

"They always kept a few hundred dollars there—when they had any," replied the agitated office girl.

"Lepstein came back here, say, destroyed all the incriminating papers he could find—"

"What do you mean, incriminating?"

"Well, unless I miss my guess, both of them were pretty deep in the blackmail racket."

"Well, if Lepstein did bump Kratz off—"

"Oi!" palpitated Miss Pulisky. "Then I'm out of a job!"

Harrison turned and scanned her keenly.

"Did Lepstein and Kratz get along together?"

"Like a cat with a dog they got along! Always they fought— sometimes they hollered so loud I couldn't help but hear, out in the office—"

"With your ear glued to the keyhole," grunted Harrison. "What did they fight about?"

"Well, everything mostly. But the last few days it was the ruby."

"Eh? What ruby?"

Bissett, pricking up his ears, quit poking among the littered papers and came over to join the conclave.

"Well, Lepstein accused Kratz of holding out on him. I don't know anything about it. But only yesterday Mr. Kratz hollered; 'I don't know what you're talking about. I ain't holding out nothing on you, you—' Only I'm too much of a lady to repeat what he called Mr. Lepstein, Mr. Harrison. And Mr. Lepstein hollered just as loud: 'You're a liar! I know you twisted that ruby out of him, and you ain't give me my cut. Are we partners or ain't we?' And Mr. Kratz said: 'You're crazy—and quit yelling like a hyena—do you want everybody on River Street to know our business?' That's all I could hear, because they quit hollering so loud then."

"Hmmm!" Harrison turned toward the mess of papers on the floor.

"I ain't mixed up in nothing, Mr. Harrison," quavered Miss Pulisky. "I just work for a salary—"

"Don't get the jitters, Miss Pulisky," Harrison reassured her. "I'm not after you. You haven't done anything—that is, anything that I can prove."

"Thank you, Mr. Harrison," she answered somewhat groggily.

Harrison bent over the heap and raked through them.

"They must have been blackmailing half of River Street," he growled, glancing at the papers. "Nothing particularly incriminating here, but too many different names jotted on to be legitimate business. But here is something!"

It was a note he had picked out of the heap, sticking half out of an unsealed envelope on which was written: "Kratz." Bissett read it over his shoulder:

Kratz:
I must see you. I have gone as far as I can. Meet me in China Alley at eleven-thirty tonight if you value your filthy life.

"And Kratz was killed at twelve! The first note said The Purple Cat, at eleven, didn't it, Harrison? Why should she change the time and place?"

Harrison thrust the note back into the envelope without comment.

"I'm going over to The Purple Cat."

They drove over in Harrison's automobile.

Harrison drew aside the proprietor—a swarthy Levantine.

"Tony, was Zaida Lopez here last night?"

"Sure, Mr. Harrison. She came in a few minutes until eleven and sat for half an hour in the back room. She told me she was going to meet Jelner Kratz. I saw him go past when she'd been here nearly half an hour, and he didn't come in. He went right on past. I went back and told her, and she left, too. I think she went following him. I didn't see either of them again."

"All right." Harrison led the way to the street.

As they drove along the street, Bissett asked: "How do you dope it out?"

"Well, according to the evidence, it looks like this: Zaida wrote a note to Kratz, asking a meeting in China Alley, at eleven-thirty. He got there before she did. Somebody—apparently Lepstein, was there too, and killed him. Zaida saw it done and fled in a panic. Then Lepstein went back to his office and took or destroyed such papers as he didn't want found, took the money in the safe, and beat it."

"But why did Zaida come and sit in The Purple Cat for half an hour, and tell Tony she was going to meet Kratz there, if the rendezvous was China Alley?"

"There are links missing, all right," admitted Harrison. "The job now is to find the maid, and Lepstein."

"How are you going to do that?"

"That's one of the secrets I can't give you—yet," grunted Harrison.

"Okay," agreed Bissett. "I'll see if I can find him, myself."

On his way back to the station, alone, Harrison stopped in a certain small establishment where curios were sold. To the imperturbable Celestial presiding over it, he said: "Joe Lepstein's hiding somewhere in River Street, I believe, Weng; find him."

The Chinaman nodded assent. Harrison stepped to a phone and called the station: "Anything new?"

The chief's voice came back over the wires: "A little. We just found Selda Mendez. Floating under a wharf in the river. She'd been stabbed."

Chapter .5.

Harrison, in his room, spread three notes before him and with a magnifying glass he carefully studied the writing. There was no doubt about it. One of the notes was genuine; of the other two, one was an undoubted forgery, and by implication, so was the other. The note found in Selda's writing desk, the one designating The Purple Cat as a rendezvous, was genuine. The name "Kratz" written on the envelope containing the note naming China Alley, was undoubtedly in Zaida Lopez's hand, but the note itself was a forgery—clever, but unmistakable to a trained eye. Harrison reflected that it was almost impossible for a right-handed person to copy a left-handed one's scrawl. He examined the note sent to him, warning him of the crime to be committed. At first glance the writing did not seem at all like the forged note. But close examination showed points in common.

There was but one construction to put upon the matter. Zaida, probably driven to desperation by his insatiate demands, had appointed a meeting place with him. She had been made the innocent bait of the trap that locked on the blackmailer. Someone had taken the real letter out of the envelope and substituted the forged note. Who should that have been but the maid? Yet if she had done this, why had she written Harrison the warning? He wondered if the maid had been one of Kratz's victims. He did not speculate on why Kratz had been blackmailing Zaida. A woman like that had spots in her past that were shady enough.

Harrison leaned back and rolled a cigarette. Perhaps in the smoke he was seeing a subtle killer who veiled himself in shadows and obscurity, hiding his tracks with corpses. A discreet knock sounded at the door.

Harrison turned to face the door, his hand on his revolver.

"Come in!"

The door opened and Weng bowed there, hands concealed in his wide sleeves.

"Any luck, Weng?"

"Lepstein hides in a house that opens upon the Alley of Bats. I can take you there, at once."

"Good!" Harrison rose, donned his coat, and instinctively touched the heavy .45 buckled beneath it. He picked up his hat. "Let's go!"

Weng was not a stool-pigeon, nor was he a member of any force or agency for enforcing law. But he and his associates had helped Harrison more than once.

It was nearing midnight when they turned off River Street into a narrow alley that meandered toward the river. Down this Harrison groped, guided by Weng's touch. Behind them a street lamp cast a glow for a short space; then they made a turn and plunged into absolute blackness. Ahead of them Harrison heard water lapping at rotting piles. The alley ended in a tangle of abandoned wharves.

"Where is this house, Weng?" Harrison muttered. There was no answer. Harrison groped for his companion, but his hand met only space. Something brushed lightly against him from an unexpected quarter. Suddenly his primitive instincts warned him of lurking peril. He recoiled with an oath, and felt the darkness come to sudden life about him. Even as he caught at his gun-butt, his wrist was locked in an iron wrestling grip. A press of bodies surged against him, fingers clawed at his limbs. He lashed out with his left, felt his fist connect and a man fall away from the impact. He drove his knee into a belly and another went down. But they were swarming over him, swamping him with numbers. He lashed out again and missed, almost throwing his arm out of the socket with the violence of the wasted blow. He lowered his head and butted a man over; the fellow went down like a ten-pin, with a tortured gasp. Harrison wrenched savagely to free his gun-arm, or to reach the pistol with his left hand. But the leverage of the hold resisted all the strength of his thick forearm and heavy biceps. With his left fist he mercilessly battered the man who held his arm, and under those punishing blows, he felt the grip weakening. But before he could quite tear free, a net with tough, unbreakable strands fell over his shoulders, entangling his left arm.

In an instant half a dozen hands grasped each arm, wrenching them back behind him. Fingers groped in his pockets, dragging forth his handcuffs. He cursed fervently as they were snapped on his wrists. His gun was drawn from its scabbard. Somebody tripped him and somebody pushed him and he measured his length on the ground. Cords were knotted about his ankles. A blindfold and a gag were added to his other bonds. He felt himself rolled onto something that felt like a bamboo litter. It was lifted, and silence followed, broken only by the soft slap-pad of sandaled feet.

Harrison quickly lost all sense of direction. But from the faint noises, and the tilt of his litter, sometimes up, sometimes down, more often level, he believed he was being carried through a succession of alleys, cellars and obscure courts. He heard a door open, and felt a light through his blindfold. Then the sandals of his captors rustled over what could have been only thick rugs, and another door opened. When the door had closed behind them, the litter-bearers came to a halt. Harrison was tilted off the litter to sway precariously on his bound legs until he was thrust into a chair. Then the blindfold was pulled away.

He was in a room whose walls were covered by black velvet hangings where gold dragons writhed. Pagoda-shaped lanterns cast a soft glow over the thick rich rugs that hid the floor. From before a great silver Buddha blue incense smoke spiraled thinly upward. But Harrison's gaze was fixed on the figure which sat cross-legged on a silken divan before him. A figure clad in a black silk robe on which dragons were worked in gilt and scarlet. A big man, with a square, immobile face like an ancient Chinese war-mask. Beside him stood a half-naked giant, on whose huge torso and massive arms the muscles stood out in knots. He stood like a bronze statue, one great hand grasping the hilt of a huge curved sword that rested over his gigantic shoulder. An executioner of Old China! But there was no need to be surprized; for this was River Street, a realm of horror and fascination and mystery, a patch of the incredible Orient transplanted into an Occidental setting, from which it was shut off by walls of inscrutable silence. Harrison knew that he was as much in the Orient now as if he sat in some secret temple or pagoda or palace in Peiping or Calcutta or Teheran.

The man on the divan wore the coral button of a Manchu mandarin, and that identified him to the detective. Harrison knew him—knew him for an almost mythical character, who moved gigantically in the shadows, seldom seen, pulling strings on which yellow men danced like puppets—strings which reached out of River Street into strange places, and across oceans. A man who lived like a feudal lord, enforcing his own laws, decreeing his own dooms, surrounded by mystery that not even Harrison had ever penetrated.

"Ti Woon!" said the detective slowly.

The coral button nodded.

"Ti Woon, foreign devil detective." There was only a hint of the flowery Celestial style of speech in Ti Woon's perfect English. He spoke without a trace of an accent. Men said he had been educated in the great universities of Europe and America.

"So you sent me the Flower of Oblivion?"

"Obviously."

"And Weng betrayed me! I trusted him."

"Weng was given his command, and obeyed as he was obliged to do," answered the Mandarin. "Like many other men, he owes secret allegiance to Ti Woon."

"But what's this all about?" demanded Harrison. "You and I never clashed before."

"Blood must pay for blood."

"What do you mean?"

"You killed the Arab wrestler, Ahmed. He saved my life once on a time. He was under the protection of the Ti Woon Tong. You slew him. My servants saw the deed done."

"So it was your men on the roof, then?"

"Ahmed sent word to me that he was hastening to protect a friend who had called on him for aid. He desired my help. I sent three of my hatchet-men to the place he named—the apartment of the woman Zaida Lopez. They went upon the roof by way of the fire-escape. As they looked through the window, the lights went out, shots were fired, and when the lights came on again, you stood over Ahmed's body with a smoking revolver in your hand. My servants hurled a knife at you, and then hurried away to tell me what had occurred. But one turned back to slay you himself. That was unwisely done, but he is a man of few wits. You broke his jaw. But I have condemned you to death, and as a sign of that doom I sent you the Flower of Oblivion, according to the ancient custom of my people."

"I didn't kill Ahmed," said Harrison. "Somebody else did. Who, I don't know. Your men were all at the window, on one side of the room. A man could have been hiding on the other side, have reached his hand through the door and turned the light out. Did your men see who turned the light out?"

"No. But they saw you standing with a smoking pistol, and they heard the shots."

"Somebody else killed Ahmed. Somebody shot him in the dark, while I was shooting blindly. Somebody knocked him down as soon as the light was turned off, and then stuck a gun muzzle against his breast and killed him. Ahmed had seen the man who killed Zaida Lopez. He would have remembered what he looked like when his brain cleared. Ahmed was shot with a .44. All River Street knows I pack a .45."

Ti Woon struck a gong; a scholarly young man in horn-rimmed glasses entered and bowed deeply, with an attitude incongruous with his American dress. He looked familiar, but Harrison could not place him.

"Go and phone Chief Hoolihan," ordered Ti Woon. "Ask him what was the caliber of the gun that killed Ahmed."

The inscrutable one bowed himself out and Harrison hoped fervently that Hoolihan wouldn't get stubborn and refuse to answer the mysterious call.

"My servant is a reporter on *The Celestial Sun*, the Chinese paper published in River Street," said Ti Woon. "He is known to Hoolihan in his official capacity. Hoolihan will answer his question."

"So that's who he was," grunted Harrison. "Thought I recognized him, but couldn't place him. You have 'servants' in a lot of different places, don't you, Ti Woon?"

"Our society is widespread," answered Ti Woon.

Harrison sat staring in fascination at the glimmer of the great blue blade in the hands of the executioner. He noticed something else—a black, curiously shaped block of teakwood standing on the floor near him, with a basket-shaped receptacle beneath it. Into that basket, the detective knew, his head would tumble if Hoolihan did not give the Chinese the right answer.

The imperturbable reporter returned and bowed deeply.

"The white devil Hoolihan says that Ahmed was killed by a bullet of the .44 caliber."

"Summon the men who were on the roof."

The reporter took up a wand and struck a gong that hung close at hand. Presently three figures filed into the chamber, and stood in a row, bowing like automatons. One, the biggest, had his lower face and jaw swathed in bandages.

Ti Woon laid Harrison's Colt .45 on the divan before them.

"Look well and make no mistake. Is this the gun the detective held in his hand as he stood over the Arab?"

"Yes, honored master," chorused two of the figures, while the third, voiceless, bobbed his head in emphatic agreement.

"You have my leave to go." The figures backed out of the apartment, and Ti Woon spoke briefly to the Chinese reporter. "Unbind him."

In a few moments the detective stood up and stretched his limbs to revive circulation. He picked up his gun and holstered it. The executioner had vanished, taking his headsman's sword and block with him.

"Allow me to offer my profound apologies, Mr. Harrison," said Ti Woon.

"Forget it," grunted Harrison, too much accustomed to River Street ways to hold resentment. "If you want to help, you might aid me in looking for Joe Lepstein."

"You think it was he who killed Kratz?"

"Looks like it."

"I had had dealings with Kratz," said Ti Woon. "He had some information he wished to sell me."

"That explains the Chinamen Miss Pulisky mentioned," said Harrison.

"It was information I wished to buy. Three months ago my brother's son, Wu Shun, was murdered in Shanghai." Harrison looked up with quickened interest, remembering the clipping he had found in Kratz's billfold. "His murderer robbed him of the great jewel, once the property of the Ming kings, called the Dragon's Heart. My brother, the Mandarin Tang, sought the slayer in vain.

"A week ago Kratz came to me. He said he knew who the man was; that the murderer had come to America, and that for a price he would name him. I told him to name his price, but he was blind with avarice. I think he feared lest he might name a price lower than the highest price I would be willing to pay. He wished me to name the price, so he could demand more."

"Likely was bleeding the murderer for the last penny he had before selling him out to you," grunted Harrison. "That would be Kratz's way."

"Perhaps. He swore he knew nothing of the Dragon's Heart, only the name of the murderer."

"Was Lepstein the murderer?"

"Possibly. Three months ago he was out of the city, for several weeks. Where he went I don't know. He said New York, but he might have been lying.

"We will find Lepstein if he is in the city," said Ti Woon grimly. "Remain at my house for a while, Mr. Harrison. Before dawn my men will have located him." He gave orders that sent a hundred men combing the city.

Before dawn a Chinese was standing before Ti Woon, bowing deeply.

"Honored master, we have found Joseph Lepstein. He is hiding in the basement of a deserted warehouse by the river. We have thrown a cordon about the house."

"Very well. Mr. Harrison will command you. Let no man dare take the law into his own hands."

In the misty darkness before dawn they approached the house, looming dimly gigantic against the black reaches of the shadowy river. They told him a man had gone in; none had come out. A window had been forced and Harrison entered stealthily, followed by a dozen lean, alert hatchet-men. He groped his way through empty storerooms, went down a stair. He heard a sudden rush of feet, the sound of a blow. A voice cried out in sudden agony. Harrison rushed into a room, just in time to see a shadowy figure vanish through a door that opened on a stair on the other side of the room. He saw at a glance that a camp cot stood near the wall; there was a camp chair, a folding table, piles of tins containing food. An oil lamp lit the room. Evidently it was a hideout kept in reserve for a long time. A figure writhed on the floor in its own blood. The man was Lepstein, and he had been stabbed in the back.

The immobile Chinese ringed them as Harrison bent over him.

"Who knifed you, Lepstein?"

The man was slender, fragile.

"I don't know!" he gasped. "He struck from behind. The ruby! The Dragon's Heart! Kratz had it—kept it in a cigar in his cigar-case. I was following him that night—look under the left foot of the camp cot."

Harrison raised it, and a tiny cavity was revealed, wherein something glowed and shimmered.

"The Dragon's Heart!" Lepstein gasped. "Kratz took it from a man he was blackmailing—I had to have it—I'd have killed Kratz for it if somebody else hadn't beaten me to it. I would have made my getaway—in a launch—tonight—" And he died.

A tall hatchet-man touched Harrison's arm respectfully.

"The man who slew him—he must be still in the building."

"Go search for him!"

"You will remain here—alone, with the ruby?"

"Yes. Go ahead."

Silently as phantoms they faded up the stairs, and Harrison stood weighing the jewel on his palm.

There sounded the footfalls of a man descending the stair, and Bissett burst into the room.

"So you beat me here after all!" he exclaimed breathlessly. "Who the devil's that—Lepstein?"

"Somebody else beat me here," said Harrison. "You wanted the dope. All right. Here's the way I dope it out. A man killed Wu Shun in Shanghai and stole the Dragon's Heart. He dodged Tang's hatchet-men and came to America. But he was broke, and he didn't dare sell the Dragon's Heart through a legitimate dealer. It was too well known.

"So he went to Kratz, and pawned the stone to him. Kratz had connections in Shanghai, though, and he learned of the killing of Wu Shun, recognized the stone, and started blackmailing the killer. He entered into negotiations with Ti Woon, meaning to sell out the killer to him, but in the meantime he was blackmailing the killer, getting back the money he loaned him on the gem, and trying to figure a way of getting him killed by the tong, without their knowing of his possession of the stone.

"Meantime, this killer was trying to devise a safe way to trap and kill Kratz. He had known Selda Mendez somewhere in the Orient, perhaps; anyway, he worked through her. Probably had her urge her mistress to have Kratz meet her somewhere. Zaida appointed a meeting time and place, but the killer substituted a false note, designating a different time and place. By chance Zaida followed Kratz. But Lepstein was trailing Kratz, knowing Kratz had a valuable jewel in his possession.

"The killer met Kratz and killed him in China Alley. Then he instantly left, not knowing Kratz carried the jewel with him. Lepstein came onto the scene a matter of minutes later, perhaps seconds later, and took the cigar out of the cigar-case, knowing it contained the jewel. He was seen by Zaida, who thought he had killed Kratz. She went back and sent for Ahmed. But Lepstein, terrified at what had happened, hurried back to their offices, stole the money out of the safe, destroyed a number of papers and went into hiding.

"Apparently the maid, having delivered the note to Ahmed, went to the killer's room and waited for him there, probably terrified by what had happened. The killer, learning that Zaida had seen the crime, and not knowing she suspected Lepstein, hurried to Zaida's apartment, slugged Ahmed and killed Zaida. He was there when I came—probably sneaked out on the roof and hid outside the room when I came in. He was there when I found the scrap of paper naming Lepstein. He thought I'd found something implicating him—by his real name—so he turned out the light, knocked Ahmed down, grabbed the paper away from me, and then while I was shooting like a blame fool, he went back to Ahmed and killed him. Afraid the Arab would recognize him.

"Later he went back to his room, found the maid there and killed her. He'd been trying to trace Lepstein, for he knew by this time that Lepstein had the ruby. He succeeded tonight, got in here and killed Lepstein, but didn't get the jewel. I got that."

"Hands up!" rasped a voice behind the detective.

Harrison did not turn. The .45 in his hand halted Bissett's sudden leap, checked the skewer-like dagger in his lifted hand.

"Easy, Bissett," cautioned the detective. "Whatever your name is."

"You knew, damn you!" snarled Bissett.

"I've suspected all along," admitted Harrison. "Ever since I looked at that gash on your head, up in Zaida's apartment. It didn't come from a blow. It was a cut by a gun-sight, pressed hard and drawn through the flesh. You had guts enough to do that to make your story real. I've seen too many wounds to be fooled."

"But you saw me on the street ahead of you when Kratz was killed," said Bissett.

"That puzzled me," answered Harrison. "But the same person who wrote that note to me killed Kratz. And you were the only one that alibi could do any good. Besides, Kratz wasn't killed at twelve. As soon as I touched him I knew he'd been dead at least a half hour. You made that yell yourself; I wanted to give you a chance to display your ventriloquism tonight. That's why I waited here with the Dragon's Heart."

Graveyard Rats

1. The Head From the Grave

Saul Wilkinson awoke suddenly, and lay in the darkness with beads of cold sweat clammy on his hands and face. He shuddered at the memory of the dream from which he had awakened. But horrible dreams were nothing uncommon. Grisly nightmares had haunted his sleep since early childhood. It was another fear that clutched his heart with icy fingers—fear of the sound that had roused him. It had been a furtive step—hands fumbling in the dark. And now a small scurrying sounded in the room—a rat running back and forth across the floor.

He groped under his pillow with trembling fingers. The house was still, but imagination peopled its darkness with shapes of horror. But it was not all imagination. A faint stir of air told him the door that gave on the broad hallway was open. He knew he had closed that door before he went to bed. And he knew it was not one of his brothers who had come so subtly to his room. In that fear-tense, hate-haunted household, no man came by night to his brother's room without first making himself known.

This was especially the case since an old feud had claimed the eldest brother four days since—John Wilkinson, shot down in the streets of the little hill-country town by Joel Middleton, who had escaped into the post oak grown hills, swearing still greater vengeance against the Wilkinsons.

All this flashed through Saul's mind as he drew the revolver from under his pillow. As he slid out of bed, the creak of the springs brought his heart into his throat, and he crouched there for a moment, holding his breath, and straining his eyes into the darkness. Richard was sleeping upstairs, and so was Harrison, the city detective Peter had brought out to hunt down Joel Middleton.

Peter's room was on the ground floor, but in another wing. A yell for help might awaken all three, but it would also bring a hail of lead at him, if Joel Middleton were crouching over there in the blackness. Saul knew this was his fight, and must be fought out alone, in the darkness he had always feared and hated. And all the time sounded that light, scampering patter of tiny feet, racing up and down, up and down . . . . . .

Crouching against the wall, cursing the pounding of his heart, cursing the patter of the scurrying rat, Saul fought to steady his quivering nerves. He was backed against the wall which formed the partition between his room and the hall. The windows were faint grey squares in the blackness, and he could dimly make out objects of furniture in all except one side of the room. Joel Middleton must be over there, crouching by the old fireplace, which was invisible in the darkness. But why was he waiting? And why was that accursed rat racing up and down before the fireplace, as if in a frenzy of fear and greed? Just so Saul had seen rats race up and down the floor of the meat-house, frantic to get at flesh suspended out of reach.

Noiselessly on his bare feet, Saul moved along the wall toward the door. If a man was in the room, he would presently be lined between himself and a window. But as he glided along the wall like a night-shirted ghost, no ominous bulk grew out of the darkness. He reached the door and closed it soundlessly, wincing at his nearness to the unrelieved blackness of the hall outside. But nothing happened. The only sounds were the wild beating of his heart, the loud ticking of the old clock on the mantelpiece—the maddening patter of the unseen rat. Saul clenched his teeth against the shrieking of his tortured nerves. Even in his growing terror he found time to wonder frantically why that rat ran up and down before the fireplace.

The tension became unbearable. The open door proved that Middleton, or someone—or *something*—had come into that room. Why would Middleton come save to kill? But why in God's name had he not struck already?

Saul's nerve snapped suddenly. The darkness was strangling him and those pattering rat-feet were red-hot hammers on his crumbling brain. He must have light, even though that light brought hot lead ripping through him. In stumbling haste he groped to the mantelpiece, fumbling for the lamp. And he cried out—a choked, horrible croak that could not have carried beyond his room. *For his hand, groping in the dark on the mantel, had touched the hair on a human scalp.*

A furious squeal sounded in the darkness at his feet and a sharp pain pierced his ankle, as the rat attacked him, as if he were an intruder seeking to rob it of some coveted object.

But Saul was hardly aware of the rodent as he kicked it away and reeled back, his brain a whirling turmoil. Matches and candles were on the table, and to it he lurched, his hands sweeping the dark and finding what he wanted. He lighted a candle and turned, gun lifted in a shaking hand. There was no living man in the room except himself. But his distended eyes focused themselves on the mantelpiece—and the object on it.

He stood frozen, his brain at first refusing to register what his eyes revealed. Then he croaked inhumanly and the gun crashed on the hearth as it slipped through his numb fingers. John Wilkinson was dead, with a bullet through his heart. It had been three days since Saul had seen his body nailed into the crude coffin and lowered into the grave in the old Wilkinson family graveyard. For three days the hard clay soil had baked in the hot sun above the coffined form of John Wilkinson. Yet from the mantel John Wilkinson's face leered at him—white and cold and dead.

It was no nightmare, no dream of madness. There on the mantelpiece rested John Wilkinson's severed head. And before the fireplace, up and down, up and down, scampered a creature with red eyes, that squeaked and squealed—a great grey rat, maddened by its failure to reach the flesh its ghoulish hunger craved.

Saul Wilkinson began to laugh—horrible, soul-shaking shrieks that mingled with the squealing of the grey ghoul. Saul's body rocked to and fro, and the laughter turned to insane weeping, that gave way in turn to hideous screams that echoed through the old house and brought the sleepers out of their sleep. They were the screams of a madman. The horror of what he had seen had blasted Saul Wilkinson's reason like a blown-out candle flame.

2. Madman's Hate

It was those screams which roused Steve Harrison, sleeping in an upstairs chamber. Before he was fully awake he was on his way down the unlighted stairs, pistol in one hand and flashlight in the other.

Down in the hallway he saw light streaming from under a closed door, and made for it. But another was before him. Just as Harrison reached the landing, he saw a figure rushing across the hall, and flashed his beam on it. It was Peter Wilkinson, tall and gaunt, with a poker in his hand. He yelled something incoherent, threw open the door and rushed in. Harrison heard him exclaim: "Saul! What's the matter? What are you looking at—" Then a terrible cry: *"My God!"* The poker clanged on the floor, and then the screams of the maniac rose to a crescendo of fury.

It was at this instant that Harrison reached the door and took in the scene with one startled glance. He saw two men in nightshirts grappling in the candlelight, while from the mantel a cold, dead, white face looked blindly down on them, and a grey rat ran in mad circles about their feet.

Into that scene of horror and madness Harrison propelled his powerful, thick-set body. Peter Wilkinson was in sore straits. He had dropped his poker and now, with blood streaming from a wound in his head, he was vainly striving to tear Saul's lean fingers from his throat.

The glare in Saul's eyes told Harrison the man was mad. Crooking one massive arm about the maniac's neck, he tore him loose from his victim with an exertion of sheer strength that not even the abnormal energy of insanity could resist. The madman's stringy muscles were like steel wires under the detective's hands, and Saul twisted about in his grasp, his teeth snapping beast-like for Harrison's bull-throat. The detective shoved the clawing, frothing fury away from him and smashed a fist to the madman's jaw. Saul crashed to the floor and lay still, eyes glazed and limbs quivering.

Peter reeled back against a table, purple-faced and gagging.

"Get cords, quick!" snapped Harrison, heaving the limp figure off the floor and letting it slump into a great armchair. "Tear that sheet in strips. We've got to tie him up before he comes to. Hell's fire!"

The rat had made a ravening attack on the senseless man's bare feet. Harrison kicked it away, but it squeaked furiously and came charging back with ghoulish persistence. Harrison crushed it under his foot, cutting short its maddened squeal.

Peter, gasping convulsively, thrust into the detective's hand the strips he had torn from the sheet, and Harrison bound the limp limbs with professional efficiency. In the midst of his task he looked up to see Richard, the youngest brother, standing in the doorway, his face like chalk.

"Richard!" choked Peter. "Look! My God! John's head!"

"I see!" Richard licked his lips. "But why are you tying up Saul?"

"He's crazy," snapped Harrison. "Get me some whiskey, will you?"

As Richard reached for a bottle on a curtained shelf, booted feet hit the porch outside, and a voice yelled: "Hey, there! Dick! What's wrong?"

"That's our neighbor, Jim Allison," muttered Peter.

He stepped to the door opposite the one that opened into the hall and turned the key in the ancient lock. That door opened upon a side porch. A tousle-headed man with his pants pulled on over his nightshirt came blundering in.

"What's the matter?" he demanded. "I heard somebody hollerin', and run over quick as I could. What you doin' to Saul—good God Almighty!"

He had seen the head on the mantel, and his face went ashen.

"Go get the marshal, Jim!" croaked Peter. "This is Joel Middleton's work!"

Allison hurried out, stumbling as he peered back over his shoulder in morbid fascination.

Harrison had managed to spill some liquor between Saul's livid lips. He handed the bottle to Peter and stepped to the mantel. He touched the grisly object, shivering slightly as he did so. His eyes narrowed suddenly.

"You think Middleton dug up your brother's grave and cut off his head?" he asked.

"Who else?" Peter stared blankly at him.

"Saul's mad. Madmen do strange things. Maybe Saul did this."

"No! No!" exclaimed Peter, shuddering. "Saul hasn't left the house all day. John's grave was undisturbed this morning, when I stopped by the old graveyard on my way to the farm. Saul was sane when he went to bed. It was seeing John's head that drove him mad. Joel Middleton has been here, to take this horrible revenge!" He sprang up suddenly, shrilling, "My God, he may still be hiding in the house somewhere!"

"We'll search it," snapped Harrison. "Richard, you stay here with Saul. You might come with me, Peter."

In the hall outside the detective directed a beam of light on the heavy front door. The key was turned in the massive lock. He turned and strode down the hall, asking: "Which door is furthest from any sleeping chamber?"

"The back kitchen door!" Peter answered, and led the way. A few moments later they were standing before it. It stood partly open, framing a crack of starlit sky.

"He must have come and gone this way," muttered Harrison. "You're sure this door was locked?"

"I locked all outer doors myself," asserted Peter. "Look at those scratches on the outer side! And there's the key lying on the floor inside."

"Old-fashioned lock," grunted Harrison. "A man could work the key out with a wire from the outer side and force the lock easily. And this is the logical lock to force, because the noise of breaking it wouldn't likely be heard by anybody in the house."

He stepped out onto the deep back porch. The broad backyard was without trees or brushes, separated by a barbed-wire fence from a pasture lot, which ran to a wood-lot thickly grown with post oaks, part of the woods which hemmed in the village of Lost Knob on all sides.

Peter stared toward that woodland, a low, black rampart in the faint starlight, and he shivered.

"He's out there, somewhere!" he whispered. "I never suspected he'd dare strike at us in our own house. I brought you here to hunt him down. I never thought we'd need you to protect us!"

Without replying Harrison stepped down into the yard. Peter cringed back from the starlight, and remained crouching at the edge of the porch.

Harrison crossed the narrow pasture and paused at the ancient rail fence which separated it from the woods. They were black as only post oak thickets can be. No rustle of leaves, no scrape of branches betrayed a lurking presence. If Joel Middleton had been there, he must have already sought refuge in the rugged hills that surrounded Lost Knob.

Harrison turned back toward the house. He had arrived at Lost Knob late the preceding evening. It was now somewhat past midnight. But the grisly news was spreading, even in the dead of night. The Wilkinson house stood at the western edge of the town, and the Allison house was the only one within a hundred yards of it. But Harrison saw lights springing up in distant windows.

Peter stood on the porch, head outthrust on his long, buzzard-like neck. "Find anything?" he called anxiously.

"Tracks wouldn't show on this hard-baked ground," grunted the detective. "Just what did you see when you ran into Saul's room?"

"Saul standing before the mantel-board, screaming with his mouth wide open," answered Peter. "When I saw—what he saw, I must have cried out and dropped the poker. Then Saul leaped on me like a wild beast."

"Was his door locked?"

"Closed, but not locked. The lock got broken accidentally a few days ago."

"One more question: has Middleton ever been in this house before?"

"Not to my knowledge," replied Peter, grimly. "Our families have hated each other for twenty-five years. Joel's the last of his name."

Harrison re-entered the house. Allison had returned with the marshal, McVey, a tall, taciturn man who plainly resented the detective's presence. Men were gathering on the side porch and in the yard. They talked in low mutters, except for Jim Allison, who was vociferous.

"This finishes Joel Middleton!" he proclaimed loudly. "Some folks sided with him when he killed John. I wonder what they think now? Diggin' up a dead man and cuttin' his head off! That's Injun work! I reckon folks won't wait for no jury to tell 'em what to do with Joel Middleton!"

"Better catch him before you start lynchin' him," grunted McVey. "Peter, I'm takin' Saul to the county seat."

Peter nodded mutely. Saul was recovering consciousness, but the mad glaze of his eyes was unaltered. Harrison spoke: "Suppose we go to the Wilkinson graveyard and see what we can find? We might be able to track Middleton from there."

"They brought you in here to do the job they didn't think I was good enough to do," snarled McVey. "All right. Go ahead and do it—alone. I'm takin' Saul to the county seat."

With the aid of his deputies he lifted the bound maniac and strode out. Neither Peter nor Richard offered to accompany him. A tall, gangling man stepped from among his fellows and awkwardly addressed Harrison: "What the marshal does is his own business, but all of us here are ready to help all we can, if you want to git a posse together and comb the country."

"Thanks, no." Harrison was unintentionally abrupt. "You can help me by all clearing out, right now. I'll work this thing out alone, in my own way, as the marshal suggested."

The men moved off at once, silent and resentful, and Jim Allison followed them, after a moment's hesitation. When all had gone Harrison closed the door and turned to Peter.

"Will you take me to the graveyard?"

Peter shuddered. "Isn't it a terrible risk? Middleton has shown he'll stop at nothing."

"Why should he?" Richard laughed savagely. His mouth was bitter, his eyes alive with harsh mockery, and lines of suffering were carven deep in his face.

"We never stopped hounding him," said he. "John cheated him out of his last bit of land—that's why Middleton killed him. For which you were devoutly thankful!"

"You're talking wild!" exclaimed Peter.

Richard laughed bitterly. "You old hypocrite! We're all beasts of prey, we Wilkinsons, like this thing!" He kicked the dead rat viciously. "We all hated each other. You're glad Saul's crazy! You're glad John's dead. Only me left now, and I have a heart disease. Oh, stare if you like! I'm no fool. I've seen you poring over Aaron's lines in *Titus Andronicus*:

> Oft have I digg'd up dead men from their graves,
> And set them upright at their dear friends' doors!

"You're mad yourself!" Peter sprang up, livid.

"Oh, am I?" Richard had lashed himself almost into a frenzy. "What proof have we that you didn't cut off John's head? You knew Saul was a neurotic, that a shock like that might drive him mad! And you visited the graveyard yesterday!"

Peter's contorted face was a mask of fury, then, with an effort of iron control, he relaxed and said quietly: "You are over-wrought, Richard."

"Saul and John hated you," snarled Richard. "I know why. It was because you wouldn't agree to leasing our farm on Wild River to that oil company. But for your stubbornness we might all be wealthy."

"You know why I wouldn't lease," snapped Peter. "Drilling there would ruin the agricultural value of the land—certain profit, not a risky gamble like oil."

"So you say," sneered Richard. "But suppose that's just a smoke screen? Suppose you dream of being the sole, surviving heir, and becoming an oil millionaire all by yourself, with no brothers to share with—"

Harrison broke in: "Are we going the chew the rag all night?"

"No!" Peter turned his back on his brother. "I'll take you to the graveyard. I'd rather face Joel Middleton in the night than listen to the ravings of this lunatic any longer."

"I'm not going," snarled Richard. "Out there in the black night there's too many chances for you to remove the remaining heir. I'll go and stay the rest of the night with Jim Allison."

He opened the door and vanished in the darkness.

Peter picked up the head and wrapped it in a cloth, shivering slightly as he did so.

"Did you notice how well preserved the face is?" he muttered. "One would think that after three days—come on. I'll take it and put it back in the grave where it belongs."

"I'll kick this dead rat outdoors," Harrison began, turning— and then stopped short. "The damned thing's gone!"

Peter Wilkinson paled as his eyes swept the empty floor.

"It was there!" he whispered. "It was dead. You smashed it! It couldn't come to life and run away."

"Well, what about it?" Harrison did not mean to waste time on this minor mystery.

Peter's eyes gleamed wearily in the candlelight.

"It was a graveyard rat!" he whispered. "I never saw one in an inhabited house, in town, before! The Indians used to tell strange tales about them! They said they were not beasts at all, but evil, cannibal demons, into which entered the spirits of wicked dead men, at whose corpses they gnawed!"

"Hell's fire!" Harrison snorted, blowing out the candle. But his flesh crawled. After all, a dead rat could not crawl away by itself.

3. The Feathered Shadow

Clouds had rolled across the stars. The air was hot and stifling. The narrow, rutty road that wound westward into the hills was atrocious. But Peter Wilkinson piloted his ancient Model T Ford skillfully, and the village was quickly lost to sight behind them. They passed no more houses. On each side the dense post oak thickets crowded close to the barbed-wire fences.

Peter broke the silence suddenly: "How came that rat into our house? They overrun the woods along the creeks, and swarm in every country graveyard in the hills. But I never saw one in the village before. It must have followed Joel Middleton when he brought the head—"

A lurch and a monotonous bumping brought a curse from Harrison. The car came to a stop with a grind of brakes.

"Flat," muttered Peter. "Won't take me long to change tires. You watch the woods. Joel Middleton might be hiding anywhere."

That seemed good advice. While Peter wrestled with rusty metal and stubborn rubber, Harrison stood between him and the nearest clump of trees, with his hand on his revolver. The night wind blew fitfully through the leaves, and once he thought he caught the gleam of tiny red eyes among the stems.

"That's got it," announced Peter. "We've wasted enough time on this job—"

"*Listen!*" Harrison started, tensed. Off to the west had sounded a sudden scream of pain or fear. Then there came the impact of racing feet on the hard ground, the crackling of brush, as if someone fled blindly through the bushes within a few hundred yards of the road. In an instant Harrison was over the fence and running toward the sounds.

"Help! Help!" It was the voice of dire terror. "Almighty God! Help!"

"This way!" yelled Harrison, bursting into an open flat. The unseen fugitive evidently altered his course in response, for the heavy footfalls grew louder, and then there rang out a terrible shriek, and a figure staggered from the bushes on the opposite side of the glade and fell headlong. The dim starlight showed a vague writhing shape, with a darker figure on its back. Harrison caught the glint of steel, heard the sound of a blow. He threw up his gun and fired at a venture. At the crack of the shot the darker figure rolled free, leaped up and vanished in the bushes. Harrison ran on, a queer chill crawling along his spine because of what he had seen in the flash of the shot.

He crouched at the edge of the bushes and peered into them. There was no sound or movement among them. The shadowy figure had come and gone, leaving no trace except the man who lay groaning in the glade.

Harrison bent over him, snapping on his flashlight. He was an old man, a wild, unkempt figure with matted white hair and beard. That beard was stained with red now, and blood oozed from a deep stab in his back.

"Who did this?" demanded Harrison, seeing that it was useless to try to stanch the flow of blood. The old man was dying. "Joel Middleton?"

"It couldn't have been!" Peter had followed the detective. "That's old Joash Sullivan, a friend of Joel's. He's half crazy, but I've suspected that he's been keeping in touch with Joel and giving him tips—"

"Joel Middleton," muttered the old man. "I'd been to find him, to tell the news about John's head—"

"Where's Joel hiding?" demanded the detective.

Sullivan choked on a flow of blood, spat and shook his head.

"You'll never learn from me!" He directed his eyes on Peter with the eery glare of the dying. "Are you taking your brother's head back to its grave, Peter Wilkinson? Be careful you don't find your own grave before this night's done! Evil on all your name! The devil owns your souls and the graveyard rats'll eat your flesh! The ghost of the dead walks the night!"

"What do you mean?" demanded Harrison. "Who stabbed you?"

"A dead man!" Sullivan was going fast. "As I come back from meetin' Joel Middleton, I met him. Wolf Hunter, the Tonkawa chief your grandpap murdered so long ago, Peter Wilkinson! He chased me and knifed me. I saw him plain, in the starlight—naked in his loin-clout and feathers and paint, just as I saw him when I was a child, before your grandpap killed him!

"Wolf Hunter took your brother's head from the grave!" Sullivan's voice was a ghastly whisper. "He's come back from hell to fulfill the curse he laid onto your grandpap when your grandpap shot him in the back, to get the land his tribe claimed. Beware! His ghost walks the night! The graveyard rats are his servants—the graveyard rats—"

Blood burst from his white-bearded lips and he sank back dead.

Harrison rose somberly.

"Let him lie. We'll pick up his body as we go back to town. We're going on to the graveyard."

"Dare we?" Peter's face was white. "A human I do not fear, not even Joel Middleton, but a ghost—"

"Don't be a fool!" snorted Harrison. "Didn't you say the old man was half crazy?"

"But what if Joel Middleton is hiding somewhere near—"

"I'll take care of him!" Harrison had an invincible confidence in his own fighting ability. What he did not tell Peter, as they returned to the car, was that he had had a glimpse of the slayer in the flash of his shot. The memory of that glimpse still had the short hair prickling at the base of his skull. *That figure had been naked but for a loin-cloth and moccasins and a headdress of feathers.*

"Who was Wolf Hunter?" he demanded as they drove on.

"A Tonkawa chief," muttered Peter. "He befriended my grandfather, and was later murdered by him, just as Joash said. They say his bones lie in the old graveyard to this day."

Peter lapsed into silence, seemingly a prey of morbid broodings.

Some four miles from town the road wound past a dim clearing. That was the Wilkinson graveyard. A rusty barbed-wire fence surrounded a cluster of graves whose white headstones leaned at crazy angles. Weeds grew thick, straggling over the low mounds. The post oaks crowded close on all sides, and the road wound through them, past the sagging gate. Across the tops of the trees, nearly half a mile to the west, there was visible a shapeless bulk which Harrison knew was the roof of a house.

"The old Wilkinson farmhouse," Peter answered in reply to his question. "I was born there, and so were my brothers. Nobody's lived in it since we moved to town, ten years ago."

Peter's nerves were taut. He glanced fearfully at the black woods around him, and his hands trembled as he lighted a lantern he took from the car. He winced as he picked up the round cloth-wrapped object that lay on the back seat; perhaps he was visualizing the cold, white, stony face that cloth concealed.

As he climbed over the low gate and led the way between the weed-grown mounds, he muttered: "We're fools. If Joel Middleton's laying out there in the woods he could pick us both off easy as shooting rabbits."

Harrison did not reply, and a moment later Peter halted and shone the light on a mound which was bare of weeds. The surface was tumbled and disturbed, and Peter exclaimed: "Look! I expected to find an open grave. Why do you suppose he took the trouble of filling it again?"

"We'll see," grunted Harrison. "Are you game to open that grave?"

"I've seen my brother's head," answered Peter, grimly. "I think I'm man enough to look on his headless body without fainting. There are tools in the tool-shed in the corner of the fence. I'll get them."

Returning presently with pick and shovel, he set the lighted lantern on the ground, and the cloth-wrapped head near it. Peter was pale, and sweat stood on his brow in thick drops. The lantern cast their shadows, grotesquely distorted, across the weed-grown graves. The air was oppressive. There was an occasional dull flicker of lightning along the dusky horizons.

"What's that?" Harrison paused, pick lifted. All about them sounded rustlings and scurryings among the weeds. Beyond the circle of lantern light clusters of tiny red beads glittered at him.

"Rats!" Peter hurled a stone and the beads vanished, though the rustlings grew louder. "They swarm in this graveyard. I believe they'd devour a living man, if they caught him helpless. Begone, you servants of Satan!"

Harrison took the shovel and began scooping out mounds of loose dirt.

"Ought not to be hard work," he grunted. "If he dug it out today or early tonight, it'll be loose all the way down—"

He stopped short, with his shovel jammed hard against the dirt, and a prickling in the short hairs at the nape of his neck. In the tense silence he heard the graveyard rats running through the grass.

"What's the matter?" A new pallor greyed Peter's face.

"I've hit solid ground," said Harrison slowly. "In three days this clayey soil bakes hard as a brick. But if Middleton or anybody else had opened this grave and refilled it today, the soil would be loose all the way down. It's not. Below the first few inches it's packed and baked hard! The top has been scratched, but the grave has never been opened since it was first filled, three days ago!"

Peter staggered with an inhuman cry.

"Then it's true!" he screamed. "Wolf Hunter *has* come back! He reached up from hell and took John's head without opening the grave! He sent his familiar devil into our house in the form of a rat! A ghost-rat that could not be killed! Hands off, curse you!"

For Harrison caught at him, growling: "Pull yourself together, Peter!"

But Peter struck his arm aside and tore free. He turned and ran—not toward the car parked outside the graveyard, but toward the opposite fence. He scrambled across the rusty wires with a ripping of cloth and vanished in the woods, heedless of Harrison's shouts.

"Hell!" Harrison pulled up, and swore fervently. Where but in the black-hill country could such things happen? Angrily he picked up the tools and tore into the close-packed clay, baked by a blazing sun into almost iron hardness. Sweat rolled from him in streams, and he grunted and swore, but persevered with all the power of his massive muscles. He meant to prove or disprove a suspicion growing in his mind—a suspicion that the body of John Wilkinson had never been placed in that grave.

The lightning flashed oftener and closer, and a low mutter of thunder began in the west. An occasional gust of wind made the lantern flicker, and as the mound beside the grave grew higher, and the man digging there sank lower and lower in the earth, the rustling in the grass grew louder and the red beads began to glint in the weeds. Harrison heard the eery gnashings of tiny teeth all about him, and swore at the memory of grisly legends, whispered by the negroes of his boyhood region about the graveyard rats.

The grave was not deep. No Wilkinson would waste much labor on the dead. At last the rude coffin lay uncovered before him. With the point of the pick he pried up one corner of the lid, and held the lantern close. A startled oath escaped his lips. The coffin was not empty. It held a huddled, headless figure.

Harrison climbed out of the grave, his mind racing, fitting together pieces of the puzzle. The stray bits snapped into place, forming a pattern, dim and yet incomplete, but taking shape. He looked for the cloth-wrapped head, and got a frightful shock. *The head was gone.*

For an instant Harrison felt cold sweat clammy on his hands. Then he heard a clamorous squeaking, the gnashing of tiny fangs. He caught up the lantern and shined the light about. In its reflection he saw a white blotch on the grass near a straggling clump of bushes that had invaded the clearing. It was the cloth in which the head had been wrapped. Beyond that a black, squirming mound heaved and tumbled with nauseous life. With an oath of horror he leaped forward, striking and kicking. The graveyard rats abandoned the head with rasping squeaks, scattering before him like darting black shadows. And Harrison shuddered. It was no face that stared up at him in the lantern light, but a white, grinning skull, to which clung only shreds of gnawed flesh. While the detective burrowed into John Wilkinson's grave, the graveyard rats had torn the flesh from John Wilkinson's head. It was an unquiet night for the dead.

Harrison stooped and picked up the hideous thing, now triply hideous. He wrapped it in the cloth and, as he straightened, something like fright took hold of him. He was ringed in on all sides by a solid circle of gleaming red sparks that shone from the grass. Held back by their fear of him, the graveyard rats surrounded him, squealing their hate and rage. Demons, the negroes called them, and in that moment Harrison was ready to agree—ghoulish grey demons, mad with cannibalistic hunger.

They gave back before him as he turned toward the grave, and he did not see the dark figure that slunk from the bushes behind him. The thunder boomed out, drowning even the squeaking of the rats, but he heard the swift footfall behind him an instant before the blow was struck. He whirled, drawing his gun, dropping the head, but just as he whirled, something like a louder clap of thunder exploded in his head, with a shower of fiery sparks before his eyes. As he reeled backward he fired blindly, and cried out as the flash showed him a horrific, half-naked, painted, feathered figure, crouching with a tomahawk uplifted—the open grave was behind Harrison as he fell. Down into the grave he toppled, and his head struck the edge of the coffin with a sickening impact. His powerful body went limp; and like darting shadows, from every side raced the graveyard rats, hurling themselves into the grave in a frenzy of hunger and bloodlust.

4. *Rats in Hell*

It seemed to Harrison's stunned brain that he lay in blackness on the darkened floors of hell, a blackness lit by darts of flame from the eternal fires. The triumphant shrieking of demons was in his ears, as they stabbed him with red-hot skewers. He saw them, now—dancing monstrosities with pointed noses, twitching ears, red eyes and gleaming teeth—a sharp pain knifed through his flesh.

And suddenly the mists cleared. He lay, not on the floor of hell, but on a coffin in the bottom of a grave; the fires were lightning flashes from the black sky; and the demons were rats that swarmed over him, slashing with razor-sharp teeth.

Harrison yelled and heaved convulsively, and at his movement the rats gave back in alarm. But they did not leave the grave; they massed solidly along the walls, their eyes glittering redly.

Harrison knew he could have been senseless only a few seconds. Otherwise these grey ghouls would have already stripped the living flesh from his bones—as they had ripped the dead flesh from the head of the man on whose coffin he lay. Already his body was stinging in a score of places, and his clothing was damp with his own blood.

Cursing, he started to rise—and a chill of panic shot through him! Falling, his left arm had been jammed into the partly-open coffin, and the weight of his body on the lid clamped his hand fast. Harrison fought down a mad wave of terror. He would not withdraw his hand unless he could lift his body from the coffin lid—and the imprisonment of his hand held him prostrate there. Trapped! In a murdered man's grave, his hand locked in the coffin of a headless corpse, with a thousand grey ghoul-rats ready to tear the flesh from his living frame!

As if sensing his helplessness, the rats swarmed upon him. Harrison fought for his life, like a man in a nightmare. He kicked, he yelled, he cursed, he smote them with the heavy six-shooter he still clutched in his hand. Their fangs tore at him, ripping cloth and flesh, their acrid scent nauseated him; they almost covered him with their squirming, writhing bodies. He beat them back, smashed and crushed them with blows of his six-shooter barrel.

The living cannibals fell on their dead brothers. In desperation he twisted half over and jammed the muzzle of his gun against the coffin lid. At the flash of fire and the deafening report the rats scurried in all directions. Again and again he pulled the trigger, until the gun was empty. The heavy slugs crashed through the lid, splitting off a great sliver from the edge. Harrison drew his bruised hand from the aperture.

Gagging and shaking, he clambered out of the grave and rose groggily to his feet. Blood was clotted in his hair from the gash the ghostly hatchet had made in his scalp, and blood trickled from a score of tooth-wounds in his flesh. Lightning played constantly, but the lantern was still shining. But it was not on the ground. It seemed to be suspended in mid-air—and then he was aware that it was held in the hand of a man—a tall man in a black slicker, whose eyes burned dangerously under his broad hat-brim. In his other hand a black pistol muzzle menaced the detective's midriff.

"You must be that damn' low-country law Pete Wilkinson brung up here to run me down!" growled this man.

"Then you're Joel Middleton!" grunted Harrison.

"Sure I am!" snarled the outlaw. "Where's Pete, the old devil?"

"He got scared and ran off."

"Crazy, like Saul, maybe," sneered Middleton. "Well, you tell him I been savin' a slug for his ugly mug a long time. And one for Dick, too."

"Why did you come here?" demanded Harrison.

"I heard shootin'. I got here just as you was climbin' out of the grave. What's the matter with you? Who broke your head?"

"I don't know his name," answered Harrison, caressing his aching head.

"Well, it don't make no difference to me. But I want to tell you that I didn't cut John's head off. I killed him because he needed it," the outlaw swore and spat. "But I didn't do that other!"

"I know you didn't," Harrison answered.

"Eh?" The outlaw was obviously startled.

"Do you know which rooms the Wilkinsons sleep in, in their house in town?"

"Naw," snorted Middleton. "Never was in their house in my life."

"I thought not. Whoever put John's head on Saul's mantel knew. The back kitchen door was the only one where the lock could have been forced without waking somebody up. The lock on Saul's door was broken. You couldn't have known those things. It looked like an inside job from the start—the lock was forced to make it look like an outside job.

"Richard spilled some stuff that cinched my belief that it was Peter. I decided to bring him out to the graveyard and see if his nerve would stand up under an accusation across his brother's open coffin.

"But I hit hard-packed soil and knew the grave hadn't been opened. It gave me a turn and I blurted out what I'd found. But it's simple, after all. Peter wanted to get rid of his brothers. When you killed John, that suggested a way to dispose of Saul. John's body stood, in its coffin, in the Wilkinsons' parlor until it was placed in the grave the next day. No death watch was kept. It was easy for Peter to go into the parlor while his brothers slept, pry up the coffin lid and cut off John's head. He put it on ice somewhere to preserve it. When I touched it I found it was nearly frozen.

"No one knew what had happened, because the coffin was not opened again. John was an atheist and there was the briefest sort of ceremony. The coffin was not opened for his friends to take a last look, as is the usual custom. Then tonight the head was placed in Saul's room.

"I don't know why Peter waited until tonight, or why he called me into the case. He must be partly insane himself. I don't think he meant to kill me when we drove out here tonight. But when he discovered I knew the grave hadn't been opened tonight, he saw the game was up. I ought to have been smart enough to keep my mouth shut, but I was so sure that Peter had opened the grave to get the head, that when I found it *hadn't* been opened, I spoke involuntarily, without stopping to think of the other alternative. Peter pretended a panic and ran off. Later he sent back his partner to kill me."

"Who's he?" demanded Middleton.

"How should I know? Some fellow who looks like an Indian!"

"That old yarn about a Tonkawa ghost has went to your brain!" scoffed Middleton.

"I didn't say it was a ghost," said Harrison, nettled. "It was real enough to kill your friend Joash Sullivan!"

"What?" yelled Middleton. "Joash killed? Who done it?"

"The Tonkawa ghost, whoever he is. The body is lying about a mile back, beside the road, amongst the thickets, if you don't believe me."

Middleton ripped out a terrible oath.

"By God, I'll kill somebody for that! Stay where you are! I ain't goin' to shoot no unarmed man, but if you try to run me down I'll kill you sure as hell. So keep off my trail. I'm goin', and don't you try to follow me!"

The next instant Middleton had dashed the lantern to the ground where it went out with a clatter of breaking glass. Harrison blinked in the sudden darkness that followed, and the next lightning flash showed him standing alone in the ancient graveyard. The outlaw was gone.

5. The Rats Eat

Cursing, Harrison groped on the ground, lit by the lightning flashes. He found the broken lantern, and he found something else. Rain drops splashed against his face as he strode toward the gate. One instant he stumbled in velvet blackness, the next the tombstones shone white in the dazzling glare. Harrison's head ached frightfully. Only chance and a tough skull had saved his life. The would-be killer must have thought the blow was fatal and fled, taking John Wilkinson's head for what grisly purpose there was no knowing, but the head was gone. Harrison winced at the thought of the rain filling the open grave, but he had neither the strength nor the inclination to shovel the dirt back in it. To remain in that dark graveyard might well be death. The slayer might return.

Harrison looked back as he climbed the fence. The rain had disturbed the rats; the weeds were alive with scampering, flame-eyed shadows. With a shudder Harrison made his way to the flivver. He climbed in, found his flashlight and reloaded his revolver. The rain grew in volume. Soon the rutty road to Lost Knob would be a welter of mud. In his condition he did not feel able to the task of driving back through the storm over that abominable road. But it could not be long until dawn. The old farmhouse would afford him a refuge.

The rain came down in sheets, soaking him, dimming the already uncertain lights as he drove along the road, splashing noisily through the mud-puddles. Wind ripped through the post oaks. Once he grunted and batted his eyes. He could have sworn that a flash of lightning had fleetingly revealed a painted, naked, feathered figure gliding among the trees!

The road wound up a thickly-wooded eminence, rising close to the bank of a muddy creek. On the summit the old house squatted. Weeds and low bushes straggled from the surrounding woods up to the sagging porch. He parked the car as close to the house as he could get it, and climbed out, struggling with the wind and rain. He expected to have to blow the lock off the door with his gun, but it opened under his fingers. He stumbled into a musty-smelling room, weirdly lit by the flickering of the lightning through the cracks of the shutters. His flashlight revealed a rude bunk built against a side wall, a heavy hand-hewn table, a heap of rags in a corner. From this pile of rags black furtive shadows darted in all directions. Rats! Rats again! Could he never escape them?

He closed the door and lit the lantern, placing it on the table. The broken chimney caused the flame to dance and flicker, but not enough wind found its way into the room to blow it out. Three doors, leading into the interior of the house, were closed. The floor and walls were pitted with holes gnawed by the rats. Tiny red eyes glared at him from the apertures.

Harrison sat down on the bunk, flashlight and pistol on his lap. He expected to fight for his life before day broke. Peter Wilkinson was out there in the storm somewhere, with a heart full of murder, and either allied to him or working separately— in either case an enemy to the detective—was that mysterious painted figure. And that figure was Death, whether living masquerader or Indian ghost. In any event, the shutters would protect him from a shot from the dark, and to get at him his enemies would have to come into the lighted room where he would have an even chance—which was all the big detective had ever asked.

To get his mind off the ghoulish red eyes glaring at him from the floor, Harrison brought out the object he had found lying near the broken lantern, where the slayer must have dropped it. It was a smooth oval of flint, made fast to a handle with rawhide thongs— the Indian tomahawk of an elder generation. And Harrison's eyes narrowed suddenly; there was blood on the flint, and some of it was his own. But on the other point of the oval there was more blood, dark and crusted, with strands of hair lighter than his, clinging to the clotted point.

Joash Sullivan's blood? No. The old man had been knifed. But someone else had died that night. The darkness had hidden another grim deed—

Black shadows were stealing across the floor. The rats were coming back—ghoulish shapes, creeping from their holes, converging on the heap of rags in the far corner—a tattered carpet, Harrison now saw, rolled in a long compact heap. Why should the rats leap upon that rag? Why should they race up and down along it, squealing and biting at the fabric? There was something hideously suggestive about its contour—a shape that grew more definite and ghastly as he looked.

The rats scattered, squeaking as Harrison sprang across the room. He tore away the carpet—and looked down on the corpse of Peter Wilkinson. The back of the head had been crushed. The white face was twisted in a leer of awful terror. For an instant Harrison's brain reeled with the ghastly possibilities his discovery summoned up. Then he took a firm grasp on himself, fought off the whispering potency of the dark howling night, the thrashing wet black woods and the abysmal aura of the ancient hills, and recognized the only sane solution of the riddle.

Somberly he looked down on the dead man. Peter Wilkinson's fright had been genuine, after all. In his blind panic he had reverted to the habits of his boyhood and fled toward his old home—and met death instead of security.

Harrison started convulsively as a weird sound smote his ears above the roar of the storm—the wailing horror of an Indian war-whoop. The killer was upon him!

Harrison sprang to a shuttered window, peered through a crack, waiting for a flash of lightning. When it came he fired through the window at a feathered head he saw peering around a tree close to the car. In the darkness that followed the flash he crouched, waiting—there came another white glare—he grunted explosively but did not fire. The head was still there, and he got a better look at it. The lightning shone weirdly white upon it. It was John Wilkinson's fleshless skull, clad in a feathered headdress and bound in place—and it was the bait of a trap.

Harrison wheeled and sprang toward the lantern on the table. That grisly ruse had been to draw his attention to the front of the house while the killer slunk upon him through the rear of the building! The rats squealed and scattered. Even as Harrison whirled an inner door began to open. He smashed a heavy slug through the panels, heard a groan and the sound of a falling body, and then, just as he reached a hand to extinguish the lantern, the world crashed over his head. A blinding burst of lightning, a deafening clap of thunder, and the ancient house staggered from gables to foundations! Blue fire crackled from the ceiling and ran down the walls and over the floor. One livid tongue just flicked the detective's shin in passing.

It was like the impact of a sledgehammer. There was in instant of blindness and numb agony, and Harrison found himself sprawling half-stunned on the floor. The lantern lay extinguished beside the overturned table, but the room was filled with a lurid light. He realized that a bolt of lightning had struck the house, and that the upper story was ablaze. He hauled himself to his feet, looking for his gun. It lay halfway across the room, and as he started toward it, the bullet-split door swung open. Harrison stopped dead in his tracks.

Through the door limped a man naked but for a loin-clout and moccasins on his feet. A revolver in his hand menaced the detective. Blood oozing from a wound in his thigh mingled with the paint with which he had smeared himself.

"So it was you who wanted to be the oil millionaire, Richard!" said Harrison.

The other laughed savagely. "Aye, and I will be! And no cursed brothers to share with—brothers I always hated, damn them! Don't move! You nearly got me when you shot through the door. I'm taking no chances with you! Before I send you to hell, I'll tell you everything.

"As soon as you and Peter started for the graveyard I realized my mistake in merely scratching the top of the grave—knew you'd hit hard clay and know the grave hadn't been opened. I knew then I'd have to kill you, as well as Peter.

"I rode to the graveyard through the woods, on a fast horse. The Indian disguise was one I thought up long ago. What with that rotten road, and the flat that delayed you, I got to the graveyard before you and Peter did. On the way, though, I dismounted and stopped to kill that old fool Joash Sullivan. I was afraid he might see and recognize me.

"I was watching when you dug into the grave. When Peter got panicky and ran through the woods I chased him, killed him, and brought his body here to the old house. Then I went back after you. I intended bringing your body here, or rather your bones, after the rats finished you, as I thought they would. Then I heard Joel Middleton coming and had to run for it—I don't care to meet that gun-fighting devil anywhere!

"I was going to burn this house with both your bodies in it. People would think, when they found the bones in the ashes, that Middleton killed you both and burnt the house! And now you play right into my hands by coming here! Lightning has struck the house and it's burning! Oh, the gods fight for me tonight!"

A light of unholy madness played in Richard's eyes, but the pistol muzzle was steady, as Harrison stood clenching his great fists helplessly.

"You'll lie here with that fool Peter!" raved Richard. "With a bullet through your head, until your bones are burnt to such a crisp that nobody can tell how you died! Joel Middleton will be shot down by some posse without a chance to talk. Saul will rave out his days in a madhouse! And I, who will be safely sleeping in my house in town before sun-up will live out my allotted years in wealth and honor, never suspected—never—"

He was sighting along the black barrel, eyes blazing, teeth bared like the fangs of a wolf between painted lips—his finger was curling on the trigger. Harrison crouched tensely, desperately, poising to hurl himself with bare hands at the killer and try to pit his naked strength against hot lead spitting from that black muzzle—then—

The door crashed inward behind him and the lurid glare framed a tall figure in a dripping slicker. An incoherent yell rang to the roof and the gun in the outlaw's hand roared. Again, and again, and yet again it crashed, filling the room with smoke and thunder, and the painted figure jerked to the impact of the tearing lead. Through the smoke Harrison saw Richard Wilkinson toppling— but he too was firing as he fell. Flames burst through the ceiling, and by their brighter glare Harrison saw a painted figure writhing on the floor, a taller figure wavering in the doorway. Richard was screaming in agony.

Middleton threw his empty gun at Harrison's feet.

"Heard the shootin' and come," he croaked. "Reckon that settles the feud for good!" He toppled and Harrison caught him in his arms, a lifeless weight.

Richard's screams rose to an unbearable pitch. The rats were swarming from their holes. Blood streaming across the floor had dripped into their holes, maddening them. Now they burst forth in a ravening horde that heeded not cries, or movement, or the devouring flames, but only their own fiendish hunger. In a grey-black wave they swept over the dead man and the dying man. Peter's white face vanished under that wave. Richard's screaming grew thick and muffled. He writhed, half covered by grey, tearing figures who sucked at his gushing blood, tore at his flesh.

Harrison retreated through the door, carrying the dead outlaw. Joel Middleton, outlaw and killer, yet deserved a better fate than was befalling his slayer. To save that ghoul, Harrison would not have lifted a finger, had it been in his power.

It was not. The graveyard rats had claimed their own. Out in the yard, Harrison let his burden fall limply. Above the roar of the flames still rose those awful, smothered cries.

Through the blazing doorway he had a glimpse of a horror, a gory figure rearing upright, swaying, enveloped by a hundred clinging, tearing shapes—he glimpsed a face that was not a face at all, but a blind, bloody, skull-mask. Then the awful scene was blotted out as the flaming roof fell with a thundering crash.

Sparks showered against the sky, the flames rose as the walls fell in, and Harrison staggered away, dragging the dead man, as a storm-wrapped dawn came haggardly over the oak-clad ridges.

Miscellanea

The Mystery of Tannernoe Lodge
[Unfinished]

Problems puzzled over in waking hours sometimes intrude themselves into a man's dreams. Just before he woke, Steve Harrison's dreams were concerned with the mysterious diagram he had been studying for weeks—the picture, the accompanying chart, and the cryptic words beneath scrawled in the hand of a dead man. In his dream a dim familiarity began to make itself evident; he seemed about to grasp some connection which whispered at the back of his consciousness. Then chaos followed, like the tumbling down of a house of cards, and he awakened.

He sat up in bed, glaring about him, his trained instincts instantly at work to tell him where he was, and what he was doing there, in spite of the unfamiliar and rather unusual surroundings. Moonlight streamed through the latticed windows, barring the carpeted floor with silver, but thick shadows lurked in the corners, along the paneled walls, with their regularly spaced tapestries of black velvet. And in the darkest corner of that room something moved.

"Who's there?" Steve demanded harshly.

There was no reply from the shadowy shape that seemed almost to merge with the gloom; yet it was tangible; the detective seemed to catch the glimpse of a pallid oval that might have been a face. And something akin to panic seized him. Snatching his .45 from under the pillow, he jerked the trigger. Only a dull click responded. With a curse he bounded from the bed, muscles tensed for a death-grapple—and even as he did so, he heard a dull impact, like that of a cleaver driven into a joint of beef; with it came a gasp, a whistling sigh. The mysterious figure toppled headlong, like an overturned nine-pin, and lay with arms outstretched. A bar of moonlight fell across the hands, which twitched convulsively.

Beyond it Harrison thought he saw a hint of movement in the gloom along the wall, but he could not be sure.

Swearing beneath his breath, he groped for the light button. A futile click was his only reward. The wires were dead. But there was a flashlight in his suitcase, and a little fumbling brought it forth. Its beam disclosed a room apparently empty except for himself and the figure which lay face down and motionless near the further wall, in a slowly widening pool of blood. Before he approached it, Harrison sent his ray dancing around the walls, over stained oak panels and velvet hangings, to rest for a moment on the door. He grunted. It was still bolted with the antique-looking bolt he had shot before going to bed. The visitant had not entered that way, evidently.

He stepped to the lattice and peered out. He looked down a sheer wall fifty feet in height, without ledges or ornaments. Tannernoe Lodge was built like a medieval castle, or at least like the builder's conception of a castle. No one could have reached his window without the aid of wings or a ladder. Suddenly he saw half a dozen dark shapes steal into the lodge.

Turning back into the room, Harrison warily bent over the prostrate figure. It was that of a man, squattily and strongly built. Queer pointed slippers were on his feet, and he wore a sort of cassock, black silk soaked in blood. A wide rent gaped in this garment between his shoulders, and disclosing a wound which brought a grunt from the detective. Lifting the man's head, he grunted again. There was a smaller wound on the breast; and he recognized the dead face which stared glassily up at him. It was a servant of the man who was his host, the owner of Tannernoe Lodge.

"Gutchluk Khan, the Chakhar!" muttered Harrison. "What the devil was he doing here? Eh—what's this?"

He stooped and picked up something—a length of silk cord, round and of a peculiarly hard yet pliant weave. And an icy trickle crawled down his spine.

"The strangler's cord!" he whispered. "He came here to finish me. But why? Is he the hidden menace? Is it his own servant that Absolom Tannernoe fears?"

He hesitated, nameless doubts crawling through his mind. The discovery of the dead man's identity roused an uncertainty in him which made him hesitate to call his host, as he would have done under other circumstances. When Absolom Tannernoe had sent for the detective and urged him to stay at the lodge for a few days, to protect him, Tannernoe, from some intangible menace, he had remarked that his immobile valet and general serving-man, Gutchluk Khan, was the one person whom he could trust.

Harrison uneasily scanned the wall before which the Chakhar had been standing when death struck him. Somewhere in that wall it was certain that there was a secret panel, through which both Gutchluk and his slayer had entered, and through which the latter had made his escape. Harrison ran his hands over the oak gingerly, with a feeling as of handling a serpent's cage. Just what sort of lurking death might be skulking just beyond that barrier, he could not know. But the wall did not give up its secret.

Turning again to the corpse, Harrison shrugged his shoulders as he again examined the wound. Evidently the implement used had been a knife of unusual size, wielded with almost incredible force, so as to drive the keen steel through flesh, muscle and bone alike. The wound in the back was as wide as a man's hand; ribs and spinal column had been severed, and in front the breast-bone had been transfixed. Death must have been instantaneous. What man in Tannernoe Lodge was capable of striking such a blow? Certainly not Absolom Tannernoe; and since his arrival, that morning, the detective had seen only the owner of the house, and the Chakhar servant.

Tannernoe had been insistent that some danger threatened him, but vague as to its nature. Harrison's ideas of what constituted a body-guard had been the act of keeping watch all night, and prowling about the premises with a six-shooter, but Tannernoe had insisted that he occupy the tower-bedroom made ready for him. Tannernoe had been very insistent, in fact; he had maintained that the mere presence of the detective in the lodge was protection enough. An ugly suspicion began to grow in Harrison's mind, rejected because it seemed so utterly reasonless and unfounded. Then he remembered something else.

Working the loading gate of his revolver, he threw out the cylinder and examined the cartridges. One showed a dinted percussion cap. By virtue of strong teeth and jaws and a vise-like finger grip, he worked the bullet free and dumped into his palm the contents of the cartridge-case. The tiny particles glistened in the light of the flash.

"Brass filings!" he exclaimed softly. "Fakes—with filings to give them the proper weight! Somebody's shifted ammunition on me. Now who—"

He sat silent, weighing the useless cartridges in his hand, as a grim expression stole over his strongly chiseled face. Steve Harrison was a strong-arm fighter by nature and choice. He seldom carried a gun; generally it reposed in his bag. But he knew that those fakes had been substituted in his revolver since he had entered Tannernoe Lodge, and, unless the lodge sheltered unknown people, only one man had had the opportunity to make that change. He had not been out of sight of his bag, containing his gun, until he removed the weapon and stuck it in his waist-band, except for a few minutes.

The cryptic Gutchluk had guided him briefly over the grounds, after which he had obtained his gun. During that time, only Absolom Tannernoe had been in the house.

"He shifted the cartridges," muttered Harrison. "But why? And then, who killed Gutchluk? Is somebody hiding in this house, that old Tannernoe doesn't know about? But if so, why did Gutchluk come after me?"

His cogitations were interrupted by a faint tap on the door. He came erect, gun clubbed in his hand. A faint whisper reached him; it was the voice of Absolom Tannernoe.

"Gutchluk! What is delaying you?" The voice was like the hiss of a serpent. "Is he dead? Why do you not answer me? I have been waiting downstairs for you to bring me the note-book? Do you have it? Has he hidden it? I know that he carries it with him—ahhhhh!"

The voice broke off in a gurgling gasp, as if a hand had been clapped over the speaker's mouth. There was the sound of a scuffle, then a shuffling noise, mingled with sharp raps. Harrison knew that sound; some one—presumably Absolom Tannernoe—was being dragged forcibly away down the hall, and it was his heels striking the carpeted floor. With a stride the detective reached the door and shot the bolt. He looked out into utter darkness into which he dared not direct his flashlight. Somewhere below him, he believed on the winding stair at the end of the corridor, he heard muffled noises, and what sounded like a murmur of voices.

He followed the sounds, walking softly as a panther, despite his bulk. As he went he revolved in his mind the words Absolom Tannernoe had whispered outside his door. The evidence of a trap was unmistakable, and obviously the reason therefore was a notebook. Harrison instinctively touched a flat package inside his shirt. He had lain down fully dressed save for his shoes. That was the only note-book of any importance he possessed. He had taken it off the body of a certain shady character known as Josef La Tour, a known blackmailer and a suspected smuggler and international thief. It bore on its pages many names and remarkable items concerning the owners of those names. It was a veritable Devil's Hand-book. But the name of Absolom Tannernoe did not appear among those pages. Why should the eccentric traveler wish for that book to the extent of doing murder for its possession?

He reached the stair and went stealthily down them, groping his way, grasping his .45 like a bludgeon. Suddenly from somewhere below came a shrill cry of pain.

He had reached the great hall on the ground floor,[1] and he saw a glimmer of light between the hangings that masked the doorway of Absolom Tannernoe's study. Gliding forward, he peered warily through.

A small electric lamp burned near the great empty fireplace, illuming a group of tense forms. In a great arm chair writhed a figure the detective recognized as Tannernoe, dressed only in shirt and trousers, his arms tied behind him. He was a spare, wiry man in middle life, lank colorless hair falling over a high narrow brow which set off sharp craggy features. There was something distinctly predatory about his great arching nose and his sharp chin. Now his skin was grey as if from pain or fear, and perspiration glistened upon it.

Five figures were grouped around him; five bearded faces hemmed him in in the circle of light. These faces were shadowed,

---

1. There is a note here in the typescript—"he fought a man in the dark"—evidently to mark an insertion to be made in a later draft.

unreal, yet tangible as a threat of death. They seemed to be crowned by a sort of cloth head-piece, alien in its suggestion. But the language they spoke was English.

"After all these years," one was saying, softly, his strange accent failing to conceal his bitter mockery, "it may be that our language is unintelligible to you. So I will speak in English, that there be no misunderstanding. I would advise that you consider your answer with care. We have showed you the feel of a lighted cigarette against your naked foot. We have the whole night before us. None will disturb us. We heard your remarks to that Mongol dog, Gutchluk Khan, just before we seized you, whereby we know that he has strangled the American detective who came here today. Very well. We left Ahmed on the stair, and he will attend to the Chakhar when he comes forth.

"You thought, no doubt, that you had hidden yourself so well that we of Lebanon would never find you? A Maronite never forgets! You should know that. We discovered your hiding place a week ago, and have been lurking in the neighborhood ever since. But you guarded yourself so well, we found no opportunity to enter your house, until tonight. Why did you send your servants away? I can guess. They would protect you against enemies, but they would not murder a sleeping man for you. That was a task for Gutchluk Khan. And so, while the house was unguarded, *we* crept in. Who died in that tower-room tonight I do not know, but he has served us well. And now you will tell us what we wish to know."

Harrison shrugged his shoulders; the affair was getting more and more bewildering.

"I can not give it to you," said Tannernoe. "It was stolen."

A harsh laugh answered him.

"What thief could outwit you?" asked the leader cynically. "You forget that I was with you when we first stole it in the place whereof you know. But my patience grows short; here, Ali, the cigarette—"

"Wait!" Tannernoe turned a shade ashier. "I see you have me. Loose me; I will give it to you."

"Loose his hands, Ali," said the leader. "And stand behind him with your dagger. If he attempts to flee, send his soul to meet the Devil he serves."

This was done; a stalwart Maronite took his place behind Tannernoe, a wicked curved knife in his hand. At Tannernoe's direction a candle was lighted. Whether Tannernoe or the Maronites had turned off the electricity, Harrison did not know.

Tannernoe pointed to a corner of the room. "Go there and press that panel, see, the fourth from the corner. Wait, I'll do it—"

"No, you won't," replied the leader, whom they called Akbar. "You will remain under the care of Ali. *I* will discover the hiding place of the Maronite gem."

Akbar began carefully running his hands over the panel, while the other three, impatient, crowded forward and began aiding him. And with appalling suddenness, a section of the floor gave way; a black hole gaped and swallowed up the four men.

Frozen by the disaster, the man called Ali cried out croakingly, and started forward, forgetting his prisoner. And quick and fierce as a jungle cat, Absolom Tannernoe sprang on him and tore the dagger from his grasp. Harrison saw the steel gleam in the candle-light as it was sheathed in Ali's black beard. The Maronite sank down, spouting blood and rolling his glazing eyes wildly, as he clawed at his crimsoned beard.

"So!" Tannernoe stood above him, knife in hand, panting, an appalling image of vindictive rage. "You think to trap me, after all these years? Ha! I'm still the same man who made fools of your tribe in the mountains of Lebanon, ten years ago! If there is still enough life in you to observe, Ali, fool, note that the trap is back in place, and seems part of the solid floor. I had that made when I built the house. Tannernoe Lodge is a honeycomb of secrets. That trap is worked by pulling that thick velvet rope which seems part of the tapestry; or when enough weight is placed upon the trap, it is thrown automatically. Your friends are now squirming in a neat dungeon under the house, waiting for the doom which I shall presently loose upon them. Then, if Gutchluk has not already attended to Ahmed who waits on the stairs, I shall do so."

It was at this instant that Harrison strode through the hanging, gun in hand. This business had gone far enough, whatever it was.

"Tannernoe!" exclaimed Harrison.

The man whirled, and his face went ashy as if he had seen a ghost. With a strangled cry he wheeled and ran straight toward the wall, caroming against it; what he did to it, Harrison did not see, but a black opening gaped, and through it plunged Absolom Tannernoe. But when Harrison sprang toward it, only the panels of the wall met his baffled glare.

Swearing, he halted, bewildered.

[. . .]

Untitled

[Synopsis]

Steve Harrison received a wire from Joan Wiltshaw, begging him to come to her aid, in Lost Knob. She had helped him solve a murder case in the hills once, and he had promised to help her any time she needed help. He went there at once and found that her husband, Brax Wiltshaw, was in jail, unable to make bail, charged with the murder of John Richardson. The Richardsons were fairly well-to-do merchants in Lost Knob, four brothers and an old maid sister— John, William, Saul, Esau, and Isabel. Their property consisted of a grocery store, the old house, and a sterile farm a few miles from town. John had worked the farm, and William, Saul and Isabel had lived in the house in town and run the store.

John had been found stabbed outside his shack and a knife bearing Wiltshaw's finger-prints on the handle had been found in a litter of leaves, to which blood-drops led. This convinced people that Wiltshaw had tried to hide the knife. He had been arrested in the river bottoms where he swore he was looking for a stray cow. The sheriff believed he was trying to escape. Wiltshaw admitted the knife was his, said he kept it in his smoke-house to cut meat and anybody could have stolen it.

But there had been an old feud between the Wiltshaws and the Richardsons, of which the present sets were the last of each line. Another family, the Barwells, had been mixed up in the feud until, harried by both Richardsons and Wiltshaws, the last of that line, a grim, gaunt woman, had gone away with her infant son, thirty-five years before, swearing vengeance on both clans.

Harrison heard Joan Wiltshaw's story, and talked with the Richardson brothers, who were taciturn and hostile, and with Doctor Dick Ellis, who was friendly and mildly cynical. He confided in Harrison that all the brothers were envious of Esau, the eldest, a tall, gangling man of great awkward strength, because he had been left the bulk of the property, having been his father's favorite son. He said Esau was a neurotic, really strong as a bull, but believing he was subject to various illments, and a free-spender only for medical treatment, which he didn't need.

It was dusk when Harrison left Doctor Ellis and headed for the jail to talk to Brax Wiltshaw. He found the jailer with his head crushed, and the prisoner gone. Apparently, judging by the position of the body, the jailer had stood too close to the cell when bringing Wiltshaw his food, and the prisoner had snatched the gun from his scabbard, reaching through the bars, and struck the man on the head. Then he had reached through and seized the keys and fled.

That night Saul and Isabel were killed, and an attack was made on Joan Wiltshaw. Thinking her husband was fumbling at the door she went to let him in and was attacked by a masked man who failed to kill her only because Harrison arrived on the spot and drove him away, though failing to capture him.

He told her that somebody else had killed John Richardson, and someone had killed the jailer and freed or captured Wiltshaw, making it appear that Wiltshaw had done it himself. Harrison believed someone got Brax out of jail so as to make it appear he had done the other murders. He suspected one of the brothers, but was nonplused to discover a motive.

Eventually he discovered that Doctor Ellis was really Joe Barwell, who had returned and lived in the town ten years to consummate his vengeance and had persuaded Esau that there was oil on the farm; Esau wanted all the money for himself.

The Silver Heel
[synopsis]

Steve Harrison, detective, received a mysterious note in a feminine hand, advising him that an unnamed crime was to take place on Water Street at midnight. The stroke of twelve found him walking along Water Street, which ran through the Oriental quarter of the city. The street was deserted except for the detective and a man trudging along ahead of him. Suddenly a scream for help rang out across the street, from behind a rotting board fence that shut off the mouth of a long-unused alley, called China Alley. The stranger walking ahead of Harrison turned at the cry and followed the detective across the street. Together they leaned over the body of a man which lay on the ground behind the board fence with a Chinese dagger in his back. Harrison recognized the murdered man as Jelner Kratz, a shady Shanghai-born lawyer, who served as a sort of link between yellow and white, dwelling as he did in the shadowy borderline between the races. (Harrison also discovered something unusual and surprizing in connection with the body, which is not at that time divulged to the reader, but which forms Clue No. 1, the first link in the chain of discoveries and deductions which eventually solves the crime.)

Searching the body he found his pocketbook intact, containing a large sum of money, and a newspaper clipping from Shanghai, relating the mysterious death of one Wu Shun, eldest son of the Mandarin Tang. The pockets had not been disturbed, but an old-fashioned silver cigar-case lay empty on the ground. Beyond the first angle of the crooked alley Harrison found the broken silver heel of a woman's slipper, wedged between cracked paving stones.

The stranger who had followed Harrison to the scene of the crime introduced himself as Jack Bissett, who had come from San Francisco in an unsuccessful effort to get a job as a newspaper reporter. He hoped to work up a story out of the murder that would land him a job.

Harrison allowed Bissett to accompany him, while he roused out the manager of an exclusive shop in the city which featured a special slipper with silver heels. Harrison narrowed his investigations down to one Zaida Lopez, a Eurasian dancing girl, and dismissing Bissett, he went to her apartment house, and learned there that she had been absent during the earlier part of the night, returning shortly after twelve o'clock.

Harrison was unable to obtain entry to her apartments by regular means, and so went on the roof, and entered by a door which he found open. (Her rooms opened on the roof.) He found Zaida dead with a Chinese dagger in her breast. Her maid had disappeared. An Arab Harrison knew as Ahmed was found lying among some potted palms outside the door, apparently unconscious, though there was no visible bruise or cut on his head. When revived he said that Zaida, a friend of his, had sent him a note—which he had destroyed— urging him to come to her at once. Her maid had brought it, but had not returned with him. The note had not stated Zaida's reasons for wishing to see him. His tale was as follows: He had come as requested, and surprized a man trying to force the corridor door of her bedroom. The man had fled and Ahmed had pursued him onto the roof, but lost him there. Zaida had opened the door to admit the Arab, but as he approached the threshold he was struck down by someone who sprung from behind the potted palms, evidently the man he had been chasing. He remembered nothing else, and claimed that he was still so dazed he could remember none of the details of his assailant.

Harrison, unable to find any evidence that the Arab had been struck, was forced to believe that Ahmed was lying clumsily, and was the murderer of Zaida. While he was questioning the Arab, Bissett came in, being determined, as he said, to stick to Harrison until he got the whole story of the crime and its ultimate solution.

In the maid's room Harrison found a note in Zaida's handwriting, urging Kratz to meet her in the backroom of a low-class cabaret "The Purple Cat" a few blocks from China Alley, at eleven o'clock. Harrison concluded that Zaida had not killed Kratz, but had been in China Alley and had seen Ahmed kill him. He accused Ahmed of her murder, believing that she had summoned the Arab to her apartments to blackmail him, and Ahmed had killed her to close her mouth. Rummaging further he found a scrap of paper on which Zaida had evidently been writing when she stopped to open the door, through which had come the man who killed her. On it was written: Ahmed: I am afraid. I have seen Joseph Lepstein—" That was all.

This changed the complexion of the matter, though Harrison did not divulge, even to the eager Bissett, just what he had found. At that moment he glimpsed a Chinaman on the roof outside, and then the lights went out, and in the dark Harrison was struck heavily and the paper was torn from his hand. (Clue No. 2.) Harrison was knocked down and fired several times in the dark. When he got on the lights again both Bissett and Ahmed were down, Bissett with a wound on his head which had addled him, and Ahmed with a bullet through his heart. Harrison at first supposed that Ahmed had been hit by one of his bullets, but the autopsy showed that he had been killed by a gun of different caliber, and further proved that the Arab had recently been struck with a sand-bag which left no external marks. That confirmed his story of having been knocked senseless. Bissett's wound was a ragged, ploughing cut in the scalp. (Clue No. 3.)

Harrison now constructed the crime as follows: Zaida had seen Kratz murdered, and had returned in fright to her apartment and sent for Ahmed. The murderer learned somehow that Zaida had seen him kill Kratz, and had followed her, attacked the Arab and killed the girl. Apparently he had hidden somewhere in the apartment, had turned out the light and killed Ahmed, fearing the Arab might be able to identify him. Suspicions pointed to the unknown Chinaman Harrison had seen, and to Joseph Lepstein, Kratz's partner.

Harrison visited the offices of Kratz & Lepstein, and found Lepstein had disappeared. Rummaging through the papers of the firm he discovered that Kratz had been blackmailing Zaida. In Kratz's desk he found a note in Zaida's handwriting, similar to the one found in her maid's room, and of the same date, but asking for a rendezvous in China Alley, at eleven thirty o'clock. Harrison discovered the note was a forgery, though the writing on the envelope was genuine. (Clue No. 4.)

Harrison visited "The Purple Cat" and found that Zaida had come there at eleven o'clock on the night of the murder, and waited for more than half an hour. Someone then told her Kratz had been seen passing the place heading apparently for China Alley, and she had followed. Evidently she had reached the alley in time to witness his murder.

The body of the missing maid, meanwhile, had been dragged out of the river; she had been stabbed with the same sort of dagger that had killed the others.

Harrison, trying to track down Lepstein, was captured by the members of the Ti Woon tong, who prepared to execute him for killing Ahmed who had been under their protection, having once saved the life of their head, Ti Woon. Harrison convinced them that he did not kill Ahmed, and Ti Woon revealed the fact that Kratz had known who killed Wu Shun, his brother's son, for whom the Chinese wished revenge. Wu Shun had been murdered and robbed of the Dragon's Heart, an ancient and valuable ruby. Kratz told Ti Woon that the murderer had come to America, and offered to name him, in return for a large sum of money. Harrison believed that Kratz had been stalling Ti Woon along while he squeezed money out of the murderer in return for silence. The Chinaman Harrison had seen on the roof where Zaida lived had been one of the Ti Woon tong, following Ahmed.

By this time Harrison had decided that Lepstein had not killed Kratz, but was hiding somewhere in mortal terror. The Ti Woon tongmen set out to help Harrison, and located Lepstein hiding in a house on the river. They arrived there just in time to scare away a shadowy figure which had just knifed Lepstein. The dying man could not name his killer, but indicated a hiding place, where Harrison found the Dragon Ruby. Bissett entered about this time, in great excitement at the turn of events, and Harrison showed him the ruby. The detective then sent the tongmen searching through the house to track down the killer, himself remaining alone in the room with Bissett.

A voice behind Harrison ordered him to put up his hands and turn around but instead, turning, Harrison covered him with his pistol just as the man whipped out a Chinese dagger. The detective then called back the Chinese, whom he had sent away on purpose, just as he had shown Bissett the ruby, to trick him into betraying himself.

Harrison presented the affair thus: Bissett, a criminal and adventurer, had killed Wu Shun for the ruby and fled with it to America. There, being broke and not daring to approach a legitimate dealer, he had pawned it to Kratz, who had recognized it and through obscure channels had learned of Wu Shun's murder. Kratz then began victimizing Bissett, while bargaining with Ti Woon to reveal the murderer of his nephew.

Bissett had known Zaida's maid in China. (As it later appeared.) He made love to her, having learned that Kratz was blackmailing Zaida for some former misadventure. He used Zaida as an unsuspecting decoy. He persuaded the maid to tell Zaida that Kratz had asked her to appoint a rendezvous, and then had substituted a forged note for the note Zaida had actually written.

Lepstein had followed Kratz, hoping for a chance to steal the Dragon Ruby, which he knew Kratz carried with him concealed in a cigar. Kratz arrived at China Alley shortly after eleven thirty o'clock, and Bissett met him and killed him with a Chinese dagger. He did not search him, because it did not occur to him that Kratz would carry the jewel on his person, Bissett had hardly left, when Lepstein came up and found his partner dead. He took the cigars out of the case and hurried away, not however, without being seen by Zaida who had waited at The Purple Cat until told that Kratz had passed going toward China Alley. She saw Lepstein ransacking the body and thought he was the murderer.

Lepstein, terrified by his possession of the ruby, went into hiding. Meanwhile Bissett, having slain Kratz, hurried to a point some distance up the street, where he waited until he saw Harrison approaching. He then sauntered down the street in full view of the detective and as they passed the mouth of China Alley, threw his voice in a shout behind the fence, he being a ventriloquist. His idea was to furnish himself a perfect alibi. There he was in plain sight of Harrison, while the crime was supposedly being committed.

Being with Harrison when the detective traced the silver heel, he learned that Zaida had been in the alley that night, and fearing she had seen him commit the crime, he hurried to her apartment and killed her. It was he who turned out the lights and killed Ahmed, fearing the Arab might later be able to identify him; and he snatched the paper from Harrison's hand, not knowing Lepstein's name was mentioned.

Later, returning to his own rooms, he found Zaida's maid there, waiting for him, and killed her because she knew too much. He then tracked Lepstein to his hiding place, realizing he must have the ruby, and killed him. He had returned after slipping away, to try to kill Harrison and get possession of the ruby.

Harrison had reached his conclusions because of the following clues: No.1: When he discovered Kratz's body he knew the man could not have screamed, because he had obviously been dead anywhere from fifteen minutes to half an hour. No. 2: Whoever snatched the bit of paper from his hand in the dark did so because he thought it contained incriminating evidence; eliminating Lepstein and the Chinaman that left only Bissett, who did not know the paper named Lepstein. No. 3: The wound on Bissett's head had been a ragged cut, not caused by a blow; Bissett had nerve enough to inflict it on himself with the sight of his pistol to make his act look real. No. 3: The writing on the note sent to Harrison, and the forged note substituted in Zaida's letter to Kratz, showed to have been the work of the same hand, and both revealed characteristics of Bissett's writing, in spite of his imitating a feminine hand. The note to Harrison had been to draw him to the scene, to act as Bissett's alibi. No. 4: A deduction rather than an actual clue. The person who wrote Harrison the note was the same who killed Kratz; therefore the only reason for the note was to establish an alibi. And Bissett was the only man present to benefit by that alibi.

Graveyard Rats

[draft; missing first and last pages]

[. . .] knew it was not one of his brothers who had come so subtly to his room. Whether Peter and Richard were sound asleep, or crouching in wide-eyed fear behind locked doors, in any event they were in their rooms. In that fear-tense, hate-haunted household, no man came by night to his brother's room without first making himself known. Nervous men are prone to shoot first and investigate later.

This was especially the case in the Wilkinson household since an old feud had claimed the eldest brother four days since—John Wilkinson, shot down in the streets of the little hill-country town by Joel Middleton, who hated them all. And Middleton had not been taken; he had escaped into the post-oak grown hills, swearing more vengeance on the Wilkinson clan before he died. McVey, marshal of Lost Knob, had failed to capture him, and Saul had little confidence in the city detective, Harrison, Peter had brought into the case.

All this flashed through Saul's mind as he groped for the ancient revolver under his pillow. He found it, drew it out, and cocked it cautiously, wincing at the loud click of the stiff spring. As he slid out of bed, the creak of the springs brought his heart into his throat, and he crouched there for a moment, holding his breath, and straining his eyes into the darkness. He dared not cry out. Richard and the detective were sleeping upstairs; Peter's room was on the ground floor, but in another wing of the house. A yell for help might awaken all three, but it would also bring a hail of lead at him, if Joel Middleton were crouching over there in the dark. Middleton had boasted that he could shoot by ear as well as by eye. No; Saul knew this was his fight and must be fought out alone, in the darkness he had always feared and hated.

Crouching against the wall, cursing the pounding of his heart, Saul tried to steady his quivering nerves. The windows were faint grey squares in the blackness, and he was standing by the wall which formed the partition between his room and the hall. There were no windows in that wall. He could dimly make out objects of furniture in all except one side of the room. If Joel Middleton were in the room, he must be crouching over there, by the old fireplace—waiting, no doubt, for his victim to betray himself. Noiselessly on his bare feet, Saul moved along the wall toward the door. If a man was in the room, presently he would be lined between himself and a window. By shifting his position he would eventually get the marauder between himself and one of those faint squares of light, and then—grimly he caressed the worn butt of the old gun.

But as he glided along the wall like a nightshirted ghost on bare feet, no ominous bulk grew out of the darkness. The faint grey squares stood unobstructed. He reached the door and closed it soundlessly, wincing at his nearness to the unrelieved blackness of the hall outside. But nothing happened. The only sounds were the wild beating of his heart, the loud ticking of the old clock on the mantelpiece. If John Middleton was in the room he was lying prone on the floor, for Saul had limned every section of the room with a window. Yet the open door proved that Middleton or someone—or *something*—had been in that room, for the open door proved it. Perhaps he was lurking in the hall outside. But why, in God's name, if he came there to kill, had he not made some aggressive move? Saul's nerve snapped suddenly. The darkness was strangling him. He must have light, even though that light brought hot lead ripping through his body. In stumbling haste he groped to the mantelpiece, fumbling for candle and matches.

He struck and lit the candle—and then as he stood blinking he first became aware of an object on the mantelpiece. He stood staring wildly, his brain at first refusing to register and credit what his eyes revealed. Then he croaked inhumanly and the gun crashed on the hearth as it slipped from his fingers. John Wilkinson was dead, with a bullet through his heart. It had been three days since Saul had seen his body nailed into the crude coffin and lowered into the grave in the old Wilkinson family graveyard. For three days the hard clay soil had baked in the hot sun above the coffined form of

John Wilkinson. Yet there from the mantel John Wilkinson's face leered at him—white and cold and dead.

It was no nightmare, no mad dream. There on the mantelpiece rested John Wilkinson's severed head. The old house came suddenly to a fearsome life with the hideous screams that brought the sleepers out of their sleep. They were the screams of a madman. What he had seen had blasted Saul Wilkinson's reason like a blown-out candle flame.

Chapter .2.
The Mad Man.

It was the screams which roused Steve Harrison, sleeping in an upstairs chamber. Before he was fully awake he was on his way down the unlighted stairs, pistol in one hand and flashlight in the other. It was his celerity in action which had contributed very largely to his enviable reputation as a man-hunter.

Down in the rambling hallway he saw light streaming from under a closed door, and made for it. But another was before him. Just as Harrison reached the landing in the hall, he saw a figure rushing across the hall and flashed his beam on it. It was Peter Wilkinson, tall and gaunt, with a poker in his hand. He yelled something incoherent, threw the door open and rushed in. Harrison heard him exclaim: "Saul! What's the matter? What are you looking at—" Then a terrible cry: *"My God!"* The poker clanged on the floor, and then the screams of the maniac rose to a crescendo of fury, and there was the sound of a blow.

It was at this instant that Harrison reached the door, and with one swift glance took in the scene, even as he went into action. He saw two men in nightshirts grappling frantically in the candle light, while from the mantel a cold, dead, white face looked blindly down on them.

Into that scene of horror and madness Harrison propelled his powerful, thick-set body. Peter Wilkinson was in sore straits. He had dropped his poker, and now, with blood streaming from a wound in his head, he was vainly striving to tear Saul's lean fingers from his throat. In Saul's eyes Harrison saw a flame he recognized. The man was hopelessly insane.

Half-way measures would be suicidal. Crooking one massive arm about the maniac's neck, he tore him loose from his victim with an exertion of sheer strength that not even the abnormal energies of insanity could resist. The mad man's stringy muscles were like steel wires under the detective's hands, and Saul twisted about in his captor's grasp, his teeth snapping, beast-like for Harrison's bull-throat. The detective shoved the clawing, frothing fury away from him and smashed his right fist to the madman's jaw with all his beef behind it. Saul measured his length on the floor and lay still, eyes glazed and limbs quivering.

Peter had staggered back against a table, gagging and clutching at his throat. There was a purplish tinge in his face. He choked, trying to talk.

"Never mind that now," snapped Harrison, heaving the limp figure off the floor and letting it slump into a great arm-chair. "Get cords, quick! Tear that sheet into strips. That'll do. We've got to get him tied up before he comes to. I don't want to have to hit him again."

Gasping convulsively, Peter obeyed and Harrison bound the maniac's limp limbs with professional efficiency. In the midst of this task he was aware of the entrance of another man into the room, and glanced over his shoulder to see Richard, the youngest brother, standing in the doorway, his face like chalk as he looked from the senseless man in the chair to the hideous object on the mantle.

"Richard!" choked Peter. "Look! My God! John's head!"

"I see!" Richard moistened his lips. "But why are you tying up Saul?"

"He's crazy," snapped Harrison. "He's beginning to come around. Get me some whiskey, will you?"

As Richard reached for a bottle on a curtained shelf, booted feet hit the porch outside, and a voice shouted: "Hey, there! Dick! Anything wrong? What's the matter? Somebody hurt?"

"That's our neighbor, Jim Allison," muttered Peter. "I'll let him in."

He stepped to the door opposite the one that opened into the hall, and turned the key in the ancient lock. That door opened upon a side porch. A tousle-headed man with his pants pulled on over his nightshirt and a shotgun in his hand came blundering in.

"What's the matter?" he demanded. "I heard somebody hollerin' and run over quick as I could. What you doin' to Saul—good God Almighty!"

He had seen the head on the mantel, and his face turned the color of ashes.

"Go get the marshal, Jim!" croaked Peter. "This is Joel Middleton's work!"

Allison hurried out of the door, stumbling as he peered back over his shoulder in morbid fascination.

Harrison had managed to spill some liquor between Saul's livid lips. He handed the bottle to Peter, who gulped a mouthful, and then sank into a chair, dropping his head in his hands.

"God!" he muttered. "I knew Middleton hated us, but I'd never have dreamed he'd stoop to this!"

Harrison stepped to the mantel, and touched the grisly object, shivering slightly as he did so. His eyes narrowed suddenly.

"You think Middleton dug into your brother's grave and cut off his head?" he asked.

"Who else?" Peter stared blankly at him.

"Saul's crazy. Lunatics do strange things. Suppose Saul did it himself?"

"No! No!" exclaimed Peter, shuddering. "Saul hasn't left the house all day. John's grave was undisturbed this morning. I stopped by the old graveyard when I went to the farm this morning. Saul was sane when he went to bed. It was seeing John's head that drove him mad. Joel Middleton has been here, to take this horrible revenge!"

He sprang up suddenly, his voice cracking as he shrilled, "He may still be in the house! Don't stand there doing nothing, man! I brought you here to capture Joel Middleton! Aren't you even going to search the house?"

"Stay here with Saul," Harrison directed Richard, who nodded, wiping his pale brow with a shaky hand. "You might come with me, Peter."

Peter picked up the revolver Saul had dropped.

"I'll get a lamp."

"Never mind. I've got my flashlight."

At the door he paused an instant to examine the lock.

"Did Saul lock this door at night?"

"I'm sure he did. Saul was always nervous and scary, especially since John was killed. The door was shut when I got to it, but wasn't locked. It fastened inside with a thumb-latch. You see that's been slipped back. These old doors don't fit very well. Anybody could stick a thin knife-blade through the crack and work that bolt back."

"Funny the fellow didn't try to force the lock on the door opening onto the porch," grunted Harrison.

"Maybe he did," answered Peter, peering fearsomely down the hall, at the shadows that lurked beyond the beam of the detective's light. "But the key was in the lock, on the inside. He'd have made so much noise forcing it he'd have woke Saul up."

"Which door is furtherest from any sleeping-chamber?" asked Harrison.

"The back kitchen door!" Peter took the flaslight and led the way. A few moments later they were standing before the door. It stood partly open, framing a crack of starlit sky.

"He must have come and gone this way," muttered Harrison. "It stands to reason he isn't still hiding anywhere in the house. If he came here to kill anyone, he'd have tried to do it already."

Peter directed the beam on the lock, and gave an exclamation, pointing out scratches on the metal on the outer side.

"Look there! The lock's been forced from the outside. There's the key lying on the floor inside."

Harrison ran his fingers over the lock, and grunted.

"Old-fashioned, ramshackle affair. A man could run a wire into the key-hole, twist the key around and push it out, then shove a chisel between the edge of the lock and the door-frame, and do the job quick and easy. It might make a good deal of noise, though."

"Nobody in the house would hear it," answered Peter. "You and Richard were sleeping upstairs, and Saul and I away off on the other side of the house."

"This was the logical door to break in at," agreed Harrison. "Breaking any other outer door would have awakened somebody. Has Middleton ever been in this house before?"

"Not that I know of," replied Peter, grimly. "There's been an old feud between our families for twenty-five years. Joel's the last one of his name left. There were killings, years ago, but none recently until Joel killed John. The Middletons were prosperous once, but they went down in the world as the Wilkinsons rose."

Harrison pushed open the door and stepped out onto the deep back porch. The broad backyard was without trees or bushes. The only place a man could have hidden himself was behind the big zinc cistern which stood under the gutter-lined eaves of the house. Harrison satisfied himself no one was hiding there. A barbed wire fence separated the backyard and the pasture lot which contained a corral, barns, sheds and a garage. A few hundred yards from the backyard fence the pasture ended at a woodlot thickly grown with post-oaks, part of the woods which hemmed Lost Knob in on all sides.

Peter stared toward that woodland, a low, black rampart in the faint starlight, and he shivered and drew back into the shadow of the porch, snapping off the flashlight.

"He's out there!" he whispered. "Hiding! Waiting! Watching us! God, how he hates the name of Wilkinson! I never suspected he'd dare strike at us in our own house. I thought he was skulking in the hills, hiding and running. I brought you here to run down a slinking coyote. I never thought we'd need your protection."

"A man could easily have come out of those woods," muttered Harrison. "He could have crossed the lot and the backyard, forced the door, gone through the kitchen and along the hall, and picked Saul's lock—just what did you see when you ran into Saul's room?"

"His cries woke me," answered Peter. "I ran into the hall and saw you coming down the stair. I ran into Saul's room, and saw him standing before the mantel-board, screaming with his mouth wide open. And then I saw what he saw. I seemed to remember crying out, and dropping the poker. Then he turned on me like a wild man. My head must have hit the table when he threw me against it—" Peter touched the abrasion on his scalp. "I was always stronger than Saul, but he was like a wild animal. He'd have killed me in another minute. Where are you going?"

"Out there," Harrison nodded toward the woods, taking the flashlight.

"If Middleton's out there he'll kill you!" exclaimed Peter, catching at his arm. Harrison shook him off and stepped down into the yard. Peter cringed back from the starlight as if it were a tangible menace, and remained crouching at the edge of the porch.

As Harrison strode across the backyard and over the fence without bothering to open the sagging wire gate, he reflected that only in the dry ridge-country could a thing like this have happened. He had been born and raised in another part of the State, but he knew something of this isolated, backwoods region which progress had passed by on either hand. It was a hard country of post-oak covered ridges and sterile, sandy valleys, where old hates smoldered and old feuds lingered among the inhabitants, descendants of clannish, hard-bitten Scotch-Irish pioneers. It was a region unique and self-contained, its very existence scarcely realized by the people of the rest of the State, except when it was brought to the public attention by some deed of appalling ferocity—such as this one.

Harrison had been brought from a distant city by Peter Wilkinson. His intended role, as Peter had said, had been that of a bloodhound tracking down a skulking fugitive, not that of a protector. Wilkinson did not believe that the local authorities were making much effort to capture the killer. Harrison believed that public sympathy leaned strongly toward Joel Middleton. But he had not had time to gather much data of any kind. He had arrived in Lost Knob late that evening, and he had been given a room in the Wilkinson house, planning to begin his investigation the next morning.

He paused at the ancient rail fence which separated the narrow pasture from the woods. They were black as only post-oak thickets can be; if an armed and desperate man were hiding there, it was far more likely that he had already sought refuge among the rugged hills that surrounded Lost Knob.

Harrison turned back toward the house. It was somewhat past midnight, and that meant that Lost Knob had been a-bed for more than three hours. But the news was spreading already, as it spreads in small hill-country villages, even in the dead of night. The Wilkinson house stood at the western edge of town, and the Allison house was the only one within a hundred yards of it. The other buildings were further away, but Harrison could see lights springing up in windows, and make out figures emerging from doors and yards.

Peter was still standing on the porch, a tall, gaunt figure, head out-thrust on a long neck that reminded Harrison unpleasantly of a buzzard's neck.

"Did you see anything?" he called anxiously.

"Not a thing," grunted the detective. "No use to look for tracks on that hard-baked ground. I don't suppose there's such a thing as a bloodhound in the village?"

"No. Nor anywhere in the county, as far as I know," answered Peter. "We've never needed any. No niggers in these hills."

Harrison brushed past him and went into the house. Allison had returned with the marshal, McVey, a tall, hard-bodied man with dangerous blue eyes. A typical hill-country type; Harrison knew he had killed several men in the line of duty. He was taciturn, and plainly resented the detective's presence. Men were gathering on the side-porch and in the yard, rushing and crowding as a city mob would have done, but standing in clusters, and muttering to each other in low tones. Their faces were immobile, and they had little to say, except for Jim Allison who was vociferous. Saul was recovering his consciousness, but the mad glare in his eyes was unaltered. He did not scream nor struggle, but he mumbled incessantly and incoherently. Harrison believed his insanity would prove permanent.

"This finishes Joel Middleton!" proclaimed Jim Allison loudly. "I wonder what them folks thinks now that sided in with him when he killed John! I reckon them that claimed to be Joel's friends ain't goin' to stand for this! Diggin' up a man and cuttin' his head off! That ain't fit for a white man. That's Injun work. I reckon folks won't wait for no jury to tell 'em what to do with Joel Middleton!"

"Better catch him before you start lynchin' him," grunted McVey. "Peter, we better get Saul to the county seat. I'll take him in my car, if you want me to. That old rattletrap of yours wouldn't hold together that far."

Peter nodded mutely. He shivered from time to time and glanced at the table where the head had been placed and decently covered. The men on the porch stood silent and expectant, looking at the marshal. As he made no suggestion, Harrison spoke: "Suppose we go to the Wilkinson graveyard and see what we can find? We might be able to track Middleton from there."

McVey lifted a mustached lip in a snarl, and answered with all the harsh, bitter vindictiveness of the hill-man.

"They brought you in here to do the job they didn't think I was good enough to do. You didn't ask for my help yesterday. All right. Go ahead and do what you want to—alone. I'm takin' Saul to the county seat."

With a few curt words he directed his deputies to pick up the bound maniac and follow him. As he strode out with them, neither Peter nor Richard offered to accompany him. Harrison heard one of the men on the porch mutter to another: "Ain't that just like the Wilkinsons? Don't give a damn about each other, and never did."

A tall, gangling man stepped awkwardly from among his fellows, and as awkwardly addressed Harrison: "What the marshal does is his own business, but all of us here are ready to help all we can. If you want to git a posse together and comb the hills, why, we'll do it."

"Thanks, no." Harrison did not mean to be abrupt. It was simply his way of speaking. "I appreciate your willingness to help, but you can help me better by all clearing out, right now. Since I'm not to have any official help in working this thing out, I'll go at it alone, as the marshal suggested, and in my own way."

The men moved off at once, silently for the most part, but he felt their resentment. As an outlander, they were suspicious of him; as an outlander who ventured to take a hand in local affairs, and rebuff native men, they hated him. "Damn' low-country mud-eater," he heard one mutter, not too softly. Harrison paid no heed. He did not mind their opinion of him, and there was no profit in taking up a senseless quarrel.

They filed stiffly out of the yard, and Jim Allison followed them, after an uncertain glance at Harrison's uncompromising face.

When all had gone, Harrison closed the door and turned to Peter.

"Will you take me to the graveyard?"

"In the night?" Peter shuddered. "It's a terrible risk. Middleton's shown he'll stop at nothing."

"Why should he?" Richard laughed bitterly. He seemed to have recovered his poise. He was shorter than Peter, somewhat stooped, and pale in contrast to Peter's leathery hue. He had a bitter mouth, eyes that seemed filled with mockery of all things, including himself, and lines of suffering were carven deep in his face. Like Peter, he was educated far beyond the mere conception of most Lost Knob men.

"Why should Joel Middleton stop at anything?" he repeated. "We never stopped hounding him, especially John. John managed to cheat him out of his last bit of land—that's why Middleton killed him. John hated him as much as he hated you! As much as Saul hated you!"

"You're talking wild!" exclaimed Peter.

Again Richard laughed mirthlessly.

"You old hypocrite! Sitting there pretending a grief you know you don't feel! At least, I'm honest! We all hate each other, we Wilkinsons! Everybody in Lost Knob hates us! The only friend I have is Jim Allison."

"No friend of mine," snarled Peter. "Worthless, drunken—"

"You have no friends," retorted Richard. "Nobody liked Saul but McVey. And McVey hates you. That's why he wouldn't bestir himself to catch Joel Middleton. You hated John—you were glad when Middleton shot him—almost as glad as you'll be when Harrison there kills Middleton.

"Saul hated you, too." He turned to Harrison. "You know, they say that insanity removes inhibitions. A secret desire to kill Peter must have always lurked deep in Saul's subconscious mind. When he went mad, the suppressed desire translated itself into action, and as a result you had to twist dear brother Saul's fingers out of dear brother Peter's gullet!"

"You're talking drivel!" exclaimed Peter. "Saul was mad. He would have attacked anybody who came into the room, poor, unfortunate wretch!"

Richard sneered like a man in pain.

"Spare us this hypocrisy! You're glad Saul's crazy. It takes you one step nearer to being the surviving heir of the Wilkinson estate, doesn't it? Only me between you and the culmination of that ambition, and you know I have a heart disease."

"You're insane yourself, Richard," said Peter wearily. "I know there has been a great deal of bitterness among us. We're an unfortunate family that way. But there's no need to spill the dirty linen of our family history before Mr. Harrison. Besides, there never was any real hatred among us. Just petty jealousies and misunderstandings."

Richard gritted his teeth in a spasm of nervous irritation.

"Petty jealousies, my God! We've hated each other like so many snakes. Oh, stare if you like! At least I'm honest. And I'm no worse than you are. You're the meanest man the devil ever made. And maybe even rottener than I thought!"

"What do you mean?" exclaimed Peter, paling.

"*Titus Andronicus* was always your favorite of Shakespeare's plays, wasn't it? sneered Richard. "I've seen you pouring over Aaron's lines:

'Oft have I digg'd up dead men from their graves,
And set them upright at their dear friends' doors!'

"You're talking like a fool," Peter sprang up, livid.

"Oh, am I!" Richard had lashed himself almost to a frenzy. "How do we know you didn't cut off John's head yourself? You knew Saul was neurotic, balanced on a hair-trigger—that a shock like that might drive him mad. And you admit that you visited the graveyard yesterday."

For a moment Harrison thought Peter would strike his brother, but with an effort of iron control, the older brother restrained himself and said quietly: "Richard, you are overwrought. I'll overlook this. As far as I'm concerned the insanity you just uttered is forgotten."

"You can't deny that Saul and John hated you," retorted Richard. "I know why. It was because of that farm Uncle Job left us, over on Wild River. I think he must have hated us all, and known that the farm would be a constant bone of contention. The rest of us wanted to lease it to that oil company, but you wouldn't agree, and according to the terms of the deed and the will, it could be leased outside the family only with the agreement of all the heirs. John believed there was a big pool of oil there. He thought we might all be rich. They got oil on the farm adjoining it.'

"I don't believe there's any oil under that land," snapped Peter. "You know why I wouldn't lease. You know I've put in thousands of dollars on my pecan orchards there—and I've paid the rest of you the stiff rents you demanded. Drilling that land for oil would ruin my trees. In the long run they'll pay more than a gusher would."

"So you say," sneered Richard. "But suppose this pecan orchard is just a smoke screen? Suppose you had dreams of being the sole, surviving heir, and becoming an oil millionaire? You never wanted to share anything with your brothers—"

Harrison glanced at his watch and broke into the altercation.

"It's been half an hour since Saul's screams woke us up. Are we going to stand here and chew the rag all night?"

"No!" Peter turned his back on his brother. "I'll take you to the graveyard. I'd rather face Joel Middleton in the dark than to listen to the ravings of this lunatic any longer."

"I'm not going with you," retorted Richard. "Out there in the black night there's too many chances for you to remove the last remaining heir. I'll go and stay the rest of the night with Jim Allison. If Joel Middleton comes there, we'll be ready for him."

He opened the door and vanished in the darkness.

Peter picked up the cloth-wrapped object on the table, shivering slightly as he did so.

"Did you notice how well preserved the face was?" he muttered. "One would think that after three days—come on. I'll take the head with us and put it back in the grave where it belongs."

Chapter .3.
The Curse of the Tonkawa.

Clouds had rolled across the stars. The air was hot and stifling. The narrow, winding, rutty road that led westward into the hills from the village was atrocious. Only a man familiar with every foot of it could have avoided the stumps and jutting rocks that littered it. But Peter Wilkinson piloted his ancient Model T Ford skillfully, and Lost Knob was quickly lost to sight behind them. After they left the straggling edge of the town, they passed no more houses. On each side the dense post-oak thickets crowded close to the barbed wire fences that lined the road. The rampart was broken only by an occasional field. Ten years before the Wilkinsons had moved "into town" from their farm. They still owned most of the land on each side of the west road.

As they bumped along Harrison questioned Peter carefully about the killing of John Wilkinson, and the disposal of his body thereafter. Peter answered readily, but kept wandering off the subject and back to the point Richard had brought up about the farm on Wild River—an old rankling sore, as Harrison suspected. Peter reasserted his faith in pecans, and spoke of the ruination of good agricultural land by the work of spudders and standard rigs— the truth of which Harrison recognized, having seen the same thing happen in his boyhood home near the gulf coast.

They had left the last house scarcely a mile behind them when they were aware of a moving figure in the road ahead of them.

"Looks like a man running," grunted Harrison, drawing his gun. "Speed up! If it's Middleton, he'll take to the woods."

But the figure turned so suddenly to face them that Peter had to jam down on the brakes to keep from running him over.

"It's old Joash Sullivan," grunted Peter angrily. "We foreclosed on him five years ago, and he's never forgiven us. He's a bit touched in the head."

The old man stood revealed in the dim glare of the headlights, a wild, unkempt figure clad in ragged shirt and overalls, bare-footed, bare-headed, with matted white hair and beard. He lifted his arms like an ancient prophet and shouted: "Are you takin' yore brother's head back to the grave, Peter Wilkinson? Take care you don't find yore own grave before this night's done! Oh, I know what's happened! Word's spread from house to house, and I come onto the street in time to see McVey carryin' Saul away!

"I knowed evil was comin' onto yore house—I've knowed it since I seen the ghost of the dead walkin' in the woods last night! I seen him as plain as I see that low-countryman sittin' by you there! Old Wolf Hunter, the Tonkawa yore grandpap murdered! He always walks when doom's to fall on a Wilkinson! He brings the doom!

"You think Joel Middleton cut off yore brother's head? Yo're a fool! Joel wouldn't no more mutilate a corpse than he'd harm a woman. You listen to me, Peter Wilkinson! It was Wolf Hunter that took John's head from the grave and laid it on Saul's mantel-board! Wolf Hunter, that yore grandpap shot in the back! As he lay dyin' he put the Tonkawa curse on yore whole line! He said Job'd die in blood, and he did! And so will you, and all yore brothers!"

"Where are *you* going this time of night?" demanded Harrison, stepping out of the car, and approaching the old man who eyed him with all the rancor of an uplander for a stranger.

"Yore friend there robbed me of my farm, five years ago," snarled Sullivan. "Are you denyin' me the right to walk the roads as I please?"

"I'd like to know just what you know about Joel Middleton," retorted the detective. "I believe somebody in Lost Knob is keeping in touch with him and giving him tips. I believe he must be hiding somewhere close to the town. You seem to be a friend of his, and—"

Sullivan shifted a bare foot as if an ant had stung it, and stooped quickly. Before the detective could divine his purpose, the old man had cast a handful of sand into his face, and was darting across the road like a chaparral bird. Cursing, Harrison shook his head, and half lifted his gun, then lowered it. He could have killed the old man before he could get out of the light, but the big detective was no man to shoot recklessly and indiscriminately. Sullivan was over the barbed wire fence and gone through the black post oaks in an instant.

"Let him go," growled Harrison, climbing back into the car. "But I'll bet the old devil is hunting for Middleton right now."

"You ought to have let the men form a posse and scour the woods," complained Peter, as he started the car again.

"Maybe," grunted Harrison, not bothering to try to explain his peculiar habit, which almost amounted to an obsession, for working alone. "But you told me McVey got up a posse the day your brother was killed, and they had no luck."

"Middleton knows these hills better than any other man," admitted Peter.

"Then chasing him is useless. We'll let him trap himself."

"How?"

"I'm not sure, yet. Remember, I only came to Lost Knob yesterday. But never yet saw a criminal who couldn't be drawn into a trap. I'll work that out later. What was that stuff about a Tonkawa ghost?"

"His name was Wolf Hunter," muttered Peter, with a strange reticence. "He was chief of a Tankawa clan that claimed all this hill country when the first white man came to settle. That was Job Wilkinson, my grandfather. He was a ruthless man. Wolf Hunter befriended him, defended him against first the Mexicans and later the Comanches, and gave him land enough to build a cabin and plant a crop on. But Job was greedy for land. He brought other white settlers in. They attacked the Tonkawas treacherously and killed them all, women and children too. Job shot Wolf Hunter in the back. They say his bones lie in the old graveyard to this day.

"As he died he cursed the Wilkinson name, as he naturally would. And in so far as Job was concerned, his prediction came true. In the '70s the herds from the lower country came through these hills on their way to Kansas, and old Job started stealing steers from them. A trail driver caught him at it and killed him, on the very spot where he killed Wolf Hunter."

"That's just coincidence," grunted Harrison. "You surely don't believe this stuff about a ghost walking, do you?"

"No!" But the denial lacked conviction. It was evident that in spite of his education, Peter Wilkinson had his share of abysmal hill-country superstition. The further along the road they drove, the more uneasy he became, though that might have been due to his fear of Middleton. Harrison did not believe he was taking Peter into any undue danger. If Middleton was out to kill, that night, he would have lurked in the hall and shot Peter as he rushed from his room. Harrison anticipated no ambush, even if old Joash Sullivan had found and warned the outlaw. Anyway, the big detective had a pugnacious confidence in his own fighting ability.

Some four miles from town the road wound past a dim clearing amidst the post-oak thickets. That was the Wilkinson graveyard. A rusty barbed wire fence surrounded a cluster of graves whose white headstones leaned at crazy angles. Weeds grew thick between the graves and straggled over the low mounds. There was no attempt at beautifying the desolate, dismal place. To the Wilkinsons, unusually callous even for hill-people, the graveyard was merely a place to lay corpses. They felt no sentiment concerning it.

The post oaks crowded close to the fence on all sides, and the road wound through them, passing the sagging gate. Across the tops of the trees, nearly half a mile to the west, there was visible a shapeless bulk which Harrison knew was the roof of a house. He mentioned it to Peter.

"That's the old Wilkinson farm-house," Peter answered. "I was born there, and so were my brothers. Some of the furniture's still there, but nobody's lived in it since we moved to town, ten years ago. Old Job built it on the site of the first log cabin that was ever built in the Lost Knob country."

If Peter was without sentiment, he was not without superstition and morbid fears. Peter's nerves were taut. He was evidently bracing himself for what he expected to see. He glanced fearfully at the black woods around him, and his hands trembled as he lighted a lantern he took from the back seat of the car. He hesitated too, a moment before he picked up the round, cloth-wrapped object that lay on the back seat; perhaps he was visualizing the cold white stony face that cloth concealed.

As he climbed over the low gate and led the way between weed-grown mounds, he muttered: "We're fools, Harrison. If Joel Middleton's laying out there in the woods he could pick us both off easy as shooting rabbits."

Harrison did not reply, and a moment later Peter halted and shone the light on a grave which was bare of weeds. The top of the mound was tumbled and disturbed, and Peter exclaimed: "Look! He filled it up again after he got what he wanted! I expected to find an open grave! Why do you suppose he went to the trouble to fill it up again?"

"We'd better see," grunted Harrison. "The head's got to go back into the coffin anyway—are you game to open that grave tonight?"

"I've seen my brother's head," said Peter grimly. "I think I'm man enough to look on his headless body without fainting. There are tools in that tool-shed in the corner of the fence. I'll get them."

Returning presently with pick and shovel, he set the lighted lantern on the ground, and the cloth-wrapped head near it. Peter was pale, and sweat stood on his brow in thick drops. The lantern cast their shadows, grotesquely distorted, across the weed-grown graves. The clouds had covered the stars, and the roof of the distant old house was no longer visible. There was an occasional dull flicker of lightning along the dusky horizons. The air was hot, oppressive, with the threat of a thunderstorm.

"What's that?" Harrison demanded, at rustling among the weeds. An instant later three pairs of tiny red beads glittered at him.

"Rats!" Peter tossed a stone and the beads vanished. "They grow big along these creeks. I hate the things. They carry plague and they gnaw carrion."

Harrison took the shovel and began scooping out mounds of loose dirt and tossing it aside.

"Ought not to be hard work," he grunted. "If he dug it out today or early tonight, it'll be loose all the way down—"

He stopped short suddenly, with a prickling of the short hairs at the nape of his neck, his shovel jammed hard against the soil. Somewhere the graveyard rats were running through the grass again. He straightened and faced Peter in the light of the lantern.

"What's the matter?" A new pallor greyed Peter's face.

"I've hit solid ground," said Harrison slowly. "This clayey soil bakes hard after a rain, and it rained hard just after the grave was first filled. Since then the weather's been dry and hot. In three days it would bake as hard as a brick. If Middleton or anybody else had dug into this grave today, the soil would be loose all the way to the bottom. It's not. The top soil was loose for a few inches down. Below that it's packed and baked hard! The top of the mound has been scratched, but the grave has never been opened since it was first filled!"

Peter staggered with an inhuman cry, throwing his pick aside.

"Then it's true!" he cried. "The old legend—the old curse! The dead walk! Now I know! Joash was right! Wolf Hunter's ghost has come out of its grave to haunt my brothers and me into hell! It took John's head without opening the grave! It reached up from hell and took his head! God! Hands off, curse you!"

For Harrison had caught at him, growling: "Pull yourself together, Peter!"

But Wilkinson struck wildly at the detective, and tore free. He turned and ran—not toward the car parked outside the graveyard, but toward the opposite fence. He scrambled across the rusty wires with a ripping of cloth as the barbs caught his garments, and vanished in the woods, heedless of Harrison's shouts.

"Hell!" Harrison paused, and swore fervently. At every turn he seemed to run into insanity, hysteria and ingrained superstition. Where but in the black hill-country would an officer of the law refuse to help track down a killer because of personal jealousy, or brothers hate each other so bitterly, or a man run yammering through the midnight woods at the tale of a ghost? Harrison cursed the woods; into them had vanished Joel Middleton, Joash Sullivan, and now Peter Wilkinson. When anything went wrong with a ridge-runner his first impulse was to take to the post oaks.

Angrily he picked up the tools and set to work again. Hill-country minds were somber and morbid. They varied from religious fanaticism—like Saul Wilkinson—to bitter atheism—like John Wilkinson. Ghosts walked and old customs of thought, forgotten by the rest of the world, still lived.

He tore into the close-packed clay, baked by a blazing sun into almost iron hardness.

Sweat rolled from him in streams, and he grunted and swore, but persevered with all the power of his massive muscles. He wanted to prove or disprove a suspicion that was growing in his mind—that the body of John Wilkinson had never been placed in that grave.

The lightning flashed oftener and closer, and a low mutter of thunder began in the west. An occasional gust of wind made the lantern flicker, and as the mound beside the grave grew higher, and the man digging there sank lower and lower in the earth, the rustlings in the grass grew louder and the red beads began to glint in the weeds. Harrison heard faint, eery squeakings all about him, and swore at himself as the memory of grisly legends, whispered by the negroes of his boyhood region about graveyard rats, came dimly back to him.

The grave was not deep. No Wilkinson would waste much labor on the dead. At last the rude coffin lay uncovered before him. Its lid was nailed fast. With the point of the pick he pried up one corner of the lid, and held the lantern close. The coffin was not empty. He saw a huddled, headless figure . . . .

Harrison climbed out of the grave, holding the lantern. His mind was racing, fitting pieces of the puzzle together. And he meant to replace the head in the coffin where it belonged. He lowered the lantern, and got an unpleasant shock. *The head was not where he had left it.*

Harrison was a brave man, but for a moment he felt cold sweat clammy on his hands. Then he remembered the red beads, the squeaking in the weeds. He lifted the lantern and shined the light about. In its reflection he saw a white blotch on the grass that was a cloth, and from beyond it a cold white face regarded him stonily. The graveyard rats had tugged the cloth from the head and were trying to drag it away. They scattered before the light like darting black shadows.

Overcoming his repugnance, Harrison wrapped the head again in the cloth. It lay near a straggling clump of bushes that had invaded the clearing from the thicket beyond the fence. He turned and carried it toward the grave. The thunder was incessant now, and the flickering of the lightning dazzled him. The thunder in his ears drowned all other night noises, but he heard the swift, furtive footfall behind him an instant before the blow was struck.

He whirled, drawing his gun, but just as he whirled, something like a louder clap of thunder exploded in his head, with a shower of fiery sparks before his eyes. Reeling backward, he fired without aim, his reflexes merely responding to his grim fighting instinct. But it was the instinct of a falling man. The roar of the gun in his own hand seemed faint and far-away as he fell heavily on the edge of the grave.

Chapter .4.
The Outlaw.

The detective's lapse into unconsciousness was brief. He was shaken out of the black abyss that had engulfed him by a sharp impact which only later he recognized as a heavy kick in the ribs. He rose groggily, aware of thunder, a constant play of lightning, and a bursting ache in his head. There was a gash in his scalp, and blood was clotted in his hair. He blinked in the light of the lantern, and wondered what was the matter with it. It was not on the ground. It seemed to be suspended in mid-air—then he was aware that it was held in the hand of a man who stood glaring at him—a tall, supply-built man in a black slicker, whose eyes burned dangerously from under his broad hat-brim. The man held the lantern shoulder-high, so its light shone full in Harrison's face. In his other hand a black pistol muzzle menaced the detective's midriff.

"Don't move!" growled this man. "I' 'low I know who you are. You're that damn' low-country law Pete Wilkinson brung up here to run me down."

"Then you're Joel Middleton!" grunted Harrison.

"Who the hell did you think I was?" snarled the outlaw. "Where's Pete, the old devil?"

"I don't know. He got scared and ran off."

"Crazy, like Saul, maybe," sneered Middleton. "Well, you tell him for me that I been savin' a .45 slug for his ugly mug a long time. And you tell him, too, that I didn't cut off John's head and stick it up on the mantel-board, neither. I know what happened in town tonight. A friend of mine told me."

"Joash Sullivan, eh?"

"I ain't mentionin' no names," snapped the outlaw. "I was told that you and Pete was headin' for the old graveyard, and I come here to tell you that I didn't cut off John's head. And then I was goin' to kill Pete. I'll kill him yet. And Richard, too, before I'm done. Don't you move. I could beef you easy as not, and maybe save myself some trouble later on. But I ain't no cold-blooded murderer. I had good reason for killin' John Wilkinson—dirty coyote, skinned me out of my inheritance, after his cussed family had done ruint mine. Where's his head? You put it back in the grave yet?"

"You ought to know," grunted Harrison, fingering his aching head. He glanced about him, and swore. The head was gone. "What did you do with it after you slugged me?"

"*I* slugged you?" There was exasperation in Middleton's voice. "I didn't hit you. I just got here. As I come out of the brush I heard a shot and then I seen a man down on his all-fours by the light of the lantern, and somethin' else runnin' off into the thickets. I come over here and picked up the lantern and seen you layin' there with yore head all bloody. If the head's gone, maybe the critter that knocked you out taken it. Anyway, I didn't hit you, and I didn't cut off John Wilkinson's head, neither."

"I know you didn't," Harrison answered.

"Eh?" The outlaw was obviously startled.

"Do you know which rooms the Wilkinsons sleep in, in their house in town?"

"Naw," snorted Middleton. "Never was in their house in my life."

"I thought not. Whoever put John's head on Saul's mantel knew. The back kitchen door was the only one where the lock could have been forced without waking somebody up. You wouldn't have known that. You didn't even know which room Saul slept in. As soon as I had time to think things over, I was sure you didn't bring John's head into the house. I figured it this way: either somebody outside the house who was familiar with the ways of the brothers broke in at the kitchen door and put the head on the mantel, or else somebody inside the house did it, and left the kitchen door open and scratched the lock on the outside to make it look like an outside job.

"Tonight Richard spilled a lot of stuff about Peter keeping them from leasing some land, and hinted that Peter wanted his brothers to die, so he could enjoy the inheritance alone. It looked logical, considering everything. I decided to bring Peter out to the graveyard, and see if his nerve could stand up under an accusation across his brother's open coffin. But he reacted differently than I thought, before I had time to spring my plan.

"I thought he'd dug up the grave yesterday. When I shoveled out a little dirt and hit hard-packed soil, I'll admit it gave me a turn for an instant. But the explanation is logical, and proves you couldn't have cut off John's head. This is the way I figure it: Peter wanted to get rid of his brothers without any risk to himself. You helped him when you killed John. I learned about the disposition of his body from questioning Peter. Less than an hour after you shot him, he was placed in the coffin, and the lid nailed down. It stood in the Wilkinsons' parlor until it was placed in that grave, the next day. He was an atheist, and there was the briefest sort of ceremony. The coffin wasn't opened for his friends to take a last look, as is the usual custom.

"Nobody was in the home the night his corpse lay in the parlor but his brothers and Jim Allison. With their usual callousness, they didn't keep a death-watch. They all went to bed, including Jim Allison, who occupied the room I slept in tonight. During the night it was easy for Peter to sneak into the parlor, pry up the coffin lid without making enough noise to wake any of them, and cut off John's head. He put it on ice somewhere to preserve it. I found that out when I touched it. It was nearly frozen. I understand the Wilkinsons have an ice-house where they keep their meat.

"I don't know why Peter waited until tonight to spring his trick, or why he called me into the case. But I reckon he brought me out here to protect him from you. I don't think he meant to kill me when we drove out here tonight. This morning he must have dug the soil on the top of the grave to make it look like it had been opened and then filled in again. He didn't stop to think that the ground underneath would be hard-packed. I gave myself away when I told him about it. I should have kept my mouth shut, gone on and opened the grave, and then laid my cards on the table.

"But that crazy talk about ghosts was in the back of my mind, and I was so sure that Peter had dug into the grave to get the head, that I didn't stop and figure out that he had the head before the coffin was put in the grave. I blurted out that the grave hadn't been open, and he was slick enough to see that the game was up. So he pretended to go into a panic and ran off. Later he slipped back and crowned me. I reckon he didn't know how bad he'd hurt me, or he'd have finished me. I remember shooting blindly as I fell. I've got a pretty tough skull. But another lick would have settled me."

"I reckon so," grunted Middleton. "But yo're plumb wrong about Pete hittin' you. It wasn't him. I come to the fence just as the critter that did hit you was runnin' off into the woods, with somethin' white under one arm. You was sprawled in the full glare of the lantern and I seen you plain. I didn't git a good look at the *hombre* that knocked you down, but I did see enough to know it wasn't Pete Wilkinson. It was somethin' that didn't have no clothes on, except feathers on its head!"

"What?"

"I'm tellin' you straight. It wasn't tall enough for Pete Wilkinson, and it was darn near naked. I'm tellin' you, it was a Injun! It was old Wolf Hunter, come back from hell! Old Joash Sullivan seen him sneakin' through the woods last night. And I seen him tonight."

"Nonsense!" snorted Harrison.

"You think so?" snarled Middleton blood-thirstily. "Well, you can go to hell. I ain't goin' to shoot you now, because I ain't no murderer, but you keep off my trail. I'm goin' now, and you better go back to the low-country where you belong, because if you try to run me down I'll kill you as sure as hell. And I ain't goin' to git caught by no man. I wouldn't stand a chance in the county court, what with all the money the Wilkinsons got. Before I go, though, take a look at what you was knocked in the skull with!"

He kicked something toward the detective's feet and Harrison, staring at it, felt his skin crawl just a little. It consisted of a smooth oval of flint, pointed at each end, and set in the cleft of a post-oak stock, tied fast with rawhide thongs—the Indian tomahawk of an elder generation.

The next instant Middleton had dashed the lantern to the ground where it went out with a clatter of breaking glass. Harrison blinked in the sudden darkness that followed, and the next lightning flash showed him standing alone in the ancient graveyard. The outlaw had melted into the woods like a shadow.

Chapter .5.
The Corpse in the Corner.

Cursing, Harrison groped on the ground, lighted by the lightning flashes. He found the broken lantern and his revolver and started toward the gate. Rain drops began to splash against his face. One instant he stumbled in velvet blackness, the next the tombstones shone white in the dazzling glare. A downpour was imminent, perhaps one of the savage ridge-country storms which flood creeks and rip up trees by the roots. Harrison's head ached frightfully, and he was shaken by nausea. The blow that had felled him had been meant to kill, and only chance and a tough skull had saved him. The killer had not dared pause for another blow, but apparently had snatched John Wilkinson's head as he fled, for what grisly purpose there was no knowing. Harrison winced slightly at the thought of the rain filling the open grave, but he had neither the strength nor the inclination to shovel the dirt back in it. To remain in that dark graveyard alone might well be death. Peter Wilkinson or Indian ghost, the slayer might return for another attempt.

Harrison climbed the gate and made his way to the flivver. He climbed in and found his flashlight where he had left it. The rain began, slowly at first, but growing in volume. Soon the rutty road to Lost Knob would be a welter of mud. It was absurd to think of driving back through the storm over that abominable road in his condition. He'd wreck the wretched flivver or stick it in the mud. But it could not be long until dawn. He decided to take refuge in the old farm house until the storm had passed.

He started the car and started along the worn road. The rain came down in sheets, soaking him, and dimming the already uncertain lights. Wind ripped through the post-oaks, showering leaves on the road, and lashing the branches. Mud puddles appeared on the road ahead of him and he splashed noisily through them. Once he grunted involuntarily, and batted his eyes, and for the third time that night, his flesh crept. He could have sworn that a flash of lightning had fleetingly revealed a naked, painted, feathered figure gliding among the trees!

A rational explanation presented itself—Peter Wilkinson had adopted that disguise for his own purposes. The road wound up a thickly-wooded eminence, rising close to the bank of a muddy creek. On the summit the old house squatted. There was no fence; weeds and low bushes straggled from the surrounding woods up to the sagging porch. He parked the car as close to the house as he could get it, and climbed out, struggling through the wind and rain. He expected to have to blow the lock off the door with his gun, but as he fumbled with it, shivering in the rain and wind that swept the full length of the old porch, the door opened under his fingers. He stumbled into a musty smelling room, weirdly half-lighted by the flickering of the lightning through the cracks of the shutters. His flashlight revealed a rude bunk built against a side wall, a heavy hand-hewn table, a heap of rags in a corner.

He closed the door and placed the lantern on the table, where he lighted it with matches from a water-proof case. The broken chimney caused the flame to dance and flicker, but the walls of the room were stout, the shuttered windows intact, and not enough wind found its way in to blow out the flame. Three other doors, leading into the interior of the house, were closed.

Harrison sat down on the bunk, holding his aching head in his hands, his flashlight and pistol on his lap. He expected to fight for his life before day broke. Peter Wilkinson was presumably prowling out there in the storm somewhere, with murderous intent. But Harrison knew that he could not be seen well enough through the shuttered windows for a bullet from the dark to find him. To get another chance at the detective Wilkinson would have to come into that room, where there was light, and no chance for a blow in the back. Harrison hoped vengefully that he would come, and soon. There were strange inconsistencies in the man's actions, all the way through. The detective believed Peter was touched with madness.

The swish of the rain on the roof, the howling of the wind, the flicker of the lightning through the shutters, beat painfully on Harrison's bruised brain. Somewhere in the old house rats were scampering and gnawing, and the sound brought to his mind the ghoulish graveyard rats. Shivering slightly he took up the tomahawk and turned it about in his hands. He believed the head was a genuine antique article, but the hills were full of such relics. The handle was of recent work, and so were the rawhide thongs. There was blood on the flint—and Harrison's eyes narrowed suddenly. Some of it was his own blood, but on the other point of the oval there was more blood, dark and crusted, and dried harder.

Frowning over this Harrison sat staring vacantly at the heap of rags in the far corner—a tattered carpet, he saw now, piled and rolled in a long, compact heap. He sat absently looking at it for some time before it registered on his pre-occupied brain. That rolled-up carpet—there was something suggestive about its shape—a shape that grew more definite and distinct as he looked—the shape of a man.

In a stride he reached the carpet and tore it away from what it hid. He looked down on the corpse of Peter Wilkinson. The head had been crushed—and he remembered the blood crusted on the tomahawk. For an instant his brain reeled with the shuddersome possibilities his discovery summoned up. Then he took a firm grasp on himself, fought off the whispering potency of the dark howling night, the thrashing wet black woods and the abysmal aura of the ancient hills, and seized and recognized the only sane and possible solution of the riddle.

Somberly he looked down on the dead man. Peter Wilkinson's fright had been genuine, after all. In the blind panic of his superstitious fear he had reverted to the habits of his boyhood, and fled toward his old home—and met death instead of security.

And as Harrison stood there, he straightened convulsively as a weird sound smote his ears above the roar of the storm. And cold chills coursed down his spine, at the suggestiveness of the sound in that hour, and under those conditions, though he well knew from whose lips it welled. For the noise he heard was one he had heard years before on an Arizona Reservation—a sound which once heard is never to be forgotten—an Indian war-whoop.

Gliding to a shuttered window that looked out upon the porch, he peered through a crack, waiting for a flash of lightning. When it came he fired through the window at the feathered head he saw peering around a tree close to the car. In the darkness following the flash he crouched, waiting—another white glare—and he grunted explosively but did not fire. The head was still there, in exactly the same position as he had first seen it. And it looked ghostly familiar. Harrison knew if that were the head of a living man it would have moved, have shifted position when he fired. It was the head of John Wilkinson, feathered and bound in place—and it was the bait of a trap.

With the realization came instant action. Harrison whirled and sprang toward the lantern on the table. That grisly ruse had been to draw his attention to the front of the house while the killer slunk upon him from behind, through the back of the building! Even as Harrison whirled an inner door began to open. He smashed a heavy slug through the panels, heard a groan and the sound of a falling body, and then, just as he reached a hand to extinguish the lantern, the world crashed over his head. A blinding burst of lightning, a deafening clap of thunder, and the ancient house staggered from gables to foundations! Blue fire crackled from the ceiling and ran down the walls and over the floor. One livid tongue just flicked the detective's shin in passing.

It was like the impact of an electrically-charged sledge-hammer. There was in instant of blindness and numb agony, and then Harrison found himself sprawling on the floor, dazed and nauseated. The lantern lay extinguished beside the overturned table, but the room was filled with a quivering lurid light, and above him there was a noise that differed from the roar of the wind, rain and thunder. He realized that a bolt of lightning had struck the house, and that the upper story was ablaze. By a freak of chance it had shocked him and knocked him down, without killing or crippling him. He hauled himself to his feet, looking for his gun. It lay half-way across the room, and just as he started for it, the bullet-split door swung open. Harrison clenched his hands; it was not his lucky night.

Through the door limped a horrific figure—a man naked but for a loin-cloth, and moccasins on his feet. A revolver in his hand menaced the detective. Blood oozed from a wound in his thigh.

"I've been expecting you, Richard," Harrison said calmly. "If it hadn't been for that lightning I'd be in a position to give you a more appropriate welcome."

Richard laughed savagely. "The gods fight for me tonight! Don't move, damn you! You nearly had me when you shot through the door—a little too low, though."

"So it was you who wanted to be an oil millionaire," said Harrison. "You damned ghoul! I understand why you killed Peter, of course. By why did you drive Saul mad?"

"Why should I share my millions with that idiotic fanatic?" sneered Richard. "I know there's oil on Wild River. While Peter lived I'd never get a chance at it. Saul was a fool. I always hated him. Ghoul? We were all ghouls at heart, we Wilkinsons—all graveyard rats, gnawing at the dead as well as the living. I've only followed my inherited instincts. As soon as you and Peter started for the graveyard I realized my mistake— I'd scratched the surface of John's grave, but as soon as you dug down a little way you'd hit hard clay, and know the grave hadn't been opened. I knew then I'd have to kill you, and it came to me that the devil had put Peter into my hands. I'd planned to kill him another way—John, too, but Joel Middleton beat me to that.

"I hurried to the graveyard through the woods, on horseback. I put on the Indian togs I'd been wearing in the woods at night to start the old legend going. It takes so long to drive that rotten road, that I got to the graveyard shortly after you and Peter did. When Peter got panicky and ran through the woods I chased him, killed him and brought his body here to the old house. Then I went back after you. I intended killing you and bringing your body here. But you were too tough to kill with one lick, and when you started shooting I grabbed John's head and took to my heels. I already had a plan to trap you with it, without any risk to myself, on the road to Lost Knob. But you've trapped yourself by coming here instead.

"I was going to bring your body here after I killed you—was going to set the house on fire. People would think Middleton killed you and Peter, when they found your bones in the ashes, and then burned the house. Or maybe they'd think lightning set it on fire! And now, by God, what I

[. . .]

ROBERT ERVIN HOWARD (1906-1936) grew up in the boomtowns of early twentieth-century Texas, eventually settling in Cross Plains where he lived for the remainder of his short life. Deciding early on a literary career, he spent the bulk of his time crafting stories and poems for the burgeoning pulp fiction markets: *Weird Tales, Action Stories, Fight Stories, Argosy*, etc. Howard's literary reputation was assured with the publication of "The Shadow Kingdom" in 1929, which featured a unique blend of Fantasy and Adventure which has since been termed Heroic Fantasy. The creation of Conan the Cimmerian in the pages of *Weird Tales* has earned him lasting recognition.

DON HERRON published his now classic defense of Robert E. Howard's Conan stories, "Conan vs. Conantics," in 1976—and the very next year he began leading The Dashiell Hammett Tour in San Francisco, which continues hiking up and down those mean streets to this day. Among other titles he has edited two critical anthologies on Howard, *The Dark Barbarian* (1984) and *The Barbaric Triumph* (2004)—plus *Willeford* (1997), a book about the books written by the cult crime writer Charles Willeford. The first of his "Mr. Hunt" stories, written in homage to Hammett and the *Black Mask* school of hard-boiled detective fiction, is included in *San Francisco Noir 2: The Classics* from Akashic Press.

MARK WHEATLEY holds the Eisner, Inkpot, Golden Lion, Mucker, Gem and Speakeasy Awards and nominations for the Harvey Award and the Ignatz Award. He is also an inductee to the Overstreet Hall of Fame. His work has often been included in the annual Spectrum selection of fantastic art and has appeared in private gallery shows, the Norman Rockwell Museum, Toledo Museum of Art, Huntington Art Museum, Fitchburg Art Museum, James A. Michener Art Museum and the Library of Congress, where several of his originals are in the LoC permanent collection.

ROB ROEHM has gone to every location in the United States that Howard mentions visiting—from New Orleans to Santa Fe, and dozens of Texas towns in between—verifying and expanding our knowledge of Howard's biography. His research has also uncovered lost Howard stories, letters, and poems, which are included in the volumes he edits (more than 20 at last count). He writes about these places and discoveries, infrequently, at howardhistory.com.

CPSIA information can be obtained
at www.ICGtesting.com
Printed in the USA
BVHW051019230622
640494BV00017B/534/J